“Wyatt?”

“Huh?”

“I loved you…long before Israel died.” The confession rocked her thoughts. She had loved Israel, but she had longed for Wyatt years before Israel had died. It had been wrong, and there were times it made her feel like she hadn’t done right by her deceased husband. She weaved her fingers into Wyatt’s, touching with tenderness where the fracture had been. “I did, right or wrong. I mean…I loved Israel, we had so much in common with his study of science and plants and my study of medicine, but I was guilty of dreaming for you long before…he died.”

His smile was tender as he lifted her chin. “I’ve known that for a long time, Doc. And I can’t count how many nights I lay awake, wishing I were holding you.”

She held tighter to him. “And when you left Cheyenne, it was all my fault. I knew I had made a mistake. I wasn’t even myself without you. It was as if I kept falling and falling, never hitting the ground to land anywhere.”

With that he wrapped his arms around her and kissed her. “I’ll always be here to catch you, Doc, always.”

Wyatt's Bounty

by

Kim Turner

The McCades of Cheyenne, Book 2

Wyatt's Bounty

Contact Information: info@thewildrosepress.com

Cover Art by *Debbie Taylor*

The Wild Rose Press, Inc.
PO Box 708
Adams Basin, NY 14410-0708
Visit us at www.thewildrosepress.com

Publishing History
First Cactus Rose Edition, 2017
Print ISBN 978-1-5092-1376-4
Digital ISBN 978-1-5092-1377-1

The McCades of Cheyenne, Book 2
Published in the United States of America

Dedication

For Mom,
who taught me the love of books,
and Dad,
who took me to the movies.

Acknowledgements

Many thanks to Maggie, Carol, Sherrie, Marcia, Jill, Kimmy, Clare, Dennie, Linda, Cheryl, and Stephanie who all at one time or another read portions or this entire story.

~

And thanks to the readers who are making this writing journey so much fun with the overwhelming response to reading the cowboys who live in my mind and heart.

Prologue

Cheyenne Wyoming, 1879

Shadows lengthened across the town of Cheyenne, adding to the uncertain confusion spreading through Wyatt McCade. He drew in a slow and steady breath, his gut clenching tight at recalling the unexpected news he'd received several hours ago. Tess Sullivan, Cheyenne's lady doctor, was going back East. Glancing across the dusty road toward her clinic, he wondered where a decision like that had come from. Cursing, he searched his vest out of habit and remembered he'd stopped smoking the fancy cigars the doc disliked. "Son of a..."

Making things worse, his mother, Dodge, had been the one to break the news. So much for a gentle blow. He scuffed the heel of one boot across the upraised wooden plank in need of repair. It was rare for Tess to mention Boston, other than the aunt and uncle who'd raised her remained there. He leaned against the porch, snatched his hat off, and ran his fingers through his hair. He'd given up long ago trying to figure the stubborn woman, but he'd never considered she would leave Cheyenne. He might as well have been hit, head on, by the afternoon train. At least that would have put him right out of his misery and for good.

Scanning across town, he slapped the hat back on

his head and inhaled a ragged breath. It was after dark and quiet, except for the echoing piano from the saloon, and the lone horseman riding toward the end of town. The clip-clop of the horse's hooves beat right along with his racing pulse. Most shops were closed, but the few lanterns hanging in doorways added to the glow that gave him a clear view of the doc's clinic. The very least she could have done was to tell him herself. *Damn it all to hell!*

How could she think of leaving when she well knew how he felt about her? And while he'd never held back where she was concerned, she had always remained an arm's length out of reach. He'd gotten several dances out of her at the spring festival, thinking he'd made a little progress. But now, her leaving Cheyenne—well, she just couldn't do that. And she'd known good and well what she was doing by telling Dodge, her best friend, first.

He stomped off the porch, spurs clinking. The doc would be madder than a wet cat at him for confronting her, but she could tell him her own version of *this* story and right damn now. A decision like that didn't come out of the blue, not for a woman like Tess who went toe to toe with the roughest men in the west. Apparently, it was time he laid it all on the line, offered her all he had and married her—if she'd have him.

Passing the livery with its coarse smells of horses, manure, and leather, he stepped up to the clinic and inside without bothering to knock, the tiny bell on the door jingling. Medicinal antiseptic replaced the earthen odors of the animals, startling his senses.

Tess called from the back, "I'll be right there."

At the sweet sound of her voice, every nerve in his

body frayed. She couldn't leave, could she? He glanced around the clinic, the place Doc called home, with its crisp white washed walls and organized office. Flowers in vases sat on her desk and the floral pictures hanging on the walls held a welcoming warmth. She couldn't leave all this behind—she couldn't leave him.

She emerged, halting as her glance grazed him. "Wyatt?"

It was clear she was wise to why he'd come this hour of the evening, and there was no sense in holding back. "Boston?"

Her eyes widened as she stepped toward the counter, resting both hands on the corner. "I decided a few days ago."

"I have to find out something like that from Dodge?" Panic scored through him at her acknowledgement of her plans, and he wanted to reach out, pull her to him, and shake some sense into her. This was all wrong.

She folded her arms but never dropped her gaze. "I was going to tell you. I'll leave…within the month, I suppose."

He jerked the hat from his head and turned away trying to gather his thoughts. He'd always been good at reading those around him, and she wasn't speaking her heart. But as upset as he was, she always melted something deep inside him, though the impact of what was happening shredded through him. He had to watch his temper. If he riled her, she would say no more and order him from the clinic. But there had to be a way to convince her she was making a mistake, the biggest of her life—and his.

She took a long deep breath, her breasts rising with

the effort, tempting his quick glance. "My uncle has secured a position for me at one of the hospitals in Boston. There are so many new practices and procedures for me to learn there."

He cocked his head, not believing a word of it. She was the best physician throughout the Wyoming and Colorado territories, and people sought her care for miles around. "You could show those big city doctors more than they could ever teach you."

She considered him, those deep green eyes holding him hostage. "There are so many new surgeries and treatments for me to learn. It's an opportunity to be with my family again. A new start."

A new start? Yeah, he'd like to *start* by pulling the pink ribbon from her long brown hair so it would spill across her shoulders. It didn't help that her soft brown skirt and pink blouse accented the fullness of her rounded curves, one of the things he loved most about her. She wasn't dainty or petite, and while it seemed to bother her, to him, she was fully a woman. He held her gaze, and her eyes glistened. Was she working up tears? Hell that would be the death of him.

"Doc, you know my feelings…for you." He whispered, his pulse exploding from his heart. God, he loved her, and this couldn't be happening. He stepped closer, close enough to inhale the sweet scent of her lavender soap.

"I can't pass up this opportunity." Her voice trailed off as she avoided his gaze.

Why couldn't she look at him? He shook his head and raised his voice to a stern whisper. "I did what you asked. I quit smoking the damn cigars. I rarely drink at the saloon, and I've turned down numerous bounties."

He lifted her chin and gave her no choice but to look at him. "And I haven't been with any woman in more months than I can count!"

It was true. He'd quit the things she'd protested and done so of his own accord. He could get over the cigars, whiskey, and even letting bounties pass him by, but giving up the pleasures of a woman…well, there wasn't anything right about that, though he'd yet to think of any woman but her for years now.

"I'm sorry." Her shoulders drew up, and her hands fell to her sides.

He backed up so he wouldn't be tempted to grab her and plant his lips right against hers. So, that was it? She was determined to leave, no matter his feelings? The tightness in his chest took all his air, and being so close to her confused his thoughts and body. He quickly faced the door, trying to make sense of it all.

"Your hat." The tenderness in her words stopped him, and he turned to her again. She held his hat in her hand, intending to hand it to him before he left. Well, he wasn't leaving, in fact he was about to change both of their lives for good. The loud click of the bolt echoed across the silent room, the bell jingling with his clumsiness. He wasn't going anywhere until she admitted her heart, whether or not he had the power to make her stay in Cheyenne.

He walked to her, stopping so close she fought to keep her footing, dropping his hat as he tugged her closer. "I know you have feelings for me and right here, tonight, you're going to admit it. *I* can offer you a new life. *I* can give you all I have for a lifetime, Doc."

"Wyatt, you have no right…" She jerked from his grasp and darted into the hallway.

"*I* have every right!" He didn't give her a chance to escape the conversation, following and wrapping his arms around her from behind. He held her against the hard length of his wanting body, inhaling. She was perfection against him, and he closed his eyes. No, he wouldn't lose her, not like this, and now was as good a time as any.

She tensed when he placed his lips against her neck in a gentle sucking kiss, something he'd never done. She tasted as sweet as he suspected she might, and her body shuddered in response as he nipped her ear and whispered. "Tell me you don't love me, Doc. Tell me you don't think of me when you lie alone in your bed each night. Tell me you don't wish my hands were touching you." His lips traced her skin once more, savoring her flavor. "I love you and you love me. Admit it."

"Wyatt…" She relaxed to his surprise, leaning against him.

His large frame shook as he tugged the ribbon from her long hair and let it splay across her shoulders, wafting his senses with the fragrant purple flowers she adored. With a gentle and fluid motion, he slid his hands to her rounded hips, the urges of his body unrelenting. "Tell me, Doc."

He kissed her neck again, and she leaned harder into him. Her pulse teased his lips as he kissed further across her exposed shoulder. Soft. So damn soft. She owed him the truth and if he had to, he'd coax it from her one kiss at a time.

She shivered as he dared to lift her blouse, his hands touching under her chemise to her soft warm belly, and his world came undone. He'd never wanted another woman as much as he wanted the doc and his hands on her bare skin drove his desire.

"You can't," she whispered, as he let one hand rise to cup her breast, her sigh causing his own breath to hitch. It occurred to him a smack across his face was in order due to his being so forward, but she hadn't pulled away. All she had to do was tell him to leave, and he'd turn and go. "Then tell me to leave."

"Wyatt?"

"So beautiful—" He spun her to face him, his thoughts disheveled as he marched her backward until she was against the wall of the darkened hallway, his tender kiss the final impact. He tasted her soft pink lips as he'd always wanted to, parting them and dancing his tongue along hers. He tangled his hand in her hair, pressing the heat in his trousers against her. "Tell me…you love me, Doc."

"Yes…" Her urgent reply cracked with emotion, as she swayed in his arms, hanging onto his shirt as if her life depended on it, "but I…I can't love you, Wyatt, not now or ever."

What kind of answer was that? What in the hell was holding her back?

"I'm so sorry, but…my uncle has gone to a great deal of trouble." She tugged away from him and steadied herself, straightening her blouse.

He'd waited years since she'd first rolled into town on a wagon train with her now deceased husband. She'd been feisty enough to convince the town council to hire her, even though she was a woman, and Cheyenne had never been sorry. And he'd been there as she'd mourned her husband, and he'd waited longer than the full year required out of respect, but now it was time.

"Wyatt…" Tears spilled down her cheeks, tearing his heart into tiny pieces.

He didn't let her finish, touching a finger to her lips and dropping down on one knee, taking her hands in his own. "Stay here—with me, Doc. Marry me." He'd taken down the worst kinds of evil without batting an eye, but asking the woman who owned his heart for her hand in marriage, he could hardly get the words out. "Let me spend the rest of my life making sure you want for nothing. We wouldn't have to rush, and you could go to Boston for your learning, then come back here…to me. Do me the honor. Let me make you my wife."

She held his gaze, struggling through her broken words. "I need to go home, and I won't be coming back. I know it isn't much of an explanation, but after Israel…I can't. I am sorry, so very sorry, Wyatt."

He stood frozen; her words jolting through him as if an outlaw had sent a bullet straight through his chest. She wasn't fickle and meant what she said and he hadn't any doubt she was set on her task. His thoughts shattered, and he sucked in what air he could force. He lifted his hat from the floor, juggling it in his hands as he stood again. There were no words, nothing he could say, but he memorized her and leaned in to kiss her cheek. He swallowed the dry lump in his throat and spoke the one truth of his heart in a whisper. "I'll always love you, Doc." And with a small brush of his hand against her cheek, he strode past her and out the door, leaving her and all he'd ever loved behind in his wake.

Chapter One

Denver, Colorado, 1880
Six months later…

Wyatt McCade dismounted. With its rowdy saloons and businesses, Denver hadn't changed much since his last run through town. He tied his horse to a hitch and pulled each of his revolvers, checking the barrels. Fully loaded. Adrenaline coursed through him, upping the ante as he peered down the cluttered street. Town was busy, making the job before him rather challenging, but it was evening, and the last rays of sun were turning the town golden. People browsed along the streets, and shopkeepers stood in doorways. Teams of wagon-hitched horses clopped along, kicking up dirt, and men on horseback, sprinkled the rutted streets.

A sudden change in wind brought a lingering stench, making him chuckle at the idea the odor could be from Abe Warner, the man he'd been tracking, instead of from the local slaughterhouse. The outlaw and his counterpart were most likely inside the saloon he'd been watching, the largest in Denver for the most part. He'd been on them for close to a month, waiting for the wanted man to slip up. Rarely did he give the men he hunted this much of his time, but Warner, at best, was unpredictable.

He glanced at the saloon. He'd have to plan with

care to take Warner alive, though he'd been less than careful the last few months since leaving home. He'd put himself in a number of gunfights with outlaws and renegades that had nearly cost him his life, but he'd landed on his feet as usual. No doubt his brothers were searching for him, but it was his mother, Dodge, who would bear the brunt of the worry. She'd understood his reasons for leaving Cheyenne, and her one request had been that he'd stay in touch by wire—something he'd yet to do. While she had always afforded him time away, this wasn't the anniversary of his father's death, or some other like event where he needed a few days to gather his thoughts. This time it had been—Tess.

He glanced down at his hands, the rounded curves of her womanly body still rode there as he'd held and kissed her the night she'd turned down his proposal. Maybe he *was* crazy, but he still tasted the warmth of her tender full lips and held the weight of her body against him when he thought of her. He tilted his hat back, using the sleeve of his arm to wipe away the lingering sweat across his brow.

He'd tried to forget her, push the doc out of his head, but it hadn't worked and he'd learned long ago there was no sense dwelling on things he couldn't change. She'd made her decision, turned down his proposal and was by now all the way to Boston, no matter her heart—and his. She loved him. She did, but something stronger than he could understand had ripped her right from his clutches.

He bent to check the knife in his boot, that, and his revolvers the surest things in his world anymore. Tess' rejection had torn him apart and not having her as a daily option would have killed him, so he'd left home never looking back. He dusted the trail from his new shirt, trying to clear his mind, as any time she entered his thoughts, all reason left him. She would be settled in Boston by now, more than two-thousand miles away, and he was in Denver, doing what most men suffering a broken heart did—work hard, every damn day.

His captures the last few months had topped any bounty hunter in the West. He'd brought in or brought down man after man, earning his name in local papers and filling his pockets. And while he couldn't care less what the news printed, something happened to a man when the woman he loved walked away.

He glanced across town once more, setting his sights on the saloon and forced the Doc from his mind. If he played it well, he'd take Abe Warner, right under the local sheriff's nose. A smile moved across his lips. Denver's sheriff, Chance Barlow, was as corrupt as the town itself and when he wasn't tangling with the likes of wayward outlaws, the man was smuggling bootleg whiskey and opium all over the west for a wealthy Chinese man called Chan. The same man who operated the slaughterhouse outside of Denver as a cover for the sale of illegal goods. And it likely didn't help matters that Barlow owned the saloon where the outlaw was spending his loot.

Patting the horse, he trotted across the street toward the saloon. He'd be known inside, so there was a short time to snag Warner without Barlow's notice. Stepping to the porch he peered inside, finding no signs of Warner or the man with him. They were upstairs with the saloon girls, giving him the advantage of surprise if he were a guessing man. His gaze settled on the far end of the long bar and swore in a staunch whisper. "Shit."

Hudson Collier sat alone, a shot of whiskey before him. That meant one thing; his sheriff brother had sent the deputy to find him. He ducked away and rounded the saloon, fighting another burst of curses. While he could use the deputy's assistance, he would do better with help of another sort. He stopped in the alley behind the saloon and fixed his sights up at Mattie's window. It wouldn't be the first time the high-priced madam had been of service, and if he moved fast no one would take notice as he climbed up the back of the building, a path he'd known for a number of years.

The alley was vacant as he pulled his six foot-two frame onto the lower roof with a chuckle. He peered through the edge of the curtained window into her plush room. Empty. Well, at least he wouldn't be interrupting her with one of the high paying men she serviced.

He lifted the window and slid the linen shade back. Struggling, he pulled himself through the half size window and stifled a groan as he stood erect again. A splash from the water closet off Mattie's room drew his attention and a smile spread across his face as he twisted the knob. Swirling steam wafted around him as he stepped inside. The tub was full, but—no madam. She couldn't be far and he stepped further into the room and froze as the blade of a knife edged his throat. *Son of a bitch!*

"Looking for someone cowboy?" Mattie's stern whisper broke the silence.

He gingerly raised his hands into the air. "Bounty hunter, no cowboy here."

"Wyatt, I've told you about sneaking in on me. I'll end up slitting your throat one of these days." She lowered the knife to her dressing table, her chocolate eyes scolding as he turned to face her.

"Oh, but what a way to die." Her scantily clad body was worth a second glance, but there was no time to spare as he shuffled past her back into the bedroom.

She tugged her robe across her shoulders, her dark hair flowing down her back. "Something tells me you aren't here for the pleasure of one of the ladies."

He removed his hat and listened against the door. "Two men came in a few hours ago. The man I'm tracking has red hair and beard."

"Wyatt, I don't want my girls at risk. Every time you come in here—" Her gaze narrowed and she threw her hands on her plump hips as he interrupted her.

"We'll watch out for your girls." He'd always made sure to keep her and the other women out of harm's way, but with Warner things might be rather difficult. The outlaw was good with a gun and not afraid to use it.

"We?" She stepped closer and flipped the badge he wore for appearance with her fingers. "At the rate *we* are going, you owe me one of these badges you wear when you're playing deputy. Red's at the end of the hall, the other man two doors down. Hudson's downstairs. Said he was waiting on you to show."

He narrowed his gaze on her knowing eyes. He was well aware why the deputy was in Denver. "When did he get here?"

She dropped her robe and fitted a full black lace gown over her dark corset as she talked. "A few weeks now. You know Sawyer sent him."

He tugged his gaze from her luscious body with a bit of reluctance. She was a beautiful woman but he had no time or interest other than the matter at hand and he didn't need his sheriff brother keeping tabs on him. "I'm sure it didn't take much prodding."

She finished the buttons to the gown with little modesty. "Your family misses you, and he's been through here several times the last few months asking about you."

"Sawyer?"

"Yes, the sheriff himself. He's worried." She winced, tightening the lacing around her middle.

His older brother wouldn't rest until he'd found him and then he'd more than likely kick his ass for leaving in the first place. "Worry is what Sawyer does best."

"Want me to get Hudson?" She trotted toward the door.

"Nope, you'd attract attention and there's no time." With her help, he could surprise the outlaw and his sidekick before they knew what was going on, and if it happened things didn't go well then Hudson could pick up the pieces.

"You know Chance will take anything you shoot up out of my pay." She adjusted her breasts, sizing up her corset with both hands and raising her brows at his lengthy view of her actions.

"I'll pay the damages." He lifted his gaze and then his left revolver. Taking in the beauty of Mattie, moved his thoughts to Tess and he shifted her from his mind. He couldn't afford to lose focus now, though a brief sense of regret washed over him once more.

Mattie grabbed two derringers out of the top drawer of the bedside stand, keeping one in hand and stuffing the other in her corset with great care.

"If Red gets wind of this, you get out of here. I'll

take the other man first." Maybe he should have let her go for Hudson and tackled the situation alone, so as not to put her in harm's way.

She gave him a smirk as was her typical air of mischief and followed him into the hallway outside the door. Pointing to the rooms he needed to invade, she took her place outside the one that held Warner's counterpart.

He winked. Some part of him was aware that not going for Warner first could be a problem, but he needed to cut the man's chances of having any help.

Mattie held tight to the small weapon as he listened at the door, grunting sounds coming from inside. Well enough. His lip curled into a smile and Mattie rolled her eyes. This would be easy, but keeping the man quiet would be the first task at hand.

He gave a series of nods. On the third, Mattie used her key and pushed the door open. He wasted no time racing across the room and placing the revolver against the man's temple. He froze between the young woman's legs, breathing heavy. Lucky enough, Mattie's girl had stifled a scream as Mattie bolted the door behind them.

"Not a word. Move off her, slow." He held the gun steady, aware one yelp from the man and Warner would be on him in seconds.

As the outlaw shifted, the young woman, motioned by Mattie, scooted out from under him and slipped into the closet across the room. The hidden escape would keep her from being noticed.

He placed a knee against the man's back and glanced at Mattie.

She opened the drawer of the dressing table behind

her and pulled out a noosed cord without making a sound.

He held it, giving her a curious grin as he worked it around the man's wrists.

"There are times we tie men—to escape." She hissed in a whisper.

"You're getting the wrong man, mister. I ain't done nothin'." The man spat, keeping his voice low as Wyatt flattened his face to the pillow.

"Not another word."

"At least give me my damn pants." The old bed creaked with his effort to turn.

Mattie took advantage by stuffing the man's own dirty sock into his mouth as he growled in protest. She used the second sock to tie the gag in place to assure his silence.

Wyatt nodded with satisfaction. Mattie was without a doubt a woman to avoid tangling with if it came down to it. He made quick work with the butt end of his revolver across the man's temple, rendering him unconscious and tying him to the bed frame.

"A little too mouthy?" She smiled, but then averted her gaze toward the closet, aiming the derringer.

Wyatt lowered his already poised revolver with a curse as Hudson emerged, hat in hand. "Shit."

The deputy smiled a big toothy grin. "Saw you ride into town right after Warner. Should've known your hind end would be up to no good. You're gonna need some back up."

"I got this." He considered the one constant friend he'd had over the years, and besides his brothers, a man he trusted with his own life if it came down to it.

"Not alone you don't." Hudson folded his arms, his

smile fading.

"Warner's in the last room. Reckon I don't need to tell you to watch yourself." He hissed, going to the door to listen once more. For months now he hadn't needed anyone or anything and it was no gamble that he never would again. Had it been months? It might as well have been years, but he shook Tess from his thoughts once again.

Hudson gave a satisfied nod, checking his revolver. "Warner's not feeling any pain, downed half a bottle of Barlow's rotgut a short time ago. How long you been on him?"

"Long enough." He growled.

Hudson glanced at Mattie. "Go on Mattie, get yourself away from this."

She tried to protest, but he took her by the elbow and urged her through the escape of the closet, turning back around. "Where ya been, Wyatt? Haven't seen hide nor hair of you in months."

He took a disgusted deep breath. "Nowhere and everywhere." It was the best answer he had for the always chipper deputy. He owed no one an explanation, save Dodge, who would most likely take a switch to him even if he was a grown man.

Hudson followed him into the hallway and asked nothing more. He pulled his second revolver outside Warner's door avoiding the urge to roll the barrel for good measure, not wanting the noise to alert the bastard. If he didn't handle it right, they were dead men. He hesitated outside the door, the silence disturbing, but there was no need to wait another minute. With a single nod to his long-time friend, he kicked the door open, bolting inside. He ducked and rolled coming up on one knee with both revolvers poised toward the bed.

The woman in the bed screamed, tugging the covers high, as a gun rested hard against Wyatt's back, knocking the breath from him. Across the room, Hudson rose to his feet, eyes wide and revolver held steady.

"Sneaking up on a man is a dangerous thing, bounty hunter." Warner poked him hard in the back with his weapon. "I've known you were on me for a while, McCade. What kept you?"

Wyatt met the deputy's gaze from across the room, no words needed at this hell of a situation. "I bide my time when I need to."

"Drop the weapon, Deputy Collier," the outlaw ordered, jabbing the revolver once more.

It was no surprise the man knew them both, but Hudson held his weapon on the red-headed renegade, a stalemate at least for the moment.

"Now, or I'll unload this gun right through him." Warner chuckled, shoving the weapon against him again. "Might just enjoy that."

Wyatt gave a slight nod, and the deputy bent with reluctance to lower his revolver, holding his hands up at mid-chest. He was fast and could draw up the weapon again in less than a second, but the situation was dire for them both.

"Now yours, bounty hunter." The bastard hissed through clenched teeth, behind him.

Wyatt held onto the revolvers for a second more. Hell, what a predicament. Warner would kill him in nothing flat one way or the other, but he wanted Hudson safe. So this was it. Fight or die.

"Nice and easy," The rough speaking bandit nudged him again.

He winked once at Hudson who gave him a slight frown. He bent to set his revolvers to the floor, taking his time to place the heavy weapons with care in order to stall a few seconds more. All he had now was the knife in his boot, but he wouldn't go down without a fight. He rose slowly, and his world began to flow in slow motion. The hard coursing of blood through his veins rang in his ears as he came to full height and without any hesitation snapped his head back, catching Warner right in the nose with the full force of his weight. The satisfying crunch was followed by the outlaw's groan of pain and the clatter of his revolver hitting the wooden floorboards.

Wyatt hit his knees, nearly senseless from the blow to his head. He shook his head, grabbed his revolver with his left hand. At the same time, Warner and Hudson exchanged gunfire. Yellow smoke and the smell of gunpowder filled the room as Wyatt spun around and cocked the hammer, firing a round toward the bastard.

Warner's body jerked from the impact of the bullet that caught him in the chest, and he fell to the floor with a thud.

Wyatt jumped to kick his gun away as he breathed his blood-gurgling last few breaths. "Justice comes to those deserving." It was a quote he'd borrowed from his father, now gone more years than he cared to count.

Warner's head fell to the side. Dead, the man's eyes still wide, his chest ceasing movement.

He turned to Hudson, who was standing but holding his upper arm, his weapon falling from his hand as blood saturated his shirt sleeve. The deputy swayed.

"Shit!" He ran for the man as his knees buckled and lugged him to the bed the woman had vacated.

"I'm all right." Hudson tried to see the wound but fell back against the pillows, pale and shaking.

"Sure you are." Wyatt ripped his shirt sleeve open. The bullet had entered the upper arm and gone through, leaving the back of his arm wide open. "It went clean through, you're good. We'll get you patched up."

"Don't hurt much." Hudson hissed through his gritted teeth as Mattie returned, derringer held high.

"Send for the doctor," she yelled and took the bloody sheet from Wyatt as Chance Barlow and several men burst into the room.

"Hands up, all of you." Barlow's evil gaze narrowed on him. "I might've known. Keep your hands up, McCade. What happened here?"

One of the men kicked Warner's unmoving body, the pool of crimson blood beneath his chest spreading across the wooden flooring.

"There's a man tied down the hall. This is Abe Warner. The same Warner on your wanted poster at the jail." Wyatt winked, wishing to curse aloud. Pissing off the sheriff was almost better than the bounty he would collect once things were cleared up.

Barlow motioned him toward the door, narrowing his sights on Hudson. "We'll see about that, McCade. Drag the deputy to the jail, the doc can see to him there."

Mattie stood in challenge. "Chance, you leave him be, or I am sure your wife would enjoy a little chat about what you're up to with my girls most nights."

Barlow glared her way, speaking in a tightened

hiss. "Get this mess cleaned up. Walk, McCade."

Wyatt touched Mattie's shoulder as he went by. "Bail me out in a few."

She was used to the routine, but the hurt in her eyes was evident. His friends weren't pawns in the game of charades he'd been playing with his own life, and he darn well knew better, though Hudson had given him little choice in the matter. He followed Barlow from the room so he could go and play the sheriff's little game of show and tell. Once things were straightened out, he'd collect the rather large bounty and later figure out just how to deal with the likes of Mattie.

Chapter Two

Wyatt startled awake in the chair opposite Mattie, who sat close to Hudson's bedside. While the doctor had patched up the deputy, neither of them had wanted to leave him alone. Hudson had stirred little, given the large dose of laudanum the doctor had given him, but he couldn't shake the stab of regret, the quick glance from Mattie his coarse reminder. He'd been sitting for the last few hours since leaving the jail and hadn't realized he'd dozed.

"Thanks for bailing me out," he whispered, though it would take some doing to wake Hudson from his medicated slumber.

"I always bail you out." Her sarcastic tone cut through him as he expected, but then she changed the conversation. "Wyatt, what are you doing?"

He rested his hands on his knees, figuring it would have come sooner or later. "Look, no lectures, all right?"

She set aside Hudson's now clean shirt she'd been mending. "If he hadn't been here, you'd be dead and it's a wonder he isn't. It wasn't like you today."

He adjusted his position in the chair. He'd known her for years now, and he had to hand it to her. She was bright and well aware of what he was up to, or lack thereof. His poor planning had been paid for with Hudson's injury, and he didn't need any reminders he'd been living rather reckless.

"The Wyatt McCade I know would never take chances like that. You've been on some downhill spiral for months now. Look at you." She got up and flipped his long hair. "You haven't had a haircut since God knows when, and you look like some kind of mountain man with that thick beard. What happened to the man I used to know?"

"Mattie—" He shrugged away from her touch wanting to curse or better yet, hit something like the wall.

"Sawyer says you haven't been home in months." She gazed at Hudson, who stirred in his sleep. "And your brother, Dawson, was through here months back. They are all worried about you."

He had expected Sawyer to hunt for him, but it surprised him Dawson would make a point to run through Denver. "My brothers need to mind their own business."

"If I know anything, and I do, you've been set on getting yourself killed for some time now." She narrowed her eyes, her tone sharp. "When are you gonna go to her and make things right?"

Wyatt's heart pounded to the surface of his chest. How the hell did she know anything about it? "Sawyer's got as big a mouth as Hudson." His older brother wasn't his keeper and his injured deputy friend should know better than to run his mouth.

"It didn't take Sawyer or Hudson to tell me about that heart of yours. A woman knows. She must be something special, this woman doctor." Mattie tossed her hands on her rounded hips.

He met her inquisitive gaze. "It's…difficult." Was

that what it was? He couldn't be sure himself. Things between him and Tess were over; he'd left Cheyenne and she'd gone to Boston and that was all there was to it.

"If you're smart, you'll go to her…whatever it takes." She gave him the slightest hint of a smile. "She's still in Cheyenne, you know."

He eyed her with caution, his gut clenching so tight he tasted bile. Why would Tess still be in Cheyenne as set as she had been on going back to Boston? He'd seen her packing up her clinic, and the number of trunks didn't indicate she was leaving much behind. He forced the words from his tightened throat. "That's no concern of mine."

"Perhaps she knew she was making a mistake." Mattie sat on the edge of Hudson's bed, careful not to wake him as she checked the dressing to his arm. "You've pined for her for years; now go home to Cheyenne, to her."

How was it women thought they knew things like this? Regardless, Tess had turned down his proposal and if she hadn't left for Boston, it wasn't because she thought she had made a mistake. He changed the subject, hoping for sweet mercy from the interrogation. "Mattie, when are you gonna get out of here, do something else?"

"Don't change the subject. Your mother is worried; your brothers are concerned. Hudson has been waiting for you like some sad lost puppy, and I'm sure this lady doctor realizes what she lost." She held his gaze, making him wish he could crawl outside the window and drop below to the hard earth with a loud and crashing thud.

"She made her decision, and we both moved on to different things. If she is still in Cheyenne, then she has reasons other than me." Even with his harsh words, his mind was spinning around why Tess hadn't left Cheyenne.

"You haven't moved ahead with your life. You're as out of sorts as I've ever seen." She pursed her lips and rested a gentle hand on his knee.

He peered down at the wooden floor to avoid her gaze. While she meant well, he didn't want or need her pity. Life was full of heartache, and this was one more thing to add to his list. "Like I said it's complicated. I—"

"Love her?" She cut him off with force, rocking her head from side to side as she continued. "Then go to her and change her mind. Don't take no for an answer, and don't come back here." She jumped up, springing to the door of the room, opening it and waiting.

Was she kicking him out? "Come on, Mattie, its damn well after midnight."

"I'll take care of Hudson and send him to Cheyenne when he's well. But at first light, you go home." She tilted a nod toward the hallway. "I mean it, you go home—to her."

He stood. She *was* sending him away, and he didn't know what to make of it. He lifted his saddle bags and tossed them over his shoulder. While he had no intentions of heading home, some part of him was curious enough to find out why Tess hadn't followed through on her plans. And Mattie was right, he was lost, living on the edge of getting himself killed, but he hadn't meant to put anyone else at risk. If he were admitting anything and he wasn't, he yearned as much for home as he did for the doc. Maybe getting back to Cheyenne would be a start. He glanced at Mattie again, meeting her intense dark eyes and turned to go, reaching into his trouser pocket and leaving the full bounty he'd earned on the dresser on the way out.

****

The front door of the clinic slammed open, hitting the far wall and knocking over the small hand iron placed there as a door stop. Tess set aside the large container of dressings she'd been sorting and ran to the hallway with a start. Several men, including Sheriff Sawyer McCade, were carrying a large unconscious man inside. Dodge followed them, grabbing a cloth and sopping up the blood which dripped to the hardwood floor from the man's belly.

"What happened?" Tess grabbed the unmoving gentleman's wrist, feeling for a pulse as the men continued into the exam room. Nothing. She loosened her grip.

Sawyer answered as he strained to help the others get the man to the table. "He took a bullet outside Marcus Benton's ranch."

Dodge tossed the bloody towels aside and poured a pitcher of water to wash her hands. "The house and property have been vacant for way over a year, Sawyer."

Sawyer narrowed his gaze on his mother as the men helping him filed from the room and back outside the clinic. "Someone's been about the place from what he said before he quit talking. Found him out by the pass, but he's gut shot."

Tess placed a hand to the injured man's face. "Can you hear me? Open your eyes." She rubbed her knuckled fist hard along his sternum, but there was no response. Not good at all. She ripped open his shirt and leaned to place an ear to his chest. The mention of Marcus Benton was startling, and the edge in Sawyer's voice was cause for concern.

"Marcus was scheduled to hang if it hasn't been done already." Dodge picked up a bottle of medication and lifted her gaze toward Tess. "Chloroform?"

Tess pressed a handful of dressings to the gaping hole at the man's belly. He'd already lost too much blood and had no heartbeat. There was little she could do. "I'm afraid we're not going to need it."

Sawyer stepped closer and inspected the unmoving man. "Benton's not dead yet, and the description was exact. Doesn't make much sense."

"What's his name?" Tess tugged a blanket across the dead man.

"Roy McCall. He started working for Brett a few weeks ago." Sawyer jerked his hat off and ran a hand through his collar length dark hair.

"I am sorry there wasn't more I could do." Tess studied the sheriff and long time friend. He was a very handsome man, and even though he was much different from Wyatt, there were times she found the similarities overwhelming enough to take her breath.

"Where's Brett?" Dodge scored her gaze at Sawyer.

Tess dropped cloths to the pool of blood still collecting on the floor. She glanced at Dodge reading the worry across her friend's brow. Marcus Benton was such an evil man, surely he was still jailed.

Sawyer headed for the door, turning back toward them both. "Already sent a rider out to his ranch to let him know. I'll have Henry take care of the body."

Tess nodded. Henry was the freed man who worked for the church to bury those who died. She glanced back to Dodge once Sawyer disappeared outside. "Why would anyone do this regardless?"

Dodge lined the table on each side of the man with more soaking cloths "I have no idea, but I didn't like the look in Sawyer's eyes one bit, and there's no doubt Brett won't round up the devil to find out who it was."

"Could Mr. Benton have done this?" Tess struggled with the idea of men being put to death for their crimes, but Marcus Benton was, or at least had been, a very evil man. He'd been sentenced to die for the long ago cold-blooded murder of John McCade, Dodge's husband, and the father of her four sons. Wyatt's father. Her heart raced inside her chest with thoughts of him.

Dodge folded her arms letting out an exasperated breath. "I don't know how that would be possible."

"Well, there is nothing more to do here, at least until Henry comes by. I can clean up once he's gone, you needn't stay." Tess tossed a few more cloths to the floor and went to the basin to wash her blood-covered hands. There was no need for Dodge, who often helped her during surgeries to remain.

"And if I didn't know any better, I would assume you were trying to run me off." Dodge stepped closer, her expression changing to that of concern.

"Pardon?" Tess turned from the basin, soaping her hands. "It wasn't my intention."

"I think the last few months, we have worked together, but we somehow haven't. We hurry when we are done with surgeries or other care to remove ourselves from each other." Dodge leaned hard against the counter and studied her.

Tess met her gaze for a moment and picked up a cloth, drying her hands. It was true. Things had taken an abrupt turn between the two of them months before, and they were both very aware of the reasons why. A sudden bolt of pain jabbed through Tess' center, crushing her breath. "I've been that obvious?"

Dodge's face softened into a smile. "Yes, and I haven't made it any easier on either of us."

Tess put the cloth aside and folded her arms. So, they were going to have the very conversation they had both been avoiding, and she should be the one to start. "It's my fault Wyatt left, and you well know it. I suppose somewhere along the way it just got too hard."

She shook her head. "Wyatt's a grown man."

Tess spoke in a forced whisper, fighting the tears that began to well in her eyes. "Yes, but it's because of me he isn't here now—his home—his family—you."

"He left because you refused his proposal of marriage?" Dodge lifted her brows in question, but it was more of a statement.

Tess held her tears at bay forcing the words from her tightened throat. "He told you?"

Dodge let out a loud sigh, shaking her head. "No, you told me. Wyatt never said anything other than he was leaving Cheyenne."

She'd never spoken to Dodge about any of it, but no matter it was all boiling to the surface now in her tears. "But, I never told you…"

"Sure you did. You packed your bags for Boston and Wyatt left Cheyenne, but you never boarded the train, though your trunks remain packed." Dodge glanced toward the hallway, where the unpacked trunks had remained for months now.

Tess wiped her eyes before the tears fell. Apparently, her very best friend knew her better than she did herself. What on earth was she to say?

Dodge, who never shied away from laying things on the line continued. “Wyatt is off dealing with a broken heart, mending it one outlaw at a time and yet the question is what are you doing about your own? Did it ride off with my son, or did you pack it away for safe keeping in one of those trunks?”

Tess bit her bottom lip, and then whispered. “You of all people should know the dangers of opening old wounds, and as much as I love Wyatt, I couldn’t do to him what I did to Israel.”

Pity filled Dodge’s eyes. “Do you think he would have changed his mind because you couldn’t have children?”

Tess held her gaze, a wave of regret coursing through her so intense she had to force herself to breathe.

“Yes, I know your reasons and while I understand how hard it’s been for you, but what’s holding you back from Boston now?” Dodge lifted her brows and nodded at the trunks again.

Tess filled her lungs with a gulp of air. Of all the things she had shared over the years with Dodge, never once had she acknowledged to her friend her reasons where Wyatt was concerned until now. Her pulse raced and her head pounded, but it was apparent Dodge had figured things out. But she had four sons. She couldn’t know what it was like to break a man’s heart because you could not have his children. She thought of her deceased husband, Israel, who had so wanted a child, and not one day of her married life had gone by without the pain of it being all her fault. She couldn't do that to Wyatt and watch another man's eyes fill with disappointment. Her head spun and her chest tightened as more tears emerged.

"Sit before you fall down." Dodge grabbed her arm and pushed her into one of the chairs and sat next to her. "I'm sorry, Tess. I've never learned the fine art of holding my tongue, and I've missed you. This can't go on, you and I avoiding each other to save the other's feelings."

"I suppose I never had to tell you how it felt to know I couldn't have Israel's children. He so wanted to be a father and took me to every doctor back East in Boston and New York and even the ones that trained me at the Philadelphia College for Women. And none of the physicians could identify a reason. I lived his disappointment every day of our married life. And I…I couldn't do that to Wyatt." She stammered through her difficult words.

Dodge gave her a moment. "Actually, I had no right, but it's time we stopped the small talk and got back to how we were, regardless. Wyatt did what he felt he had to do and now, it's time you thought about you."

"Me?" She tilted her head and frowned.

"Your uncle, I assume could still hold that position or gain another for you, it's time you decided what to do. Either to gather those trunks and go to Boston to learn all you can, or unpack them and get yourself back in order—no matter Wyatt's return." Dodge's voice dropped an octave.

What on earth did she mean? Go to Boston. Stay in

Cheyenne. Wyatt hadn't returned, and maybe he never would. She'd seen the hurt in his eyes when she had told him she couldn't accept his proposal, and it had all but crushed her heart in hurting him.

Dodge took her hand. "Look, you are not home while your bags sit waiting, and you aren't working in some fancy Boston hospital while you go through the motions of being a doctor here in Cheyenne. One day, Wyatt will come home, and when he does, he doesn't need to be the brunt of your regrets. If you're going to Boston, then go, one hundred percent ready for the challenge, but if you stay, you need to make sure the reasons that kept you here are the right ones, children or none. Now, so that we are past this nonsense, I will be going with you for the rest of the week when you see your patients."

She leaned in to hug Dodge, grateful to have her friend back, and undergoing a much needed sense of relief.

"You are here every day, going through all the motions, but you have to find yourself again, regardless of Wyatt." Dodge squeezed her hand.

She waited for a long moment, pondering things. Wyatt had been gone for six months, the longest time she had ever known him to be away from Cheyenne. There was no way of knowing when or if he would return. Her throat tightened at the effort to speak. "But what if he doesn't come home?"

Dodge never batted an eye. "And what if he does?"

She couldn't utter a word as Dodge patted her hand and left the clinic, leaving her to her thoughts. After a moment, she moved idly to her bedroom, peering outside the window. The landscape of mountains in the distance always attracted her attention. There had been times in the past she'd stood in this same window, waiting for Wyatt to return from one of his bounty hunts. But what if Dodge was right?

Her heart pounded at the thought. Wyatt could be a hard man, and even if he did come home, it didn't mean he would offer her any forgiveness. She'd known for some time now that walking away from Wyatt was a mistake—the biggest of her life, but there were no guarantees in matters of the heart. She let the curtain fall back over the window. She eyed the three trunks which lined the hall outside her bedroom. She'd more than disappointed her aunt and uncle by not returning to Boston, but when it had been time to leave, she hadn't been able to make her legs walk the short trek to the train depot. Thoughts of leaving Cheyenne had crushed the very breath from her, and so she had sat and listened for the train to blow its whistle and depart. Only then had she wept the tears over the fact she had loved Wyatt more than life itself.

"Oh, what am I doing? I am waiting on him, knowing full well he will never forgive me." She lifted the lid of the largest trunk. It was true, she had seen the hurt in his deep blue eyes and she'd spent months wondering what a man did when the woman he loved caused him to ride away shattered and broken. Did he have any idea that she consumed the local and surrounding papers for any news of him, losing herself to tears when he was mentioned and praying for his safety?

"It's my fault, though I don't know what to do about it." She shut the trunk again and headed to the front of the clinic. No number of sleepless nights had ever caused her guilt to flee. As much as she did love him and had loved him for more years than she should admit, she couldn't become his wife. Even if Dodge had figured her reasons, it didn't mean Wyatt would understand. Men wanted children, and he would be no different. She had been married to Israel for eight years, and in all that time, she had never once conceived a child. A stab of physical pain gripped her center.

"Oh, Wyatt, I'm so sorry." It had been six months and seven days since he'd departed Cheyenne. She peered at the clock on the wall. "And eight hours or so."

Maybe she should have tried to explain things to him, but he would have told her that children didn't matter and at first it might not have, but it would have—to her. No one could know how hard it was to be a physician who brought children into the world, but would never hold her own. God had miracles for some, but she wasn't one of them. Well, she'd long given up on praying for such an event in her life, but as Dodge had told her, Cheyenne was her home, and if she was going to stay, she needed to find herself again. She had to quit pining at the window and work on putting her life back into some kind of meaningful order. Life in the West for any woman was difficult, and she wasn't going to lose all she'd worked to gain.

She faced the mirror. She *was* a mess, tired eyes and hair falling loose around her face. If Wyatt did come home, he'd keep right on riding; she was so out of sorts. Picking up the brush, she took the pins out of her hair smoothing it. It was time to unpack, get back out seeing her patients more often, and with Dodge riding along, it was apparent she had her friend back. And she would quit waiting for Wyatt, but make sure when and if he did return, she was the woman he would remember, even if there were no guarantees he would be the same man.

Chapter Three

The heat of the afternoon sun played across the prairie, the bold orange sun hanging low in the sky as Wyatt rode the trail leading him home to Cheyenne. Mattie's advice had gotten to him, and it was time to go home. He didn't have to try hard to remember how damn long it had been. His strength with figures had not let his mind rest in counting every day since he'd been on the trail and since he'd last seen her—Tess.

More than six months had passed. He wasn't sure what explanation he'd have for his brothers, but Dodge would be angry to say the least. He missed home, but going back to Cheyenne, with Tess still there…his gut tightened and his heart raced. What had kept her from leaving? It couldn't have been him alone? That bridge had already been crossed, and the rushing water beneath it was gone and along with it, any rights he had to ask just why she'd remained behind.

Ahead of him the outpost south of Cheyenne appeared, which meant he would be home by late evening. Once there he could figure out how best to deal with Dodge, who wouldn't take it well that he hadn't wired even once. Lost in his thoughts, he slowed his horse, glancing ahead as two men on horseback rode toward him from out of nowhere. He stopped the animal as two more rode up on each side of him with two at his back. Outnumbered, and it didn't appear they were of the friendly sort. *Shit!* There was no way to make a quick bolt with his horse, so he waited, glancing a full round at the men surrounding him.

"Dismount and drop the revolvers." A voice behind him barked, and he turned, the dark hat shading the face he knew well.

"What the hell?" he whispered out loud, not believing the man before him still roamed the earth, the purest of unearthed evils. Marcus Benton? He steadied his horse and eyed the man he'd thought long dead. Rage scoured through him, and he held tighter to the reins. Nothing good could come out of this. He'd put Benton on the train back East for sentencing himself, and he'd relished in reading he'd hang for a long list of crimes including the murder of his father. He should have known the man was powerful enough to swindle his way to freedom, and now he'd be the one who paid for not killing the bastard himself.

"Wyatt McCade, fancy meeting you like this." Benton's lip curled into a smile, and his sadistic dark eyes narrowed. "I said dismount and drop your gun belt."

He said nothing, glaring at the men closing in around him. There were six in all, including Benton. He contemplated his predicament, keeping his mount. He could reach for his guns and no doubt take out four of the men, but he couldn't get them all. He could easily shoot Benton and lose his life, which might be damn worth it.

"Now!" Benton's voice echoed across the prairie, with its thick coarse grasses of green and brown, whipping in the heated wind.

Escape was futile, and off his horse with no

weapon other than the knife in his boot, he was a dead man. He dismounted, never taking his gaze from the man he'd hated his entire life as he made short work of lowering his gun belt to the sandy trail.

Benton circled his horse closer. "You've done right well for yourself, bounty hunter. I've read about you in the papers. Tell me; what puts such drive and determination in a man?"

"Weren't you scheduled for a rope?" Wyatt raised a brow, turning a circle of warning to the men who dismounted, all of them keeping their distance as they surrounded him.

Benton gave a hearty laugh. "Interesting thing about courts and law. There is always a loophole. It was your father who taught me that. I've been pardoned, and now, it's your turn for justice. Your brothers will follow as will Brett Morgan, for the death of my brother."

"Your brother killed my father and tried to kill Sawyer; he had it coming." He held his ground, tightening his fist, contemplating an escape, though his fate was sealed. "And I should have swung a rope and hung your ass right then and there." He'd thought about it at the time, wanting to make sure Benton rotted in hell, but his sheriff brother had insisted the law be followed.

Benton climbed down from his horse. "I believe Eleanor, once told me the same thing. Such a pity she will suffer the loss of her sons and Brett Morgan for swindling me out of land that was to be mine."

"That's right; Brett got the property you wanted, and you only gained your land at the mercy of my father." Wyatt spat loud and clear, turning again as the men began to close in around him. Benton's failure to gain the land he wanted years ago had been behind the man's plot of evil against the McCades and Brett Morgan, his father's trusted ranch foreman.

"Brett's a thief," Benton rebutted with a snarl.

Wyatt cursed to himself. "Brett's taken nothing from you and neither did my father."

Benton pulled gloves on each hand with care, his dark eyes stoic as he stepped closer. "Your father kept a number of questionable counterparts, and Morgan was one of them."

Wyatt narrowed his eyes on the circle of men getting closer, and a few stopped or backed up a step. It was clear they knew who he was, his reputation for a good fight preceding him. "Nothing you do here today will get you that land. Not one damn thing."

"Idle talk, but now it's time to, let's say, teach you a little lesson a long time in coming." Benton pulled a bull whip from his saddle bags and turned back to him.

The men moved in, and Wyatt turned another slow full circle, eyeing each of them. They might get the best of him, but the man who made the first move would suffer as would the one behind him. Shit, the air felt tight as he sifted it through to his lungs anticipating the first move. Son of a bitch, but he wouldn't go down without a fight. He turned about the time that Benton's whip slapped around his ankle, jerking him to the ground in a cloud of dust, the men falling in a heap across him.

He swung hard with both fists and resisted with all he was, pulling from the primal man deep inside him. Fight or die. He punched with purpose, knocking one large man back but feeling the snap of bone in his right hand. Another he kicked aside, the man yelping with the impact to his belly. Too many. A boot caught his side, and the crunch of bone sounded a second before the pain scorched through his ribs. He growled through the pain to keep fighting. All around him was a blur as he was subdued, with three men holding him to the hardened earth and Benton's boot across his neck, cutting off his air. He struggled to breathe and sucked in a short painful breath, gripping his side. His hands were pulled together before him, and he pulled against the burn of the rope as he was tied, the painful right hand causing him to cease the fight.

"Why resist, Wyatt, you know death is coming." Benton taunted near his face as the men held him to the ground. Frankly, he'd figured Benton to hang him or at least string him up to be whipped, which had been the man's calling card in the past.

Wyatt struggled at the burn of the rope. His hands were his one defense, and tied he had nothing but the pain. He struggled to breathe, the weight of the men holding him too much. He coughed again at the dust, narrowing his gaze on Benton, who stood above him.

"You've always annoyed me, not as smart as your older brother in keeping the proper…respect. That land belongs to me and so do the mines on *Brett's property*." Benton spat and kicked his side hard enough to knock the breath free of his body. He sucked in a cluttered breath of dust with a wheeze. Nausea plagued him with the impact of another kick. His mind focused on the searing pain, his ribs were broken and his hand throbbed. He lifted his head and forced out the words. "My respectful brother…will kill you when…this is over."

"Well, now this is far from over." Benton coiled the whip and tossed it to one of the hands, who bobbled to catch it.

They were going to kill him, and that he'd not be using the bull whip made little sense. Maybe he would be hanged or shot, but Marcus Benton would get away with nothing. The rage built up inside of him again. "McCade lands…were never yours and neither are those mines. Your scheming…against my father backfired long ago."

"John McCade created his own little web of deceit and it's his sons who will pay, starting with you." Benton kicked him again and nodded to the man who had taken the whip. "We could negotiate a bit on just how to do this more humanly, but John McCade's sons deserve the worst kind of death. Such a pity for Eleanor."

Wyatt glared and focused hard, every muscle in his body tight. It had been no secret that Benton had once loved Dodge but lost her to Brett after his father had been killed. Hell, he'd never understood the past where his mother tangled with the man before him and chose Brett. There were some questions you didn't ask.

"It's going to be a long evening but given this heat, it shouldn't take you long to meet your maker." Benton directed a glance into the heated sky and then back down at him. "No water for miles, and the heat will parch you like a roasting pig."

He'd be left for dead. He glanced around, four men still holding him to the ground. He gave another struggle with all his might. He clenched his jaw against the pain scorching through his side as he tried to take a solid breath, his strength ebbing. The bastard might kill him, but he'd never get the land he wanted. Forcing air from his lungs, he let a slight smile play across his lips. "I'll see…you in…hell."

Benton snarled with an evil grin. "Well then, let's see who gets there first."

Funny, he had always known he would die hunting down a bounty but never had he thought it would be Marcus Benton who would have the honor. His father's words echoed in his mind as they always had since his death. *Fight, Wyatt, fight son, never let up, never show fear.*

"Boss." One of the men spoke to Benton with a bit of hesitation in his voice. "Not sure I want murder on my hands or one of those McCade boys coming after me, with all due respect, sir."

Benton shoved him away from them all. "I decide the plans here." He turned to the others. "Any one of you who see reason not to be a part of this may leave right now without fear of reprimand, but you leave without further pay."

One of the men holding Wyatt stepped away. "When I followed you here, this wasn't what I signed on for, and I'd rather not cross Sheriff Sawyer McCade." The edge of nerves to the man's voice was evident as the others still held him to the ground.

He fought, but with his hands tied, he was useless, and he could hardly breathe. Hot and thirsty already.

The men backed idly toward their horses, the latter speaking again. "And I've heard men talk of that McCade who dresses like an Indian, even the Cheyenne have a fear of him."

"Both of you get out of my sight and let me not see your faces again." Benton roared this time, stomping near them.

In seconds, the men rode off on their mounts, a flurry of dust settling across them all, choking what breath Wyatt had taken. He pulled at the ropes, shoving at the men once more, but to no avail. His body shook in fatigue.

Benton turned back to him and kicked him to get his attention. He blinked his blurry eyes to a squint, coughing and sputtering, unable to speak.

"Wyatt, a bullet, nahhh or even a noose. Too easy. Too…kind. But scorching out here on this hell of a prairie should be punishment enough. By the time you fight through the heat, you won't last the frozen night with no horse or weapons. Just you and the buzzards by noon tomorrow." Benton nodded at the man nearest him.

The large man dragged a log over and shoved it under Wyatt's boot at the ankle. He tried to wrestle away, but the men held him still. They were going to break his leg, and he had no fight left. Hell, Benton knew just what he was doing in breaking his leg and leaving him to die. It wouldn't take long at all. *Son of a bitch!*

Then there was no delay. The man jumped above the log, just at his ankle. The snap of the bone took what little breath he'd managed. He lost his bearings, shaking in unbearable pain as he stifled his scream. The man stomped once more across the leg for good measure. This time, with the crunch of bone, his mouth opened, but no sound escaped him as the world closed around him. He struggled to grasp the growing abyss of darkness with his tied hands, reaching for the one place he might be safe from the pain—Tess.

Chapter Four

Tess jotted down the medications she needed to order from Chicago. Running low on laudanum and chloroform wasn't a good thing, and the container of powdered quinine was getting rather low. She scolded herself that until Dodge's lecture, she had let a lot of things fall behind without realizing it. Well, now she was cleaning up and getting the clinic and her life back into some semblance of order.

Voices mingled in the office where she returned after folding the list into her apron pocket. The front door of the clinic remained open, and Dodge trotted toward her with a large crate. She was followed by Zane, her grandson and Sawyer's eldest son, who was carrying two more of the large crates from the mercantile.

"Oh, Dodge, let's put it on the counter." She grabbed one side of the crate and helped Dodge heave it to the counter with a clunk.

"Whoa, these are heavy." Zane toggled the crates he held and plopped them on the counter beside the other, then dusted his hands.

"Thank you, Zane." Tess smiled. He was the spitting image of Sawyer, and she often caught herself watching him for the small hints of Wyatt that shone through when he smiled. Only a year and half before she'd done what she could to save his life after he'd taken a spill on his horse and his extended stay in the clinic had given him a special place in her heart.

"You're welcome, Doc." Zane tilted his hat back, his gray eyes bright.

Dodge wiped her brow. "I had most of what was on your list at the mercantile, but I took the liberty to order some of the items out of Denver. Might take a few weeks."

Zane took a stroll around the clinic, shoving his hands into his trouser pockets. He glanced outside to his dog, Sirius, who waited at the door, pink tongue hanging from his mouth as he panted in the heat.

"That's fine. Want to make sure I am stocked, and I have a list of medications I need to wire for from Chicago, though these days it can take months." Tess sorted through one of the crates, eyeing the contents which included bandages, ties, splints, and a few liniments and oils that should have long been ready inside the clinic.

"Zane, head on to school. I don't want you late again." Dodge planted a kiss on his cheek "Evan wants you out with the herds this afternoon, so no fishing after school."

"Yes ma'am." Zane grabbed a belted pile of books from the top of one crate and trotted out the door jumping from the porch, the dog barking as he followed.

Dodge turned back to Tess. "He missed school yesterday when one of the horses foaled and Evan needed help. Sawyer wasn't too happy, but Evan has taken time to teach him a lot about the ranch and caring for the animals. He's right good at it."

Tess smiled, aware that Evan, the youngest of

Dodge's four sons, had taken the task of teaching Zane to heart. "He's growing up so fast; he looks more like Sawyer every day."

"Well, he'll be off to university in Denver in a few years to study law." Dodge added, laying items from one crate onto the counter.

"I'm sure he will do well. He's such a smart boy." Tess took another look around the clinic. It did look much better and without the clutter of her trunks in the hallway. Things almost seemed back to normal—all but the part where there had still been no word of Wyatt.

"Yes, but I am afraid I will miss him, though he is set to return and open Cheyenne's first law office." Dodge put a bundle of dressings aside.

"Lawyer by day, musician by night?" Zane's proficiency with the violin was remarkable for a boy his age. He'd been taught by his mother at a very young age, and when she'd died, he'd taken on the journey of finding Sawyer, the father he'd never known. And while the boy had been an incredible surprise to everyone, he had molded with ease into all their lives just as if he'd always been there.

Dodge turned abruptly but continued talking. "He was playing on the porch last night, and I had to stop and close my eyes and listen."

"Dod! Dod!" Nicholas bolted into the clinic ahead of Sawyer's wife, Rose, the toddler jumping for Dodge to pick him up. "Dod, candy?"

She scooped up her youngest grandson and kissed his rosy cheek. "No candy, but why don't you help me unpack these boxes?" She set him back down and handed him a smaller box of dressing cloths. He squatted to open the box, blond curls hanging across his tiny brow.

Rose ambled toward Tess and placed a small vase of fresh cut flowers on the counter. "Nicholas and I picked some wild flowers for you, knowing how you love having them in the clinic."

"Flo…wer." Nicholas chanted without looking up from his treasure.

Tess had to smile. She and Rose shared a fancy for pretty flowers and that Nicholas had helped made them all the more special. "Thank you, Rose. They're lovely."

"Oh and this package came for you. I had to go by the post office to pick up telegrams for Sawyer, and I dropped off a few articles for Mr. McDonald at the paper." Rose handed her a small parcel.

Tess took it, tugging at the brown paper packing. "This will be the bitter root and some other herbs I sent for. How are things at the paper?"

Rose beamed with excitement. "I've managed to write a few articles a week. Sawyer tolerates me interviewing the prisoners sometimes, and I've even written about the circuit judge's visit, but it's difficult what with chores and a busy little one."

"I enjoy the paper every week; in fact it becomes my bedtime reading." Tess pulled layers of cotton from around glass vials, the truth being she scoured any paper she could get her hands on for news of Wyatt.

Rose rubbed her swollen belly. "I hardly read at all anymore, my days are so full that I fall asleep as soon as my head hits the pillow."

Tess admired her for a moment. She was radiant, expecting her second child soon, her cheeks pink and full and her blue eyes bright with hope. "Well, at this point you need your rest. Nap when Nicholas sleeps. Doctor's order."

Rose smiled at Nicholas, who was still busy with the box of items Dodge had given to him. "No worries, Sawyer hardly lets me do a thing these days."

"Sawyer is right." And though she was happy for Rose and Sawyer, a sudden pain scored through her at the reminder of her own body's inabilities and the fact that Wyatt still hadn't returned home. She turned back to the crate she'd been unpacking, willing the tears that welled in her eyes to dry. Dodge had continued to reassure her of his return, but that had done little to ease her regret where he was concerned.

"Sawyer will hardly let her out of his sight." Dodge took off on a full run across the room and unhanded a pair of scissors from Nicholas, putting them out of his reach. "No-no, these might hurt you."

"No, no, noooooo." Nicholas mocked her with a giggle but was distracted when Sawyer stomped through the door of the clinic, spurs clinking along with the heavy sound of his boots.

"Papa." The toddler ran to wrap himself around his father's leg, grinning at them all from under the shadow of the man before them.

Sawyer picked up his small son and sat him in the crook of one arm, speaking to Rose and stepping closer. "Did you go by the post?"

Rose pulled the folded papers from her smock, handing them to him. "I was coming by the jail but stopped by here first."

"It's fine." He unfolded the telegrams, urgency crossing his face as he kept Nicholas from touching the memos, by handing him off to Rose.

"Sawyer?" Rose sat Nicholas to his feet on the floor. "Sawyer, what is it?"

After a moment, he crumpled the notes in his fist, turning back to them. His lips flattened and he jerked the hat from his head, his gray eyes serious and dark. "Son of a bitch," he whispered, not meeting anyone's eyes, lost to the news he'd just read.

Nicholas scampered across the room chanting after his father. "Son…bits, son…bits."

"Sawyer, really! Bad words Nicholas. No, no." Rose scolded them both, but let the boy continue to play. "What on earth?"

It was more than obvious that Sawyer didn't want to say. His face was serious, but it was Dodge he turned to. "It's from Hudson who is fine, but he was shot helping Wyatt capture an outlaw in Denver. Wyatt left early the next morning. I suppose it's been several days ago."

Tess grabbed the counter to steady herself, unsure her next breath would come. Wyatt was as close as Denver and—Oh God. Her pulse raced and she fought to keep from shaking. He would come home now, wouldn't he? Denver was several day's ride by horse—so close she shivered.

"That would explain Hudson's delay, but where is Wyatt now?" Dodge glanced at Tess but then turned back toward her son.

Sawyer clenched his fists, his gray eyes narrowing. "There's more…"

Dodge stepped closer and Tess' breath held in her tightened throat.

He ran a hand across his face, blowing out a disgusted breath as he spoke, "Marcus Benton has been pardoned."

The quiet in the room was deafening. Tess took a step back, shaking her head. How on earth could that have happened?

Dodge's mouth dropped open, and she spoke in a flurry of words. "That's not possible, but that would explain Brett's ranch hand that was shot."

Tess grabbed the counter, breath leaving her lungs all together. How could an evil man like that have been pardoned? Worse, Wyatt remained elusive while Marcus Benton was free to roam. This could not be happening.

"What are you going to do?" Rose grabbed the crumpled telegrams from Sawyer and began reading them for herself. She handed them off to Dodge, who scrutinized them for a moment.

"Get to the bottom of things for starters." Sawyer's hands gripped into tight fists.

"I should have known that Marcus had enough money to swindle his way out of death one more time." Dodge crumpled the notes once more, keeping them inside her own fist.

"We all should've known." Sawyer folded his arms. "I'll send a few wires; see what I can find out."

A wave of nausea clamored through Tess. "Sawyer?"

He turned and settled his gray eyes on her.

"Wyatt's out there…" She held more words at bay, bile rising in her throat.

"We'll find him." Sawyer held her gaze a moment more and turned to kiss Rose on the cheek before heading out the door.

Nicholas bolted to follow, but Rose lifted him into

her arms.

"Papa. Papa." The small boy began to cry, but Sawyer was gone.

"Come on, we'll go after Papa," Rose coaxed, hugging him as she scurried after her husband.

Tess turned, exchanging brief glances with Dodge. Lord, but she was going to be sick. She raced for the back door where she stepped off the porch and heaved, clutching her chest. How would Sawyer find Wyatt when none of them had any idea where he was? If Marcus Benton had returned and he didn't know, things could be very bad for Wyatt. It was no secret that Mr. Benton hated all the McCade's, but there had been times in the past that things between he and Wyatt had gotten more than heated.

Dodge touched her back, handing her a cool damp cloth. "Here."

"I'm all right." She wiped her mouth and tried to sound convincing, but Dodge had always seen right through her.

"No, you're not and I'm not, either. The boys will find him. They have to." Dodge stepped off the porch and hugged her close.

"Mr. Benton hates Wyatt, what if—" She held her words, tugging from Dodge's embrace.

"Marcus is the equivalent of a horse's ass, and if he so much as lays a hand on Wyatt, I will string him up by the…Well, I will personally string him right up and he knows as much." Dodge folded her arms and talked between her clenched teeth.

Tess couldn't stop the chuckle that escaped her. She covered her mouth. Nothing about the situation was funny, but if she didn't laugh, she would cry real tears.

Dodge giggled with her. "I can come up with worse."

Tess let her smile fade. "I shouldn't be laughing given it's my fault he still isn't home, but Denver…he has to be close, Dodge."

"Wyatt loves you. I know my son, and you are his heart. We both just need him home, and the rest will figure itself. The boys will find him somehow." She sounded certain.

Tess peered across the mountains. *Oh, God please let him be safe.* "What must I have done to him?"

"He will love you as he always has, Tess." Dodge took the cloth and used it to wipe the tears from her cheeks. "And when he returns, you can tell him your reasons and see that you have worried for naught."

She so wanted to believe it would all be fine. Maybe one of his brothers would find him, or maybe he would ride back into town from behind the mountains she still searched each evening. Explaining her actions seemed simple compared to Wyatt being at Marcus Benton's mercy. But he was so close. If he'd been to Denver and he did return soon, how on earth would she ever explain why she had broken his heart and shattered her own?

Chapter Five

Wyatt...you must live, fight son. Fight. You will settle the West one man at a time. There is more to do, push hard in all things. Fight, Wyatt. Wyatt jolted awake, a baby's cry in the distance, disturbing his thoughts. Father? His vision blurred to the darkened sky, the pain in his ankle drawing him to a confused state of consciousness. A wolf howled, not a baby, and for a moment he wasn't sure where he was, until he made the mistake of trying to move. "Ahhhhhh…" Marcus Benton had left him for dead, the rotten coward. His thoughts were lost as he traced a hand to his thigh, seeking relief from the unrelenting pain in his left ankle and foot. The man had known what he was doing, sentencing him to a slow and painful death by breaking a lower leg and leaving him to die.

He tried to focus on his surroundings, not that it helped his blurry mind. He should have woken in Hell by all his expectations, but it seemed Hell was right in the middle of the Godforsaken prairie. His face ached, and his hands were so swollen. He couldn't make a fist or feel his fingers, his right hand painful even at rest. His ties had been cut, but the ropes remained around his wrists, and he struggled to free them. Nausea plagued him with the effort, and he gagged, bile rushing to the back of his throat. Breathing hurt the stretching of his broken ribs. How long had it been? His body shivered involuntarily, the brute cold somewhat the lesser of evils plaguing his broken body.

He pulled himself up, cradling his right hand, but the pain in his leg scorched through him without mercy. "Aaahhhhhh." He closed his eyes, sucking in the night air and shivering, numb with cold. He held his boot, the leather tight around his lower leg, barely able to move.

He'd dreamt of his father as if he were real again. But John McCade had been gone for years and could help him no more than he could help himself. *Thirsty, so tired and thirsty. Cold.*

Gathering his strength, he held his leg and dug his right boot heel into the thick grass, determined to move. He might manage to crawl but he wouldn't get far and it was miles to anywhere.

He fell back once more, curling to hold his leg. He'd hurt before but never like this, and the dreams of his father's voice were mingled with the faces of Dodge, his brothers—and Tess. He pictured her face, her green eyes, and long brown hair. So beautiful. He smelled the lavender. She was still in Cheyenne, hadn't Mattie said so? Perhaps if he'd stayed home, he wouldn't be lying on the cold prairie, serving up his own version of last rights. His breath caught, and he fought the bout of coughing that pounded his tender ribs. He tensed, and pain shot through all the muscles of his calf contracting in spasms.

Groaning, he tried to move again, but it was useless. He pained when he didn't move, but it was unbearable when he did. His body shivered, and he gave in to closing his eyes. Tired. He had to rest, for a little while. Thirsty, so dry he couldn't swallow his own saliva. Death would take him soon with any luck at all.

He sighed and held his leg, giving into the sleep that scrambled his dreams, his father calling to him once more.

****

Wyatt didn't want to rouse from the confinement of deep slumber though his father drew him, calling to him over and over. *Wyatt?*

His father called to him, and he forced his eyes open, squinting at the glare of the sun. He grabbed his father's shirt with both fists, but… "Daw…son?"

"It's me, brother." Dawson placed a canteen to his lips, lifting his head. "Drink, take some water."

The cool metal touched his parched lips, and he tried to drink, but his mouth didn't seem to work, and the liquid spilled down his chin and neck. He coughed and gulped, then gagged, the pain in his leg unmerciful. How on earth had he survived the night, or had it been days?

"Drink, brother. I'm here." Dawson tried again, forcing the canteen once more.

Wyatt forced his eyes open again. The sun rode high in the sky, and the heat roasted him, though he shivered. His ribs hurt, and breathing was a struggled effort, but he wanted the water and this time gulped, trying to take the canteen for himself.

"Just a little at a time, you'll get sick." Dawson pulled the canteen away. "Who did this, Wyatt?"

He couldn't focus. "Water…"

Dawson gave him more of the cool liquid, though his voice was stern. "Look at me Wyatt, who?"

He swallowed until he lost his breath and pulled his lips from the canteen, watching the buzzards circle high in the sky above him. "The buzzards…are waiting."

His brother glanced at the sky. “I’m taking you home; you wouldn’t make good buzzard food anyway. Who the hell did this, Wyatt?”

He groaned in pain, but gathered his breath. “Benton.”

Dawson eased him back to the ground, rage crossing his face. “Benton? Son of a… Sawyer sent word he’d been pardoned, guess he didn’t waste any time getting to you.”

“Bastard…” He coughed and grabbed his ribs with a groan.

His brother’s voice softened as he began to use water from the canteen to clean the blood from his cheek. “I’m taking you home, Wyatt, leastwise we both gotta get out of here with Benton on the loose.”

Wyatt winced as his leg cramped, the muscles of his calf drawing tight. “My…leg. Aaahhh…Son of a bitch!”

Dawson traced his hands over the twisted boot of his leg causing him to yelp and try to shove his brother away. “The leg’s broken above the ankle. I’ll have to get you splinted so we can move you.”

“It’s too…late.” His voice cracked as he opened his eyes again. His head pounded from the heat, and while he could no longer feel the foot in his boot, his leg shot unrelenting pain clear to his knee. His ribs hurt with each breath, and his hand was twice its normal size, his fingers swollen so tight he could grip nothing.

“You fight Wyatt; this isn’t enough to bring you down.” Dawson tugged the tail of his leather tunic from his breeches and began cutting away strips of leather with the knife from his belt.

Wyatt focused on his brother. He had no doubts

he'd die as he already should have, but the least he could hope was his brothers would avenge him by putting Marcus Benton six-feet under. "You get…him."

"You fight, Wyatt, and we'll get him together. I'll be right back. I've got to find splints for your leg." Dawson surveyed around them and took off on a trot.

He closed his eyes and time slipped from him again.

"Stay awake, brother!" Dawson patted his bearded cheek with his return, and then spoke in Cheyenne of all things.

He opened his eyes and focused on Leaning Bear, who stood behind his brother. He might have known. As far as he was concerned, the sharp-tongued Cheyenne Medicine Man, that his brother called friend, was nothing but trouble.

"Gotta get the boot off with all the swelling." Dawson tugged on Wyatt's left boot.

He gritted his teeth at the back lash of pain, his eyes watering as the foot he hadn't been able to feel, carried a burning heartbeat of its own. Pain scorched through his entire being, and a groan escaped him as he struggled not to pass out.

"Sorry brother, it's gotta be done." Dawson patted his face again, rousing him from the brink of darkness.

Leaning Bear chanted in Cheyenne, then spoke in English, tossing down splints. "The spirits say very bad."

Had he the energy, Wyatt would have cussed. The last thing he needed was the medicine man praying to the Cheyenne gods over his fate. "Don't need a thing…from his spirits." It was all he could do to get the words out of his mouth, but damned if he'd give the

Indian the satisfaction.

"My brother doesn't have much faith in the Cheyenne ways," Dawson explained as he readied the splints.

"White man's God never speak. I will build litter to carry him to his mother." The Indian turned away from them, the crunch of the high grass under his moccasins a scurry of wisps.

"Don't need his…help." Wyatt cursed. He'd always found Leaning Bear annoying and a cheat when he came to town to sell his pelts.

"He means well. He's the one who spotted you." Dawson shook him when he closed his eyes. "Sawyer said you were in Denver; is that the direction you came from?"

Wyatt gave a slight nod. His brother would never get him to Cheyenne before he died. He groaned and closed his eyes again in defeat. He hadn't the energy for much more and to die all he had to do was let go.

"Wake up, Wyatt. I've gotta get your leg splinted." Dawson moved to his left side. "I need you to stay awake."

"Trying." He forced his eyes open. He'd lost consciousness and even dreamt for a moment, but it had seemed like years. The canteen touched his lips, and he gulped twice, the damn Indian helping him this time. *Bastard.*

Dawson placed the splints along his leg and tugged the leather straps in place tying each one secure.

He yelped with each, the pain taking his breath. "Ahhhhhhh…can't…"

"That's all, deep breaths, brother." Dawson pushed him back down to the grassy earth.

Fighting tears he hadn't the moisture to shed, he shivered. "Cold."

"No, you're burning up with fever." His brother placed a hand to his forehead.

"Not…gonna make…it." He wasn't giving up, but his leg and ribs hurt, and he struggled to breathe. Death would be easier than this by far, and he had no fear of the darkness anymore.

"You're going home, now you hang on!" Dawson patted his face and uttered in a syllable or two of the Indian's tongue. The two were debating his survival for the trip, and the medicine man wasn't certain.

"Tell his…sorry ass to…speak English." Wyatt growled, sure Leaning Bear spoke Cheyenne to rile him further.

The Indian peered at him and back to Dawson, handing over the reins to his horse and speaking in Cheyenne again.

"I can't take your horse." Dawson's voice softened, and he shook his head. "The litter will work if we secure his leg and tie him tight enough."

Leaning Bear put the reins of his unsaddled horse into his brother's fist. "He is your brother. He is my brother, even if sorry…ass…brother."

Wyatt didn't know whether to curse or laugh but didn't have the energy for either. He and the Indian had never had a true liking of each other, but a respect that Dawson held them both to.

Leaning Bear bent, peering at his splinted leg, and pulled out a pouch from his leather tunic. "Willow Bark tea for pain and fever."

"Whiskey?" Wyatt whispered then cursed, "Damn it."

Dawson shoved the pouch of tea into his tunic, shaking his head. "We got no whiskey. I'll let the tea rest in the canteen for a while. Leastwise you won't feel every bump on the way to Cheyenne with both horses carrying you. We gotta move you brother. Bite this." Dawson placed a small shaved stick he'd been working on the last few minutes in between his teeth.

He groaned but kept it in place, tasting the bitterness of the green stem as Dawson and Leaning Bear lifted him with one steady move to the litter. He gritted against the wood, his teeth sinking deep as he yelped loud enough to scatter the impending buzzards overhead. His eyes filled with tears as the pain in his leg shot to his knee and throbbing big toe. He gave into a loud cry as they settled his litter to the horses. He'd never make the ride to Cheyenne.

The Indian spoke his good-bye and turned to walk away, leaving him and his brother to their journey.

"That's all for now, brother. I'll give you some tea in a bit." Dawson wiped his face with a cool cloth.

He gazed at his brother through his blurred vision and gave a nod. His younger brother taking care of him was surreal. He'd spent a lot of time worrying over Dawson's escapades in Indian negotiations, but he was his own man, doing what he thought was right. Somehow, his quiet younger brother commanded a respect from Indians and white men with no more than his actions. And now his brother was his savior, not that he'd live to thank him.

"We're not that far from Cheyenne, a little more than half a day's ride. Should be home by nightfall. Looks like you got a good punch in." Dawson tugged the bandana from him and wrapped his paining hand

and tucked it against his chest. "It won't be long brother. Rest."

He grimaced as the horses struggled to find their cadence. The foot of the litter was tied to the Indian's horse and the head to Dawson's animal. Perfect, he'd die with a horse's ass in his face. He tried for a chuckle and grabbed his side, it not being worth the effort. The endless rocking plagued his leg in spite of the splints. Well, he'd never make it five miles, but then who the hell was counting anymore?

Chapter Six

The golden sun dropped behind the mountains, casting Cheyenne into the darkness of late evening. Tess pulled her buggy into town on the main road, not having meant to be out after dark. Sawyer had continued to warn her not to take too long when leaving Cheyenne to check on her patients, and he'd been adamant she not go alone. But Dodge had received a large shipment of items for the mercantile and had been too busy to ride along. Besides, she had stayed close to town and she was back now, safe and sound.

She urged Annie, her mare and her constant companion along toward the clinic, stifling a yawn and noticing the flurry of men moving toward the clinic. Someone was hurt, no less, given the body of a man on the litter. She scrambled from the buggy. Reaching inside, she grabbed her medical bag, turning back to them.

It was Dawson who met her gaze as the men, including Sawyer, closed the distance, but what caught her attention was that Dodge was with them. She was hanging on to the head of the litter, scrambling to keep up. When she glanced up, Tess' heart dropped to the floor of her chest, beating no more.

"Wyatt?" It was a slight whisper that escaped her, and she froze, unable to move. Every fear she had ever had and every prayer she had ever uttered for him came full force to the surface. *Oh, Lord in heaven.*

"Leaning Bear and I found him early this morning, not far from the outpost," Dawson explained, as the men met her at the stairs to the clinic. "Marcus Benton got him, looks like yesterday sometime."

Tess said nothing as she went to the head of the litter, glancing at Dodge and resting her gaze—on Wyatt. He was shivering and moaned as she rested a hand across his fevered brow, fighting to keep tears at bay. Sawyer and the other men were talking, and she was aware Dodge was speaking to her, but she heard none of it. *Wyatt? Oh, God what have I done to you?*

Dodge touched the sleeve of her blouse as the men continued inside with Wyatt. She couldn't move and somehow she had no words, but then Dodge grabbed her, shaking her from her stupor.

"Tess?" Dodge shook her harder. "You must care for him."

Tess tried hard to gather her scrambled thoughts, Dodge's words sinking in. "I'm all right. I'll…I'll need your help."

Dodge tugged her along, leading the way as they followed the men inside.

"Easy, Wyatt." Dawson held his splinted leg, moving it at the same time the others, including Sawyer, got him to the table.

He yelped in pain his voice dry and raspy.

Tess washed her hands in the basin, drying them as she went to Wyatt's side. His eyes were closed, and he moaned with each ragged breath. His hair was long and his beard thick and his face was bruised. He hardly looked like Wyatt at all, but it was him and she touched his brow once more.

"His ribs are broken, and he's favoring his right hand there. I wrapped it. I guess Benton broke the leg for good measure. He's a fever, in and out." Dawson offered as he lifted his leather tunic away from Wyatt's chest and cut away the shirt he was wearing with a large knife.

"Wyatt?" Her voice cracked as she spoke to him, but she held her tears. She was a physician and her options to fall apart were limited even if every ounce of her body wanted to crumble to the floor.

His eyes blinked open and he squinted. "Doc?"

"You're home, Wyatt." She slid her hands through his hair, feeling for cuts or bruising along his scalp and finding none.

He grimaced. "Doc?"

"I'm here, Wyatt." She traced from his shoulders and downward toward his hands, taking the one without the wrap. "Wyatt, squeeze my hand."

He did as she asked, which meant the rope burns around his wrist hadn't caused the damage she thought they might have. She tried to let go, but his hand held her tighter.

"Never…saw an angel…till now." His voice was soft, but it was apparent he was seeing well enough to know it was her. Some part of her wanted to burst into tears at his words and the chance they offered forgiveness.

She brought her face close to his again, her pulse racing and her thoughts still running at random. "Wyatt, you have to tell me where you hurt. Do you know where you are?"

"Home." His eyes were closed again, but he answered.

"You have to tell me what's worse." She placed her hands along each side of his chest, stopping Dodge, who turned to rinse the bloody cloth she had been using to clean up his chest, but not before she held Tess' gaze.

She could only offer her friend and Wyatt's mother a simple nod of reassurance as she pressed on his chest and worked her way down to the purple bruising on his ribcage. He grimaced, trying to push her away, the old wooden table creaking with the struggle.

Sawyer grabbed him, stopping his fight. "Let the doctor work, Wyatt."

Tess traced the ribs beneath the purple skin. Fractures, at least two of them. She grabbed her scope and listened to his breathing. At least his lungs weren't punctured, but the bases were diminished. Pneumonia. "Two ribs fractured. We'll wrap him last, and his fever is likely from pneumonia."

"Cold." He struggled against Sawyer's strength, shivering hard.

Tess assessed his belly, pressing with some depth, but he never tightened or showed he was in any pain. It occurred to her that she'd seen his naked chest in the past when she had treated his injuries, but now she caught herself admiring the perfectness of the tight muscles of his abdomen. Such a strong man to have survived the night alone in such condition. He'd probably been in terrible pain.

Dodge wiped Wyatt's lips with a cool rag. "It's all right, son."

"Water." He rasped without opening his eyes, still trying to tug free of his brother.

With Tess' nod, Dodge lifted his head to place a

small tin cup of water to his lips, and he drank it down in gulps. He coughed, and his face wrinkled into a frown as he managed to pull from Sawyer's grasp and hold his side.

Tess unwrapped his injured hand, tossing aside the rags. His fingers were all puffy, but there was a slight protrusion to the bone of the hand where the small finger connected. A boxer's fracture with the skin already blue on both sides of his hand. He'd fought back, and she would have expected no less. She grabbed splints and ties, and as she placed them on the hand, he groaned but didn't pull away. The bone wouldn't need to be set, but it would need to stay wrapped for a time. The less he moved it the better. She tied the stays in place and made sure the fit was snug.

Dawson caught her gaze. "He's had Willow Bark tea. Should I take the splints from the leg? It'll need setting."

"Yes, cut his trouser leg away. And Sawyer, send one of the men for ice from the saloon. Jacob keeps any he has in the cellar, wrapped in canvas." She glanced at the sheriff who tilted a nod to one of the men waiting outside the door.

She moved to the other side of the exam table to Wyatt's left leg, waiting on Dawson to cut the pants away. His skill with the weapon was evident as he made short work to free Wyatt's leg of the ties and splints.

Tess cringed at the sound of Wyatt's guttural cry, so primal and unlike the strong man she had always known. His pain was severe and no doubt, given the oddly twisted appearance of his lower leg just above his ankle. Setting the leg was going to be difficult, given the chloroform she'd ordered still hadn't arrived. She had no way of rendering him unconscious, and while laudanum would help, it wouldn't touch pain like that. She tugged his socks off and grasped both his feet. "Wiggle your toes, Wyatt."

She waited, and after a long moment, the toes of both feet moved. His ankle and foot held gross purple swelling which was the most likely sign that both leg bones had been broken. How had this been done? She nodded to Sawyer who held Wyatt tighter as she manipulated around the lower leg, ankle and foot.

Wyatt cried out again cursing them all. "Just…leave it, damn…it to hell!"

She turned and grabbed the metal syringe, drawing up the laudanum from a glass vial in a hurry. Satisfied at the amount, she went to Wyatt, touched his brow, and spoke tenderly wanting to be certain he understood. "I have laudanum but no chloroform. Wyatt, do you hear what I am saying?"

He squinted at her, but it was a long moment before he spoke. "It's all right…Doc."

Evan roared into the room, his heavy boots clomping along the floor, metal spurs clanking as he jerked the hat from his head. "What the hell happened?"

Sawyer glanced up, the sheriff's gray eyes cold and dark. "Benton got him."

"Pardoned my ass, we should have all handled his sentencing right here in Cheyenne when we had the chance." Evan spat in response, glaring at his eldest brother.

"It's not the time, Evan!" Sawyer cut him off before he could say anything more.

Tess ignored them. Evan should well know what

Mr. Benton was capable of doing. “Wyatt, I’ve got the laudanum.” She went to his right side, and he never made a sound as she stuck him and injected the thick medicine into his hip. Returning to his lower left leg, she hesitated. This would not be easy, and she needed to give a bit of time for the medicine to work.

A thud sounded, alarming Tess who glanced around. Evan was on the floor. The youngest McCade brother had never been fond of the sight of blood, and Wyatt’s misshapen purple leg hadn’t helped matters.

“Shit.” Sawyer let go of Wyatt, scrambling to get Evan to his feet. “Come on, get up. You should’ve known better than to come in here.”

“Well, I just…wanted to check on Wyatt.” Evan allowed his brother to assist him from the room, swearing and rubbing his head.

Tess turned back to Wyatt’s leg. Somehow she had thought longing for him was her punishment for what she had done to him, but she had never once thought this would be her suffering. What if he didn’t survive? Pneumonia was always a fifty-fifty chance of survival. He was strong and that he was still alive showed his will to live. No, she wouldn’t think of that, she would force him to live and give him no other choice.

“I’ll set your leg as fast as I can, but…” She fought the urge to wrap her arms around him and hold him until there was no pain for either of them. That he was before her, still caught her breath, and she had to remind herself she was indeed his physician—at least right now.

“Whiskey.” He groaned, holding his chest.

“Not with the laudanum.” She halted the idea, shaking her head. Mixing alcohol and the medication wasn't safe at all, even if he didn't appear to have any severe head injury. Why had she let her supply of chloroform drop to nothing? This too was her fault, and she would never forgive herself.

"Whiskey or this here…ain't happening." Panic took him, and he stiffened holding his upper leg. "Son of a bitch…whiskey!"

Tess jumped. His roar filled the room, vibrating all the way through her chest. Beside her, Dodge jumped as well.

Dawson whistled toward the door, and Evan tossed a sliver flask from his shirt pocket. He caught it with one hand and landed his gaze on Tess. "It can't hurt in his state."

Tess resolved his brother was right. There was little more she could do to ease the pain, and if the mix of both the medication and the alcohol made him lose consciousness, then at least he would be out of pain for the time being.

Dawson held the canister to his lips and he growled through a few swallows and lay back but then spoke. "Sawyer? You get Benton and…you…get him good."

Sawyer gave a reluctant nod and he closed his eyes again.

Tess glanced at Dodge and whispered, "He'll still be in a great deal of pain. Frankly, it will be awful. Sawyer, you and Dawson hold him to give me counter pressure, and Dodge you will have to help." Lord, could she even do what she had to? Hadn't she hurt him enough already?

"Dawson and I are gonna hold you, Wyatt, don't hurt the ladies." Sawyer laid his grip across his chest above the broken ribs, holding him to the table as

Dawson held his right hip and leg, with the weight of his body.

"Why, do…I think, this isn't going to…be good." He panted in raspy breaths, struggling against his brothers. "Can't breathe."

"Relax brother, don't fight us," Dawson coaxed.

Tess placed one hand above Wyatt's ankle and the other at his heel, the movement causing him to cry out as she adjusted to the position needed. *Dear God in heaven...*

He threw his head back against Dodge who held him tighter with a nod for Tess to go head. "It will be over soon, son."

Tess' hands were shaking, but she tightened her grip, tears filling her eyes. If she didn't do this right, it would take more than once, and she couldn't allow that. "On three." Her voice cracked as she gave the first nod, then the second. On the third nod, she griped tighter and pulled with the full weight of her body, the crunch of bone under her hands enough to cause her stomach to knot, but she didn't let up.

"Ahhhh…damn it…to…hell!" Wyatt went rigid, gagged, struggling to free himself, though his brothers held him still.

Finally, the bones in his leg lined up. Satisfied, she laid his leg back to the table, his retch being from the intense pain which brought on nausea. She placed her hand to his bearded cheek wishing she could take the pain from him. "It's over, Wyatt; it's all done now."

His large frame shook hard, and he fought to take his next breath, tears flowing down the side of his face. She'd never seen him cry, and the pain scored through her as if her own.

"Breathe, Wyatt." Sawyer shook him. "Come on, brother."

"I'm so sorry." She wrapped her arms around him and clung to him as his eyes rolled back and his head slumped against his mother, unconscious.

"He's passed out, probably best." Dawson let go, as did Sawyer, the room quiet.

Dodge eased him back to the pillow and covered him with a blanket, though Tess didn't move. She couldn't. She continued to hold him, his body hot with fever and damp with sweat. She brushed his shaggy hair away from his face, placing her cheek next to his oblivious of those around her. He was nothing like himself, so fragile, but she would be here, day and night to cool his fever and tend his injuries, and she wouldn't let him die.

She burst into tears as the men left her alone with Wyatt and Dodge. She sniffled and wiped her tears. She had to splint his leg and get his ribs wrapped which would be easier given he was out cold. She needed to prepare quinine for his fever and one of the men had brought in the bucket of ice that would decrease the swelling of his hand and leg. Yet, even though there was much to do, she could not tug herself to the task. She leaned closer to his ear and whispered as she ran her hand into his thick long hair, even with Dodge looking on. "I won't let you die, Wyatt McCade." With that she placed her lips to his for the brush of a kiss her heart needed and turned to the task at hand.

****

The golden light of the lamp flickered across the room, casting yellow shadows over the white washed walls onto Wyatt's damp bronzed skin. Tess pressed the cloth once more into the cool basin of water and wrung out the excess, the splash a comfort covering Wyatt's raspy, rapid breathing. She ran the cloth across his chest. Pneumonia could be deadly, but his fever had lessened, though it hadn't gone entirely. The quinine helped, but he fought against his dreams day and night.

She stared at his face as she continued with the cloth. He was such a handsome man, though she wondered about the thick beard and long shaggy hair that were so out of character for him. He'd always kept his hair and beard trimmed. She didn't have to wonder if the changes were due to her, and she didn't have to guess that he was in this very condition because she had walked right out of his life.

She was a fool to have turned down his proposal of marriage and all she'd ever wanted—even if her reasons were real to her. But then for him to be brought back to Cheyenne in so much pain. She shivered at remembering the cry he'd made when she had set his leg. At the time, the physician inside her had taken over, denying the guttural scream that wanted to escape the woman who loved him.

He moaned, shuddering against the chill of his fever. She pulled the blanket higher and tossed the cloth back into the cool water and picked up the tin cup of powdered quinine mixed with water. She placed her hand under Wyatt's head and lifted, touching the cup to his lips.

"Drink, Wyatt…" She allowed the liquid to pour from the cup into his mouth until it spilled over the sides of his face. She grabbed the cloth to dry him and rubbed his throat. "Swallow, Wyatt."

Finally, his throat moved and he gulped, coughing.

Moaning, he turned his head. She tried for more, at least some of the bitter liquid would be better than none and he swallowed again. "Good, Wyatt. Rest, I'll be right here. I'll be right here, always."

He escaped back to his raspy breathing, restless for a time, but then stilled. She touched his brow, wondering if he had heard her or understood he was safe. Did he even know he was home in Cheyenne, given his state of fever? He'd called for her in his dreams, but he'd fought against the darkness, swinging his fists.

Dodge trotted into the room. "Tess, I'm so sorry, I meant to nap a short time, but it seems I slept for longer than I intended. I know you need to rest."

It had been hours since she had closed her eyes, but that hadn't been Dodge's doing. "I am fine." And she was for the most part, more so than she might have expected she would have been on Wyatt's return.

Dodge touched his brow. "Still fevered."

"He took a bit more quinine." Tess wrung the cloth once more and laid it across his forehead.

He groaned, the bed creaking under the weight of him, and he mumbled with restless urgency. "Fire! Fire!… Da…Ming!"

"Wyatt?" Tess touched his arm, glancing at Dodge.

He wrestled against the blankets, fighting. "Da Ming…no, the fire…father!"

And then, he settled, as still as he had been moments before.

She didn't know what to make of it. "Dodge? Why is he remembering Da Ming in his dreams?"

Dodge's concern was apparent, fear and worry plaguing her features, though she dropped her gaze and touched his cheek. “Wyatt, it’s all right, son. It’s all right.” She sat in the chair beside the bed and took Wyatt’s large hand in her own.

Tess watched her; sure Dodge was avoiding her question, but why? Da Ming was one of the Chinese men who had worked for John McCade years ago. He had also been husband to Mei Ling, the Chinese woman who Dodge claimed as a sister. The woman had remained on the McCade ranch to this day, and Wyatt had often spoken of her as if she were family. But why was he calling for Da Ming, and why was Dodge reluctant to say more?

“You must go lie down and rest.” Dodge stood again, letting go of Wyatt who was now sleeping soundly.

She brushed away her thoughts, shaking her head. “I can’t leave him.”

“I’ll wake you if I need to.” Dodge gave her no choice, coaxing her to rise and follow.

“He never left me, when I had the influenza.” Tess studied him, tears coming to the surface. “While I was caring for Israel and all the others who were sick, he was there, helping me and making sure I ate and slept and…when I got sick, he never left me once, and all I did was hurt him.” She burst into tears, covering her mouth with her hand. It was all too much, and fatigue had long taken her.

Dodge tugged on her arm. “You are no good to him if you can’t think. You must rest, and you are going right this minute.”

She allowed Dodge to lead her out of the room and across the hall. Well, at least she could hear from there, should he wake.

"You rest, until morning." Dodge pushed her to the bed and took a moment to remove her boots, tossing them aside and covering her with a blanket.

The tenderness was a reminder of how her aunt had always tucked her into bed at night even after she was a grown woman. Boston seemed so very far away now, and without Dodge, she might have succumbed to the loneliness of missing her family. The blanket warmed her, and the softness of the bed seemed to consume her, but she needed to understand the reasons for what had happened to Wyatt and the reasons he fought so hard in his dreams.

"Dodge, Mr. Benton…" She chose her words with care, "there was always something bad between him and Wyatt. Anytime he came to town, I watched Sawyer push Wyatt back to protect him, and I never understood it."

Dodge took a long deep breath, folded her arms, and leaned against the door frame. She was such a beautiful woman for her age, with her light hair and blue eyes much like Wyatt's. "Marcus' hatred of John has brought evil to my sons. He couldn't let John win at anything."

Tess thought on her words, but that much she already knew. And she had asked the same question of Dodge a short time after Sawyer had almost lost his life at the hand of Marcus Benton's half brother. None of this made any sense, but she'd seen Wyatt posture any time Marcus Benton showed up in Cheyenne. "First Sawyer and now Wyatt, when does this stop, Dodge and these dreams of fire and Da Ming? It's not the first time he's said those same words."

"I'm afraid, with Marcus receiving a pardon, this is

just the beginning…" Dodge shook her head and Tess figured she wasn't saying anything more. Dodge was like that, sharing what she could and harboring things best left unsaid somewhere deep inside.

"Dodge?" Tess whispered, tugging the blanket higher. "I loved Wyatt…long before Israel died."

Dodge let a slight smile spread across her face, her eyes softening. She dimmed the lamp. "That comes as no surprise. Wyatt is plagued with fever, his dreams are just that, but I do know this. He didn't return home to die. He came back to you. Rest, Doctor."

Tess' throat tightened. She wasn't sure what had made her share her thoughts other than her need to tell someone. Despite his injuries and fever, he had called for her, more than once. That had to mean something, didn't it? He was still very ill, but he was aware she was caring for him.

Dodge pulled the door closed, darkness falling across the room. Shadows danced on the ceiling from the lanterns in town. Tess stared at the ceiling praying Dodge was right, that he had returned because of her remaining in Cheyenne. And she would rest for a time and then return to him and care for him until the fevered dreams no longer haunted him, and until she could tell him the same thing she had disclosed to Dodge.

****

Wyatt rose from the depths of deep slumber, fighting the pain that pulled him to the surface. He tried to open his eyes and made the mistake of moving. He'd forgotten his leg, though it hadn't forgotten him. Paralyzing pain shot up through his calf and foot, and he grimaced. Breathing was an effort, pain so coarse he panted to avoid inhaling deeper. He blinked hard, making out the room with its white washed walls and dark wooden beams above. His heart pounded, and his ears rang as if someone hammered metal pans around his head. Dreams, so many distorted images of chasing and being chased, hunting and being hunted. Where the hell was he? He squinted to focus once more. The doc's clinic—she hadn't been a dream, had she? He called for her, a whisper at best. He hurt, and she could stop the pain. "Doc?"

He closed his eyes, the effort to keep them open overwhelming but then her tender voice surrounded him; muffled, and he reached out to touch her wanting to make sure she was real.

"It's all right, Wyatt. You're safe at the clinic." She rubbed his upper arm, her gentle touch as soft as her beautiful voice.

He opened his eyes to the blurry confusion of heaven or so he thought. Tess? Why was she still here, not that with his pain and confusion he could rationalize the thoughts of the stubborn woman? But she was here and somehow just being near her eased his suffering.

A cool cloth touched his brow. He shivered at the chill which scorched his skin. He couldn't see her very well, but he could smell her, the sweet scent of lavender flowers wafting around him as she moved around him.

"It's all right." Her voice was soft and distant, but now it all came back. Dawson had gotten him home, and Tess had set his leg. He tried to push air from his lungs to speak, but his voice wouldn't come, the pain in his side pounding right along with his aching leg.

"Shhh, rest. You've a fever." She traced the cool rag across his chest, her voice a comfort in his paining world. “I’m here, Wyatt.”

He lifted his left hand and touched her cheek, needing relief from the unrelenting pain. She could help him, take away the hurt. “My leg…”

“I’ll get you something for pain.” She coaxed, putting his hand down and returning promptly. “I’ve got laudanum, Wyatt.” Her sweet voice coaxed him to relax, and she turned to the draw up the medication.

The jab to his upper arm was masked by the spasm that cramped his calf, pulling tight and drawing his toes. “Ahhhhhh…my leg.” He tried to reach his calf, but couldn’t.

Tess jerked the blanket aside, exposing his leg and foot. “You’ve got muscle spasms…let the medicine work.” She tenderly massaged his calf and the tightened muscles eased.

“I have quinine to help with the fever.” She brought the tin cup to his lips, urging him to drink.

He gulped at the foul tasting water until she took the cup away. He stared at her deep green eyes as long as he could, wanting answers of which he had no right to ask. And letting it all go he spoke, wanting her near, no matter her reasons. “Don’t…leave.”

“I’m not leaving, not ever.” The bed dipped as she sat close to him.

Had he heard right? He didn’t understand, as she had been set on going back to Boston. He shivered, unable to understand his situation or her thoughts. The cold cloth touched his face again, and he closed his eyes, the beautiful shadow of her fading. Somehow it was enough to know she was near and the warmth of her being close might stave away the haunting dreams that would return—or perhaps he’d choose to dream of her where he might stay warm and safe from the fight inside himself.

Chapter Seven

Tess touched Wyatt's long shaggy hair, stroking her fingers through the length of it, still shocked at his appearance. He was hardly the man she remembered. Touching him, so much of her heart needed forgiveness that wouldn't come if he didn't improve. How could she have known and worse yet, how would she ever explain it all to him when he was better?

Tears filled her eyes, and she whispered continuing to run her fingers through his silky dark hair, something she could only remember doing when he'd held her the once, smothering her in heated kisses and then asking for her hand. But his hair had been short then and as she touched him now, it was more than apparent he was no longer that man. "Oh God, what have I done to you and me? I'm so very sorry." She lay her head beside him on the bed, so fatigued she couldn't even sob as the tears flowed. She stifled and inhaled to avoid making a sound and her body shook in her sorrow as she sniffled.

"Don't…cry." Wyatt's hand touched her head and stroked her hair.

She lifted her head and dabbed at her eyes with her sleeve. "Wyatt?"

He never opened his eyes as his fingers tangled further in the length of her hair. "No…tears."

"Wyatt?" She whispered his name again and touched his brow. He was cool, the fever broken somehow without her notice.

He coughed hard with congestion and grabbed his side. "Water."

She hurried and lifted the tin cup of cool water and held it to his lips. To her surprise he drank until the cup was empty, though he shivered. "So…cold."

"I'll get you another blanket." She stood, but he grabbed her arm, stopping her.

"You…keep me…warm." He tugged her closer, his teeth chattering, as he focused on her for the first time, seemingly aware.

She hesitated, but sat on the bed as he pulled her beside him. "Your leg."

"Cold." He'd been through so much pain and hurt. How could she not do as he'd asked? He was so vulnerable, and perhaps he needed the warmth and comfort he hadn't found in his unsettled dreams. She leaned until she was lying in the crook of his arm, trying to cuddle closer as gently as possible. She pulled the quilt across them both. Lord, but she fit to him in perfection, and when he massaged her upper arm with his hand, she was the one who shivered. It was late and she was exhausted, and Dodge wouldn't return until morning. Lying beside him was all right, wasn't it? He needed her and never again would she not be there for him—if he'd still have her.

"Doc?" His weak voice summoned.

She raised her head, it being the first time he sounded like himself.

"My…leg?"

She was aware what he was asking. Badly broken legs never healed well and left a man crippled. It had already occurred to her that a man like Wyatt wouldn't want to live if he couldn't be a whole man, one who walked without a crutch or other help. "You'll heal, Wyatt. Little by little. You'll heal."

"Can't…ride…if not." He lost himself to a strong bout of coughing, holding his side.

"Rest. Your body has to heal one day at a time." She laid her cheek against his shoulder, listening to the steady beat of his heart and tucking his injured hand across her hip so as not to hurt him more.

He didn't like her answer. "Not gonna…be much of a man."

"No, Wyatt, you may have a slight limp, but you will walk again. You are healing, even if it doesn't feel like it." She tried to explain though he shook his head.

"Limp?" His tone sharpened. "Crippled."

She touched his cheek to make him look at her and then she rested a hand to his thigh. "You will walk again, Wyatt, and yes maybe with a limp and maybe not, but you will not be crippled."

He surveyed her for a time and glanced down at his leg where their hands were almost touching. Tess sucked in a deep breath as he raised his hand and traced his fingers along the back of her hand, saying nothing more. He never looked at her as he continued, tender and swirling across her skin. Some part of her heart leapt at the gesture.

"Should…have died." He more than growled it from his throat.

"But you didn't, and I won't let you." She held his hand, relishing in the temporary closeness.

He closed his eyes, and Tess curled back into him. The fatigue had taken her long ago, and she meant what she said. She wouldn't let him die. Worse she wouldn't let him lose his spirit, and so she held him until the light in the room begin to fade and the night engulfed them both.

****

Tess woke from a dream she couldn't remember, but one that had scared her abruptly from her slumber. She'd been lost and Wyatt was calling her, trying to find her but she was hidden in the darkness. He couldn't see her even though she had screamed and screamed. She batted her eyes to the early morning grayness seeping through the shutters of the window, relieved it had only been a dream. She remained still, not wanting to disturb Wyatt's rest and relishing in lying against him, something she'd been doing for several weeks now at his insistence each night. It hadn't taken much prodding. It was the part of each day she looked most forward to, where it was only the two of them.

He had dreamt during the night but held tight to her, not fighting the dreams, nor asking for the laudanum. Some part of her should have known not to ever lay down with him as it wasn't the proper thing for a lady, much less as his physician. All the days of caring for him while he was in so much pain had somehow been her punishment—and this, lying beside him each night after Dodge left for the ranch was her reward. And no one could take this closeness from her.

"Why did you stay in Cheyenne, Doc?"

She jumped, startled by his deep, soft voice that vibrated through her. She had thought him sleeping but turned to meet his drowsy gaze. Her anticipation of his questions had come, but now was a bit of a shock. He'd never been a man who held his tongue, but how on earth was she to give him the answers he deserved where he might understand? Her pulse raced.

“I did plan to leave, because I thought it best. I packed my trunks and purchased my ticket.” She sucked in a slight breath and pushed it out through pursed lips.

He fluffed the pillow behind his head, regarding her with clear blue eyes that read right through her. “Must’ve taken some doing for you to stay.” He groaned adjusting his leg which rested on a pillow outside his blankets, but there was no mistaking his tone. Hurt and anger, rightly so.

She took a breath and sat up, never taking her gaze from his. “I couldn’t leave my clinic, my home, and my friends, Dodge, Mei Ling, and Rose and even though you were gone, I couldn’t leave—you.”

“You didn’t stay…for me.” The expression on his face held uncertainty.

She swallowed hard, though her words came in a whisper. “I did, Wyatt, but you never came home.”

He tugged himself up in bed beside her, groaning and holding his leg. He took a moment to catch his breath and met her glance once more.

The quiet in the room was broken by the old clock on the wall that ticked along with the pace of her heart. He said nothing for a long moment, and then whispered. “I watched you the day you arrived in Cheyenne, all those years ago. Sittin’ up on that wagon, dressed fancy and as beautiful as I’d ever seen.”

Tess faced him, curling her legs beneath her. Why was he telling her this? Did he truly remember her arrival to Cheyenne?

He hinted at a smile but dropped his gaze as he

talked, wiggling the toes of his injured leg. "And I kept my distance, never stepping too close to you, afraid if I touched you I might never let go. And I never wished for Israel's death, not once."

"Oh, Wyatt, I never thought that of you," she interrupted, touching his arm.

He glanced at her hand and then took it. "But watching you grieve after he died was as hard as wishing you were mine. And when you were ill…" He leaned back against the oak headboard, and she was sure he was fighting tears.

"I shudder to think of my fate had you not cared for me when I had the influenza." She'd been plagued with fever, and his callused hands had cared for her with great tenderness.

"I sat by your bed for days…just as you have cared for me." His drowsy eyes closed for a moment.

"You've done so many things for me, and I never meant to hurt you by leaving…by not accepting your proposal." How on earth could she explain? He was already shaking his head, not believing her.

"Best you should've gone to Boston. Not sure I'll be worth much after this." He nodded toward his leg.

"Wyatt, your leg will mend if you let it heal before you try to walk…it will. But I didn't go to Boston, because I knew I couldn't leave things between us so…broken, with my mistake, but…"

He squinted, blinking hard.

She wiped her eyes. She had to explain, tell him what was no in her heart. "I know I hurt you, and have given you little as to the reasons why."

His voice was soft as he touched one of the tears spilling down her cheeks. "Rather take another beating than see your tears."

She gathered her voice, whisper that it was, and all she had inside her. "I was married to Israel for eight years and never once did I conceive a child. I couldn't marry you, Wyatt, because I hadn't been honest enough to tell you I'd never be able to have your children. I am barren, Wyatt."

He tilted his head and placed his palm to her wet cheek, his thumb tracing her lips, studying. "All I ever wanted was you, Doc. You are so beautiful and smart and that word hardly defines the woman I see before me."

"Men want sons, Wyatt, and I had thought while it might not matter for a time, it would be something we would both grow to regret." She tugged his hand away, but he held tight not letting go as she continued. "You can't know what it's like to be a physician; to bring a baby into the world, knowing you will never hold your own child." She burst into tears, covering her face and of all things; he tugged her into his embrace allowing her tears.

****

Wyatt took a struggled breath, trying to make full sense of Tess' words. All this time, her reasons for avoiding him and turning down his proposal was because she couldn't have children? They had never discussed the issue, but regardless what she was thinking, her tears would be the death of him, that or the unforgiving pain in his leg. He'd spent the last half a year missing her so much he thought he might die, and it seemed she'd suffered in her own silent hell.

He held her tighter for a moment and pushed her back to look at her. She was trembling in tears, and he tucked a strand of her hair that had fallen, behind her ear, gazing into her sad green eyes. Those eyes should never hold any pain, not even for a moment. "I loved you, Doc. I love you still. Even lying on the God-forsaken prairie, in the dark, all I could think about was you."

"I'm so sorry, Wyatt…it's all my fault or this wouldn't have happened to you." She sniffled again, wiping her face with the blanket.

He refused to let her think thoughts like that. "Unh-huh, Doc, you didn't do this. What happened to me has nothing to do with you at all."

She clung to him then. He inhaled as deeply as he could his body awakening, not that he could do anything about it. He'd hurt like hell sometime in their tangled slumber last night but hadn't asked for the medicine, not wanting to disturb her as she slept in his arms again. But now, his leg was paying the price.

"You're hurting?" She tugged from his grasp.

"I hurt here." He took her hand and touched it to his chest, placing their hands over his heart. "Knowing you carried this for too long. I would've understood, Doc, and it wouldn't have made any difference where children are concerned. I love you, Doc, nothing could ever change that."

She wiped her eyes again and sniffled. "Then what of us?"

He figured the question for a moment. "That all depends on you, Doc. I want what makes you happy." He hadn't woken this morning to work out all the details, but he could think how he'd like things to be, given the long night with her warm body lying so close.

"Perhaps, time to allow you to heal and—me too."

She smiled, tender and sweet, her cheeks remaining pink.

He wrapped his arms about her, placing his lips against hers as tenderly as he could. She trembled as he took her mouth, running a hand into her hair. Breaking the kiss, he pulled her against him, and in spite of his pain whispered, “All I’ll ever need in this life is you, Doc.”

Her gentle nod was his reassurance. He closed his eyes, fatigued. He was hurting, but the pain could wait and he would heal and give her the time she needed and then—he’d never let her go again.

Chapter Eight

"I'm damn tired of being in this bed. If I were up, I'd sure as hell get to the bottom of things." Wyatt hissed at Sawyer, who had yet to put together any of the details related to Marcus Benton's pardon. So much for his damn careful planner of a sheriff brother.

"There's been no sign of him. Hudson sent a telegram that Denver is clear, but you're in no condition to mount a horse, regardless." Sawyer slammed a hand against the doorframe gaining his full attention.

He could have bitten nails at the wasted time he'd been laid up with his leg. Eight damn weeks to be exact. Tess had said three months, but he wasn't about to give it one more day than that. Every moment he sat idle was another that Marcus Benton graced the earth, though the man still hadn't showed.

"I'm working on things, be patient; if we don't do it right, we lose him again. No one's seen him in Sterling, Gillette, or clear back to Council Bluffs." Sawyer's gray eyes narrowed as he held his hat and gritted his teeth.

"That's doesn't mean he's not watching." He regarded his brother with caution but spoke his mind anyway. "I should have killed him when I had the chance, and you stopped me, brother, but this time…the son of a bitch! He took my revolvers, rifle, and my damn horse; good thing I never named that one either.

Maybe I should name the next horse so when I ride up Benton's ass I can let him know the name of the animal I'm about to shove that way."

Sawyer inhaled an exasperated deep breath. "We'll do it right this time, but not if you take things into your own hands."

"We should have done it right the first time!" He snapped, irritated at the whole damn thing. "Always so patient, well, I can taste blood on this one brother, and I swear to God if I could get out of this bed I'd unleash the wrath of hell on the man." His heart pounded in his chest, and he wanted to hit something, hard!

Sawyer's eyes narrowed, and he said nothing for a long moment. "You think I don't know the same blood you thirst for? I've been there, and you aren't angry at anyone but yourself. You're damn lucky to be alive, and we have a family and a town to protect. Sooner or later, he'll show up. That's what he does and you'd best remember, sometimes revenge don't taste so sweet."

He glared at Sawyer and held his harsh words, the struggle overpowering his thoughts. He slung everything off the bedside stand, tin dishes falling to the floor and the large water pitcher spilling. He was stuck and might as well be dead if he had to lie in this damn bed any longer. He caught his breath, vowing away the pain in his leg turning his gaze away from his all-seeing brother. It was true, Sawyer had been gunned down by Marcus Benton's now dead brother, and he'd almost died. Somehow, now that he was the one on the other end, it didn't feel the same. He and his brother were different. Sawyer was a law man, abiding by the way of the West, but he was a bounty hunter. And there were no rules he'd follow to put Marcus Benton right into the pits of the hard earth.

"What happened?" Dodge rushed into the room and glanced at the mess of food and scattered plates on the floor. She waited, glancing back and forth between them, slinging her hands on her narrow hips.

Sawyer turned and stomped down the hallway, leaving Dodge to pick up the mess. She was quiet as she cleaned up the spill and laid the tin plate and pitcher on the tray. "He's working on things, Wyatt. He's got men scouting, telegrams to lawmen in the area and men from town are searching."

"Not damn fast enough." He spat, then bit his tongue, grabbing up his knife and stone from the bed beside him.

Dodge sat the tray aside and folded her arms as he began sliding the blade across the flat rock. "Evan is handling the ranch, and Brett's out on his own mission of getting himself killed by searching on his own for Marcus. Zane is staying out of school to watch the house and stay with Rose, his little brother, and Mei Ling. Sawyer has his hands full, and it's your job to support him."

As a bounty hunter, he was bound to no power of a sheriff, but he was loyal to his brother, and she was calling him out. Sawyer studied things and planned them well, and he had the patience of Job if it came right down to it. He took a pained breath, giving in. "He and I don't do things the same."

Dodge tossed the soaked rag on the tray she'd set aside. "No, you don't, but that is where you complement each other when you work together. One picks up where the other leaves off." She stopped and sat beside him on the bed, changing the subject. "Wyatt, where did you go?"

He swallowed hard. She had aged since he'd been gone, a few more wrinkles around the edges of her eyes, but she was still a right handsome woman with her slender build, light hair, and his own blue eyes. He sighed and leaned back against the headboard in defeat. He hadn't any answers. Where *had* he gone? A little bit of everywhere and a lot of nowhere. "I rode north. Wound up following a bounty all the way to Gillette and then Sterling. I made it to Denver twice, and there were a lot of days I'm not sure I knew where I was."

Her eyes softened, and she rested a hand on his thigh. "I worried day and night. I'd read about you, praying you were safe. You promised me you'd wire."

"I know." Guilt plowed right through him as rough as the afternoon train plowing up the earth at his feet.

"You will find your way, Wyatt; you always did, but listen to your brother. The two of you together could always do anything." Dodge smiled, lifting her brows and continuing. "And Tess waited, just as miserable as were you."

He relinquished a nod, not that he still understood anything where the doc was concerned. "It just got too hard and she's still here and I don't know what the hell to make of it. Children?" His mind hadn't stopped whirling around their tender exchange when she'd confessed her reasons, but it had become apparent to him she hadn't forgiven herself, even if he was long past the moment she had walked away.

"Bearing children is a woman's reward for love, Wyatt, and Tess' pain over never having children is real to her." Dodge met his gaze once more, standing to move about the room. "And how would you feel about the fact, should the two of you marry, there would be no children."

It was a bold question, but he knew the answer. "Never wanted anything save her."

"Then you have to show her. Tess is strong willed and independent but all she needs is reassurance that you do love her no matter. And your leg will heal, and Marcus Benton will be brought to justice in time, but you need to stop feeling sorry for yourself and stop sharpening that damn knife of yours all day." Dodge faced him once more and he stopped swirling the weapon across the stone in his hand.

Hell, he'd learned long ago, figuring out a woman was something a man didn't do and while his mother seemed to think she had to explain things to him, he knew his way around Tess. If, and when he healed, he would show her how much he loved her, but he was ready to drop this conversation. He glanced at the knife. Sharpening gave him reassurance of the task before him where Marcus Benton was concerned—the thin edge of the blade was his promise of revenge.

"She waited, watching for you every day, knowing she'd made a mistake. Talk to her. Do your mending and think hard about what it means to love her and at the same time what you might lose by seeking out Marcus alone." She headed to the door, not looking back.

He knocked his head back to the headboard and swore silently. Son of a bitch! Leave it to Dodge to dig deep. He held his leg, which throbbed most all the time. How could she or Sawyer, either one expect he wouldn't go after Marcus Benton? If the man wasn't stopped, the family was at risk and the war that had raged inside him since his youth would never end. His father's voice would continue to tell him all the reasons why he had the mission before him. What kind of man would he be for Tess if he didn't take his revenge? Couldn't they all see that? Well, he was no coward and in another month, he'd do what he had to with or without his brothers—and of that he was most certain.

****

Deep purple clouds gathered across the unforgiving sky. The rain would come. Tess climbed up the steps to the porch of the clinic shaking off the water that caught her on a run from the livery. She'd managed to get Anna stalled before the rain but the short walk to the clinic had soaked the shawl she had used to cover her head and shoulders. While she was exhausted from the day at the McCade ranch assisting Rose in the delivery of her second child, her heart was full. She smiled. If every woman delivered as fast as Rose, her job as a physician would be incredibly easy. After six hours of hard labor, Rose had delivered a healthy baby boy. Dodge and Mei Ling had assisted, but it had been her that had placed the tiny bundle in his father's arms. Funny that Sawyer's eyes had filled with tears, the sheriff holding Nicholas in one arm and the newborn in the other.

She sighed. It was a picture she had often dreamt she would see in Israel and even—Wyatt. But that wasn't meant to be. Wyatt had said it wasn't an issue where children were concerned, but to her it always would be. She turned to go inside. The storm would make for a long night and she needed to let Wyatt and Dawson know that they had a brand new nephew and that mother and baby were doing well.

She'd spent most of the ride from the ranch in thought of Wyatt. He'd been restless and angry most of the time, so she had given in to letting him try bearing weight on his leg the once. The moment had proven futile with him falling back into the bed cursing as loud as ever and holding his leg. She'd assured him it would take time to get him walking even with a crutch and that hadn't been what he'd wanted to hear. It was hard to see his continued struggle.

Thunder echoed across town, making her jump and take one more look at the dark sky behind her. Inside she met Dawson, who'd been staying at the clinic on guard most nights. His presence was a comfort of sorts, because he helped calm Wyatt when he got riled over his leg and spoke of revenge. The thought scared her, but leastwise there had been no sign of Mr. Benton.

"Doc." Dawson set the book he'd been reading aside with his greeting. "I thought you might wait out the storm at the ranch."

Tess lifted the shawl from her shoulders and hung it on the back of one of the clinic chairs to dry. "I thought it was best I got back, but Rose did very well. A boy, near nine pounds. They've named him Uriah."

He chuckled with a shake of the head. "I'm sure Dodge is happy about that, heard more stories about her grandfather than anyone over the years. Uriah's a strong name."

Tess folded her arms with a bit of chill. "I think it's the first time I've seen her speechless, when Sawyer told her."

He picked up the book again. "She says he was the best man she's ever known, it's a fitting thing for Sawyer to do."

Tess glanced at the book in his hands. Odd, she'd never seen Wyatt open a book of fiction, Sawyer neither, but Dawson often had a book shoved in his back pocket or saddle bags. "A Tale of Two cities, Charles Dickens."

Dawson glanced up at her, his deep blue eyes serious. "My father read this to me when I was younger, it's good remembering."

"Your father read it to all of you?" She stepped closer. Wyatt had often talked of his father teaching he and his brothers their lessons and works of fiction had been part of those requirements.

He nodded, his shoulder length brown hair falling across his upper chest. She'd seen women in town who were frightened by his appearance, assuming he was an Indian. Even tonight he had on a buckskin shirt and trousers and a small feather was braided into his hair. He'd always worn a medicine pouch around his neck on a leather cord and it was there now. She hardly noticed these things about him any longer; she'd grown so used to him. He was the quietest of the brothers, soft spoken and thoughtful, but she'd always enjoyed conversations with him. He had an incredible mind with answers and ideas few others had ever thought about.

He glanced away as evidently the memories flooded him. "He'd choose a story and start reading out loud after dinner. Sawyer would say he had studies and Wyatt found another place to disappear, but I listened, sometimes for hours, imagining the stories in my head and making sure to learn the lessons from each. I remember this one in particular."

"It's an incredibly hard story with its many truths." She'd read the story more than once herself.

"Each time I read it, seems I learn a bit more. You don't mind?" He questioned his use of the book, offering it back to her.

"Oh, no, please, I have a library full of books, all collecting dust. I offered Wyatt a few, but I think he doesn't care for much of anything save sharpening his knife." She sighed. Any time he was awake, he seemed to have a hold on the stone and the large bone handled blade, but of more concern was the distant gaze he held when he slid the blade across the smooth stone. It frightened her that he was so set on revenge even after the beating he'd survived. He had to know that Mr. Benton was best left alone, though she feared the evil man was no more done with the fight than Wyatt.

"Sitting idle isn't easy for him." Dawson opened the book, thumbing through to where he must have been reading.

She shrugged uncertain. "I hope you're right. I've never seen him like this."

He rested his elbows on her desk. "Soon as he is up on the crutch I made, he'll see he can walk and that's half his battle."

Tess wanted to believe his brother was right. "The crutch is beautiful but it's still too soon for him to try and I think he knows that. Enjoy the book and thank you, Dawson for helping me with him the last few weeks. He listens to you."

Dawson stood with a nod, taking the open book with him to the porch. His buckskin tunic was belted and a tomahawk rode at his side. She'd watched him throw the weapon and unhand an outlaw of a gun once, but now his belt also held a revolver. In the corner of the clinic was a loaded rifle, there for protection. She shivered that such was needed but this was Cheyenne and Marcus Benton was nowhere to be found.

She turned toward the hallway to check on Wyatt. The pneumonia was gone and his ribs, while still tender, had mostly healed, but his lower leg was still too swollen to get inside his boot. While she wanted him well, it remained in the distance of her thoughts that while he was healing in bed he was safe.

She found him sitting up in bed, his injured leg straight before him but now free of the splints. He was dressed in a white shirt and dark trousers, the shirt open, showing the fading bruises on his chest and the rippled muscles of his belly and—he was sharpening the knife.

She stood in the doorway, not understanding his need for revenge, but then she hadn't been the one left for dead and she didn't fully know the past where Marcus Benton and John McCade had tangled in negotiations over land deals.

He glanced up, but went back to the stone. Thunder crashed in the distance and the patter of rain sounded across the tin roof of the clinic.

She started the conversation, hoping his mood had changed from the wee hours before dawn when she had readied her things for Rose's delivery. "You tell me the storms make your leg hurt, do you want laudanum tonight?"

He didn't answer at first, continuing with the knife. "Some pain's a good thing." Lightning lit the room with a quick flash, allowing her the glance of his dark blue eyes. So, his mood had changed little from the early morning, where he was short on answers and quick on temper. She picked up the tray of food from beside him and moved it. Well, at least he had eaten. She said nothing more, setting the tray aside.

"Sorry. How's Rose?" He lessened his tone, and his apology surprised her.

"Your brother has another son, nine pounds, Uriah. And Rose did very well." She began tidying the room for the night and was all too aware he watched her.

"I am sure Dodge gloated over that." He glanced at her but went back to sharpening the knife, though a chuckle escaped him. "Did you have to medicate Sawyer?"

"He had his hands full caring for Nicholas, while we stayed with Rose." She poured more water into the tin cup by his bed.

He watched her then, something more in his questioning gaze, a knowing, and she set the pitcher back on the table and waited.

He took a deep breath, let it out slowly, and shook his head slightly. "You and I haven't talked so much of late, and I'm thinking maybe that's my fault."

She held his gaze. It was true as each day felt more and more as if they were just going through the motions. They hadn't managed much on progress other than idle chatting. She'd tried, but he'd become more angry and withdrawn over the weeks, and she hadn't known how to handle him, but maybe it was time. "Well, perhaps you should spend less time sharpening that weapon."

His gaze held her hostage as he set the knife and stone aside, eyes stoic.

Tess glanced from the knife back to him and sat on the edge of the bed. "I know how hard it is for you to sit here for so long, but perhaps in a few days you can try the crutch again if Dawson helps you."

He cocked a glance at the crutch leaning against the wall beside the bed, but then he picked up her hand in his own. "This here's not so hard, Doc. It's harder watching you whirl thoughts through your pretty head day in and out and not hear you speak them."

What was he saying, not that she could concentrate with his tender caress? "I suppose I worry of you getting to your feet and going on some mission to get yourself killed."

He chuckled, still rubbing her hand with his callused fingers. "Doc, I would hardly be the man worthy of you if I didn't do what needs to be done."

"I would love you no matter. He almost killed you and I couldn't…" She didn't finish her statement that should he die at Marcus Benton's hands she would never take another breath.

He took his time to respond, the way he did when he was organizing his thoughts. "And that is how I feel toward you, no matter…children, Doc."

Tess swallowed hard at his change in subject. No, she wouldn't allow more tears over the matter, but she managed a nod. Somehow, her regrets over the issue wasn't her lack of being able to produce a child. She worried about him. He wasn't the same man she had known, but then again, maybe she wasn't the same woman either. "You came back to Cheyenne, Wyatt, but I miss the man you use to be, the man who knew there was power in the law and in more than one. You and your brothers have always fought together, not alone."

He dropped his gaze to his hand that held hers. "Not real sure I know that man anymore."

She whispered, wondering of the words that seemed to escape her on their own. "It scares me when you sit for hours with that knife, and I know what you are thinking. I didn't hurt like you, physically, but I do think we have to talk more, Wyatt."

"I'd like that, Doc." He drew her hand to his mouth and kissed the back of it and then placed a tender kiss to her palm before tugging her ever closer and placing his lips to hers for a short gentle kiss.

Her heart beat stronger inside her chest at his tenderness, and she leaned against his chest and held on as he wrapped his arms around her. She inhaled the scent of soap and Wyatt, and closed her eyes. In his arms, so many things were right, and her worries always seemed to fade.

"And I would have found my way all the way to Boston to bring you home where you belong." He squeezed. "Just took me a bit of thinking."

She listened to the beating of his heart, a constant thump that matched the thunder in the distance. Rain played harder across the tin roof of the clinic, and a slight chill plagued the room from the open window. "You would've hated Boston."

"Think they would've kicked me right out, do ya?" He eased his grasp, holding her face and touching his lips to hers as tender as a feather.

She lifted from his embrace and brushed back the thick strands of hair hanging across his brow, pushing them back. "They would have taken one look at this long hair and jailed you right away."

He ran a hand through his shaggy dark locks. "Not to your liking, huh?"

She sent him a pair of raised brows and shook her

head with a smile.

"That bad?" He rubbed his beard and let a grin slip as he trailed his hand up her arm and to her neck and cheek, leaning toward her. He placed his lips to hers again and she shuddered, tasting the flavor of coffee. His warm breath exchanged with her own as his tongue danced against hers, his hands roaming her body. Lord, but his touch sent a rush of heat through her entire being and for that moment all the world was right once more. He ended the kiss with a tender pull of her bottom lip and leaned back. "I'll get hair a cut one of these days, and when I do what needs done, I'll take you to Boston for a visit."

She let her mouth fall open. The thought of seeing her aunt and uncle made her hopeful and homesick all at once. "You would go with me?" Somehow she doubted he would have any desire to do so. He would have nothing in common with anyone in Boston, but her uncle would no doubt be fascinated by conversation with him.

"I would go to the ends of the earth to see you smile just like that every day." His whisper melted her further into his warm embrace. "I love you, Doc, but neither of us can continue to dwell in the past. I'll stop being such a bastard…sorry…but you have to make me one promise, right here and now."

Tess opened her mouth, shaking her head but he placed a finger to her lips then lifted her chin to make her look into his deep blue eyes. "No more worries about what is behind us. I can't go another day watching you care for me as if you have to pay for what happened between us. That's over, Doc. Gone. Forgotten. Forgiven the minute I saw you again. These beautiful green eyes should never be sad again in this lifetime."

She'd bordered between regret and hope for so long now, she hardly knew where she stood. He was right, and the tenderness of his spoken forgiveness offered a bit of relief, though she couldn't hold back her emotions.

He used his thumbs to catch her tears as they fell and smiled lifting a brow in wait on her answer.

Her chest was tight, and her pulse raced. "I promise, Wy…"

Before his name left her, his lips touched hers again, and she melted into his embrace, savoring him and weeping despite her promise. How had he known what she needed was permission to forgive herself? He'd always read her so well even when she eluded him, and now was no different save the part where she would never let him go again. She would hang on now as tightly as she ever had and take each day with him as a gift, forgiving herself and stepping forward into the future, whatever it would bring.

Chapter Nine

Wyatt stared at the crutch Dawson had made. His brother had taken to being his personal caretaker to the point of becoming annoying. He whispered a curse, but eyed the crutch again, and glanced down at his leg. As worthless as a damn lame horse. They should have hauled him off and put him down, just like any injured animal. He scooted closer to the edge of the bed, little by little, thinking it might be worth another try.

More than a week ago, when Tess had been out visiting her patients, Dawson had helped him up, supporting him and letting him try the crutch. It hadn't worked, as terrible pain had scored through his ankle and the muscles of his leg had drawn tight in spasms, making him curse his brother and give up on the idea once more. But his brother had refused to give up on him with a good scolding. *If you try a little bit each day, Wyatt, you'll get there, but you can't give up.*

Well, he'd managed to make Sawyer angry over not knowing anything more on Marcus Benton's whereabouts and with Dawson frustrated with him, he might as well shoot for Evan next. But it seemed if he wanted things to change it was up to him. He shifted to the side of the bed with some effort, using both hands to ease his leg down until his heel touched the floor. He'd do it this time, or break his damn leg again by trying. Twelve weeks now he'd been lying in the same room in the same bed and he'd been counting each and every day since he'd gotten his wits about him back.

He grabbed the crutch and steadied it at his left side, running his hand along the smooth oak his brother had polished to a shine. Pressing his socked feet to the hardwood floors, his body shook as he expended the effort to stand on his right leg, while allowing the slightest pressure to his left. He tucked the bow of the crutch under his left arm and sucked in a few panting breaths clearing his head, not sure one more week would make a difference. Sweat trickled down his cheeks as he contemplated the first step, nausea scoring through him in anticipation of the pain. He cursed in a harsh whisper, "Son of a bitch!"

And with that, he stepped placing pressure on his left leg and biting his lower lip to stifle the growl. The pain rolled through his foot, ankle, and calf taking his breath. He slammed his weight to his right leg, bobbling with the crutch and stepping through again with another swear. He balanced on his right leg thinking if he fell, Tess would have a good scolding for him as she was just down the hall.

Well, he'd had enough of lying in the damn bed, except of course where she lay with him during the night, and that had damn near made him insane with want of her. He'd kissed her time and again, and the tenderness they had shared was consuming. God, he loved her, everything about her. All his injuries had healed, and if he could manage to walk, he might also manage to find out just how luscious the curves under her petticoats were. Well, at least if nothing else, she was a rather interesting distraction, and as soon as he was on his feet, he'd marry her, giving her no chance to ever slip away again.

He shuffled again through two more steps, losing his balance. He caught himself on the small table that turned over, spilling the pitcher of water and tin cup. He hopped hard on his right foot, aware he'd made too much noise.

"Wyatt, are you all right?" Tess made her way down the hallway, the pattering of her boots suggesting she was on a trot.

Shit! No time to get back to the bed without a great deal more pain. He steadied and eyed the bed as she turned the corner into the room. He fought to keep his weight on his right leg and smiled having no hell of an idea how to bet back to the bed.

"What on earth?" She raced to support him as he hopped again on his right leg, growling, the bed too far.

He grabbed hold of her grateful for the assistance of not having to put his left leg down again for the moment. "I can do it, if you help a bit."

"I've told you that you should wait until one of your brothers is here." She held to him as he stepped through once more, groaning hard at the pain in his ankle. Holy damnation it hurt!

"Gotta…get up sooner or later." He pushed through another step and made a dive for the bed, taking Tess with him. The impact to the mattress made the large bed creak as Tess fell on top of him. In a brief second it occurred to him she would hop off him quickly, so he wrapped his arms about her, ignoring his ribs and his damn leg.

"Wyatt?" Her whispered question was tense though she relaxed against him, holding her upper body off his chest.

He smiled. Well, that was rather darn convenient. He'd never had her in a horizontal position except when she had slept beside him each night, and even then she lay on top of the covers and used a blanket from her room as a top cover. And he'd kissed her each night, re-igniting the fire within him, having her so close in the daylight, he stopped to stare. She had the greenest eyes, but there were also the tiniest brown specks. He'd never studied another woman as much as he had her over the years.

He brought his hand to the back of her head and pushed her toward him, capturing her lips with his own. His groin tightened as he parted them, and she gave no resistance. Exploring her further he let his hands wander down her sides to her hips, tugging her tighter against him with a growl. The rounded curves he'd always know existed enticed him further, and he deepened the kiss.

She moaned as he rolled her beneath him, never breaking the kiss as he fitted himself to her once more. If anything on this earth had been close to perfection, it was her body pressed against his own.

Suddenly, she pulled from his kiss, breasts heaving. "Wyatt, what are you doing?"

He chuckled, tangling his hand back in her hair. "Kissing you with fervent passion."

"Oh, well…are you finished?" She didn't move as he might have expected, but instead kept her face close to his own as she whispered.

"Hardly." He took her mouth again, the want in his trousers more than fierce. He rocked his hips against her and groaned at his leg, pulling from the heated kiss and rolling to his back not speaking the curse he was thinking. Damn his ankle.

"Wyatt, your leg."

She turned to her side. The leg had gotten his attention, but damn if touching her with her obvious acceptance caught him off guard. He had wanted her for years now, and the reality that it was no longer a farfetched dream made him stop and just look at her, taking in the beautiful features of her high cheek bones, arched brows and the tender plump lips he'd just tasted.

She was puzzled at his continued stare. "Why did you do that?"

He smoothed the hair from her face and brushed his lips across hers again. "Because I've been laid up in this bed for God knows how long, watching you, hearing you, smelling you, and waiting so long to touch you like this. And if I were an able man…"

She stopped him with a tender finger to his lips. "I was asking about the crutch, you knew better than to try that, much less alone."

"It's time, Doc, like a lot of things, and when I'm well, nothing this side of heaven or hell is gonna stop me from loving you proper," he whispered as he kissed her cheek and watched her as she rose and stood by the bed, straightening her rumpled dress. She looked at him and turned and left the room, leaving him crooked on the bed, holding his leg and somehow, for the first time, a part of her.

Chapter Ten

Wyatt sucked in a puff of the skinny cigar he held between the fingers of his left hand; with the full knowledge Tess would scold him, should she find out. That he could now manage to move about the clinic on his crutch she'd returned to seeing her patients, which left him a bit unnerved. It wasn't safe, but her insistence had won out, the need for her around the community great.

Sitting on the porch of the clinic was a nice change of scenery. He'd forgotten there was even a sun to watch, and he stared at the orange ball in the sky and blew out white smoke savoring the hint of flavor he'd missed. Evan had helped him outside and handed him the lit smoke. Moving hadn't been easy, but his younger brother was built like a grizzly with the strength of ten.

"Howdy, Wyatt. Don't you look like a brand new shiny penny?" One of the saloon girls stopped on the street before him, out perusing customers if he were a guessing man.

He eyed her scantily clad body, taking another long drag on the smoke. "Hello, Eliza."

She stepped closer, batting her made up eyes at him. "I heard you were on the mend. You know, if you need a little help recovering, I'm sure I could have all you need."

He laughed. Eliza's attentions just might ease a bit of his pain, but he'd never had any interest in the gossiping whore. "Eliza, you know I am hardly man enough to handle a woman such as yourself."

She narrowed her gaze. "Doc Tess must be handling things fine, seeing you haven't made your way back home to the ranch since you are up and around."

He held his poker face. She *was* a gossip and could make things not so nice for Tess if she chose. "Doc says I have a bit more recovering to do. Don't let me stop you from your evening, Eliza."

She adjusted her corset, pushing her breasts higher and grinning at him. "Well, I suppose I'll save it all for that little brother of yours, then."

He took another long draw on the cigar. There was no secret in the fact that Evan frequented the local brothel, spending his hard earned money inside. "You do that."

She flashed her chest at him once more and swayed her hips as she sashayed away with apparent purpose.

He picked up the revolvers that Evan had purchased for him on a recent ride to Ft. Collins. He'd paid his little brother to purchase a set on his recent trip when Sawyer and Dawson had only scoffed at the idea. The revolvers were heavy and were similar to the ones Marcus Benton had taken from him. It wouldn't take much to get used to them, those and the rifle leaning against the wall. He gripped a revolver with his left hand and placed it in his right. His broken hand was healed but his grip was weak and it would take some doing to get his aim just right. Well, as soon as he was on his feet, he'd get in some target practice outside of town.

He turned to study Cheyenne. The town hadn't changed much during his absence. Lang, the old man at the livery, had added another corral, and from the piano music that floated across the wind, Jacob had hired someone who could play better than the last man. Evan had said he was going to listen to the music. He chuckled. Evan wouldn't be back before dawn, and that had nothing to do with the music.

The train had whistled moments ago, and now the black smoke of the engine filled the sky behind the buildings before him. The engine from Council Bluffs had increased to arriving several times a month, bringing more settlers into the area. Cheyenne was growing, and he'd always held a sense of pride that one day it would be a big town now that it was a main hub of the Union Pacific. He took another puff of the smoke, and his thoughts wandered back to Tess.

Something had changed in her or maybe he had been the one who was different since they had fallen across the bed together. Hell, it had made him damn near insane, and all he'd thought about was having her as his own—she being the one thing in his life that made any sense at all. She'd smiled more of late, perhaps having taken his advice for not dwelling on the past and every day he watched her made his heart full. Most men didn't admit so easily to love and while he spoke little of it, loving Tess, well, that was the easy part when it came right down to it.

Children? Some men wanted children, but he'd never thought past his want of her. Children changed a man, but then again, so did a woman. He was a bounty hunter, not given privilege to knowing much about the fate of his future, but he'd been thinking about less bounty hunting and the possibility of just deputying for Sawyer, as he did a lot of the time anyway. Tess well knew he'd never change his line of work, nor would he expect her to stop her doctoring, but her sadness over having no children was real. Dodge had told him children were a woman's reward, and if he could change things for Tess, he'd take any punishment needed, though there was little he could do, other than make sure he was with her all he could be.

"I'm figuring the doc has no idea you are out here smoking." Sawyer stepped up to the porch and leaned against the railing, squinting into the sun.

"Nope. She's out seeing her patients." He darted a glance at his brother, then adjusted his leg.

Sawyer figured him for a moment, gray eyes serious. "How'd you get out here, Evan help you?"

He sucked the cigar for a long moment and then ground the butt into the arm of the wooden chair. "Wasn't easy, but getting better by the day." Sometimes he wasn't so sure, but he was making slow progress.

"I reckon not, at least you have some color in your face," Sawyer added.

"Lying around gets old fast." He eyed his brother who watched the scurry of people beginning to filter through town from the arriving train.

"What the hell?" Sawyer ambled to the edge of the porch, shoving his hands into his trouser pockets.

Wyatt glanced the same direction. A large entourage of men in business suits and hi-top hats, escorted women in finer dresses than he could remember ever seeing, toward the hotel. "The damn circus arrive?"

His brother said nothing, watching until they all

disappeared inside.

"Wait a minute, I know that look." He met his brother's gaze when Sawyer turned.

"It's nothing, those New York types roll into town, and there's trouble at the saloon or bank." Sawyer glanced back over his shoulder.

"Nahhh, you know one or more of them." He waited, with Sawyer not talking.

Sawyer sucked in a deep breath. "The taller man, the one with the red vest. He's Miles Rollins. New York senator, or at least he used to be years ago."

He shrugged. "Enlighten me."

Sawyer removed his hat and wiped his sweaty brow with the sleeve of his shirt and returned his hat. "When Father died, Rollins was there with the group of us who were riding."

"And?" Dread plowed to the surface of Wyatt's chest. Since the beating he'd taken, his father's voice had haunted him. At first he'd thought it was from the confusion of the medicated dreams, but of late, even fully awake hints of his father's voice echoed at unrest.

"While Marcus Benton and his brother schemed to kill father, I could never be sure Senator Rollins was there for the right reasons." Sawyer kicked at a loose board on the wooden porch.

"He was in on it?" Wyatt gripped his fists into tight balls, ignoring the remaining soreness in his right hand. His father had led an expedition into Nebraska to sell land to those who wanted to invest in the building of railroads. At the time, men with gold-lined pockets were headed west to find their waiting fortunes. Sawyer had been seventeen while on the trip, and he'd witnessed their father's murder in cold blood.

"I can't be certain…" Sawyer didn't finish his statement, toeing the loose board once more with the nose of his boot

"Of what?" Wyatt pulled himself to the edge of the chair with a groan.

"What's he doing here, all these years later." Sawyer squinted toward the hotel once more.

"Might be passing through." Wyatt didn't think so given his brother's concern, but people from back East came through Cheyenne all the time, most on their way farther west.

"Nahh, if he's here in Cheyenne, he's up to no good." Sawyer folded his arms. "You best let me help you back inside. I see Evan took care of your purchases at the fort."

Wyatt pulled himself up, balancing on one leg, and Sawyer grabbing the rifle with a questioning glare. "Benton took the best revolvers I ever owned. A man's gotta have protection." He shoved the revolvers in each side of the holster around his hips and grabbed his brother with one arm and used the crutch with the other.

"Well, don't get any ideas just yet." Sawyer tugged harder at his belt helping him gain his balance as he leaned on the crutch and bore what weight he could on his socked left foot. "Try to stand straight."

"Easier said than done…damn it…" He hung onto his brother's shoulder, and after a bit of struggle, the two managed. He could bear weight about every third step and bit his lip to stifle the groan he wanted to let go of with each painful step.

Sawyer hissed. "Damn it, brother, try to help, if I let you fall, Tess and Dodge will skin me alive."

"Just hang on. Did you go to Benton's?" He'd

known Sawyer was checking on Marcus Benton's property from time to time, but the house and surrounding barns had remained vacant.

"It's deserted, but some tracks have been through, near the barn. Probably just a passerby." His brother held the door for him to make his way inside.

"Any chance it's him?" Wyatt's pulse pounded at the prospect.

"Looked like a lone set of tracks, and you and I both know he's never alone." Sawyer sent a warning glare his way. "But I don't think you are apt to go anywhere fast."

They made it down the hall, and he plopped on the side of the bed, holding his leg. "No, but it's just a matter of time, brother. Anything else from back East?"

"The pardon is official, signed and dated about a month before Dawson found you." Sawyer folded his arms.

"Pardoned? He paid someone off." That made sense if nothing else was coming together.

"Let it go for now, Wyatt." Sawyer lifted his leg and helped him to bed. "You're lucky to be alive. He's had it in for you for a while, but I can't say as to why he left you without doing you in as he hasn't ever been one to play games for too long."

"There's a lot more pain to rotting on the prairie than dying by a bullet or swinging by a rope. Likely he thinks me dead, and that just might come in handy when I'm on my feet." He smiled with sarcastic satisfaction, but gripped the sheets at the burn of rage he held back.

"I see it, your ache to end this, Wyatt, but you have to wait until we know what's going on and where the hell he is. Benton's never been a patient man; he'll slip up sooner or later." Sawyer stomped toward the door and stopped, glancing back.

"If I had done it right he wouldn't be here to be so elusive." He fired back, his pulse racing. "You want it done by the law again brother, you best find him before I do. Otherwise, when I'm walking, there won't be any side of the law that can stop me from ending the bastard's life."

"And that's why you are laid up, for not being careful. But I think you have more to consider here than yourself. Leastwise, that's the way it should be." Sawyer's brows lifted

"It was six men against one, and I gave them all a run for their money, two went high-tailing it away from there. And as for considering more than myself, that isn't any of your business, brother." He hissed. He was used to Dodge talking to him where Tess was concerned, but his brother had no right to this topic of conversation.

Sawyer held his gaze for a long moment. "Well, if you aren't going to worry about things here, maybe I should remind you Hudson is still healing in Denver, though he's done some spying at Chan's compound and Benton's been sighted going in and out of the place."

"Son of a bitch! I knew it. But I never asked for Hudson's help with Warner. That plan went awry because your deputy can't leave well enough alone, but you and I both know he has no business at all poking around Chan's alone." He spat in defense, though the guilt over compromising Hudson still plagued him. But the deputy had to know better than challenging Chan; most who did wound up no better than pig food.

"Both of you and even Mattie should have known to stay clear of Warner, and Hudson knows better than to venture too close." Sawyer blew out a long hard breath. "I wasn't going to tell you, but I haven't a doubt Benton will surface soon and we all need to be ready and I don't need you jumping the gun on things."

He glared at his brother. He didn't need a lecture, but they'd long suspected Benton of working deals with Chan, delivering bootleg opium and Chinese liquors to contacts in various towns throughout the West. "Likely Benton is working with Chan, and the price of opium just took a climb."

"If Chan and Benton are working together on anything, it's not the price of opium we have to worry about. Chan's mind is burned up with the drug, and it's his son, Zihao that runs things now, protecting him and their business endeavors." Sawyer turned for the door, lifting his hat to wipe his brow with a sleeve. "I'll be by tomorrow to help you up again, leastwise, as long as you are still slow to move, I have you nailed down."

"Well, don't count on it for long." He threw a pillow toward the door as Sawyer slammed it closed. He gritted his teeth. He still had a ways to go in order to heal but it wouldn't be that long, and the first place he'd start would be Denver with or without his brother's approval. He jerked up the knife and stone, searing the blade across the smooth rock once more.

Chapter Eleven

Wyatt sat in the jail office reading the paper that Rose had brought by. His sister-in-law continued to write for the paper each week, even after her recent delivery. She'd been vibrant and happy, carrying her tiny infant and showing him off around town with Nicholas toddling alongside, hanging onto her skirt. It gave him a glimpse of what Tess would never know, and somehow her pain was his own, not so much because he wanted children but because he wanted what made her happy.

Last night, the doc had been so tired after her daily ride outside Cheyenne to check on a few of her patients who needed attention, she'd fallen asleep across her bed without having any of the stew she'd left simmering earlier in the day. He'd removed her shoes and covered her with the heavy quilt that hung on the footboard. He hadn't wanted to intrude, but he'd stayed there in the chair by her bed most of the night, listening to the sound of her soft breathing. It was a sound he'd come to enjoy given the weeks she had lain close beside him. The night had been short, and when the dawn brought the first signs of morning, he'd slipped from her room. She'd been beautiful and taking in the sight of her in her bed, lying on her side, tender and soft—

"Shit." He wasn't sure what was worse, waiting to heal or living with the urges of his body at her presence most all the time. Having tasted the silkiness of her skin, he was well aware of what he was missing, and if his damn leg would heal, he'd have her too. He went back to the paper, wanting the distraction.

Sawyer bolted through the door trotting to the cabinet across the room and jerked open a drawer that contained information on outlaws and important documents. He slung papers aside and dug deeper into the drawer with a flurry of curses.

"I assume you have a reason for trashing the files?" While he hadn't been in the office in a while, he was the one that kept things in order, and since his long absence, things had been left in disarray.

Sawyer never turned around but kept rustling through the handfuls of papers. "Do you know anything about the land deeds for the ranches, ours and Brett's?"

He shrugged. "They aren't here. Dodge keeps those at the ranch in the safe. What do you need them for?"

Sawyer threw down the remaining papers on the cabinet and faced him. "You remember the top hats that got here last week?"

He nodded, the look in his brother's eyes more than concerning.

Sawyer ran his hands through his dark hair in frustration. "Apparently, *Rollins and Associates* are carrying a deed that gives him the rights to McCade and Morgan lands for the whole six-thousand acres together."

He tried to comprehend, shaking his head. "Father divided the land a long time ago, deeded it out separate."

His brother's expression tightened. "Evidently, there is something to it. One of Brett's men rode out to have him come in. Rollins wants to meet to discuss *the terms of his ownership* of both ranches, calling himself a business entrepreneur. I knew the damn bastard was back for a no good reason."

"He came right out and said this?" Wyatt leaned back in the chair to straighten his leg again. No one had any rights to McCade land save he and his brothers,

"He and his men were cleaning out the winnings and running off Jacob's customers at the saloon, bragging about a railroad spur from Cheyenne all the way to Rapid City." His usually calm brother paced across the room and hung his hat by the door, more than agitated.

"Rapid city? That would go right through both ranches if he tracks it from the Cheyenne hub. They'll never get a track across the Black Hills anyway." He hissed. No one was getting McCade or Morgan lands. This was a farce.

"Oh, he has it all mapped out, right around the edge of the Black Hills all the way around to put a hub right there outside the falls in Rapid City. I'm sure Rollins will more than explain what he has up his damn sleeves. Brett knows nothing, and I expect you to behave, as if you are in any condition anyway. You look peaked." Sawyer warned and went back to sort through the cabinet once more. "It would help if I could find the damn deeds."

He took offense. "I've got enough fight for the likes of this man, nothing peaked here. The deeds have always been in the safe, ask Dodge. She's at the mercantile today anyway."

"Let me handle this until we see what the hell is going on." Sawyer glanced back to the papers he lifted from the drawer before him, tossing most aside on top of the cabinet.

"Best you get Dodge here if Brett's on the way." He cocked his hat back and folded his arms. It wouldn't be wise for Brett to lose his temper—nothing good would come of that, and Dodge had the uncanny ability to keep him in check when needed.

Sawyer gave him a glare of frustration.

"She can keep Brett under control." He stood, holding the edge of the desk and grabbing his crutch, gaining his balance. While he and Sawyer had enough about them to at least listen, Brett wouldn't take the news sitting down. Morgan had been his father's ranch foreman, loyal and hardworking and had done as much in raising him and his brothers as their own father. But he was a man of few words, proud of the cattle business he'd built on the land he'd been given by John McCade for his years of service.

Sawyer shrugged and moved to grab his hat again. "I'll get her, not that she'll behave any better than you or Brett."

"I got it brother, but I don't care who the hell he thinks he is. This is our land." Wyatt's heart pounded in his chest, but he forced himself to relax. Getting riled only fatigued him further now that he was able to get around on his own.

"I'll be back." Sawyer raced out the door, muffled curses following him.

Wyatt had the strong urge to chuckle. It wasn't often he could remain a bit calmer than his brother. He used the crutch to make his way to the door, peering across town. It seemed Rollins had entered town for a purpose after all. How could there be a deed that someone else owned their land? That made little sense, given his father had been meticulous about legal papers, his Chinese notary, Da Ming more than efficient with all the paperwork and deeds involved.

Out of the corner of his eye, he spotted Brett riding up on his mount with a cloud of dust behind him. Wyatt's mind whirled for a moment with a quick thought. His father had deeded land to Brett at the same time he'd given a portion to Marcus Benton. Son of a bitch, this was no coincidence, with Rollins hitting town and Benton receiving a pardon. Something didn't add up.

Brett dismounted and tied off his horse with a nod. He traipsed inside the jail, rigid with a stoic face. "Wyatt. Good to see you out and about. How's the leg?" His gray hair swirled in loose curls from under his hat, and his mustache thick and white moved as he talked.

"I'm healing." That was an understatement. He was getting better, but it was a damn slow process that he was growing tired of.

"You know anything about these deeds?" Brett turned back to the door and spat a plug of tobacco off the jail porch and turned back.

Wyatt met his gaze, leaning harder on the crutch. "The gentleman is the same senator that was with you and Sawyer on the expedition when father was killed says he has a deed for the six-thousand acres together."

Brett balled his fists. "He was trouble then, but how the hell does he have deeds to prove that? John gave me my land outright. I have my deed and your mother has a copy as well."

"Sawyer went for Dodge. Apparently, this Rollins

wants to explain his ownership and takeover plans." He explained with some sarcasm, hopping away from the door.

"Whole lotta hell he'll catch in trying." Brett scowled and turned as Sawyer allowed Dodge to enter the jail office before him.

"You can't be serious." Dodge tossed her bag aside on a chair, swinging around to glance at Wyatt and then back to Sawyer.

"So he says. I've not seen the deeds." Sawyer gave a nod to acknowledge Brett as Dodge moseyed toward the man and ducked to place a light kiss to his cheek.

Wyatt dropped his gaze. He didn't know why his mother didn't go ahead and marry Brett. The two had carried on for years, not bothering to be discreet about it, and most in town were well aware of the situation. But on the other hand, Dodge could be a handful and Brett might have his own reasons for not pursuing things further.

"I've got the deed to the land I own outright. It's forgery." Brett tugged the wrinkled document from inside his vest.

"I have our deeds, quite a number of them in the safe on the ranch," Dodge said with certainty. "I'm sure we can straighten this whole thing out."

Brett lifted a single brow, offering a sarcastic smile to Sawyer. "So, the cocky bastard returns, and he'd better have a damn army with him."

Sawyer focused a warning glare on Brett. "I don't need any one of you to bristle until we iron things out."

Wyatt studied his brother who right along with Brett had carried a lot of secrets from the day his father had been killed. The truth behind his father's murder had surfaced after Sawyer had almost lost his life. And that had been at the hand of Marcus Benton's now dead brother. A picture was beginning to build in his mind, and he wasn't sure he liked it.

Dodge turned to Brett again, placing her hands on her hips. "You know him? Both of you?"

Sawyer sucked in a deep breath and let it out in a puff of lips. "He was on the expedition when father was killed."

Wyatt leaned on the desk, giving his paining leg a bit of rest. The crutch helped him balance but did nothing for the constant ache and fatigue.

His mother didn't miss his struggle. "Wyatt, why don't you sit?"

"I'm good." He lied, but he wasn't about to sit down for this kind of news.

She touched his sleeve, gaining his full attention. "You will rest when this is over. You are hardly well."

He gave her a slight nod as Rollins and three men all dressed in fine suits entered the jail, in a haggle of voices and commotion. It might as well have well been the circus. He wanted to chuckle, though his nerves were more than on end with the thoughts working through his head.

"Sheriff McCade." Miles Rollins removed his hat with a nod to Sawyer, then reached out to grasp Dodge by the hand. "And my dear, Mrs. McCade, I presume."

"I *am* Eleanor McCade, and I'm quite interested in how you could own *my* land." Dodge promptly removed her hand from his.

Rollins dropped the smile. "Well, I'm not a man to take things slowly, so I appreciate your willingness to hear the full plans for this institution of Rollins and

Associates, which while upsetting will have some provisions you will find more than acceptable given the circumstances."

"Provisions?" Sawyer's jaw set, and his stance widened. "Let's take a look at the deed first. And I can assure you, we'll be meeting no terms of anything today."

Rollins gave him a look of speculation and glanced at the other men who had followed him inside. "Well, then as I said, right to the business at hand. I'd first like to introduce you to the business partners in this endeavor. Mr. Frank Lloyd of Lloyd Copper Corporation and Mr. Barton Jessup with the Rapid City Railroad Commission and, of course, my attorney Mr. Randall Cook." The men all acknowledged as introduced, but not one of them said a word—an air of deceit riding the room.

"My brother, Wyatt, and this is—" Sawyer's introduction was interrupted.

"Mr. Morgan, it's been a number of years, sir." Rollins extended his hand toward Brett who only folded his arms.

Wyatt continued to sum them all up, studying each man. Rollins spoke clear and sure, but the attorney with him made little eye contact, likely a puppet in the charades. It was the copper man, Lloyd, who gave him concern. The sinister smile the man held was a dead giveaway of poor character if anything else, and Jessup fidgeted with his tie, unnerved by the proceedings. Bounty hunting had taught him a lot over the years but mostly about the little signs that gave way to the truth behind a man. These men knew they were up to no good.

The attorney reached into his rather large leather carrier that hung from his sagging shoulder. "I have the deed here, and it is the official certified copy." He pulled the document free of a folder he tossed aside. "Ahh, here it is and it is signed by one John Zachariah McCade. Fifth of April, eighteen hundred-forty-six. Said deed allows for ownership of the lands at hand, to one said Miles Rollins with and according to the death of his father, Jefferson Rollins, original purchaser of said lands, eighteen hundred-forty-six."

Sawyer took a step closer as the short attorney laid the document on the desk. Dodge leaned in for a view but stifled Brett's curses by sending an elbow to his ribs. Brett grabbed his side, giving her a stern glance.

His father's full name spoken aloud gave Wyatt a momentary reminder of the pain he would carry for the rest of his life. He leaned off the desk onto his crutch to allow room and viewed the deed for himself. His father had always signed in his full name, and for a moment he was taken back to his childhood, where he'd watched the care John McCade had taken in each document he'd signed. His father's voice came to him again. *Always take pride in signing your name, son, you are the only one who will ever carry it.*

"And Mrs. McCade, if I may ask that you take a look for verifying this is your late husband's signature." The cowering lawyer glanced at Dodge and adjusted his tiny spectacles, dropping his gaze back to the documents.

Dodge shook her head. "John would never give up this land or put it in jeopardy."

"Turn it over." Sawyer commanded with a nod, the shadow of his hat playing across the wooden desk.

"I assure you this is a legal item. My father purchased this land from John McCade as stated and on my father's death a few years ago, it became mine." Rollins flipped the deed with a staunch glare at Sawyer.

Wyatt squinted leaning closer. More signatures remained along the back of the document. The precise signature of Da Ming was just below his father's. The slant to the signatures had been very distinct. John McCade's left-handed slant leaned to the right and Da Ming's right-handed signature held perfect up and down lettering. Something wasn't right. Wyatt lifted the deed and brought it closer. This was his father's writing, but John McCade had a signature like no other, with swirls and penmanship few men were able to mimic. The signed black ink curled in close replica, but the slant of the penmanship leaned left instead of right.

He let a smile curl across his lips and glanced at Sawyer and then Rollins. "This isn't my father's signature; the slant isn't correct."

Rollins burst forth with rebuttal. "I assure you and all present this document came from my own father's files, and this land is legally mine."

Wyatt smirked, shaking his head. "Try again. The slant of my father's penmanship wasn't to the left but to the right."

Sawyer stepped in front of Wyatt, separating him from Rollins and the other men. "You want this land, then it's up to you to prove this document isn't forged."

Wyatt pushed against his brother, cursing under his breath. What the hell? He'd wanted to let the jackass know that his father's left hand wrote in a slant that leaned to the right. Hell, he could show the man as he wrote like his father with his own left hand. He folded his arms and leaned back, not happy at all for the moment.

Rollins and the men with him eyed each other. “This is absurd. It will hold up in a court of law as legal.”

Wyatt grabbed a scrap piece of paper from the desktop. He dipped Sawyer’s quill in the ink well and put the ink to the paper, but his brother slammed a hand down to stop his progress. Son of a bitch! He could prove the point right now with his own left hand.

“This is preposterous,” Rollins growled in frustration.

“We’ve owned this land since before there were towns out here and long before either of us were ever born, deed or not. I think it’s time you move on with your idea, Mr. Rollins.” Sawyer finally let a smile play across his lips.

“Well, now.” Rollins hissed. “I assure you the deed is legal in the eyes of the courts and upon my father’s death, the land now belongs to me, regardless of whatever proposal of scheming you are not sharing.”

Wyatt pushed around his brother, his pulse racing in the effort. Hell, he’d been ready for a good fight for some time now. “Why now? You’ve known of the land clear back to the ride you took with our father, and we all know how that ended.”

“Well, I never purchased any land from that expedition, and you all have my deepest sympathy for Colonel McCade’s untimely death, but my investments took me farther north, to more profitable lands as my father saw it. But my need of my father’s land will allow access for the rail as well as other profits to be had on these lands.” Rollins accented the last of his words, his dark eyes narrowing as he took a step forward.

Wyatt leaned off the crutch, meeting the challenge. Did the bastard think being assertive would give him any advantage in this room?

Sawyer interrupted the exchange with a stern glance at Wyatt. "The government isn't paying money for land to build spurs if you are planning on the railroad plowing from our land through to Rapid City as you mentioned, and I'm guessing a man like you cares little for the ranching business."

"That would be where the mining of copper will be a source of payment for building the spur through to Rapid City, at least at first. With the current investors and productive mines, the full bill of the rail would be paid, and it should stand to be a very profitable adventure for us all." Rollins spoke in a superior tone and unrolled a map he jerked from his lawyer's leather bag.

Brett folded his arms, red faced and tight lipped. "You plannin' on that copper coming from my land?"

Sawyer stepped in front of Brett as Wyatt leaned to glance at the map. Brett's land held three mines, two that had never been opened and one that lay dormant.

Rollins glanced at Mr. Jessup, who had yet to speak. "Mr. Jessup has mapped out the tentative spur plans to Rapid City as…well, you explain, will you."

Jessup eyed Brett and pointed to the map in various places. "As you can see by the crossed lines of the rail, the spur will leave Cheyenne tracking north, here, here and here, laying the track around the outskirts of the Black hills and winding up just outside Rapid City. The copper mines will assure financial stability and later profits will be divided according to the plans laid out by Rollins & Associates."

"This takes the rail less than an acre outside our home." Sawyer slammed a fist onto the table.

Wyatt held steady, finding it unusual that Sawyer would lose his temper that quickly.

"Well, now Sheriff McCade, we have the legal push of the Wyoming and Dakota Territories behind us on getting this railroad built. Enough investors are already on board to make it happen. It's a connection that will be made despite your rejections." Jessop spat in a flurry of southern English.

Sawyer never flinched but met the man toe to toe. "But you will not take it through our land."

Brett shoved Sawyer aside to move in closer. "You won't be mining anything. The open mine ran dry years ago, the other two are not for the taking. And it was Jefferson Rollins who originally sold this land to John McCade. Got your facts a bit mixed up near as I can tell." Brett tilted his hat back and continued, "And you've got yourself one deed there. Two years before this, John McCade divided his six-thousand acres, unless you have three deeds, you are out of line on this bit of deceit."

"Well now, I assure you that the land in full is on this one document, reissued by the United States government to my father after that original attempt at land divisions." Rollins pushed out his chest, slinging his hands to his hips. "Because of those mines."

Jessup took a step back, but Frank Lloyd gave Brett a sly smirk. "With the equipment and man power of my company, it will be right profitable for you as well when those mines are opened."

"Like hell it will. What's the purpose of a railroad across the Black Hills anyway? The gold rush there played out years ago, and there's not much need for a rail to Rapid City." Brett spat as Dodge tugged him back.

Miles Rollins picked up the conversation again. "This has nothing to do with gold; this is to grow the Dakota Territories. And you will retain your land and collect twenty percent of the mined copper market price for the duration which could be more than lucrative if we are guessing right on the condition of the mines. This, I assure you, gentlemen and madam, is a very generous offer to my now taking over ownership of the land, which will happen. Oh, and part of the trade off will be ten percent of the cattle profits toward my investments on the railroad for my allowing you men to continue marketing the beef back East by the Union Pacific rail." He glanced in turn at each of them, his features smug and sure. "As I've said, this is a very fair offer and means you will not lose your homes or lands and at the same time can maintain your current way of life. It might mean a little less cattle profit for a time and hearing the whistle of the train closer to your homes—"

Brett swung a fist and caught Rollins in the side of the jaw. His head, popped back, and he lost his stance, falling backward at the impact. The men with him struggled to catch and lower him to the floor. Sawyer grabbed Brett with a curse and dragged him away.

Wyatt nodded with satisfaction. Rollins had it coming, and Brett had put the man in his place with one punch.

The attorney yelled as Rollins came back to

himself, trying to stand. “Sheriff, I demand you detain this man for battery.”

Sawyer placed a hand on the little man’s forehead and shoved him aside. “Quiet.”

“Yes sir, by all means, Sheriff.” The lawyer grabbed the deed and shoved it back into his leather bag as Jessup rolled up his map.

Rollins held his jaw and wiped blood from the corner of his mouth with a fancy embroidered handkerchief. “No, no that isn’t necessary. Perhaps raising the percent of cattle market requirements to twenty percent will gain your attention as well as dropping the copper percentage by five.” Rollins tugged free of Lloyd’s grip, staggering to keep his balance. “Gentlemen, when I play poker, I do not bluff. The stakes have changed and each time our demands are not accepted, I will be changing the game of play. My attorney will have the official papers drawn and ready within the week. I bid you all good day.” He glanced toward Dodge and turned to go, the entourage of men following him.

Sawyer slammed the office door of the jail once they were out of earshot and turned to Dodge. “Do you know where the deeds are?”

“In the safe at the ranch, that holds most everything in the form of documents your father had,” Dodge responded, folding her arms. “This is fraud.”

Wyatt hobbled to one of the chairs and sat, his leg throbbing. All of this made little sense, but one thing was sure. No one was getting McCade lands. “I take it you had reason enough not to let me show the slant of how father wrote?”

Sawyer nodded and explained, “We might just

need that trick if they take this far enough to need the courts."

Wyatt figured as much once he'd had a moment to think about it, but he would have thought pushing hard now to thwart Rollins' plans.

Sawyer turned back to Brett, who rubbed his knuckles. "Back on that expedition with Father, Rollins was looking at land like all the rest, but that I remember, he didn't make the purchase at the time due to the war and financial instability of the shredded government. And all we needed was you to send a fist at the man."

Brett's rough features were expressionless, his green eyes cold and dark. "Someone needed to see that the bastard was listening. As I remember it, Jefferson Rollins sold John the lands we now own because he thought a section in the Dakotas worth more. He was already planning for a railroad spur north even back then. He, like others, thought Denver instead of Cheyenne would be the Union Pacific's choice for a main hub. So he made his purchase of land in Colorado but never got the funding to make Denver happen, which makes me wonder just how there are investors now. Rapid City makes no sense at all, but Rollins plows through our land, places the spur around those Black Hills. He makes his money selling the land back to the railroad, makes a profit off railroad stock at the same time he's mining copper to foot the bill. Sounds like a damn fine plan if you ask me."

"Why that no good rotten jackass!" Dodge added her own colorful thoughts on the subject.

All the men turned to look at her at once, Wyatt stifling a chuckle. Dodge was one woman who spoke her mind and could have a fouler mouth than any drunkard cowboy if she'd a mind to.

She slammed her hands on her hips. "Oh, none of you look at me like that, I call it like I see it, but the government isn't paying for building the spurs any longer."

Brett twirled his hat in his hands. "Not for the spurs farther West, but they are paying on the connections to the northern lines they want to build. But there's more to it. You have John's deed for the four thousand, and I have mine for the thousand John gave me. So there's one deed missing…"

"The deed held by Marcus. What about it?" Dodge questioned.

Wyatt sat forward in the chair. "I smell a rat and he has an official pardon and we all know he has land in northern Wyoming, all the way to the Dakota line."

Sawyer rested his gaze on Brett. "Benton's been seen in Denver a short time ago. Any chance that Chan has a play in all this?"

Brett nodded in agreement, glancing at Sawyer. "Benton has too much at stake to show himself. Chan's son might be into things, but leastwise his compound is an easy place for Benton's coward hind-end to hide. You keep that deputy of yours lookout there. Might just need him."

Wyatt bristled on the inside, his pulse racing at the mention of Marcus Benton. So the bastard had remained in the vicinity for all this. He gripped his fists tight, trying to calm the fight that surfaced. He'd long figured Benton to have followed him out of Denver before the beating, but now, he'd waited and his need for revenge weighed heavy.

"I want you all home tonight for dinner. Wyatt, have Tess bring you in the buggy." Dodge grabbed her bag and wandered outside, motioning Brett to follow. He rolled his eyes and went out the door behind her, mumbling curses as usual.

Sawyer turned, glaring. After a moment, he shrugged, disgusted. "Punch first, ask questions later. Should have known Brett wouldn't hold a fist. We need to follow the law on this, or we could lose far more than we think."

"We all know what we stand to lose. And Benton, the damn bastard, I figured him behind it just like you did. We haven't seen him, but he's been here all the time." Wyatt snapped, resting harder on his crutch, his mind whirling around it all. "I'll tell you, Sawyer, I'm done sitting idle. I'm not like you brother. Not the sheriff minding all the rules. Bounty hunters play by no rules, and Marcus Benton set the tone for that long ago."

He grabbed the crutch in his hand and limped past his brother and outside on his own. It was true, he'd not fall victim to the laws of the court in losing his father's land. Besides, there were too many things that had started to add up, and he was sick and damn tired of waiting to heal so he could get to them. He stared across the town of Cheyenne as he made his way back to the clinic. This was his home, and the ranch belonged to his family. Come the wrath of the devil. It was time to bring down Marcus Benton.

Chapter Twelve

Tess glanced at baby Uriah in her arms as she sat next to Rose at the McCade dining room table. The meal had been enjoyable though tense. She glanced across the table. Wyatt had cursed through gritted teeth at most of what was being said. Dodge had located the deed copies for McCade, Morgan, and even Marcus Benton's lands. All had been signed before the date of the deed that Rollins held. It was also true that the slant of John McCade's signature had been altered and leaned in the wrong direction. She'd noticed Wyatt's sense of pride over sharing his father's left handed script.

The baby flailed his tiny arms, freeing himself of the swaddling blanket. "Oh, are you tired of being all wrapped up?" Baby Uriah yawned, and his eyes drifted to watch the flame of the lamp at the table.

Wyatt met her gaze, and she wondered if his thoughts were the same as her own. Holding the infant, all she could think was that she longed for her own child—Wyatt's child though that would never be. Dread worked through her, but she pushed it aside and relished in the brief conversation she and Wyatt had shared on the ride to the ranch.

They had found some semblance of living at the clinic together, which hadn't gone unnoticed by those in town. The whispers seemed to follow her, but she'd yet to mention it to Wyatt. She'd asked him once when he would be returning to the ranch though she hadn't wanted him to go, and his response had brought tears to her eyes. *Not leaving you ever again, Doc.* He had assured her that they would marry, but he wanted to be on his own two feet, and today he'd been adamant about giving up his crutch, though he limped in terrible pain he denied.

Dodge angled her glance at Sawyer. "What's the law on our deeds being dated prior to the one Rollins has?"

"It's hard to say. Father's deeds are dated August of eighteen-hundred forty-four and Rollin's one deed, eighteen-hundred forty-six. Father sold a lot of land in Nebraska that year from the records here, but the good thing is these deeds prove Jefferson Rollins as the person of sales, so that part of the story is straight." He flipped one of the deeds taking a closer look.

Brett snorted, stroking his mustache. "That took all of a handshake and an exchange of stocks John no longer wanted. He always preferred to invest in land."

Tess glanced at Dodge who sat next to Brett. When she'd first come to Cheyenne, she had been shocked to learn the nature of their relationship, but after a time it seemed to matter little. It was no secret to anyone in town that Dodge often stayed with Brett at his ranch. Wyatt had never had much to say on the issue, though he spoke highly of Brett. Perhaps her life at the clinic with Wyatt was much the same, though she feared if the whispers continued, she might very well lose future patients who might need her help.

Sawyer's son Zane glanced up from the book he'd been thumbing through. "From what I've read it is the more current document that is used in courts to compare with older documents thought valid, though some of the older documents were not government issued. But possession of the land most often wins, so that's two things in our favor."

"Add the slant of Father's signature and there won't be much fight left in Rollins, but then we all know this is far from over." Wyatt folded his arms, posturing, his voice laced with anger.

Tess' heart sank. All that meant was Wyatt being one step closer to his quest where Marcus Benton was concerned.

Nicholas, who'd been sitting in Rose's lap eating a bowl of stew, picked up the bowl and turned it up like a cup to drink the remaining juices. The chubby faced toddler set aside the empty container and patted his tiny brother in Tess' arms. "Baby brover."

Tess had to smile. It was sweet how much the toddler seemed interested in the tiny bundle. "You want your baby?"

The boy held his arms out. Tess grinned at Rose, who took the baby and helped his big brother hold him. The toddler smiled, eyeing everyone around the table to make sure they had seen him.

Sawyer tousled his son's light curls and the giggling toddler pushed the baby to his mother and got down to play, howling as he took off.

"The deeds we have were government issued with your father's signature. How and where would Miles Rollins get the document he has for the full six-thousand acres unless it was a forgery from some other document with John's signature?" Dodge's blue eyes showed the strain.

Sawyer sipped his coffee and turned back to the conversation. "We need to do what we can to track down any details, more documents, try to place together what happened when the first deeds were signed. I'll send off a few wires to the land offices tomorrow."

Brett's frustration reached its peak and he glanced from Dodge to her sons one at a time as he spoke. "John deeded my land to me right in front of the judge. No illegal deed or crooked New York top hat is gonna take it from me, and no one is mining the land I own. I can also tell you no one is taking your land either, boys, because your father and all of us have worked too hard over the years to build this cattle business." He stood and tipped the brim of his hat, to the ladies, speaking to Rose. "You did mighty fine with that one there, Ms. Rose. I am glad all is well with you and the little one."

"Thank you," Rose whispered as Brett left the room, Dodge following him outside.

Wyatt stared into the flame of the lamp on the table, lost in thought when Tess turned back to face him. He was a man who had to keep busy and wanted the truth of things without waiting, and his frustration was evident. That was the part of Wyatt that scared her at times, not because he would hurt her, but because when he was like that he cared little for himself, likely the reason he'd been caught off guard by Mr. Benton when he'd been attacked. She'd stitched and patched him up a number of times though the latest one had all but stalled her heart. He wasn't fully healed, but he still thought he could take Marcus Benton with his bare hands.

Evan appeared at the doorway of the dining room. "So what the hell is going on about this Rollins having a deed? This is our land by-God!" He slammed into one of the chairs.

Sawyer slid the deeds toward Evan. "These are Father's original deeds. Rollins' plans are to run the railroad right through here and mine copper off Brett's land, so he can take the railroad all the way into the Dakota Territory. He's got a deed that looks legit, but for the full six-thousand acres, not the division of land we know Father made."

Evan arched a blond brow. "The hell you say?"

"We're sure of nothing for now. He wants to pay Brett a portion of copper prices, and he wants you to pay him a portion of the cattle market, so we can remain in our homes…for now." Sawyer's sarcastic explanation made Evan shake his head.

"Ain't no one dealing the cattle around here save me!" Evan slammed his fist on the table.

Baby Uriah screwed up his tiny face and emitted a shrill cry. Rose stood and bounced the infant shushing him with her whispers as she hurried from the room.

"Sorry, Rose," Evan called after her and turned back to his brothers.

"I'm gonna ask you like I have Brett and Wyatt, keep it down until we get this figured out. There is something crooked, forgery for sure, but we're gonna have to prove it." Sawyer glanced from Wyatt back to Evan.

Evan slung his chair back, standing. "Those are our cattle, this is our land and home or have you forgotten how hard Father worked for all of it!"

"Sit!" Dodge shouted from the doorway.

Evan plopped in the chair once more, his lips pressed into a thin line of anger as he glared toward her and then Sawyer.

Tess remained quiet, thinking matters of the family needed to remain just that. Evan was young, and he and Sawyer had often struggled at their relationship from the things Wyatt had shared. For the most part, he thought it had to do with Sawyer acting the role of father and Evan resisting.

"I'll talk to Brett. He loves his land as do we, and no one is going to lose it. We have the deeds of proof. I expect you all, including Dawson to rein in your tempers and work with Sawyer. Do I make myself clear?" Dodge waited, meeting the gaze of each of her sons and then stopping on Evan who gave a reluctant nod.

It wasn't the first time Tess had watched Dodge call down her sons, but it always amazed her that she could silence them with her words alone.

Wyatt cleared his voice. "Where the hell is Dawson anyway?"

"He's hunting with Leaning Bear. He'll be back by Monday," Sawyer answered, shaking his head and picking up one of the deeds.

"Some things never change," Evan whispered, folding his arms across his chest.

Tess met glances with Wyatt. It was no secret that his brothers cared little for Dawson's involvement with the Indians. Wyatt had often cursed Leaning Bear, though of late she had been quick to remind him that it was the Medicine Man who had given up a horse to make sure he got home when he'd been injured.

"Let it be, if Leaning Bear hadn't found Wyatt…" Dodge stopped. "None of us want to think about what might have happened to him and let it be a reminder to you all to watch yourselves."

Wyatt met glances with his mother as Mei Ling entered from the kitchen. The elderly Chinese woman set a plate before Evan. "Mind you eat too much. Get fat." She poked him in the belly and picked up Zane's empty bowl and returned to the kitchen.

Tess exchanged smiles with Dodge as she sat back at the table. Mei Ling always felt the freedom to speak her mind no matter the situation. She glanced at Evan who ignored her and dug right into the heaping plate of food. He technically wasn't fat, but he was taller and heavier than any of his brothers.

He scooped another large bite of stew and gulped. "Well, I suggest you boys with badges, get to it. No one is driving a railroad through this land, and I sure as hell won't be paying off profits from the cattle market to some swindler from back East."

Sawyer narrowed a gaze on his youngest brother. "None of us want that, but I've got a few things to check into, and Zane's researching the law. I'll contact the land offices in every territory to see what I can uncover."

"You do that brother. I've got some things to check out as well." Wyatt nodded to Tess, and with great effort got to his feet balancing to take weight on his bad leg.

Tess stood and straightened her skirt, wondering at the abruptness with which he had moved, his tone so cold.

Sawyer stood, folding his arms aware of the same. "Best you watch your step, Wyatt."

Of all things, Wyatt laughed and gave his brother a serene smile, tilting his hat. "I'm not stepping. I'm riding in a damn buggy."

Tess exchanged glances with Sawyer. It seemed his brother could read Wyatt as well as she could. Because he no longer lay in bed each day sharpening his knife against the stone, didn't mean he had given up on the idea of revenge, and he'd always hated riding in wagons, though he never named his horses which had always seemed strange to her. But given his mood, it would apparently be a long ride home. She turned and followed him to her buggy where Anna munched oats from a bucket.

She wasn't sure what she should or shouldn't say, but Wyatt seemed fine and assisted her into the buggy with a smile. "I'll drive."

"If you like." She settled back as he fidgeted his large frame into the buggy, letting his left leg hang out the side, then easing it in.

He snapped the reins, and the buggy moved into motion, Anna reluctant to leave the oats behind at first.

"She's not used to being spoiled with the oats." She made small talk, assessing his mood further. He had to be upset as much as any of the family. She was still shocked over it herself, and the worried look on Dodge's face hadn't helped her feel any better about it all.

He glanced at her and then the road ahead, though the silence was deafening. Well, she couldn't take not being able to speak her mind if it came right down to it. "I'm sorry for what is happening, Wyatt, but I just can't see this man taking anything, given Dodge has the proof of deeds."

"Not your doing, we'll get to the bottom of things soon enough." His tone was lighter but not his expression. “Look, a lot of things from the past are coming to the surface, and it has nothing to do with you.”

“So much of it I’m not sure I understand, and it scares me, thoughts of you getting hurt again.” She whispered the last few words hoping not to upset him further.

He stared at the road ahead for a moment, grimacing as he held a hand to his knee. “I’ve got some healing yet to do, Doc.”

“I know your leg still hurts, your limp is worse by evening, perhaps using the crutch some of the time.” It was still too soon for him to walk without the added help, though she’d be hard pressed to ever have him admit he needed any assistance from the crutch or her. She worried that she’d let him walk to soon as well as giving up the crutch which had been his own idea.

“I don’t want you worrying about my leg or other things. I’ve got some leads, just not sharing that with Sawyer yet.” He took a deep breath and let it out, sweat collecting along his brow. “You know the other night, Doc, when you woke me from dreaming?”

She nodded, having been startled several nights before with him lying next to her and fighting something in his dreams. Once again he’d said Da Ming’s name and screamed of fire. She’d asked him about it later, but he’d made the excuse he didn’t remember.

“When I was twelve, I was with Father at the railroad office. It was late, and he had business to attend to. He told me to stay inside the railcar until he returned, but it took a while. Dawson fell asleep. I got bored. Ventured out anyway. I walked around the tracks and climbed on a pile of wood, but then I heard a man screaming and snuck closer." He stared straight ahead, but his hands were so tight on the reins his knuckles were white.

Sweat gathered across his brow as he continued. "Mei Ling's husband Da Ming was being whipped by Marcus Benton, and I watched, unsure where Father had gone or how to find him. Then I watched as Da Ming's own brother, Chan, set fire to the railcar where they put Da Ming and sent it down the tracks…"

Tess reached for his hand as his voice cracked. This was some part of the dreams he carried, but she had to wonder why he was telling her now. "Oh, Wyatt…"

He swallowed hard, his body shaking. "His own brother. And I can still hear his screams from that burning railcar, even after all these years, the damn dreams never stop, Doc."

Tess let go of his hand and wrapped her arms around his middle. "I thought Da Ming's death was an accident. Mei Ling told me that."

He shook his head against her. "She doesn't know. I ran back for my father, and he grabbed me out of the night, his hand on my mouth, getting me away in case Benton heard me."

"Wyatt, that's horrible. I'm so sorry." She glanced up at him, holding his gaze.

"My father never laid a hand on any of us, never thought physical punishment was due a child, but that night he threatened to beat me if I ever spoke of what happened again. I had bruises on my arms for weeks where he shook me so hard…" He shrugged, and he was trembling, sweat pouring down his cheeks. "And I never said a thing until telling you this right now, but the worst part of it all, even worse than Da Ming's death…"

Tess' heart melted into tiny pieces. Wyatt had real tears streaking his face. Lord, but except when she'd set his leg she'd never seen his tears.

He went on, looking ahead at the darkened road before them. "I had words with my father, years later, right before he was killed. I called him a coward for not standing up to Marcus Benton when Da Ming had been killed. I was so young and stupid. I just never understood why he hadn't done something, but it wasn't until all these years later that I understand…"

"He deeded Marcus Benton the land to keep you safe." Tess finished for him. It was a shock to hear Da Ming, who she had never known, had not died of an accident. But Wyatt's tears crushed her. She grabbed the reins and stopped, Anna, the buggy bobbling to a halt. She turned back to Wyatt, whose gaze was lost, and she placed her hands to both his cheeks making him look at her.

"You were a child, a frightened child who should have never seen such a thing. And your father had to know you were a young man who didn't understand the fullness of the situation when you argued." She tried, but he was shaking uncontrollably.

"I was so angry, he wouldn't fight and put Marcus Benton in his place and then, it was Benton's brother who killed him. Marcus Benton has pushed all these years to have what he wanted…but he'll never get this land, and I know he's behind all of it." He ran his hands into his shaggy dark hair, his hat falling at their feet inside the buggy. His fists were gripped so tight his knuckles shown white as they shook. "And Da Ming should've never died like that, and then Sawyer almost died, it will never stop if I don't do it, can't you see?"

She still held his face, but he wasn't with her. He was reliving Da Ming and his father and Marcus Benton as lost as she'd ever seen him. She held him tighter, "Wyatt, look at me! Wyatt!"

He struggled out of the trance and focused on her, his breathing so fast she wondered if he might pass out.

"It's all right. Wyatt, look at me." She tried. "Your father loved you, and you were a child who never should have seen what happened to Da Ming. It's not your fault, Wyatt, and your father was protecting you as best he could."

Wyatt tried to tug away, wiping his face with his sleeve.

She didn't let go. "You cared for me when I couldn't take care of myself. Let me be there for you now. Let me be where you turn when you hurt, not those horrible dreams."

He turned then and held her gaze, blinking hard as if he was trying to understand her words. And then he grabbed her in his embrace, holding her as tightly as he ever had and resting his cheek against her own, the tension in his body easing. "And all these years, since my father…I hear his voice. *Wyatt, you have to fight with your head, not your fists. Wyatt, you have to settle the West, bring down the men who would corrupt her. Are you listening to me son? Fight harder, work harder, you have more in you son…always do good by men, Wyatt.* I have to end this or my father's death, all he ever stood for was in vain. I have to do this."

Tess tugged him closer, rocking him as the night

closed in around them. How could she have ever known the story he'd just told her? No wonder Wyatt had been such a hard man over the years. To have seen that as a child was a horrible thing. And then the fight with the father he had always adored hadn't been resolved before John McCade had died. How could he have held onto secrets with so many scars for so long? He'd almost died at the hands of Marcus Benton, but the man she held wouldn't rest until he'd avenged himself for the sake of his family and all his father had ever taught him. How could it be that she would ever stand in his way, though her fears of losing him were real?

Chapter Thirteen

Wyatt ran a hand through his short hair and trimmed beard. It was strange to be somewhat normal again, though he feared things would never be normal again. Somehow his recent disclosure of things from the past to Tess had left him fatigued but in sorts, relieved. He wasn't sure what had happened to him that night, as he remembered little of his confessions, but Tess had explained to him it was something close to suffering a soldier's heart. The shock of witnessing Da Ming's horrifying death as a child had been held inside for too long, and while he hadn't been a soldier, he'd suffered the same state of stress. He wasn't sure he understood, but no matter, his head was clear for the first time in months.

After a full day of being stuck in the jail, sending out a few telegrams and studying the details related to the deed issue, he'd concluded the answers would be found in Denver—for the right price. He'd made a quick stop by the bank earlier, taking out a large sum in Golden Eagles which now weighed down the saddle bags across his shoulder. If he played his cards right, the coins would be a payoff for information from the past and the remainder would purchase the best wedding dress Denver had to offer.

He crossed the street to the clinic as the last of the sun dipped behind Cheyenne. Tess would be back from her patient visits by now and would have found the flowers he'd filled in vases all over her bedroom. Never mind he owed Zane six-bits for searching for all the wildflowers he could find. His nephew had given him a suspicious glare but returned a few hours later with two buckets full, though he ventured some were weeds. Ah, she wouldn't mind when it came down to it and it required something special for him to make things official with her and this time with an answer he could accept.

Somehow the things of the past mattered little. He'd held out on her a bit, waiting until he had done more healing, but she'd hinted now and again about when they might marry. He thought to wait a bit longer, but given that he needed the quick jaunt to Denver, it was the perfect time to make things right and this time for good. Besides, he could barely keep his hands off her, and town folk were beginning to chatter. And he'd waited about as long as he intended to wait to have the doc as he'd always wanted her—naked and beneath him.

He kicked off his boots with a bit of effort and slipped inside as quietly as he could. Surprise might be to his advantage. He limped toward the hallway leading to the doc's bedroom and stood in the doorway. She was before the mirror brushing her hair. She'd bathed and was wearing her robe and nightdress though it was still rather early. He gulped a forgotten breath.

"Nothing wrong with the view from here." He held onto the door frame. He'd been cautious of her privacy in staying at the clinic even though she lay down with him at night in the bed he'd occupied for a time now. But this glimpse of her left his body aching with the need to touch her.

She turned toward him, a flush of pink across her cheeks, and then her mouth dropped open. "Wyatt, you cut your hair."

He supposed it was a shock to her and smiled. "Yep, and I've never seen anything so beautiful as you, Doc."

She turned back to the mirror and stroked the brush through her hair once more with a frown. "I didn't know you were spying on me, but the flowers are lovely. I had thought my birthday forgotten." She touched the petal of a purple flower in a vase on the edge of her small dressing table.

He limped closer as she continued with her hair. He wanted to do that. He'd brushed her hair before, when she'd been ill and unable to do it for herself. He stopped behind her and took the brush from her hand as he met her gaze in the mirror. He'd never let one of her special days pass him by, always leaving her flowers, even when she'd been married though he'd often left them anonymously. "I've not forgotten your birthday in all the years I've known you, Doc."

She shivered as he ran the brush the length of her long brown hair. "I know."

He pulled the brush several more times, never looking away from her deep green eyes. He ran his thick fingers through the length of her hair and lifted strands into his fingers and inhaled the scent of sweet lavender soap. Placing his hands along her hips, he whispered near her ear. "I've been thinking, Doc. I need to go to Denver, see about things related to that deed. Maybe we could take the train, you go with me." Hell, he'd asked her once. He could do it again, couldn't he?

"I thought we could see the judge there and make things official. We can get a nice room in Denver and eat at the finest restaurants, and I'll be buying the most beautiful dress to be found."

She said nothing for a moment, but it was apparent she was fighting tears. Well, he couldn't allow that, now could he?

"No tears." He turned her, pulling her the length of him, holding her as he spoke. "Only want to make you happy, Doc. Can't have the people of Cheyenne gossiping about things not of their concern."

"Well, maybe these are happy tears." She brushed away the one that spilled to her cheek, though she smiled.

"I know my not going home to the ranch has the ladies in the quilting circle chattering. And I've still got some healing to do, but I'm not waiting much longer to make you mine, Doc." With that he touched her lips, tracing his thumb across them, lips he had memorized over the years. He wanted to consume her in one motion, take her right where they were and never let up until her legs quivered and she called his name, but that would wait.

"Denver sounds like a beautiful plan, but…" She shook her head slightly and opened her mouth, but he cut her off.

"Children don't have to come from your body, Doc. From time to time, babies lose their mamas or folks are looking for a home for a small child with no parents. We can cross that bridge later."

She placed a hand to his cheek and in the softest whisper answered, "That's even more beautiful, but I have to…make this right."

Wyatt wrinkled his brows, what wasn't right about any of it? Things were perfect, all except her tears, which for good or bad reasons could cut him at the knees.

She gave him a hesitant smile and placed her hands to his, pulling them away from her body and keeping them in her grasp. "When you asked me to be your wife, you said you would do it only once."

He tried to protest, but she touched his lips with her finger, keeping his words at bay. She smiled a mischievous grin, perplexing him even more at what she was up to.

"So…Wyatt Zachariah McCade, would you do me the greatest honor of my life by becoming my husband for the rest of our lives?" Her voice cracked, though she still held the smile along with her tears.

He lifted her into his arms, turning around with her. He inhaled the sweet lavender and closed his eyes, burying his face in her neck, never wanting the moment to end.

"Wyatt, your leg…" She protested in a whisper but never let him go, clinging so hard to him he had to sneak in the next breath.

"My leg's no trouble with you, Doc," he whispered, and he could have walked to the ends of the earth with her finally in his arms for good.

She danced her fingers through his short dark hair, kissing his cheek and whispering into his ear. "No cigars, no whiskey, and no women at the saloon, but I know you've been smoking and taking a nip from Evan's vial. Remember, I'm a physician, Mr. Bounty Hunter, and nothing gets past me."

"I believe I can hold up my end of that bargain."

He continued turning a slow circle, the weight of her pleasing in his arms, and though she was right about his leg, he'd never admit it.

"But…" Tess held his face and planted her lips right on his own for a gentle kiss that caused him to shudder.

He chuckled at her. "But what?"

She fidgeted from his embrace, stepping back as she pulled the robe away from her body. Wyatt sucked in a ragged breath.

She laid the garment aside, leaving him the full view of her dark nipples playing across the white linen of her gown. And with a bit of hesitation, she placed her fingers to the buttons of her night dress and with trembling fingers unfastened the first button, meeting his gaze again. "I…don't want to wait until Denver for you and I…"

He lifted his brows shocked at her boldness but amused with the shade of pink that fell across her cheeks. "Doc, you don't have to do that…" Hell, he'd waited this long that another few days would be nothing, well at least until she'd allowed the gown to pool at her feet.

He steadied himself. It was apparent the doc had done a little planning of her own. He scanned the beauty of her. Full breasts and rounded hips, more breathtaking than he'd ever imagined. He stepped closer and lifted her chin, waiting until her green eyes found his again. "I've seen a lot of sunsets, Doc, but I've never seen anything like you."

Her smile was well worth the words that escaped him in a tightened breath. She was full of the curves and fullness of a woman, and right now, his hard body was proof enough of that. Something told him that the doc wasn't thinking rational and it might be best if he stopped her, tucked her into bed and then dunked his entire body in the water trough out on the street. "I should run is what I should do…we'll get to this, Doc…"

She shook her head. "My body craves your touch."

Ah, hell, he wasn't walking away from that. She was to be his wife and as far as he was concerned she already was. He jerked his vest and shirt away, never taking his gaze from hers, tossing them aside. He was surprised and groaned as she fell into his embrace, her breasts crushed between their bodies as he took her lips again. He closed his eyes, enraptured that her kisses were as urgent as his own, wanting the press of her body against his rigid groin. He tasted her plump lips and danced his tongue along hers until she tugged from the kiss, gasping for a breath and swaying in his arms.

"You're trembling, Doc," he whispered, as he settled her against him again, his heart pounding to the surface.

Her hands flattened across his chest. "It's been a long time."

He touched her cheek, tracing to her chin. "It's all right. Just me and you, Doc."

"I know." Her sweet voice filled his ears and he sucked in a breath as she let her hands slide down his torso. He closed his eyes, her gentle caresses easing over his ribs and sliding around him. Bending, he traced his lips across the warm flesh of her neck and shoulders, holding her as he tilted her further, nipping across the tops of the tender roundness of her breasts.

She sighed; slight enough to cause his britches to

tighten further. He dipped his head taking a nipple into his mouth and rasped his tongue across the taut peak, until her breath shortened and her hands played with urgency along his scalp.

He was surprised when her hands slid to his trousers buttons, tugging. Hell, if that didn't set him on fire, heat shooting through his groin. He placed his hands with hers and together they undid the buttons. He stepped from the pants and jerked his socks off, ignoring his leg. He stood to embraced her again and traced his hands down her back and across her rounded buttocks, pressing her against the hardness of him. Nudging her, she laid back on the bed and he covered her with his body, taking her mouth again, his hands roaming her torso. He'd do his best to rush nothing. He'd take his time; explore her beautiful body as he'd waited a damn lifetime to touch her like this.

He kissed her chest and made his way to her breasts, nipping and sucking the pert nubs until she took in a fervent breath, tangling her hands in his hair. Kissing underneath each breast, he savored a trail of exploration across her ribs and her belly, his hands massaging everywhere they rested, the doc writhing beneath him. Well, he could manage this for a lifetime. He slid lower, pushing a hand across the mound of soft brown curls causing her to tremble, though her legs opened for him. His fingers parted her, slipping across the bud of her pleasure. He stifled a groan as the doc's upper body lifted off the bed with her urgent sigh.

"Easy, Doc." He coaxed, placing his lips back to her belly, kissing down to her hips with tender nips as his fingers continued to touch her intimately. She was beautiful as he savored the smooth taste of her flesh.

And when he pressed his fingers inside her, he was rewarded with a deep sigh of satisfaction, her body clenching around them. Apparently, the doc *did* know what her body was capable of as she pressed against him. He chuckled and obliged, withdrawing his fingers and pushing her thighs apart to lie between the heat of her.

She was breathless, her breasts heaving as she wrapped her arms around him, kissing his shoulder. He could have worked her longer, enjoyed watching her bliss, but right now he wanted her. He wanted to hear her cries as her body let go with him buried deep inside and he wanted to find his own release with her clinging tightly to him.

She wrapped her legs about him as he probed, then filled her full and deep with one swift thrust of his hips. He swallowed her gasp, savoring her mouth again as he moved against her slow at first, the rhythm of his hips steady and sure. He'd expected this moment to take his breath, but he hadn't expected it to near suck the life right out of him. He tangled a hand into her hair and sucked in a ragged breath as her silky heat engulfed him again and again. She was perfection.

She traced her hands down his back, pressing herself against him, urging his pace with small cries of pleasure. That did it. The doc well knew what she wanted and he was going to give her all he could. He moved with fervent purpose until each impact of himself against her caused her gasp. Holy damn, but she was beautiful with her breasts bouncing and her dark hair splayed across the pillow. She clung to him, meeting him stroke for stroke and then her warmth tightened around him.

"Ah…ah…Wy…att…" Her body shuddered and clenched as he rode through her release, his own body shattering with the last of her cries. He fell against her, his body wracked in spasms and she held him as they both struggled to recover.

Sweat streaked and breathless, he was certain he'd never catch his wind or his heart again. And he dared not to move, holding her gaze, not wanting to part from her. He kissed her and she held him even tighter, keeping him tucked between her legs still buried deep inside her. He touched her cheek and brushed the hair back from her damp face unsure he could see enough to take in all the beauty of her and certain he'd never again be the same man. He kissed her forehead and then each cheek and then her tender swollen lips, as his body jerked time and again with the aftermath of his climax. Holy hell, but he loved her.

She panted, a raw whisper escaping her. "Never…let me go again, Wyatt, not ever."

He chuckled, breathless and squeezed. "Not ever, Tess."

She touched his brow with the back of her hand as if she were checking his fever. "You never call me, Tess. Are you sure you are feeling well?"

He thought about it, resting on his elbows and relishing in her breasts pressed tight between their bodies. Had he never called her by her given name? Well, maybe it was time he remedied that. He'd always thought her name elegant and somehow as beautiful as she was, but she'd always been, *Doc*. He smiled and kissed her tenderly and then held her gaze, the light from the low-lit lamp flickering across her face. "All I have ever needed in this life is you. Never gonna let you go again. I love you, *Tess*, always have, always will."

Chapter Fourteen

Wyatt glanced across Denver as he helped Tess step from the train. He'd never taken in the view from the depot until now, and it took one second for him to spot Sheriff Chance Barlow in the distance. The man was having a smoke, leaning against the porch railing of one of the local businesses. Barlow gave him an evil nod as he blew out a puff, the sinister look in his eyes a warning. He held the man's gaze but kept his poker face. It might be that getting married in Denver was one thing, but seeking out what he needed from Chan would be another with the sheriff already on him.

Tess turned a full circle taking in the sites of the beautiful city, tugging his glance from the knowing sheriff. "I haven't been to Denver in more than two years, my how it's grown."

Wyatt grabbed their bags, limping along behind her, a bit on edge with Barlow on them that quickly, but it was rare the crooked sheriff didn't meet those entering town by rail. "Walk's not far. I'll get us checked into the hotel, and I've got a few errands to see to, you being one of them."

She smiled, and her fascination was worthy of a chuckle, but somehow being in Denver was too quick a reminder of what lie ahead.

She glanced at him, taking his arm. "I know you told me no questions, but this is making me nervous, as you are so very sneaky. We are to be married this very night, and I haven't a thing, not even the required old, new, borrowed, or blue."

It had occurred to him that she deserved a wedding where their families could attend, but that would take a bit more planning than what he'd managed to pull off for her in Denver. He wasn't waiting any longer to make her his own for all time, and he hadn't spared any expense in doing so.

He stopped outside the Windsor Hotel in the center of town, the one that he wanted her to be able to say she'd stayed in at least once in her life. While he'd leave Denver with lighter pockets, it was as it should be. She had stayed in finer hotels in Boston or New York, but it had been a while and this was as fine a hotel as the West had to offer and it hadn't come cheap.

Tess' mouth dropped open at the fancy rock-work building with its sidewalk red carpeting and elaborate marble etchings. "Wyatt…" She turned to face him, her eyes wide as she whispered, "This must be very expensive."

"Let me worry about that." He'd made decent money over the last few years, but the months when he'd left Cheyenne he'd managed to build up a good savings. He'd eyed the new hotel from his previous walks through the town. Taking up a complete city block it boasted the only in-room tubs, and he'd made sure they had the best room available. Tess would like that.

He allowed the bellman to open the door for them and led her inside, setting their bags on the fancy hardwood floors. The lobby was dressed in plush red carpeting and fancy drapes that hung from ceiling to floor. Even the stairs had a layer of plush red carpeting across each step.

The clerk at the desk, a small man with tiny spectacles, smiled his best grin. "Yes, sir. Might I be of assistance to you and your lovely wife?"

Wyatt leaned on the counter and pulled a roll of money from his trouser pocket. "McCade. I wired a few days ago from Cheyenne for a *special* room."

The man scanned his agenda and glanced back up. "Yes sir, Mr. McCade. You are set for room twenty-two on the second floor one of our finer rooms. Here's the key and if you will sign here." The man laid a piece of paper on the desk, and Wyatt signed it glancing at Tess who had yet to close her mouth.

"The southpaw bounty hunter." The man's voice held a knowing admiration. "You have a remarkable record, practically famous all through the West."

Wyatt motioned the man closer as he took the keys. "Practically. I'm uh, not here on business though, so let's keep things quiet." It wasn't a surprise that the man recognized him, but he was hoping to remain rather out of sight on this trip, even if Barlow was already aware of his arrival with Tess.

"Oh, by all means, sir. I'll have your bags brought upstairs to your room." The man fidgeted with his glasses scanning the lobby and nodding his head toward one of the bellman.

"I got our bags, thanks." Wyatt winked at the frazzled man, grabbing the bags and taking Tess by the hand, leading her to the stairs.

Tess hesitated at the bottom. "Wyatt, your leg…so many stairs."

"It's fine, go ahead." He eyed the climb as she

went ahead, thinking maybe she was right but his leg had been reason enough to request a low floor. Being cramped up on the train and now this jaunt hadn't helped matters and he hadn't brought the crutch. He forced his mind not to count them and took one step at a time leading with his right leg and holding the railing with his left hand for support. While he no longer needed the crutch, the leg still throbbed and ached most days and was so swollen at night he could hardly get his boot off.

She waited on him at the top, and he led the way to their room, fidgeting with the heavy key and opening the door, allowing her the first peek at the luxurious room.

She wandered inside, touching the vases one at a time. "Wyatt, did you? How did you? So…beautiful. You spoil me with the flowers at home and here."

He set their bags down on the high bed and wrapped his arms around her from behind. "I know you love flowers as much as I love you."

"So thoughtful." She leaned into his embrace and tugged from his grasp to stroll around the room, touching the different flowers in vases.

He backed against the dresser, following her with his gaze. "After this evening, you are stuck with me for good, Doc."

She glanced at him with a sly smile. "Can't think of anywhere I'd rather be."

Damn, she was beautiful enough to take his breath, but that would come later and he was damn looking forward to it. "Grab your bag, I'm taking you someplace, but remember no questions. We're a bit behind schedule."

Tess flitted around the room, first to her packed items and then to her shoulder bag, scrambling to unearth things she might need and slinging others. He wanted to chuckle at how hard it was for her to not ask what he was up to as she hadn't liked one bit that she wasn't aware of every detail.

"You promised me a dress and lord knows leaving that choice to a man…" She shook her head, viewing the contents of her bag one more time before slinging it over her shoulder and turning to face him.

Wyatt pulled her to him and touched her lip with his fingers to stop her words. "Trust me, Doc?"

She narrowed her eyes in speculation but stifled a slight grin.

"Come on." He took her hand in his own and led her from the room.

"You are making me very nervous and I still need to bathe and my hair is a mess from the train." She followed, her flurry of words making him smile all the more until they reached the stairs once more.

His leg throbbed inside his boot, which was already tight. She slipped under his left arm and helped take the pressure off his leg, reading his mind. Out on the street he held up his elbow to escort her, wondering if she might have a fit about where he was taking her. In all likelihood…that would come, but he'd smooth things over later and when it was done she'd be too happy to think much on it with what he'd planned.

"Wyatt, slow down." She trotted to keep pace with him, adjusting her bag to stay across her shoulder.

"Sorry, we're a bit late." He weaved them across two streets and back behind the main road, Tess shuffling in a flurry of skirts to keep up. Music from one of the saloons echoed as he turned another corner to the back of it—and toward the brothel.

Tess jerked to a stop, jarring his leg, her mouth dropping open.

Wyatt hopped for a second, easing his leg back to the dusty ground. "Doc, it's all right, come on." He tugged her hand, limping worse, but she held her ground, digging in her heels.

"Wyatt?" she whispered in challenge, glancing before them. Scantily clad women hung from the balconies, paying them no mind. The wash was hung to dry across rungs of rope and several of the ladies were smoking, leaving the air filled with a slight haze that mingled with the distant scent of alcohol.

Wyatt took her by the arm. "Just trust me, will ya?"

She continued to whisper as they made it up the porch stairs, more damn stairs, where she halted again. "Wyatt, this is a brothel for goodness sake…"

"You promised no questions." He chuckled at her irritation and tugged her behind him, gripping her hand tighter for reassurance as he led her inside anyway.

"Wyatt?" She tried again, but he didn't turn, pulling her to follow him up the stairs inside. More damn stairs, at this point he wouldn't be worth six bits when he got her back to their room later.

Inside was dark but incredibly fancy for such an establishment. Purple velvet curtains hung to cover windows, and the air was heavy with perfume, alcohol and smoke. Women in revealing fancy dresses sat around talking with men who were more than friendly with their wandering hands. Tess would scold him later, though she held tight to his hand, dropping her gaze.

He knocked at Mattie's door, which jerked open

with his third rap.

"Well, it's about time. I figured the train got held up." Mattie was dressed in a fine red gown, and he had to wonder if it was because of the favor he'd asked.

"Hello, Mattie." He urged Tess into the room behind him, shutting the door. "How's Hudson?"

"He's out and about." Mattie smirked at him, placing a hand on her rounded hip and turning to Tess. "I might have figured the woman to capture Wyatt McCade's heart to be a pretty one, but my, my I had no idea. You're a real beauty. I'm Mattie." She extended her hand.

Tess smiled and hesitantly took her hand. "Thank you."

Mattie turned back to him. "Well, at least you cut your hair. And your injuries?"

"Took some doing but my personal physician is the best." Wyatt winked but didn't glance at Tess for fear of reprimand. "Give us a minute."

"I'll check the bath water." Mattie made a hasty exit through the door by the window, not looking back.

He rested his gaze on Tess who scolded in a whisper. "Wyatt?"

"She's a good woman, Doc." He tried. "She's pulled all this together for us to marry."

Tess shook her head, still keeping her voice low and folding her arms. "Wyatt this is a brothel, and I know what she and all these women are. I suppose I know better than to ask any further questions about how you know this place."

He defended Mattie, though he couldn't blame her for her thoughts. "She's a friend. That's all."

She ambled away from him to touch the wedding

dress hanging against the back of the door. He'd spared no expense. It was a beautiful garment, a natural color with lace and sculpted buttons, a narrowed bodice and a high neck with puffy sleeves and next to it on the table, a pair of tan flat boots both in just her size. Now was the time, and he had just the item to smooth things over with her. He followed her and took her hand in his, placing in it a necklace Dodge had given to him, one that had belonged to the mother she'd never known. The delicate jewelry was braided silver with sapphires lining the metal heart at its center. While he hadn't added the purpose of the trip to Denver to his family's knowledge, Dodge had come to him the night before they left, giving him the necklace. One of these days he was going to pull off something his mother couldn't figure out.

Tess glanced down. "Wyatt, what's this?"

He smiled. "Something old, new, borrowed and blue. It belonged to Dodge's mother."

"Oh, Wyatt, surely I can't..." Tears rimmed her lower lids.

"She wanted you to have it, so I suspect she knows what we are up to and when I see you again, I'll make you my wife, Doc. Mattie will get you where you need to be in just a bit." He kissed her hand that held tightly to the jewelry and nodded at Mattie who'd returned. He held Tess' gaze a moment more, and as he made his way back out into the hallway, he figured one of two things. The doc would have more words with him about this, or she'd be so caught up in becoming his bride she would go easy on him. Either way he was at her mercy. Right where he'd always wanted to be.

Chapter Fifteen

Tess sat on a stool while Mattie used a hot iron on her hair, section by section. The two had chatted as she'd bathed, dried, and dressed, making small talk. It hadn't been a very comfortable thing, but she had gotten through it and very soon she would be outside the establishment on her way to becoming Wyatt's wife. Anxious nerves flittered through her stomach; though there wasn't anything more she wanted in the world.

"You have such lovely hair, doctor." Mattie dropped a loose curl and grabbed the next section, using a large comb to smooth it.

Tess glanced at her in the mirror. "Thank you for doing all this for me and for Wyatt."

Mattie smiled but spoke hesitantly. "May I ask of Wyatt's injuries?"

Tess nodded uncertain.

"Is he well after…what happened? The beating I mean. Hudson was still recovering, and we heard so little." She continued with Tess' hair but held her gaze in the mirror.

"He was near death when his brother, Dawson, found him, but he has a bit more healing to do. His leg was badly broken, and he may always carry the limp he has now, and while he'd never admit it, he tires easily."

Mattie shrugged. "So tough, Wyatt McCade, and of

course he will have his revenge. I have felt responsible as when he was here in Denver, I pushed him to go home—to you."

"To me?" Tess asked her mind wandering across the prospect of Mattie knowing Wyatt so well. Had this woman before her insisted Wyatt return to her?

Mattie dropped another lock of her hair and used a comb to raise a tendril above her ear, leaving her as fancy if not fancier than some of the ladies she had seen sitting downstairs "It didn't take much over the years to know Wyatt had lost his heart over the likes of you."

Heat rushed to her cheeks as she held Mattie's gaze adding a knowing smile.

The madam giggled. "Oh my…well don't worry, he and I are only friends, there being few people you can trust in a town like Denver these days. He and Hudson have both watched out for me and my girls for some time now."

Tess touched the long strands of ringlet's hanging across her shoulder. "I'm sorry I didn't mean to…"

Mattie interrupted, moving before her and curling the last tendril of hair. "I make no excuses, for who I am, but Wyatt McCade is a special kind of man and without a doubt he adores you." She turned to the wedding dress. "One of the Chinese ladies at the seamstress shop made it special, and it will fit you like a glove."

"But perhaps there is something more you could do besides this…line of work," Tess asked, though it was hardly her business, and she regretted asking when Mattie shrugged.

"Someone has to stay to make sure the younger girls get out of their contracts of forced servitude." She said it with confidence, as if it was the full purpose of her life. “They bring them in younger and younger these innocent girls, and in a few months, their lives will never be the same. No real chance for any future. Soiled doves they call us, but some can leave, and I can help that happen.”

Tess gave a hesitant smile, aware of the life such women lead, many dying of disease at very young ages. She used the mirror to see the back of her hair which Mattie had scooped together and swirled with ringlets hanging from the ribbon placed around the gathering on top of her head. “It’s so lovely, thank you, Mattie.”

“I don’t think I’ve ever seen a finer dress.” Mattie lifted the beautiful garment off the hook and held it up.

Tess touched the dress tracing the carved buttons and off-white taffeta material.

“Let’s get you dressed, and we need to get you to the courthouse.” Mattie worked open the buttons on the back of the dress and assisted Tess to pull the garment over her head, careful of her hair. Tess’ pulse raced at the idea of such a fancy dress, and the fact that she was about to be a married woman once more. She stared at herself in Mattie’s long mirror that stood beside the bed. What would Wyatt think when he saw her? She could hardly believe the reflection before her was her own. How on earth did he know just the right size, the dress fitting her to perfection?

“By tonight, hearts all over the West will be breaking with Wyatt McCade getting hitched.” Mattie tucked a stray piece of lace into the buttons on the back of her dress and adjusted the bustle.

Tess gave into a slight smile. While Mattie meant well, she wasn’t sure she wanted to know how many hearts might be broken with that kind of news. No matter, he was about to make her his wife, and she'd never again wonder of his past. She stepped into the boots admiring the quality, fine leather with lacing on the sides at the ankles.

"Well, I think we have you about as ready as can be." Of all things Mattie kissed her cheek and gave her a hug.

Tess moved her arms to embrace the woman, hesitant at first and then with an added tightness. If Wyatt thought enough of her to allow her to ready his bride for marriage, then who was she to judge? "Thank you, Mattie."

Mattie studied her. "It's been my pleasure. I've never seen Wyatt happier."

"No, I thank you, more than you know." She touched her hand. "If I can ever be of service in the care of you or your girls, please ask."

Mattie's face softened into a smile. "That's very kind, Doctor. Are you ready?"

Tess glanced in the mirror once more. She did look beautiful. Well, she shouldn't be surprised. Wyatt had always been a man of great detail in observing those around him and that included his study of her for all those years. She took one more deep breath and followed Mattie outside to meet the man she had loved for more years than she was able to count.

****

"Well it's a pleasure to be able to serve you, given the men you've hauled in right under our noses." Judge Benjamin Harwood sat behind his large rosewood desk, smoking a thick cigar and preparing the marriage license.

Wyatt sat across from the judge, dressed in a new starched shirt and dark trousers. His leg hurt in the new shiny black boots he'd purchased, and the stiff leather was unforgiving to his swollen ankle. He'd found Hudson in Barlow's saloon, and the deputy had promised to stand up with him. He glanced at his pocket watch. Late as usual.

The judge glanced up from the paper he'd signed and gave Wyatt a sly grin, leaning back in his large leather chair. "Wyatt, I've known you for years now and your father since before you were born, never thought you much on the idea of marriage."

Wyatt raised a knowing brow toward the judge. "It just takes the right woman."

The judge picked up his glass in toast. "Here, here." He sucked down his liquor and asked, "I understand she's a physician, the one in Cheyenne. Seems I've heard folks speak of her great abilities as a surgeon."

"She's the best there is." He adjusted his leg, leaning back farther in the chair. Hell, she was the best of everything, and all he'd ever need in this lifetime. Marriage was a big step, but he'd been ready to hold her the rest of his life, for years now.

The judge grabbed his pocket watch and stood. "And you'll still hunt down men for bounty as a married man?"

It was an honest question, and the judge had every right to ask. Bounty hunters lived on the trail of one man or another, never tied down by a woman. "Still got some healing to do, but I'll be out on the trail here and there, and she will continue her doctoring."

"I heard of your injuries, Wyatt. Maybe it's time

you let the bounties go and took your bride home. Found yourself some kind of other work." The judge challenged, blowing a puff of white smoke above them.

Wyatt offered a smile. He might give up bounties on some men but not the one who almost took his life. "A man's gotta make a living. I'll deputy for Sawyer some."

"Ah, well it's hard to change overnight. But if you are ever a mind to it, I could always use a good man on my team here in Denver. Any son of John McCade's would be welcomed on my staff; leastwise you'd make a better sheriff than Barlow, the bastard. Not sure how he manages to get the vote every time he runs. Denver might very well benefit from a doctor such as your wife too. Think about it." The judge smiled, extending his hand.

Wyatt gripped the man's hand. "I appreciate that, Judge, but Cheyenne's home."

"That it is. Shall we?" Judge Harwood put his watch back into his vest pocket, ground out his cigar, and led the way toward the courtroom.

Wyatt followed him down the narrowed hallway to the left. Inside, he stood beside the bench as the judge separated documents and reached for his Bible, fumbling through and opening it to the Psalms. The judge busied himself with the details and dusted off the vest of his fine suit coat.

The entrance door of the courtroom opened, and Hudson scampered inside. He took his hat off and grinned as he slowed his pace and stopped beside him, smoothing his unkempt light hair. Wyatt folded his arms. Hudson had always been there when needed, but had more times than not, arrived just in the brink of time, keeping no clock but his own.

"Sorry, got stopped by Barlow; bastard's got men watching you and me." Hudson dusted his trousers off, whispering.

Wyatt glanced at the judge who was paying them little attention. "Chan?"

The deputy leaned closer. "He's got the slaughter house tight as a drum. You'll pay hell getting through that son of his, Zihao."

Wyatt narrowed his eyes. He'd get through to Chan one way or another, but Chan's son Zihao was a problem and the one running things in the compound these days. "I already paid hell once, won't be paying it again."

Hudson nodded and changed the subject as the judge approached. "Never thought I'd see the day, Wyatt McCade was a married man."

"Shut the hell up!" Wyatt gave him an elbow to the ribs. Hell, he might as well have his brothers riling him as the likes of the deputy.

"Ahhh, the lovely bride." The judge bowed, glancing past them.

Wyatt turned and the world stood still, time stopping all together, except for the beating of his heart. Tess waited at the doorway of the courtroom gazing at him. In all his life, he'd never seen anything to the likeness of her dressed in the wedding gown he'd had made. She was magnificent and downright breathtaking, and she would be his. Her hair was rolled with spindles of curls, and while he'd never seen an angel, he imagined they looked something like the beautiful woman before him.

She dropped her gaze and the blush of her cheeks

gave him a thought or two he shouldn't entertain. He was speechless as she stopped beside him. Many men had stood as he had and watched a woman walk to him to wed him, but none would ever have what he had in Tess. She was so beautiful all he could do was shake his head in sheer admiration as he glanced up and down the length of her body.

"So beautiful, Doc." His heart pounded against his chest as he forced words to the surface, not expecting that this moment would take his breath away.

Tess touched his shirt. "And look at you, with a new shirt and trousers. Boots too. I've never seen you wear a tie."

Yeah, the damn boots needed breaking in, and the ribbon tie at his neck was coming off soon. He offered her a smile, still struggling to breathe.

Judge Harwood cleared his voice, and they both turned to face him. "We are gathered here today to see the union of this man and this woman to be married under the jurisdiction of the Colorado territory, and remaining legal in the states, of course." The old judge chuckled.

Wyatt took Tess by the hands, never taking his gaze from hers as the judge continued. Her brown eyes glistened and her cheeks held a rosy shade of pink, but he'd never seen her wear a happier smile.

The judge went on. "And so with that being said, do you, Wyatt Zachariah McCade, take this woman, Elizabeth Jane Sullivan to become your lawful wedded wife from this day forward and for all of your life, forgoing all others and until death do you part?"

Hell, that was the easy part, but getting his voice to work. "I do." And he would, for all the days of breath he ever took in this lifetime or the next.

The judge turned in her direction. “And do you, Elizabeth Jane Sullivan, take this man, Wyatt Zachariah McCade, to become your lawful wedded husband from this day forward and for all of your life, forgoing all others and until death do you part?”

Tess’ green eyes found him again, her hands trembling and her voice shaking. “I—I do.”

The judge cleared his voice. “Who gives this woman to be wed?”

Tess drew her gaze from Wyatt to the judge and back, her mouth dropping open slightly.

“I have this, a wire…” Wyatt dug in his trouser pocket and extracted a telegram and unfolded it. “Tess’s uncle, Thomas Sullivan gives permission for her to wed with the blessings of himself and her aunt.”

The judge took the telegram, adding it with the marriage license in the middle of his Bible with a smile.

Wyatt turned back to Tess who wiped her tears. He might have figured as much, but no matter how tears came to her, he carried them deep inside as he’d always carried a part of her. Somehow he wasn’t even whole without her and now, he never had to be without her again.

She mouthed the words. “Thank you.”

The judge continued by reading a few verses of the Psalms and then looked up from his Bible. “And the ring?”

Wyatt held his hand out, never dropping his gaze from her. Hudson struggled to remove the small ring from his little finger with some effort and dropped it into Wyatt’s hand.

He took his time placing the ring on her finger, the

impact of the moment all consuming with her hands in his own, and the marriage almost complete. He'd waited years to have her, had lost her, and would now have her for his lifetime. All he wanted, and all that was right stood before him, and she was downright amazing, wasn't she? He placed a palm to her cheek, forgetting the others in the room. She was his wife. His home. His heart.

"Then by the power vested in me I pronounce you husband and wife. Wyatt, you may kiss your bride." The judge took a step back, removing his spectacles and smiling in approval.

Wyatt took Tess' face in his hands and kissed her with passion, savoring the taste of her tears and the tenderness of her lips until the judge cleared his voice.

Tess pulled from the kiss, the blush across her face extraordinary.

"I give to you, Mr. and Mrs. Wyatt Zachariah McCade. And my business here is done. Let me be the first to congratulate you Dr. McCade." The judge took Tess' hand and placed a tender kiss on the back of it and then handed Wyatt the completed paperwork.

"Thank you, Judge." She beamed, radiant, admiring the thick golden band on her finger.

"Congratulations, Wyatt, Doc Tess." Hudson placed a kiss on Tess' cheek and took a step back.

She smiled. "Thank you, Hudson; it's good to see you are well."

"Hey, I'll catch up with you both at the hotel for the festivities." Hudson didn't wait on Wyatt's response but found his way outside.

Wyatt turned back to Tess.

"Wyatt, the ring, I had no idea. It's so beautiful and

the wire from my uncle. You thought of everything." With that she fought her emotions and fell into his embrace.

"Hey, we aren't nowhere near done for tonight. I'm taking you to the best meal Denver has to offer which is in the hotel. There will be cake and dancing and music and a photographer for a few pictures."

"Pictures? Oh, Wyatt." Tess touched the beautiful wedding dress. "And I've never seen a finer dress."

He took her hand and kissed it. "Nothing at all is too good for you, Doc. I know you would have liked your family here and mine too, but I won't have the town folk talking and we can have a reception. Dodge and Mei Ling will probably invite the whole territory."

She kicked a boot out from under the length of her dress, admiring it. "You did all this for me, and I had no idea. It's been beautiful, and I would want nothing more."

He pulled her into his arms. "I told you I will spend until my dying day making sure you want for nothing, Doc."

She wrapped her arms around his middle laying her head against his chest, and he held her tighter. Life would be different but full of possibilities each and every day. He chuckled.

"What's so funny?"

"Nothing, come on, Doc, we got a party to go to." He held out his arm. "Doctor McCade, may I?"

"Of course, my husband, Mr. McCade." Tess took his arm and allowed him to lead her outside the courthouse and to the first evening of the rest of their lives together as husband and wife. Some things were well worth the wait, and the doc had been one of them.

Chapter Sixteen

Tess shuffled across the room, still wearing her wedding dress, which had caused a bit of spectacle at the fancy meal at the hotel's expensive restaurant. And Wyatt had beamed, looking on as various couples and staff offered their congratulations and good will. He'd even made sure that a large cake had been brought in for all to share, never mind the fact they didn't know any of the guests in attendance, save Hudson. Wyatt had danced with her as the small orchestra played in the corner of the room. And now, she was Mrs. Wyatt McCade, and no matter what life brought, she would never take that fact for granted.

"The meal was wonderful, Wyatt. I can't remember the last time I had such a fancy iced cake. Perhaps when Sawyer and Rose married." She put her small bag on the bed table and turned to him.

He limped closer, wrapping his arms around her. "I could hardly take my eyes from you tonight."

"It was the most wonderful day of my life, and you make me so happy." She squeezed her arms around his middle and leaned into him. "I still can't believe it."

He tossed his hat aside, holding her tight. "Hey, now, no more tears, though I suppose it's been a long day."

Well, she might be a bit tired from the travel but the excitement was flowing and this was her wedding night. She took his hand and led him to the bed, wiping her eyes. “Happy tears are a good thing. Love me, Wyatt McCade, all night long if you like.”

“Well, that’s quite an invitation, Doc.” He tugged his dress shirt from his trousers and kicked from his new boots, favoring his ankle with a quick rub.

“It’s such a relief to say it. Mrs. Wyatt McCade. Doctor McCade.” She frowned and then smiled. “I suppose I am Doc Tess either way.”

“My Doc. My Tess.” He growled, jerking off the shirt and turning her to begin with the carved buttons on the back of her dress.

“There are so many buttons, it may take a while.” She shivered as Wyatt’s breath heated her neck. Lord, but her body knew when he was close and warm heat flowed to her center in anticipation of his touch.

“There are exactly eighty-four buttons and they are all mine to take care of one at a time.” He kissed her ear and whispered, tugging the first through. “One.”

She giggled with a shiver. Another button. Another kiss.

“Two.” He growled.

She closed her eyes. She’d never make it through that many buttons or kisses.

“Three.” He turned her, and his lips touched hers tender and warm. “You know, Doc, I thought you might still be miffed at me for taking you to the brothel.”

“Well, I should be angry at using the tub there instead of the nice one here in this room, but Mattie was so very nice.” She still worried of the plight of such a kind woman. She’d treated women in brothels, most who ended up with terrible infections to the point of dying. “Why would such a beautiful woman live like that?"

"Mattie's a good person, and she had her reasons. Besides, I needed help pulling all this together." His answer was short, as he unbuttoned his own shirt.

"She told me you and Hudson have helped her with getting some of the younger ladies out of that…line of work." She whispered the last part, though it was admirable what Mattie was doing.

Wyatt added, "We help her when we can."

She'd thought Mattie mighty resourceful to have gotten all she needed for the wedding ready. "She is a woman of means, and she worries so little about herself."

He shrugged. "She sees it as a mission, I suppose, always has."

"She was worried of you." She knew better than to ask questions best left unanswered. Perhaps he had spent time with Mattie.

"Probably, but…" He took her hand and put it to his chest. "Mattie and I are friends like I told you, no more. Besides, my heart has been occupied for years now."

"My heart and my life will always be yours, Wyatt." And she meant it. Too much time had been lost in the last few years where she had thought herself not worthy of his love because she couldn't have children. Perhaps she would never forgive herself for that, even though he had reassured her children weren't necessary. But she had held to her promise to keep all that behind her and it was time she simply loved him and lived her life regardless of children.

"Raise your arms," he whispered with urgency, done with the buttons, and with his height, he lifted the gown over her head and off. He draped it across the small chair by the bed and turned back to take her in his arms once more, kissing her fervently. Tess opened her mouth and allowed him access, dancing her tongue along with his, inhaling the sweet hint of mint.

He made quick work of her chemise and bloomers, tossing them aside and pulling her against him once more. A few weeks ago, she'd been incredibly nervous, but now, she anticipated what Wyatt's touch would bring. And standing before him naked was beginning to seem very natural.

He tugged his fancy trousers down and tossed them aside, bending to remove his socks and standing again. He was over six feet and carried thick muscles across his wide shoulders, and his chest was sculpted with a scant amount of dark hair scattered across it. His belly rippled with muscles that stayed drawn tight even when he was at rest. She knew that because she'd bathed his fevered body so many times months ago. And even though his ribs and his leg still held the hints of faded bruising, he was the most incredibly handsome man she had ever seen. And now, he was her husband.

He moved toward her, a beautiful man if there were such a thing. She shivered as he traced kisses to her neck and shoulders, then down to her breasts. He sucked a nipple deep into his mouth, his thumb finding the other. Exquisite. She let herself melt to his caresses and closed her eyes relaxing at his touch. She ran her hands into his hair, holding him to her and savoring the pleasure of his heated mouth.

He moved back up, nipping at her bottom lip and nudging her. "Lie back, Doc."

She sat, expecting him to follow her, but he pushed

her back with a gentle mischievous grin. He bent then, leaning over her and ran his palm the length of her body, following his hand with his lips, making her squirm in delight.

She wrapped her arms around his neck but he escaped her capture, riding lower to her breasts and tugging with his lips to each nipple in turn, heat scouring her middle.

"So…nice," she whispered.

He covered her body with his own, slipping lower and placing his lips to her belly and then scooting to lift her thigh over his shoulders. What was he doing? But then she knew. Her eyes sprang open as he kissed the insides of her thighs, one and then the other. Lord, but Israel had never done what he was about to do. She might have expected this, as the last few weeks all the questions of Wyatt McCade had been answered. She'd learned that there was more than the regular position when a man like Wyatt made love and much of what he'd done had never been detailed in her medical books, but he hadn't done this. Oh, but…

His fingers parted her and he placed his heated mouth against her, sucking in a gentle tug.

"Ohhhhh," she gasped, placing her hands into his thick dark hair. "Oh my, Wyatt."

His answer was a slight moan of satisfaction, his tongue roaming the depths of her and returning to the tortuous pleasure. Lord, she couldn't bear it as he continued. She hissed and writhed in the bed. Never had she felt anything like it and as if of its own will, her hips moved in motion with him. Over and over he sucked and teased until her legs were quivering, and his name left her lips in an unexpected gasping cry. She tightened as the heated tendrils of release bolted through her, his name riding across her lips in a hint of a whisper she couldn't speak.

Floating down from her bliss, she landed in his arms as he scooted back up against her body. She rested her head back against him, closed her eyes and thought she might even weep; it had been so intense and intimate.

"Right beautiful, Doc." He kissed her shoulder, splaying his large hand across her breast.

Tess let out another sigh. This had to be one of the mortal sins, but she was now married and supposed all was allowed in a husband's bed. "I've never…done that before. Good Lord, Wyatt, what you do to me."

He raised an inquisitive brow. "Never?"

"Well…no." She shook her head. Israel had always made love to her the normal way, and while it had often been pleasurable, it seemed always to be the same. That was not the case with Wyatt.

"I'm thinking you liked it?" He waited. The glow of the lamp shown copper on his skin, and she touched his cheek as a smile curled across his lips.

"Yes." It was all she could manage as she lay in a heap at his side.

"Well, before this night is over…" He smiled and brought her hand to him, urging her touch. She took to the motion he'd shown her tracing her hand the length of him several times watching as he closed his eyes and moaned. She continued for a time and until he grabbed her hand and rolled her beneath him, his blue eyes serious and wanting. Entering her, he tossed his head back and sucked in a deep breath, his body held above her. He moved again, just as slow, and this time it was she that sighed.

She tightened each time he filled her, wanting the weight of him crushing her body. He shook with restraint, as he thrust with concentrated focus. She held his hips, urging as he rocked into her. His muscles were tight and his body damp. She kissed his shoulder tasting the salt of his skin and relished the brief thought that she was after all these years, finally his wife. There was a beauty in their joining that she hadn't expected as if all she held was good and right. And she moaned as her body began to draw tighter to what he was bringing her once more.

He tangled his hands in her hair, his kisses passionate and as tender as their joining. He swallowed her sigh as she began to spiral, giving into the cry of release. Wyatt's breath came hard against her neck as the scorching pleasure shattered them, Tess clinging to him as he gave his own roar of pleasure.

Where did she end or he begin? It was like that with Wyatt. It wasn't purely physical, but while he made love to her body, he did so also to her mind and heart. And this was love; she was sure of it and held him as his body convulsed several more times.

He didn't move from her but kissed her chin and cheeks and tugged her hair back from her face, keeping his close to hers. His grin was contagious as he ducked his head to suckle along her breasts once more. "Doc, I believe that was loud enough to summon the law."

She covered her mouth, sitting up. There were times with Wyatt the pleasure was so intense, she didn't know what sounds she made. "Was I too loud?" Good lord, if anyone at the hotel had heard her, she would have to hide her embarrassment.

“Well, I liked that part.” He kissed her brow and gave a hearty chuckle.

She pouted. “What if someone heard me? Wyatt, it’s not funny.”

“No.” Wyatt let go of his grin, touching her cheek and kissing her with passion once more. “No, it’s not funny; it’s downright breathtaking is what it is. I love you…Tess, and you are perfectly enough.”

Tess snuggled in closer to him. “And I will always love you, Wyatt. Today has made me happier than I have been in a very long time.”

He was serious then, shaking his head, his deep blue eyes holding her. “I’ve spent a lot of my life not knowing where or what I was supposed to be doing, until you.”

His words were so tender she fought off the urge to allow tears. “I’ve always known there was a side of you that was gentle, Wyatt McCade.”

“Shhh, don’t tell anyone.” He kissed her, rolling to his back and pulling her across him.

She braced on one elbow. “Oh, I am being serious. You are sweet whether you like it or not. But there are so many things we haven’t talked about, like my working at the clinic, where we should live, and our work. I suppose we never talked about every detail and—”

He touched her cheek, his smile as tender as she’d ever seen. “The clinic is fine for a home, the ranch is crowded these days anyway and besides, it’s better I am in town to watch things for Sawyer to be home on the ranch in the evenings. You will still do your doctoring, and I’ll bounty now and then, and we’ll have many, many nights like this.”

She took a long deep breath. Even though Wyatt cared little for the business of ranching, he still loved the ranch and the home where he'd been raised. "But the ranch is your home."

His gaze held her own, unblinking as he traced a finger down her cheek to touch her chin. "My home will always be where you are, but I've got an idea about a place to build a real nice home for us on the ranch. Maybe next spring, besides, I've lived in town for a while now."

"That would be so nice. We could ride into town each day together." She settled against him again. He did have a soft side and she'd always known it. How could she have ever walked away from him regardless her reasons? She laid her head against his chest, listening to the hard thump of his heart. "Wyatt?"

"Huh?"

"I loved you…long before Israel died." The confession rocked her thoughts. She had loved Israel, but she had longed for Wyatt years before Israel had died. It had been wrong, and there were times it made her feel like she hadn't done right by her deceased husband. She weaved her fingers into Wyatt's, touching with tenderness where the fracture had been. "I did, right or wrong. I mean…I loved Israel, we had so much in common with his study of science and plants and my study of medicine, but I was guilty of dreaming for you long before…he died."

His smile was tender as he lifted her chin. "I've known that for a long time, Doc. And I can't count how many nights I lay awake, wishing I were holding you."

She held tighter to him. "And when you left Cheyenne, it was all my fault. I knew I had made a mistake. I wasn't even myself without you. It was as if I kept falling and falling, never hitting the ground to land anywhere."

With that he wrapped his arms around her and kissed her. "I'll always be here to catch you, Doc, always."

Chapter Seventeen

Tess woke with a start; not remembering for a moment where she was, but then she smiled thinking about the lovely night before and the fact she was a married woman once more. The sun was bright behind the shuttered hotel window. Mid-day. She'd slept longer than planned though she'd woken at dawn to find Wyatt watching her sleep. Without a word he'd crawled between her legs and made love to her, slow and searing and until they had both been sated. She smiled to herself and hugged the blankets closer inhaling the remaining manly scent of him.

He'd dressed and kissed her, heading out on errands, telling her to sleep. Some part of her worried, as he didn't have the protection of his brothers in Denver, but he'd assured her he still had Hudson and that would be enough. He seemed to think he might find a bit of information related to his father's land dealings with the man everyone called Chan. All she knew about the elderly Chinese man was that he ran the slaughterhouse and imported illegal opium from the Orient and bootlegged it all over the West. With what Wyatt had confessed about Da Ming's evil brother, she didn't like at all he might have dealings with the man, his son, or the Chinese that worked for him.

She dropped her thoughts. It was best, or she'd drive herself crazy with worry. She glanced around the room, the flowers creating a freshness that covered the odors of the expensive hotel rugs and new curtains. She touched the petals of a vase of purple wildflowers, her favorite color and how Wyatt had accomplished all he had for her special day, she would never understand.

She turned to the knock at the door and grabbed her robe, wrapping it around her as she got out of bed. “Yes?”

“Hot water for the tub, ma’am.” A young male voice came from outside.

Tess opened the door hesitantly. “Thank you.”

She watched as the thin boy, who couldn’t be more than fourteen, rolled in a cart of large steaming buckets of water.

He gave a bashful glance and went about filling the tub in the washroom and returned. “It’s quite hot, so give it a few minutes, ma’am.” He spoke as he advanced back toward the door, avoiding direct eye contact.

“Oh, wait.” Tess reached for her small purse and began digging for coins.

“No ma’am, Mr. McCade has taken care of everything. And if there is anything else you need, please ring the bell there on the table. I’ll be right down the hall.” He closed the door as he left.

She smiled. Wyatt hadn’t missed a detail, seeing to every need, including the needs of her body and he did that all too well. Lord, but he had a voracious appetite for her. She opened her bag and pulled out her long brown skirt and tan blouse and in no time, had finished the elaborate bath and was on the streets of a Denver afternoon.

Wyatt wouldn’t return until it was evening, and she

had been excited to visit with old Mr. Murphy at the apothecary. While physicians back East would frown upon any non-traditional medications, she'd found that many of the herbs did indeed work for her patients. A lot of those she used, Mr. Murphy obtained from the Indians or shipments from as far away as the orient and India.

The five minute walk to the Apothecary took nothing at all. She entered, and the strong smell of herbs, plants, and mushrooms wafted into one strong scent she couldn't identify although she could smell eucalyptus as bold as any. On the small stove, several boilers of plants were bubbling along, and the steam from all the pots mingled to a slight mist across the dim storefront.

"Ahh, Doctor Sullivan, it's been such a long time, dear." The old man spoke in his usual Italian accent which was loud due to hearing loss. He took her hand before she could clear her vision of the blurry hovering mist. He was as round as he was tall, but the smile on his face was of sheer joy.

"I am now Doctor McCade. I was married yesterday, here in Denver. It's so wonderful to see you again, Mr. Murphy." She let go of his sweaty hand and unfolded the small paper list from her bag.

"Well, then, I should bid you the most of congratulations there is." He took her list and read. "I believe I have all this in fine quantities. I'll take a look and pull it for your inspection." He turned to the shelf behind him, muttering to himself and reaching in a variety of places for tiny bottles and tins. He settled several to the counter before her and then packed some of the dried plants in brown paper which he folded with great care.

Tess picked up one of the bottles and opened the lid sniffing gingerly. “Silkweed,” she whispered and added it to the collections of bottles. Silkweed was a diuretic for those who retained fluid from heart dropsy. She could order Digitalis from back East for steadying the heart, but it always seemed to be on short supply, and silkweed was a help in between orders for the patients who needed it.

“That’s a new batch, rather strong, got it from the Indian I think of your acquaintance. The Cheyenne Medicine Man, Leaning Bear.” The man turned back to the shelf, searching bottles once more.

Tess had to smile. Dawson’s friend, the man who’d found Wyatt, was still selling herbs and pelts in Denver. If not for him, she would hate to think what might have happened to Wyatt.

“And I believe this is all on your list, Doctor Elizabeth.” He set down the remainder of the items.

Tess searched the list again, comparing it to the bottles and packages of plants. “How much do I owe you, Mr. Murphy?”

The rotund man figured in his head and came up with a more than fair sum. “Two dollars and sixteen cents. And might I ask if you married one of those McCade boys from Cheyenne, dear Doctor Tess?”

She dug into her purse for the folded paper money, handing it to him. “I am afraid so. I married Wyatt McCade.”

“Ah, a very lucky man to wed such a beautiful lady.” The man’s smile was contagious as he bowed.

A rush of heat stole across Tess’ cheek and she grinned. “Thank you, Mr. Murphy. It has been so good to see you." She hugged him and placed the wrapped items in her bag, careful of the glass bottles and turned to go.

Back outside, she entered the small bakery past the apothecary; the fresh smell of baked bread reminding her she was famished. She moseyed inside and made the purchase of a small loaf with honey and butter. She ate as she strolled along the dusty streets glancing inside the variety of storefront windows. Denver had grown and the streets were cluttered with more people than she'd seen in a long while.

She'd been thinking of making a purchase for Wyatt, something special for their marriage he might keep to remember. But he collected little, other than a fancy shirt or two, but he had plenty of those. She wandered into a shop that carried tools and items that would interest any man, unsure of what she might be looking for.

The glass encased counter she found farther inside the store held a large assortment of knives. Nope, he was too fond of the one he'd sharpened over and over while he'd been healing. He still carried that one in his boot, but she'd yet to see him sharpen it of late. She shivered. No weapons. He carried arsenal enough to make her cringe, though he had left the new rifle he'd gotten from Evan at the clinic.

Scanning the top counter, she spotted a small wooden box with a compass sitting on top. It was a replica to those on the ships in Boston's harbor. She shook her head. Wyatt needed nothing for direction save the stars, and he knew those well. He was a man who required little by way of things, and she doubted he would wear a ring as she scanned the ones lined in a beautiful black velvet case.

"Might I help you?" A store clerk approached on the other side of the counter.

"Uh, well I was looking for something special for my husband, but I am afraid he is rather difficult to buy for." She paused for a moment, met his alert gaze and continued to browse.

"Cuff links, a tie, a ring, a knife? Men love knives." The young man lifted one of the fancy knives from the enclosure. She wanted to cringe but shook her head instead.

"No, I need something unique, something useful." She would know it when she saw it.

"Well, there are some nice hats in the back, herdsman and ones for the city, along with good winter coats." He tossed a thumb over his shoulder.

"No…I don't think so." She continued to browse and came across the pocket watches. Wyatt had lost his father's watch during the attack by Marcus Benton. He'd never said anything about it, though Dodge had mentioned it to her. One of the watches on display held a horse and rider in raised gold on silver. Some part of it reminded her of Wyatt when he was riding the new horse he had purchased right before the trip. He'd bought the palomino from a man who came to town for the sale of several horses. He'd seemed proud of the mount though the animal remained nameless like all the others. "What about this watch, the one with the rider?"

"Yes, well this one is quite expensive." He pulled it from the cabinet and displayed it for her. "It has a small diamond in the sky for the rider to know his way and once you open it there is protective glass over the face. Very fine quality, sturdy too."

"It's quite beautiful." She admired the weight of it in her hand. "What is the cost?"

This man hesitated and lowered his voice an octave. "It's priced at six dollars. The trim around the watch and the horse and rider are set of gold."

"Six?" Tess spoke to herself. She didn't care, expensive or not. "I'll take it."

"Yes, ma'am, and I'll have it wrapped special for you if you like."

"Yes, please." She smiled; satisfied with her find and sure Wyatt would like it.

The man returned with the small box wrapped in thick brown paper. "Here you are, ma'am."

"Thank you." She paid him the correct amount and exited the store, crossing the street to head back to the hotel. One day, Wyatt would go back out on the trail for hunting bounties, and he could carry the watch close to him and remember it was from her for their wedding.

A smile slipped along with the heat to her cheeks. She was married and happy, and it had been a long time coming. And making love with Wyatt was beautiful. He was attentive to her every move and sigh as if he was reading her like a well written story. And her body reacted to his touch over and over, but it was her heart that remained full.

She adjusted her bag over her shoulder, careful of the glass vials inside and glanced into a window shop that carried fancy dolls. Reminded of her childhood in Boston, she studied each of the dolls and their fancy dresses. She leaned closer, looking at the smallest dolls sitting in the front of the window. They were beautifully adorned in real clothing, and their china faces made them seem alive. She smiled, but then noted the reflection of a man in the glass, and he was not too far behind her.

She turned from the window, not looking at him and trotted ahead with several other women who appeared to have been to market. She caught a glimpse of him in her peripheral vision, and he was gaining on her. Her pulse raced, and her breathing felt short. The streets of Denver were full of people, and while it was concerning, he couldn't do much of anything with so many witnesses, could he? Confronting trouble was best. Dodge had always said so herself.

She stopped abruptly and turned, eyeing the star on his lapel. Chance Barlow. While she'd been to Denver numerous times, she'd never met the sheriff, Wyatt thought so little of.

He lifted the hat from his head, tugging the cigar from his mouth. "I'm sorry, ma'am, wasn't aiming to startle you." His brown eyes narrowed, and his tone was condescending as smoke left his mouth with his words.

"Pardon me, but you have followed me for two blocks or more," she challenged, though her pulse raced.

He let a smile curl across his lips. "It's my job to make sure that all the citizens of Denver remain safe, especially the wife of Wyatt McCade." He stepped closer. "It would be very wise for you to let the bounty hunter know it's time to leave my town. And it would be very important that he take Deputy Collier with him." His smile grew wide and evil as he ground his cigar out on the bottom of his boot without breaking his gaze.

Tess swallowed a lump of fear, standing her

ground. "I assure you that I am very capable of maneuvering the streets of Denver on my own, but I'll let my husband know of your concern." She held his gaze for a moment longer and turned back for the hotel, forcing herself not to check if he was still there. His concern had not been genuine and his intentions were not good and she had to wonder of his warning.

She could hardly remember entering the hotel and climbing the stairs. Somehow she never even took a breath until she closed the door to the room behind her. She leaned against it, the bottles of medicines and herbs in her bag clinking together. She'd broken some in her haste, but she stood still, focusing to slow her breathing. After a moment, she sat her bag aside, careful to set the pocket watch away from the broken bottles. Telling herself things were fine, she moved to the window to peek outside. She froze, below, across the street from the hotel; the sheriff tipped his hat at her. She slammed the fancy wooden shutters closed and sank to the floor in tears.

Chapter Eighteen

Wyatt trudged along the back alley toward Chan's slaughter house on the outskirts of Denver. While he hadn't been there in a while, the stench of blood and animal lingered strong. Rambling through the back alleys had freed him of Barlow and his men, who watched everything on the main roads, though throwing Hudson off his trail hadn't been easy. Now he had to hope he could get through Chan's son, Zihao to see the man. The temperamental Chinese son lived to protect his aging father and nothing more.

He was surprised Sawyer hadn't thought of Chan and the possibility of finding copies of his father's deeds with Da Ming's belongings. Even though Dodge had found the family's deeds of proof, he hoped this trip to prove a bit more of history related to the purchases and sales of land by his father. But neither his brother nor his mother had been present to witness Da Ming's cruel death, and neither had heard the screams coming out of that blazing railcar, that had haunted him all these years.

And he'd watched as Chan and Marcus Benton had removed crates of items belonging to Da Ming prior to setting the railcar on fire. Many of those documents had belonged to his father, and while John McCade had questioned the issue, nothing had been returned. And years later that had been the brunt of the argument he'd had with his father, the last words he'd ever spoken to him in hate. His heart ached to make that right but words in anger couldn't be taken back and his father had been killed at the hands of Marcus Benton's half brother before he realized what a fool he'd been.

But now, it was up to him to see if he could coerce his way into Chan's compound and with any luck find what he was looking for, though there wasn't any doubt it would cost him. Chan was long past rational thought given his age and his mind burned up from years of opium use. The only ace he'd have in this game of draw was asking for Da Ming's personal items for Mei Ling. Her brother-in-law had denied her the items long ago, angered at her lack of following Chinese custom and joining his household on Da Ming's death. Instead, she had remained on at the McCade ranch as much a part of the family as any one of them.

He turned the corner, checking behind him as he approached the slaughter house, resisting the urge to pull a revolver as several Chinese men narrowed the gap behind him. Chan had men posted all over town, and these two had been on him for a couple of minutes, though they weren't the reason the hair on the back of his neck stood. Marcus Benton had been riding his mind all day. There was no doubt the man was involved in the fraudulent deed issue, and he might just find proof enough of that today.

His father had always had Da Ming make two exact copies of every deed, without question. One was placed in the safe at the ranch, another was at the railcar office, and he suspected it in the boxes that had been taken before Da Ming was killed. He hadn't wanted to chance the loss of his purchases and sales to fire or other kinds of loss. If the second copies of the deeds were in those crates along with Da Ming's personal affects, then he'd have proof enough that Rollins' one deed for the full six thousand acres was falsified. And that was all he needed to prove.

Reaching the outside of the meat market, the rotten scent of pig shit and blood filled the air. The Chinese men working the market glimpsed at him without stopping their work of hacking up parts of animals and adding them to pots that were stewing in large boilers on several fires just outside the porch. They would play the game well, pretending not to speak English, but most were capable if it came down to it.

He stepped closer to the opening of the market, its large wooden doors propped open for the days' business. He waited until several of the men made eye contact, never stopping their work. "I'm looking for Chan."

The men ignored him, going back to their work. *Shit.* He moved closer, but was stopped by the two men who had tailed him. "I am looking for Chan, and I won't be repeating myself." The bastards were aware what he was saying and they damn well knew who he was. When no one said anything, he took a step toward the door, meeting Zihao head on.

"Bounty Hunter have business with my father?" Built like a wall of stone, the man's voice was a guttural growl of English. He was framed up with large, bulky muscles and a long braid of dark hair all the way down his back.

"I would speak with him regarding his sister-in-law, Mei Ling." Wyatt narrowed his gaze, holding it steady.

"My *auntie* is well?" Zihao questioned with no emotion at all in his almond-shaped eyes.

"She is." Wyatt glanced at the men moving in behind him. He couldn't afford at this point to stir things up as he was plenty outnumbered, and even though he was left-handed, his right would be no good with a revolver yet.

Zihao tilted his head, his eyes drawing to mere slits. "Drop weapons and follow me."

He'd expected as much and with reluctance loosened his gun belt, allowing the two men who approached from behind to take them. Well, at least he still had the knife in his boot, but this visit wouldn't call for anything more than conversation and money for the most part. He entered the warehouse, which held the same stench at a staler state. It was dark inside where women and men were cooking up pork dishes with a score of heavy Chinese herbs mingling in the air. He might be hungry but he'd never be hungry enough to partake of anything inside this butcher's shop.

He followed Zihao up a small flight of stairs and into what appeared more like an actual home. Through a narrow hallway, they entered a large parlor, smoke filtering in a haze—opium. He stifled a cough. Several Chinese women in various colored silk robes, lounged across the furniture, giggling with each other at his presence. One rose from her pile of pillows and swayed up to him with a great show of opening her robe. He eyed her luscious young body but pushed past her to follow Zihao to Chan's room. The woman hissed, then laughed, joining the other woman, cursing him in Chinese. He didn't speak much of the language, but he'd been around Mei Ling enough over the years to understand a good Chinese swear word.

Reaching Chan's room, with its spinning fans and heavy incense to cover the stench, he removed his hat. Damn Chinese and the required respect. Zihao disappeared around a slatted bamboo paper screen and spoke in deep guttural Chinese. Moments later, Chan appeared at the divider, giving him a brief once over with his good eye, the other glazed silver—a souvenir from the fight that took Da Ming's life and one he had witnessed. He was dressed in his usual black silk and offered a slight bow. Wyatt followed with the same, not that he was respectful of the man, but he would be required to play the game.

"Much image of father." Chan spoke in broken English walking closer.

"I'll take that as a compliment." Wyatt held steady, surprised that Zihao hadn't returned to be a part of the proceedings.

Chan motioned to the table which sported an opium pipe and a bottle of some kind of Chinese liquor. He sat. "Words like father."

Wyatt sucked in a deep breath and took the chair. The old man's hands shook as he poured two small glasses of the clear alcohol. He had to play his cards right, let Chan lead things or the visit would be over quick. Hell, he'd have to have at least one drink with the man, to get what he needed. Damn Chinese etiquette. Chan took his glass, and Wyatt lifted his own. They both drank. The old man growled and laughed as if things were funny. Wyatt made no sound as the foul liquid burned all the way to his belly. Chinese rice whiskey was worse than any rotgut he'd ever encountered.

"You have come with word of sister-in-law?" Chan started the conversation, his silver eye glistening.

Wyatt gave a slight nod. "She is well."

"And honorable mother." The old Chinese refilled the glass and held it high. That Chan would ask about Dodge wasn't a surprise, but the honorable part wasn't meant in respect. The man had tangled with Dodge a time or two in the past, and he despised the friendship that Dodge and Mei Ling shared. "Dodge is good."

Chan studied him a moment. "I read paper, Bounty Hunter left for dead."

He cursed to himself. His beating had made the papers, but that wouldn't be where Chan had learned of his fate. He ignored the comment. "I've come to ask about Da Ming's personal belongings for Mei Ling once more. It's right that she should have them as she is growing older and needs to make her peace."

"Da Ming dead. Why sister-in-law not come ask?" The old man glared at him, his silver eye unblinking.

Wyatt wanted to curse, having no patience for this hand of poker. "She doesn't know I am asking once more on her behalf."

"Da Ming keeps too many unimportant item. No money find in box." The old man waved his hand in dismissal, downing his second shot of the foul whiskey.

Leave it to the old man to think he was looking for money. "Not looking for money, just items taken from his railcar the night he died."

The man's one eye set on him for a long moment and then he growled. "Cost money."

"Mei Ling has a right to what belonged to her husband." Wyatt avoided gripping his hands into fists or raising his voice. Patience wasn't something he held, but had no choice with the elder Chinese. If he didn't give the proper respect, the negotiation would be over.

"Owner of box, Da Ming. Da Ming dead. Owner of Da Ming's belonging now Chan." The old man's hearty laughter echoed around the room.

Holy hell! This was worse than a game of dead eye poker. He'd hoped Chan would have been a bit more confused from opium. "Name the price."

"Four crate. Fifty gold eagle for look and one-hundred for take Mei Ling what she will have." His gaze held steady, as he nodded, the laughter gone.

One hundred dollars. Son of a bitch! That was insane, but the old man knew he had the money. He leaned back and pulled the pouch of gold coins from his trousers and plopped it on the table, uneasy without his weapons and the ease of the negotiations.

Zihao appeared from behind the screen and lifted the pouch without a word and disappeared again.

Wyatt gritted his teeth, but that was progress even if the rising hair on the back of his neck continued to warn him. He should have brought Hudson along with him, but this was his alone to do.

Chan stood. "Bring crate."

"Four crates," he corrected as the old Chinese man steadied on his feet.

"Very much like father." The old man cackled, then mumbled in his native tongue.

Wyatt nodded. He'd spent most of his life wishing he was more like his father, so he'd own up to it now. Perhaps what he was accomplishing right now would have somehow pleased the father he'd lost.

Chan made another command in Chinese, bowed, and left the room. The old man was getting soft, giving in for the sake of golden eagles that would make the purchase of more opium from the Orient.

Zihao brought the crates in one at a time and sat each down on the table and after the fourth, he didn't return. Amazingly, Chan had left him alone as well, but he couldn't shake the feeling he was being watched. The crates were packed full, covered in dust, and he made swift work of the first two, wondering if this had been a futile attempt at insanity. He glanced around the room again. He was alone, but he wasn't stupid, and nothing went on at the compound that Zihao didn't watch.

Thoughts of Da Ming brought back the instant guilt of betraying his family for the secrets he'd held since he was a boy. Mei Ling believed her husband died in a railroad accident, but he'd never forget the sound of Da Ming's cries as he'd burned to death in the railcar at the hands of his brother and Marcus Benton. His gut clenched at the memory. He'd never forget his father's face when he'd sworn him to secrecy over what he'd seen. It had been the one time his father had scolded him enough to scare the hell right out of him, and he'd heard his father's words over and over. *This is the time to keep your mouth closed, Wyatt, and by doing so I am asking you to be a man. You will never speak of this again; Wyatt, ever, or I will be forced to take a strap to you.*

He opened the third crate, the lid cracking further as he pulled the dry rotted wood away, noting the new penny nails. The shiny silver nails indicated recent tampering. He'd been right. He dug into the stacked items, tossing aside various maps and surveys. It was still strange the ease at which he was permitted to browse the contents before him. It occurred to him that Chan had the one hundred golden eagles and might still shoot him in the back on the way out.

He pulled the tin of deeds free. His pulse raced as he lifted two, proving Jefferson Rollins' purchase of land through Rapid City. Digging farther he found the deed that granted Brett one-thousand acres and behind it the one his father wrote to Marcus Benton—Eighteen-hundred fifty-five. His hands shook holding the deed that had paid the price for Da Ming's death. Now, it was all coming together. Benton didn't get the land he wanted to connect the railroad through to Rapid City. Working the mines on Brett's land was needed to foot the bill for the spur, with the government's lack of paying for miles of track. It was a perfect plan. Benton would profit from his land being sold, with Miles Rollins filling his pockets at the same time for building the rail. And Chan would make his money taking his illegal goods farther north.

He lifted the next few deeds from the box. "Well, I'll be damned." It was the copy his father had signed for the purchase of the full six-thousand acres in Cheyenne, Wyoming—from Jefferson Rollins. Behind it, a second deed from eighteen-hundred forty-six an exact replica of Rollin's fraudulent document.

Son of a bitch! He'd done it. He could now put an end to Miles Rollins charades and wait, because there was no doubt Marcus Benton would finally surface. He tucked the deeds into his sleeve, and then perused the other contents of the crate.

He grabbed a braided red cord freeing it, and the circular piece of jade it held. It was the necklace Da Ming had always worn for luck. Along with it were his black silk hat, leather gloves and a bundle of letters scrolled in Chinese from and to Mei Ling. Very little to prove the man had existed but enough to give Mei Ling a few things to cherish.

He stood and glanced around. Getting inside the compound had been easy enough, and he hoped getting out was the same. He waited a moment and entered the hallway only to meet Zihao. There was no more need to see Chan.

"My father trusts you find what you seek of Da Ming?" Zihao's deep guttural voice held an edge of challenge.

Wyatt nodded, saying nothing, the narrow hallway a limited escape if it came down to it. He held Da Ming's silk hat with his other items tucked inside, the deeds still riding his sleeve.

Zihao nodded. "And you find father's deeds?"

Wyatt narrowed his gaze. He'd been watched, but he said nothing. What a hell of a predicament, though Chan never opted to side with anyone save the one paying the highest price.

"Deeds prove owner of land but not who get land." Zihao laughed, leading the way. "Bounty hunter not very wise to dig up past."

Wyatt clenched his teeth and followed, still uneasy. The comment from Zihao meant he well knew what was going on where those deeds were concerned. It seemed the deeds hidden in his sleeve weren't worth much to Chan or his son who had likely collected payment from whoever had been in the crate before him. And there wasn't a doubt in his mind that had been Marcus Benton, as his presence in Denver hadn't been for idle reasons.

Zihao stopped on the porch and waited as Wyatt was given his weapons once more. "Bounty hunter become pig slop if he returns. Greetings to my *auntie*."

Wyatt held the man's gaze. He'd have no need to return if it came down to it, and he'd gained what he came to find. Outside the compound, he took a deep breath as he strolled onto the streets of Denver once more. That had been too easy, and he wasn't sure what to make of it, though the falsified deed for the full six-thousand acres would have been all that was needed for Miles Rollins to push for ownership of McCade and Morgan land.

It was early afternoon as he rounded the corner at the saloon nearest to the hotel—and came to an abrupt halt. Chance Barlow blocked his way, smoking a cigar and giving him a nod. He could have done all afternoon without meeting the bastard face to face.

The sheriff blew a long exhale of smoke into the air above him, pursing his lips. "You've business with Chan?"

Wyatt bore a hard look at the man. "The crime in Denver not enough to keep you busy these days?"

"The crime in Denver climbs a notch every time you show yourself here, McCade," Barlow added with sarcasm in his southern accent.

Wyatt pressed. Toying with the sheriff when he was in Denver was half the fun and there was no doubt the jackass had already tired of Hudson's extended stay. "I could always show you boys the ropes if you need a little help."

"You know, I heard you like to've died. Been wondering what kind of man brings down a bounty hunter? Might like to meet a man like that, a man who takes what he wants. What's rightly his own." Barlow snorted in laughter and stomped out his cigar on the wooden plank at his feet.

Wyatt narrowed his gaze, gripping his fists tight, the deeds crinkling inside his sleeve. "You let Marcus Benton know I'm coming."

Barlow raised a slanted brow in threat and bit the end off another cigar, spitting the butt to the ground. "You'll want to watch yourself in my town. Why I just escorted that pretty lady doctor back to the hotel, not sure why my presence startled her so. It would be a shame for a woman like that to find herself in trouble she never asked for."

Wyatt slammed a left hook across the man's jaw, without batting an eye. Barlow's head snapped back, and the cigar flew as he pushed into Wyatt. Both men rolled to the ground, Wyatt fighting for leverage, his leg paining at the effort of slinging the man from him. Barlow scrambled for his gun, placing his hand on the revolver.

"Too late." Wyatt stood over him, his own revolver aimed hard at the man's head. "Stay away from my wife, or I'll bury you so deep, the scavengers won't find your bones."

"Put your weapons away, boys, we're apparently in the broad daylight of a lovely Denver afternoon." Hudson with his usual smile stepped in front of Wyatt and held his hands up to keep Barlow at bay as he got to his feet.

The sheriff froze, noticing the people who gathered across the wide dirt road. He faced the small crowd. "It's all right folks, a little misunderstanding. Go on about your business."

The crowd of men and a few ladies thinned, leaving Barlow to face Wyatt once more. “This is my town. You’d both be wise to be on your way before dawn or there will be serious repercussions!”

Wyatt glared, trying to catch his breath and wanting to hold the harsh ache in his ankle.

Hudson straightened the badge on Barlow’s lapel, adding to the tension by patting his face. “So, when you gonna retire that badge you wear? It’s not serving you too damn well.”

Barlow slapped his hand away and sent one last warning. “Not sure what kind of deputy Sawyer McCade approves for his services, can’t be the son of a coward drunk could add up to too much.”

Wyatt was quick to grab Hudson, shoving him back and putting himself in between the two. Things were already heated, but Barlow knew where to throw his slurs to rile his partner. Hudson’s father had often been jailed for his public drunkenness right here in the town of Denver, where Hudson had been raised. The man had succumbed to the alcohol, leaving his son an orphan at a very tender age.

Hudson tugged free as Barlow turned to go, the sheriff’s laughter filling the air as he reached for a cigar from his vest pocket. “By dawn, gentleman.”

Wyatt cursed. “Shit! The train isn’t due for a few more days, but I’ve gotta get Tess out of here and you too from the looks of it.”

Hudson tilted his hat back, studying him. “You can get a wagon at the livery for cheap if you return it within the month. And I know just where you’ve been. You’re damn lucky Zihao didn’t slit your throat.”

“Thank you, mother.” Wyatt hissed.

"Jackass! You turned up a deed you needed, didn't you?" Hudson folded his arms, curious.

Wyatt tugged the deeds free of his sleeve. "Enough to shut the whole damn thing down."

The deputy glanced at the saloon and back. "Then you'd better have eyes in the back of your head. If Benton is behind it, he'll waste no time finding the likes of you."

"Then he better get to it." Wyatt turned to go. "I'll see you in Cheyenne."

"Nope." Hudson tilted his hat back. "Your brother has me staying here on business."

Wyatt angled an arched brow. "Business enough has been done in Denver, what does he need you here for?"

Hudson's gaze darted away for a second. "Just business, watching for Benton, who must've dug himself into the earth somewhere between here and Cheyenne."

Wyatt sent him a curious glance. How was it Sawyer still needed a man in Denver? "Guess you better get to it, but heed your own warning of eyes in the back of that stubborn head of yours."

"I'm part weasel, can hide with the best of them, besides, my staying in town keeps Barlow from following you." Hudson chuckled. "I'll see ya, Wyatt."

Wyatt nodded, uneasy at the idea Hudson would remain behind. He'd already left his friend here to recover once. The young deputy could very well handle himself with Barlow and his men, but if he meddled too much around Chan's, he could find himself in a bad situation. He rubbed the knuckles of his left hand and turned toward the hotel once more, thinking of Tess.

She was at best, scared out of her mind and given Barlow's warning, he needed to get her out of Denver. He'd scored and big with Chan, but didn't need to push his luck where Barlow was concerned. Now all he had to do was shut down Rollins and wait in Cheyenne for Marcus Benton to show—and that was only a matter of time.

Chapter Nineteen

"Storm's gonna catch us." Wyatt pulled back on the reins. The wagon clinked and clamored to a stop as the team of horses halted under a small spread of modest trees. "I'll get the canvas up. Not much shelter in the middle of nowhere."

Tess glanced at the scrolling gray clouds that lined the sky for miles behind them. "It's moving fast."

Wyatt climbed down and lifted the large oiled canvas from the back, glad he'd asked the gentleman at the livery to add it, but content to have gotten the doc out of Denver. She'd been scared half to death over the incident with Barlow, and he'd found her sitting on the hotel bed shivering. He'd held her then, assuring her things would be fine and though she had recovered quickly, she had agreed to leave town without any fuss at all. But now with the storm about to take them, he had to wonder if dealing with Barlow would have been a bit easier.

He'd been hoping to make better time, to put some distance between them and Denver. Given the fact he'd gotten the deeds out of the compound, he wouldn't be surprised in the least if Zihao didn't come riding right up on them, but the Chinese had little to gain related to the deeds. That whole scene still played as very odd in his mind, the ease at which he'd taken what he wanted from the damn compound.

The storm had been rumbling behind them for an hour or more but it was gaining, the thunder growing closer and the horses anxious. Shit! This was turning bad fast and his thoughts on the deeds were replaced with the task at hand.

"What do you need me to do?" Tess stood in the buckboard raising her voice against the storm.

Wyatt glanced at her. Beautiful was an understatement and her smile was enough to settle the fight that was still raging inside him. She wore a blue skirt and her long brown hair tossed in the wind. And she was now his for all his life, and somehow he was looking forward to that—just life with her. He stopped amid the whirling winds and impending rain to smile and just look at her.

"Wyatt?" She placed her hands to her hips at his delay.

"Just lookin'." He grabbed the rolled canvas stretching it out and pulling himself up in the back of the wagon. It had cost him six dollars to borrow the overused wagon and tired horses, which he had promised to have one of the McCade ranch hands return to the Denver livery within a few weeks.

He tossed Tess the end of the canvas and went to work putting the bows of hickory in place for tenting it. As she held to it, he pulled the canvas across each and secured it as large drops of rain began falling from the sky around them.

He jumped down from the rear of the wagon, cursing the forgotten soreness of his ankle. "Get the front ties and get inside." He yelled against the wind and thunder. He unbuckled his holster wrapping it around itself and set it inside the wagon. Adjusting his hat, he grabbed his oiled duster and tossed it on.

Tess leaned across the buckboard on one side and then the other to tie the stays and tucked the flaps before climbing into the wagon. Wyatt waited until she was safe inside. She'd be dry and he needed to get the horses unhitched and hobbled under the larger trees that would cover them and the wagon. He stepped into the road with heavy boots, pushing down with his right leg. The mud would be thick after this rain.

Tess glimpsed from the back of the wagon, having tugged open the flap.

"Hang on, I'm gonna move the wagon." He urged the horses ahead taking the wagon farther under the cover of trees and into higher grass off the muddy road. Lightning snapped all around them and while trees weren't that safe, they would offer them and the horses a little more protection from the high winds.

The horses were already spooked and difficult to lead. They had been making good time but in rain like this they would have to sit still for more than a day if not longer. Wagons. If they were on horseback instead of the damn wagon they'd have had a hell of a better chance to beat the storm home.

Water poured from his hat, and his body shivered from the cold rain that had saturated his shirt prior to adding the duster. Thunder rumbled above and lightning streaked the sky once more. This storm wasn't short lived. He cursed as he unhitched the team and struggled to secure one horse at a time.

The second horse bucked with the thunder but settled with his coaxing. His boots mired into the mud. Hell, he should have worn the new ones that hurt his feet to break them in. This was the worst rain he'd been caught in for a while now, and it was strange, the feeling that came over him. Had he been alone he would have ridden out the storm or made his way somewhere dry, but his worry wasn't for himself, but instead, for Tess. Married meant she came first as it should be, and he worried more of her comfort.

Thunder clapped above him causing him to duck, waiting on more. The duster kept him from getting drenched further, but his boots were full. He turned back once more before returning to the wagon to eye the horses and stopped dead in his tracks, the rain pelting around him. He hadn't been on this road back to Cheyenne since he'd been beaten. And there it was. The old tree where Benton had beaten him snapped his leg and left him to die. He turned a full circle, the whole scene playing through his mind. His pulse raced, and a cold sweat took him. The need for revenge was strong enough to make him shake, his breath rapid. *Holy damn!*

He forced himself to inhale deeply, pushing away the pictures in his mind. He trotted to the wagon, the rain pounding across him. Pulling up on the back of the tail gate, he laid it down and jumped up, tucking himself inside. He scooted a box out of the way speaking to Tess as he shook the water from his hat and duster. "This is a good one. Looks like we might as well sit here until it passes. It'll be a day or more before we can make the roads again." He pulled off one boot and dumped the water and turned to look at her, trying to mask his worry.

She handed him a cloth to dry with. "You're limping worse."

"Ahh, well the horses gave me a bit of trouble." He

dumped water from the other boot struggling with his left leg which was paining with the effort of dragging the horses along, and the recent fight in Denver he hadn't bothered to explain to her.

"Is it safe here?" She sat on the small barrel of water.

Wyatt struggled to his knees, holding onto on his bad leg to get inside the wagon and rubbing his ankle once inside. "We're good, and if any Cheyenne are in the area, they probably know Dawson or Leaning Bear." He made it sound simple, but no one was safe out on the prairie alone, and she knew it.

"We haven't much in the way of bedding, but I think this quilt will work to lie on, and we can use the lighter blanket as a cover." She moved a few things around in the wagon and smiled. "I suppose there is no chance of a fire in this?"

He winked at her. "I like cold beef and biscuits."

She smiled. "Well, cold food on the way."

Tugging his socks off, he wrung them and hung them to dry across the crates at the end of the wagon.

"Well, we have plenty of food if we are stopped for a few days." She handed him a biscuit with dried beef inside.

"Maybe a day or two." He ate, leaning back against the wagon's side, looking on as she made up a place to sleep. She sat then and picked off pieces of her own biscuit.

The noise of the heavy rain and thunder drowned out their conversation and she talked louder. "I'll be glad to get home and get us settled in the clinic. I was thinking if you wanted, the room I am in is a bit smaller than the one you stayed in when you were injured.

Maybe we could move there and it has a back door, which might make a bit more sense."

"That's all up to you, Doc." He glanced outside again, lifting the canvas as thunder blasted. Lightning hit the horizon behind them and his pulse bounced hard once more. He hadn't expected his reaction to being where he'd almost lost his life. He shook his thoughts and turned back to face her as thunder battered down on them again.

She lifted her shoulder bag and pulled out a small brown package, handing it to him as she scooted in beside him.

He held her gaze, curious. "What's this?"

"I had wanted to give it to you in Denver, but we left in such a rush. It's something I got for you, my husband, for our wedding." Her smile was contagious as she threw her hands together in anticipation.

Wyatt opened the small box and tossed the brown paper aside. He then removed the top. A pocket watch and a very fine one. He lifted it and held it in his palm. The case was laden with a horseback rider in gold and a diamond of a star above him in the sky. Right beautiful. He glanced back at her.

"I know you lost your father's and it can't be replaced, but I hope you like it. I thought the rider looks like you. And the star, you always talk about following the stars so you don't lose your way." Her words were a flurry as she explained using her hands in gesture.

He turned it in his hand, the silver back shiny with the edged textures in a darker metal. "It's a right fine watch. I'll never lose my way to finding you again."

She regarded him as he opened it, the Roman numerals thick for an easy glance. She'd gone to a lot of expense for such a watch. He grinned, taking her hand. "It's uhmm, very nice, but it's missing something."

She frowned.

"Inside my father's watch, I carried a picture of you, right here." He touched the inside of the cover.

"You had a picture of me? Where did you even get one?" Her brows knitted together in puzzlement.

"Some secrets are best kept." He'd been in her clinic some years ago, and several pictures of her were lying on the counter where she had been going through a box of things her aunt had shipped to her. He'd not asked but taken the smallest and never said a word.

Her smile was tender.

"Had to have something beautiful to look at each day when I was on the trail." He kissed the back of her hand.

"I suppose you can put one of our wedding pictures there now." She ducked against him following a boom of thunder right above them. "It's so loud. It may be hours don't you think?" She finished her biscuit and wiped her mouth with the edge of her handkerchief.

"Looks like it. Might as well get some rest." He tugged his damp shirt over his head and leaned back against the sack of feed he had for the horses. He'd had worse for a pillow. He took the last bite of the dry biscuit, chewed, and swallowed as Tess settled in beside him.

"I'm not very tired. I suppose we could think of something to do." She kissed his lips, running her hands along his chest.

He let go with a smile. "All you ever do is ask, Doc."

She kissed his chest as he rolled her to her back, wedging up her skirt, his erection hard and wanting with the feel of her exposed thighs. There was no point in finding their way out of clothing in such a storm.

She sighed as his fingers found her and she tangled her hands into his hair.

He chuckled. “If I didn’t know better, Doc, I’d think you planned on no pantaloons.”

She tried to hide her smile, working at his trousers. “It makes things easier when on the trail, husband.”

He pushed his britches down his hips, making short work of joining their bodies. “I love the watch.”

“So glad you do.” She was already drawn tight, and he wasn’t going to last long at this rate. He’d never have his fill of her; never get enough of touching and exploring her womanly curves and tender olive skin. He pushed her back, flat beneath him and rocked into her, burying himself deep. Thunder crashed around them and the rain beat hard across the canvas.

In a few strokes, she moaned, and he upped the pace, pushing her legs further apart and raking his hands into her hair, holding her face. God, he loved to watch her when her body gave way. He pumped harder and she traced her hands down to his hips, pressing him to her firmly, taking him with her. He shuddered clinging to her as if she were life itself and her urgent whispered cries were his triumph. He collapsed atop her and rolled, pulling her across his chest once more. She snuggled into him, breathless and limp.

“Will we be safe if we sleep?” she whispered, still catching her breath.

“I’ll be awake.” He wasn’t so sure, but he needed to make certain she didn’t worry needlessly and in this kind of storm, there was no one for miles.

"All night?" She toyed with the hairs on his chest.

He kissed the top of her head and enveloped her in his arms, hanging onto her as tightly as he'd ever held anything. "All night long, Doc."

Chapter Twenty

Wyatt sipped his coffee, gazing across the table as Sawyer and Dawson studied the deeds he'd brought from Denver. He'd arrived home with Tess in the wee hours of the night, and he'd carried her to his old bed, kissed her, and joined his brothers. Evan stood in the corner of the room, leaning against the counter sucking down his own cup of the thick black liquid, quiet for once.

Sawyer pushed the deeds around and flipped the blank one that mimicked what Rollins' held, all but the wrong slant of his father's signature. "Why would Chan still have the deeds after all this time and not realize what he was privy to?"

"The better question is why he made it so easy, even though Zihao knew I'd taken these." Wyatt set his tin mug to the table, still puzzled at how simple it had been.

Sawyer pushed the deed toward Dawson, who lifted it to take a closer look.

"You said the crates had been tampered with recently…" Dawson lifted his gaze.

Wyatt interrupted. "Someone has been in the one crate of late. Shiny penny nails had closed it up, and it wasn't as dust covered as the others. And Zihao hinted Benton had been there, but we all know Benton would know of the copies and the correct slant of Father's script."

"So Zihao and Chan are playing both sides. But I'd lay odds Rollins did the forgery and paid little attention to the direction of Father's penmanship. Those true copies of the deeds, the three-way split of the land should hold up in court." Dawson shoved the document back to Sawyer and settled back in his chair.

Sawyer nodded in slow succession. "Pretty damn good chance, at least enough to stall Rollins' plans for now. Dodge and Brett have the second copies as proof." He set a thumb on the deed that Rollins had likely copied for their father's signature alone. "Father bought six-thousand acres from Jefferson Rollins, not the other way around. And he split that land up in eighteen forty-four. This deed from eighteen forty-six won't stand up in court with what we have."

Evan stepped forward, folding his arms. "You know Rollins says he is going to re-open the copper mine next week."

Wyatt narrowed a skeptical gaze on his youngest brother. "When the hell did he decide that? Does Brett know?"

Evan's brows lifted. "He's sittin' idle, but I don't think for long. He's also thinking it was Marcus Benton who killed his new hand, Roy McCall weeks back. Those tracks Sawyer had seen around the place were likely him."

Sawyer scowled at Evan. "Brett, like all of you has been told to keep things quiet. I let Rollins know yesterday that until the circuit judge arrives he isn't to make any move to do anything."

"I'm good brother, but you might have a little chat with Brett, he's got a mind to put a halt to the man if he steps one foot on Morgan land." Evan's deep voice echoed across the kitchen.

"Brett has been warned." Dodge pranced into the room followed my Mei Ling, taking chairs at the table, both in robes covering their night clothing.

Wyatt glanced at Mei Ling, dreading the exchange of Da Ming's belongings and that he might have to explain more than he'd like to. She might have been their second mother, having a hand at raising him and his brothers from a young age. And now, after all these years, just as much a part of the family as anyone.

"Brett gets it in his head, won't be much stopping him." Dawson shrugged and leaned forward again laying his palms flat on the table.

It was true, Brett wasn't a man to sit and wait on trouble. If Rollins and his men stepped foot near the mine, he'd not bat an eye at taking them out one by one. He was most of the time a calm man, expecting little, but he had a strong love of the land he had worked most of his life, the same land he'd also owned for years now.

Sawyer rubbed a hand across his tired eyes. "No one is giving up or giving in. I think we have proof enough to halt things, but we all need to be aware of retaliation. I should've known you didn't go to Denver just to get married. How the hell did you know to look for the deed there?"

Wyatt surveyed all his brothers. They were waiting for an answer, but he rested his gaze on Mei Ling. He'd not hurt her for any reason in the world and some things were best kept.

"He knew where the deeds were because when he was a youngster, he was in the wrong place at the wrong time." It was Dodge who answered the question.

Wyatt's entire body tensed. What the hell did she know about it? He met his mother's like blue eyes, confused because his father had sworn him to secrecy and besides Tess he'd never shared the story with anyone.

"I knew when you were going to Denver what it was all about." Dodge's let out a soft sigh. "This family has held enough secrets over the years."

Wyatt said nothing, glaring. Sawyer had kept the secret of Benton's brother being the man who had gunned down their father years before. He and Brett had been there and told the family at the time they had killed the man, until he returned set on revenge nearly killing Sawyer. It was a miracle Tess had saved him, though Benton's brother had met his end, and that was part of Benton's need for revenge now.

"I've warned you boys to stay away from Chan. How much did it cost you?" Dodge looked at him waiting.

"Enough." He wasn't about to answer that question. Knowing he was a fool was one thing but being called one by his mother was another.

"As I suspected. Chan never deals fair, and I suspect that he had as much to do with Da Ming's death as those who did it." She glanced at Mei Ling who gave a slight nod, her almond shaped eyes attempting to hide the sadness that lay behind them.

Wyatt angled his head, listening. After Da Ming died, he'd heard some of the discussion by men at the railroad who suspected Chan at being responsible for his own brother's death, but he'd never heard his father speak of it again.

"It's time for the truth, Wyatt." Dodge turned. "Mei Ling?"

Mei Ling lifted her gaze and held Dodge captive for a long moment. The two had been close friends since they were young women bound to a West that neither understood at the time. Dodge had married John McCade and traveled to the unforgiving country where Mei Ling had become her first friend.

His mother took a deep breath. "Chan took Da Ming's things from the railroad when Da Ming was killed. I thought your father, Mei Ling, and I were the only ones who knew that."

Mei Ling tilted a nod of response. So they had both known Da Ming's death was no accident, all this time? And Dodge wanted the truth from him now? What the hell? His heart pounded. He'd suffered nightmares and anguish as a youth over all that had happened and hadn't had anyone to confide in, save the father who'd forbidden the discussion.

"Chan kept what was in the office of the railroad car where John had Da Ming complete his deeds, the same car that was set fire with Da Ming inside." Dodge's blue eyes focused on him again. "And I know you saw what happened. Your father told me Wyatt, but he thought it best we never mention it again."

"What I saw is best left unsaid." He waited, unable to look at Mei Ling, the air thin.

"Wyatt, I know Da Ming die at hand of brother. You speak it to solve family problem with land." Me Ling spoke sure and proud, her chocolate eyes calm.

He struggled for a moment to fill his lungs with air, his mouth going dry. "Mei Ling."

"Please, Wyatt, speak it." She raised her tone an

octave, not giving in.

He shook his head, the pain inside his chest visceral enough to crush him with the thoughts of hurting her. He took a deep breath and studied each of his brothers and turned back to Dodge. "I was at the rail yard with Father who told me to stay there where Dawson was sleeping."

He met Dawson's gaze. He wasn't sure if Dawson even remembered that night but he continued, "Of course, I didn't do as he said. I wandered around and played on the tracks everywhere I wasn't supposed to be as it got darker outside. I climbed on top of a wood stack and sat for a time, and that's when I heard…Da Ming."

Mei Ling folded her hands together, and he wanted to cringe, watching the skin of her knuckles tighten. That wasn't even the half of it. He went on, "He was screaming in pain, and I got down and crept along, hiding behind rail cars and wood piles. Scared out of my mind as I found them. Da Ming was tied to one of the posts, and Marcus Benton was whipping him. I couldn't run. Afraid to move. I didn't know where Father had gone. When they dragged Da Ming to the railcar, it was moments later they ran from the car with all the crates of Father's papers, leaving the railcar in flames." Wyatt's pulse raced in remembering and his voice cracked, but Mei Ling met his gaze with a nod for him to continue.

"I could hear Da Ming's cries from the car, and I ran to find Father, who grabbed me out of the darkness and held his hand over my mouth until he could get me back to his railcar." He shook his head. "He'd seen what happened and the men who did it and swore me never to mention it again. I know that's how Benton got his plot of land out of Father, even if it wasn't the land he wanted at the time."

Dodge let out a tense breath and raised her brows. "Your father gave the land to him to protect you, Wyatt. To protect all of us. But he was aware that Chan and Marcus were up to no good. And you are right, not the property that Marcus was hoping for which is why he has returned with this preposterous scheme."

Wyatt fought his emotions. All this time, his fears as a youngster and the damn nightmares and his father's voice that had never let him rest. *Settle the West, Wyatt. You and your brothers will keep her from being corrupt. Fight hard, son to find the truths.*

"It is true," Mei Ling answered.

Sawyer shrugged. "Benton and Chan go way back. Chan smuggling opium and Chinese whiskey, the same whiskey we know Benton had his men run all over the West."

Wyatt agreed with a slight nod, but how could a man find hate enough to participate in his own brother's brutal murder? He might like to kick one of his brother's asses from time to time, but he'd never thought about watching them die at his own hands.

"Those crates held copies of Father's deeds. We all know that Da Ming made two exact copies of each and sometimes a third. There were deeds and property documents from Denver clear through the Northwest, Dakotas and more, but the stakes were high on stuffing more in my pockets with Chan's son Zihao watching, and we have copies of them all here at the ranch anyway," Wyatt added, with a glance at Sawyer.

Mei Ling lifted her gaze. "I know Chan responsible

in Da Ming death. Da Ming fear this at times. Chan, know many bad man. Marcus Benton lead Chan to deceit."

"That's the pot calling the kettle the jackass he is," Dodge spat.

Dawson rolled his eyes, and Evan chuckled, then sipped his coffee. No one was ever surprised at what escaped their mother's mouth, and even Sawyer shook his head.

Wyatt adjusted in his chair, tired from the trip and ready to snuggle in beside Tess in his old room for the little remainder of the night. "So the question remains we have enough to stop them now, but then what?"

Sawyer shrugged. "Then we wait."

Wyatt studied his brother who hadn't spoken the rest of what they were both thinking.

Dawson took the deeds looking them over again. "The ink is older on the deeds signed by Father, but the paper for the copy of the six-thousand acres is older, while the ink is newer. It's clear forgery."

"Go on." Wyatt leaned on the table for a closer look.

Dawson squinted angling the deed to the light of the lamp on the table. "I think you are right in that Rollins' copy matches this blank one, forged, which makes it look real. But at the time lots of unofficial land dealings were happening without government involvement. Years later, the government reissued some land deeds, but from what I recall, not in Wyoming."

Wyatt fidgeted with the papers. "And all this Rapid City planning, taking the rail right across our land, lets Rollins make money off the stockholders he's been courting. So while the government isn't paying much for the spurs, he'll get his money one way or the other."

"And he takes the copper all the way to the bank." Sawyer slammed both hands flat on the table before him.

"Damn good set up, but what's Benton's stake in it all?" Evan asked.

Dodge answered the question. "He owns a great deal of land in northern Wyoming and the Dakotas just sitting idle. I would bet my hind end it's Miles Rollins who had him pardoned so they'd both profit. That or he would've been hanged on schedule, the filthy goat!"

"So the question remains, where the hell is the filthy goat?" Wyatt said it and caught the glare from Sawyer. His older brother was aware of his thoughts where Marcus Benton was concerned as were all in the room.

"Ahhh, enough. I'll see you boys in the morning. Goodnight Dodge, Mei Ling." Evan slammed from the room, spurs clinking down the hallway.

Wyatt watched him go. Evan wasn't much for small talk and would rather settle things with a good old fashioned fight, much like himself. He turned back toward the table meeting gazes with Mei Ling.

"Thank you, Wyatt." Her voice was soft.

He reached into the pocket of his trousers and pulled the green circle of jade on the red cord free. He held it in his fist and reached across the table to take Mei Ling's hand turning it palm up and placing Da Ming's necklace in it.

Mei Ling opened her hand and glanced back at him. "Da Ming wear this always."

"I found it in one of the crates, and I have a few more things in my saddle bags," he whispered.

She bowed, holding the jade close to her heart and leaving the room in silence.

"I'd rather have cut off my arm than to do that." Wyatt met his mother's gaze, tears rimming her eyes.

"She'll be fine." Dodge blinked.

Dawson got up from the table and stretched with a yawn. "I'm heading out in the morning to Casper, be back in a couple of days."

"Casper?" Wyatt questioned, figuring his brother taking off to more Indian business.

Dawson pulled his long brown hair into a band as he talked. "Meeting Sam and Will Hagen. Made the purchase of a mare from them."

"Gonna breed Viho?" Wyatt asked about the horse, a mustang mix Dawson had gotten from the Hagen brother's a few years ago.

Dawson beamed with pride. "Gonna try, of course Samuel wants the first foal if it's a male, to get some of Viho back into the mustangs he's raising now."

Sawyer spoke then, propping back and stretching out his legs. "I ran into Adam Hagen in Sturgess, said he was interested in meeting Tess as he'd heard of her."

"Adam's a good man, has a medical practice in Rapid City, but I've seen his wife more often, her name is Alicia, and she works with the sick Indians on the reservation just outside the city." Dawson leaned to kiss Dodge on the cheek.

"Careful, son. Wire when you can." Dodge touched his hand as he nodded to his brothers leaving the room.

"How's the leg?" Sawyer turned back to Wyatt.

"Fine." He lied. The fight with Barlow and the storm and days with the wagon had set him back a little.

Sawyer gave him a warning glare but said nothing

more. His brother knew once he was back on his feet, the stakes of the game would change and quick. He'd gotten a good start on that with his jaunt through Denver.

"John worked hard for this land." Dodge began talking, taking the heat away from him and Sawyer. "He saved for years, gained the money his father left him, and worked in mapping the railroads, selling the land he had for profit to continue, but he never wanted to give up any of the land here."

"We're not giving up this land." Wyatt gritted his teeth and shook his head. "But why now, after all this time?"

"The transcontinental railroads had to be completed first, before all the spurs." Sawyer leaned forward and wrapped his hands around the tin mug of coffee, slowly turning it where it sat on the table. "I believe the fight at the river was a start, and I think Benton was just waiting for the government to pay or have a need for a rail through to the Dakotas. But then when his brother was killed, those plans fell apart. My guess is back then Da Ming wouldn't forge the deeds. I am sure Benton thought with Father dead he could go ahead with his plans but didn't count on Dodge and Brett being in the way."

Wyatt thought it through for a moment. It all made sense to that point, but all the years in between didn't add up. It was true that Marcus Benton thought that if John McCade was dead, he could forge documents to complete what he'd started and then gain Brett's land through forged deeds. Add Miles Rollins who had the funds and backing to build the railroad spur and the government would be on their side if it came down to it.

He shook his head, his heart pounding inside his chest. He gripped his hands into fists, so tight they shook. "Rollins is in it for the money, and Chan will be able to ship his goods all over the northwest, but Marcus Benton won't rest until he's buried us all. We stop Rollins with the deeds and he'll show and I'll be waiting."

"If Rollins can't raise the funds through investors, that rail won't be built, and now we have proof enough to stop him, but this is not your permission to seek out Marcus on your own Wyatt." Dodge got up. "You have to work tomorrow Sawyer, go on to bed."

Wyatt glanced at Dodge, who no doubt had cleared the room on his account. That meant only one thing—a lecture. He slumped in his chair, with the odd inkling to protect his ears from a good thump at having taken on Chan alone. Sawyer stood and made his way out of the kitchen with one final glare at him.

Dodge's light blue eyes read him like a book. "You knew better than to approach Chan."

"I did what I thought best for the family. You knew all along about Da Ming," he challenged.

"Your father shared enough, but Mei Ling knew much from Da Ming before he died. He had been worried for John's life as well. My guess is he knew what they were planning or at least guessed they would try to kill John, not knowing his own death would be first at the hand of his own brother years before your father was killed." Dodge brushed her short gray locks behind her ear.

"Father and I had words over Marcus Benton before he died." He'd only ever told that to Sawyer and later Tess. "He warned me again of not crossing

Benton, but I was young and stupid and didn't want to hear what he was telling me. I called him a coward for not doing something about Benton long ago."

Dodge touched his hand from across the table. "He loved you, Wyatt, and words and disagreements mean little in the scheme of things. I know you want revenge, but your world has changed, Wyatt. You need to start thinking with care in being a married man. Everything you do will affect Tess and you can't take chances where Marcus is concerned. You can't get him alone, nor should you try. He will fall victim to his own doings soon enough but you…you have a new start, a wife and your life. Play your cards right, Wyatt, and play them well."

She rose, leaving him alone in kitchen. Sawyer and Dodge were well aware of what he was thinking. And Dodge was right. If he got himself killed, he left a wife behind. He made his way down the hallway to his old room. Tess was lying on her side sleeping soundly. Regardless what Dodge or any of his brother's thought, it would never be over until Marcus Benton was dead and with or without his brothers he had no choice but to see that it was done.

Chapter Twenty-One

Wyatt watched from the jail office door as Miles Rollins and two of his men entered the bank. This was the third time this week the man had gone inside, taking investors with him and remaining for hours at a time. The three had just returned from outside town, which made him wonder just what they might have been up to.

He swore a whispered curse. The man was walking around town, greeting those that got off the train every few days and even taking wagon loads of men out to see the property that would never be his. Dodge had reported he'd ridden very close to the house a few days before, but Evan had fired shotgun blasts in the air as a warning, turning the men away. Things were getting more heated, but the eye of the storm lived inside him—and it wasn't related to Rollins, the copper, or even the land. Where the hell was Marcus Benton?

He and Evan had spent a few weeks tracking Rollins, some of which seemed to take place in the direction of Denver—which meant somewhere the man was meeting with Marcus Benton. At least the federal circuit judge had been delayed, buying them a little time, and Hudson had reported nothing much with telegrams he sent from Denver.

He turned back to go inside but stopped short catching a glimpse of Dawson slumping in the saddle, his horse ambling along slowly into town. Something was wrong. "Dawson!"

He took off on a run to catch the slow walking animal as Sawyer exited the jail running behind him.

"What the hell happened?" Sawyer yelled as they got to Dawson, whose leather tunic front was covered in blood.

Wyatt stopped Viho and grabbed his brother, sliding him from the saddle. Dawson growled in pain but stood to the ground, swaying and holding a bloody cloth to his forehead.

"Who did this?" Wyatt steadied his younger brother with Sawyer's help.

Dawson blinked several times, taking a deep breath. "Benton. At…the pass."

"So the son of a bitch is here." Wyatt belted out. He'd felt it for a time now, even though he suspected Benton to remain hidden in Denver.

Dawson grimaced as Sawyer pulled the cloth back from his head. A bullet had grazed a deep gash across his forehead above his left brow.

Sawyer placed the bloody rag back to Dawson's head.

"You saw him? Benton?" Wyatt threw Dawson's right arm over his shoulder and Sawyer took his other side.

Lang, from the livery, ran over giving Wyatt a nod grabbing the reins to Dawson's horse. "What the hell happened to you?"

Dawson lifted his gaze, holding his head. "Benton."

"Nothing but trouble's gonna come now." The old man headed toward the livery with Viho in tow.

"Hey, Lang?" Sawyer called over his shoulder.

"Get Dodge at the mercantile, send her to help the doc."

"I'll get her." The old man scampered along, mumbling to himself. "Bastard's got a lot of nerve showing his ass around these parts again."

"Benton fired the rifle, and there were two others." Dawson groaned. "Knocked me right out, but the horse…got me…here."

"You had no business out there anyway," Sawyer scolded.

Dawson was quick to respond. "It's a shorter ride to town…by the pass."

Wyatt tugged his brother harder. "Then they meant to find you, or they were waiting on any one of us."

Dawson groaned and held his head, staggering.

"Guess you'll wear a hell of a headache for a while." Sawyer struggled to keep him upright. "Tess at the clinic?"

"Yep. Stand up, brother." Wyatt tugged Dawson's arm tighter as he swayed again.

Sawyer raised his voice. "Did you get a good look at the other men?"

"Didn't see much of anything. I think they were those clowns with Rollins." Dawson swayed at the stairs of the clinic needing their full help. "If he wanted me dead, I would…be."

"He aimed for your head for God's sake; if he was playing, he'd of shot the horse," Sawyer scolded.

"Doc!" Wyatt called as they stormed into the clinic. So, the connection was made. Rollins and his men had been meeting with Marcus Benton somewhere out by the pass, the perfect spot to catch any of them at random.

Dawson growled, gritting his teeth. "Had to cut the

mare loose, they…were on my heels. Gave me chase until…the ridge."

Tess came running from the back. "Dawson? Get him to the table." She followed them into the exam room. "What happened?"

Wyatt met her gaze as he helped his brother up.

Sawyer busied himself with removing the cloth from Dawson's head but answered the question. "Marcus Benton got him. It's deep, but he's got a damn thick skull."

"I'm all right." Dawson sat upright and braced himself as Tess touched his brow and studied his eyes.

It was then that Wyatt got a better look at the wound. It was deep and a wonder it hadn't taken his brother's head clean off. The deep open stripe went from his brow up into his hair line, and the swelling around it was growing purple and thick. It dripped a steady stream of crimson blood down Dawson's face, spilling further onto his leather tunic.

"I will kill him before this is over." Wyatt wasn't sure he'd spoken it until Tess' head snapped around, and her green eyes narrowed on him.

She turned back to Dawson. "Well, it's quite a bit of swelling, and there won't be much I can do to stitch it. I'll dress it, and you need to lie down until the bleeding stops. There is no doubt I'll need to check on you every few hours for a few days." She cleaned the wound and placed the dressing.

Tess steadied Dawson's head with both hands. "Look up, and down."

He followed her orders but swayed, Wyatt and Sawyer both grabbing hold of him and laying him back across the exam table. He closed his eyes. "Dizzy."

Tess propped a pillow under his head. "That means your brain has sloshed around inside your head with the impact of that bullet, and you have to let it rest. It's very dangerous."

He groaned, his eyes staying closed. "See to my horse will you, Wyatt?"

"Lang took him to the livery, just a minute ago." Wyatt glanced at Tess.

She gave him a slight nod of reassurance, walking across the room to close the shutters. "He just needs rest, and in the darkness, to keep the light from making things worse."

Dodge raced into the clinic. "Who in the hell did this?"

"One guess." Wyatt snarled, meeting gazes with his mother, wondering that Lang hadn't told her.

"Marcus?" She shook her head in disbelief as she took Dawson's hand and inspected the bandage, fussing over him. "Good Lord, are you all right?"

"Fine, Dodge." He opened his eyes, blinking to focus.

"Dawson, I've dimmed the room, but it's best you keep your eyes closed, and I've got some herbs that might help with the dizziness." Tess went to the cupboard across the room.

Dodge placed a hand to Dawson's cheek. "I'll stay with you. Just rest, son."

Dawson lay still, his eyes closed, and Wyatt focused on him, his hands curling into fists.

That Benton was as close as the pass, he thought hard about taking off on his own, but he'd watched as, moments before, the men working with Rollins rode into town and went into the saloon cackling and jostling with each other. There was no doubt in his mind the men had been there when Dawson had become a target. Well, it had been damn long enough he'd sat idle waiting to heal. He slipped from the room, heading toward the saloon.

Stepping to the streets of Cheyenne, he stomped that way, not looking back. Oh, he fully expected his sheriff brother to follow, but enough was enough.

He pushed through the saloon doors and scanned the tables of men playing cards, exchanging glances with Jacob, who lifted his shotgun from beneath the counter. He could always count on the old saloon owner to back him. Now the odds were more even. He moved closer to the table, having not been in the saloon much at all since his injuries. He stopped before the table. "You boys know anything about shots fired out at the pass near the Morgan ranch?"

The men passed cards. They knew. Lloyd, with his dark hat and fancy suit, never batted an eye and laid down another golden eagle on the table, but Jessup decided to answer the question with a smug smile. "A shot was fired at an Indian, some kind of savage in the distance. Who's asking?"

Wyatt curbed his temper for a second. They knew good and damn well why he was asking. One of the miners at the table lay down his cards and eased up from the table, backing away. The other followed suit, both aware of what was about to happen, and neither interested even in the money they had both left behind on the table.

Well, that cut the numbers down a bit. Wyatt leaned down on the table with both hands gripping the edge. "I'm asking." And before any of the men could react, he tossed the table on its side, slinging cards, coins, and paper money across the floor.

A fist caught his jaw, and his head popped back, but he righted himself thrusting a fist across Lloyd's cheek and elbowing Jessup across the brow sending him backward. The man danced for stance, falling across the upturned table and coming at him again. He gave him a left hook, hanging onto him and punching again with all the power of his left fist. He turned and took a hit to his mid belly from Lloyd. He heaved a breath grateful it hadn't been his still tender ribs.

He punched again with his left, his right fist not worthy of a good hit, and Jessup grabbed his side and doubled over, coming up with a pistol and holding it in his face. Lloyd jerked away and punched him across the cheek. Wyatt dove to avoid the gun and tackled both men. The three landing in a pile and the pistol unloading with a sharp blast.

Wyatt wrestled and punched, thinking if they were all fighting this hard, none of them were hit. And somehow, out of the blur of writhing bodies around him, he had the advantage. Lloyd rolled aside, holding his jaw. He hit Jessup once more, and the man held up his hands in defeat, the pistol lost.

"Wyatt, that's enough." Sawyer had him by the shirt, pulling him away.

"I'll say when it is enough." He grabbed Jessup by the collar and lifted his fist once more, but Sawyer grabbed his gun belt to sling him back. He hopped on his leg still not giving up the fight. "Damn it to hell, Sawyer, you see what they did to Dawson!"

"Enough." Sawyer was between him and the two men who climbed to their feet, both bloody and breathless.

Miles Rollins sprinted into the saloon shouting and glancing at his men. “I want this man arrested sheriff, right now—he’s a danger to the citizens of Cheyenne.”

Sawyer sent a warning gaze to Wyatt, but he turned to Rollins. “That’s enough from all of you.”

“Sheriff, you will arrest this man at once,” Rollins spouted. “He came in here with intent to kill, and I insist justice be done.”

“Justice?” Wyatt took a step closer and was stopped by Sawyer again. “Tell me you bastards know nothing of a bullet grazing my brother’s head.” Wyatt yelled, and Sawyer fisted the front of his shirt.

“No, I would not and neither would my men,” Rollins shouted. He slammed his fancy cane on the wooden floor with each of his words, but he took a step back with Wyatt pulling Sawyer along toward him.

“And I suppose you would know nothing about Marcus Benton pulling out his rifle this afternoon or being on the other end of the deed you keep flashing around. You will never get our land.” He snatched himself from Sawyer’s grip and nailed the man right in the jaw.

Rollins staggered back, knocked senseless, his men keeping him on his feet. He sputtered and coughed coming back to his senses with a whirl of anger. “The first time I was assaulted, I let it go. Now I insist on arrest sheriff, and it is your duty to do so.” Blood dripped down his mouth. and he pulled a pressed handkerchief from his lapel pocket and placed it to his lip.

“I said enough, Wyatt.” Sawyer hissed slamming him against the wall and knocking the breath from him.

Had he been at his best, it would have taken more than his brother to handle him.

"Sheriff, I want the fullest extent of the law against this man even if he is your brother." Rollins spat, blood gathering at his lip once more.

"I asked you men to clear out," Sawyer yelled. "Now!"

Rollin's glare was cold. "I will be contacting the federal marshals." He turned to go, the men with him following.

Across the room, Jacob lowered the rifle.

Wyatt tried to pull free again, but Sawyer held him against the wall, cursing. "Damn it, Wyatt, you never learn."

"Son of a bitch, Sawyer." He cursed his brother as Sawyer tied his hands behind him. But his brother had every obligation as sheriff to arrest him. He'd gone into the saloon and done what he knew better than to do. But if he had it to do again, he would have done things the same. The ache in his fist was well worth the fight, though his ankle wasn't holding up as well. The ache had already started, and his boot was tight.

"I can walk without being tied." Wyatt glanced over his shoulder, every nerve in his body tense.

"You are being detained for starting this mess. Shut up and take your medicine." Sawyer turned him around. "You had no business coming in here, Wyatt. It's bad enough you and Evan are out doing your own thing and look what it got Dawson for snooping around…Damn it."

"Well, at least we are doing something." He spat with a growl.

His brother shoved him harder. "Walk!"

****

Wyatt sat inside the last jail cell in the darkness. The rage displayed at the saloon had calmed all but the part where he still cursed his brother in silence. It wasn't the first time he'd been on the wrong side of the iron bars, but most often it was Sawyer giving him a minute to let off steam. This time though, if Rollins came in to sign the papers, charges would be pressed. A fight wouldn't get him much, thirty days, being no one was hurt. Fine. So be it. But this time, when he did get out, the game of play had changed.

Sawyer whispered to someone in the office, and Tess' voice responded. He wasn't sure he was ready to see her yet, but he apparently had no say. The door opened, letting the yellow light of the office lanterns cast a glow across the darkness.

"Wyatt?"

He glanced up and stood, going as far as the bars allowed. It was apparent he'd scared her, but he hadn't meant for that to be the case, though she well knew his reasons. How was it just the sound of her voice settled him further, even if her disappointment was evident?

"Sawyer said I should check on you." She held up the cell keys and put one in the lock, turning the squeaking black iron.

"Nice of my loving brother." He smirked and sat back down on the bed as she let herself inside, leaving the gated door open behind her.

She set her medicine bag down beside him. "Are you hurt?"

"Nope." Actually, a scratch on his shoulder was burning, as was his cheek and lip, but he'd expected a lecture and not the tenderness she was presenting.

She touched his cheek, and he winced. Reaching in her bag, she dampened a cloth with antiseptic and touched his face with it.

He stifled a groan at the sting. "How's Dawson?"

"Resting. He'll be fine in a couple of days," she answered her voice void of emotion.

She was angry. Guilt ran through him. She added more antiseptic to the cloth and touched his lip. He pulled back at the burn, but she held it in place and he closed his watering eyes.

"Wyatt?"

"Don't ask me to explain what you can't understand." He didn't need the lecture, or her tears if it came down to it.

Her gaze settled on him. "Wyatt, you can't take this all on yourself and going in the saloon to start a fight…"

"I did what I had to do." He'd made her no promises, and he'd been clear about that.

"If Rollins presses charges, Wyatt…" Her voice broke slightly.

"Then I'll do my thirty days." That was how it worked; besides his brother was sheriff and not much more would happen.

"Let me see your shoulder." She tugged back the rip in his new shirt.

Shit, he couldn't keep one clean of blood these days. He unbuttoned the torn garment and pulled his right arm from the sleeve.

She frowned. "This is deep. They cut you?"

"Nahh, I got scraped somehow. It's not bad." He hadn't even felt it until he had settled into the cell and had time to think about it.

"It'll need stitching." Her voice softened as she reached into her bag and pulled out her suturing needle and after cleaning the wound started with the first stitch. He tensed but didn't move. Hell, some pain was a good thing, except where she was concerned. She worked the next suture and the next without saying anything more, her focus on the detail. She prided herself on perfect stitches, more so than the women who sat outside the mercantile quilting on Saturdays. While the needle bit each time, it didn't bite as hard knowing he'd let her down.

When she was done, she glanced at him again. "Anywhere else?"

He shook his head. He wasn't injured as much as disgusted with himself for sitting still for so long while he'd healed.

She sat beside him and after a moment lifted her gaze. "I know who you are, Wyatt, and I know why you did what you did. I'm not asking you to change. I'm not asking you not to do what you feel you have to. But I am asking you to not do so alone, ever again." She shook her head, and the tears came. "You are one man, Wyatt, the one man I love, and I can't lose you, not after all we've gone through."

She was beautiful with her hair down, across her shoulders, but the sadness her eyes held nearly broke him. "I've done a lot of things in this life that I regret, but I make no apologies for any of them. I'm a bounty hunter."

He leaned to kiss her cheek and kept his face close to hers, their foreheads touching. "When this is over and Marcus Benton gets what is coming to him and Miles Rollins is sent back to New York with his tail between his legs, I will make whatever promises you need of me, but if I don't stop this, it never ends for any of us like I told you before."

The silent tears dropping down her cheeks crushed through his heart, but then she whispered, "I know you are right, but there has to be a better way. I love you, Wyatt, and I can't lose you, ever." With that she left the cell, hesitating to lock him back in.

"It's all right; if I wanted out I have a key. I run deputy here. Had a key in my boot for years." He offered an uncertain smile.

"So you didn't let yourself out?" She seemed puzzled by that.

"Nope." He chuckled at the thought, but his brother had been so angry it wouldn't be a wise choice.

She shook her head but kept eye contact with him and gave in to the smile he needed. Well, he'd gotten himself into trouble once more, but it would be short lived. And with her smile and his promise, thirty days would pass. He turned back to the cell window when she disappeared back into the office. He glanced north of Cheyenne, behind the city searching the darkness. Benton was near, and now there was no doubt of his connection to Miles Rollins.

"She deserves a husband who is going to be here. Bide your time, and Benton will mess things up soon enough. He's never been much of a patient man." Sawyer stood in the doorway, arms folded.

Wyatt turned from the barred window. "I will be bringing that bastard down as soon—"

Sawyer moved closer, his spurs clinking across the wooden flooring with each step. "As soon as what, as you heal, as you get out of jail. You can't take him alone, Wyatt. He doesn't play fair, never has. I have some leads and you brought the deeds, we have the ammunition, but I can't take him alone either. I need your help, not that wild spirit you can't control."

Wyatt leaned an elbow against the windowsill. What was his brother saying? "Leads? Those leads have anything to do with Hudson still nosing around Denver?"

Sawyer rested his hands on the irons, his gray eyes serious. "Have you ever thought I withhold information to keep you out of trouble? You never listen, Wyatt, always taking on the world all by yourself."

Wyatt narrowed his gaze on his brother and moved closer. "You know where Benton is?"

"You were right on top of him in Denver. He's checking in there and riding out every few days to meet with Rollins—in the line of trees a mile away from the pass. Likely, why he caught Dawson off guard." Sawyer raised his brows and let out a deep breath. "He'd been to Chan's just before you. You might have missed him by a day. And Hudson is following orders, though he hasn't seen Benton as of yet."

"Why the hell are you telling me this anyway?" Wyatt hissed. If he'd missed Benton by *hours,* it just added to his rage over the matter.

Sawyer shook his head. "Not sure I know, but things are about to come to a head, and with Dawson taking a bullet, I'd like to know you aren't going out alone to get yourself injured or worse."

Wyatt considered him. Leave it to Sawyer to pull the family together in a crisis. "All right, brother, but I'm telling you like I told the others. When the time comes, Marcus Benton is mine. Mine!"

"I reckon you deserve that honor, but getting yourself locked up's not helping things, and if you kill Benton, you'd better do it right or you'll find yourself in a box constructed by Henry." Sawyer glared hard, still gripping the bars.

Wyatt studied his brother who was always right about things. Henry was a freed man who took care of all the burying the dead in Cheyenne and the man made a right good living at building the wooden caskets.

"Miles Rollins signed for your arrest to press charges." Sawyer tilted his hat back, letting out a heavy sigh.

Wyatt gripped the iron bars tighter. "All right, thirty days. then I rip out Marcus Benton's throat."

"Damn it, Wyatt!" Sawyer slammed his hands to the bars. "Haven't you heard anything I've said? No, because you can't see past your own drive for revenge. Father didn't teach you that, and you'd better start thinking about the things he did teach you."

Wyatt bristled, holding his entire body tight. "Like what, honest law and following the rules?"

"Yes!" Sawyer shouted, his voice echoing the jail to silence.

Wyatt jerked away, gripping his fists into tight balls. "Look what following the damn rules got us. Dawson shot, my ass kicked, and you gunned down. This time brother, I am playing by no rules." He hit the bars hard and turned away from his brother and back to the window, done with the conversation.

Sawyer stood there a moment more and turned back for the office, slamming the dividing door to separate them, leaving him once more in the pitch black darkness.

He threw himself into the small bed and put his hands behind his head, his heart thumping hard inside his chest. What part of this did Sawyer not understand? Marcus Benton didn't follow the rules of engagement, and he'd been harassing them all for long enough. Apparently, he'd have plenty of time to think on things. Thirty days, all he had to do was wait for thirty days and then, if he didn't find Marcus Benton, he had no doubt the man would find him.

Chapter Twenty-Two

Zane bolted into the jail office, out of breath, stopping before Sawyer. "Pa. There's men…out at Brett's, starting the mining. Evan sent me. They've got rail cars and tools and machines, and Brett is fit to be tied. You have to go."

Wyatt trotted over to the iron bars, glancing into the jail office. "Son of a bitch, Sawyer let me out of here."

Sawyer jumped up from the desk, grabbing his hat. "How long ago?"

Zane shook his head. "Evan thinks since dawn."

Dawson bolted from the chair across the room and set down the paper he had been reading. "Evan posted a few of the hands out by the pass. Is anyone at the ranch?" He moved closer, his medicine pouch hanging around his neck and a small dressing still across his brow.

Sawyer was quick to respond. "Evans got a few men there. Zane, go to the ranch and stay with Rose, Mei Ling, and your brothers. Get my rifle from the shelf and stay posted on the porch and watch the back. Send one of the hands to town to sit with Tess at the clinic. Are you riding Shadow?"

Zane nodded.

"Then you ride like hell until you get to the ranch, don't stop for anything." Sawyer waited for his son's nod, and his gaze followed Zane until he was on the horse and headed out of town.

"Want to let me out of here so I can help?" Wyatt called from the back, shaking the heavy iron bars. He'd been sorting through files for twenty days now, serving his sentence and to be honest, ten more days sounded like torture.

Sawyer ignored him and glanced back at Dawson. "Can you ride?"

Dawson's lip curled into a hesitant smile. "Rode in worse shape than this."

"Take off and hit the back side of the pass on Brett's property and watch from the tree line. Might need you there if things get out of hand. Go ahead, I'll be along and take this with you." Sawyer tossed a rifle to him and grabbed his hat.

"Sawyer I know you hear me. Let me out!" They would need his help and he wasn't going to sit idle for something like this.

Sawyer came to the cell door after Dawson was gone. His brother had been able to negotiate a deal to keep him jailed in Cheyenne, and Rollins had agreed to the sentence, being the circuit judge was delayed further. "I needn't warn you to watch yourself. Do we understand each other?"

Wyatt gave a reluctant nod, holding a curse. He didn't need Sawyer's continued display of acting as his father.

Sawyer turned to leave, checking his revolvers without letting him out of the cell.

"Hey, hey, open the damn gate." He hissed, slamming against the bars with both hands.

Sawyer adjusted his hat, glancing back at him

through the office door. "Let yourself out and hurry about it."

Wyatt was dumbfounded for a moment. So, Sawyer had known all along he had a key. He jerked up his trouser pant leg and reached inside the split leather of his boot to retrieve the key, opening the lock and tucking the key back in his boot.

In no time at all he rode alongside Sawyer toward the pass near Brett's ranch on the new palomino he'd purchased some weeks ago. He'd yet to take the horse to a gallop, but the animal was a sturdy ride. He'd been in a cell for twenty days, and riding let him know how stiff he was, not to mention using his left leg to climb in the saddle still wasn't easy. But the idle time in jail had been good for his mind, and it might be that he would well miss the evenings where Tess came to sit and talk with him after the sun had set. She usually brought him supper and they would chat until late into the night, then he'd escape the cell to return her home each night. It had been last night, she'd asked him to stay and he had, long enough to hear her cries of pleasure more than once.

He urged his horse ahead, needing the run more than the animal beneath him. Moments later Sawyer halted them. Zane had been right. Outside of Brett's property was a line of wagons loaded with mining equipment, some with a couple of large machines for digging. So, Rollins and his men were serious. Frank Lloyd, the one heading up Rollins' mining campaign, was standing at the front using a scope for surveying the land around the mine. And there was Brett and his hands, before the mine, wagons overturned for cover to block their way.

He caught a flash of light from the trees behind the mine. Dawson signaled, using his small mirror to reflect the sun. Wyatt couldn't see him at all, but the mirror reflected once more, and he lifted the brim of his hat twice in returned signal. "Dawson's set."

"Well, they aren't on Brett's property yet." Sawyer summed up the situation. "Best I run them off before Brett pulls any tricks, and of course Evan is right in the mix. Holy hell."

Wyatt spotted his youngest brother near Brett behind one of the wagons. Evan was best at acting first and thinking later. He was reckless and unguarded most of the time, and while it was Brett that kept him in line, this was one time it might be the reverse.

"Best you turn both sides back," Wyatt said under his breath figuring Brett not easily persuaded.

"I have a feeling neither side will budge." Sawyer studied the scene with his own scope. "Seems Lloyd knows the lines well and hasn't crossed yet."

Wyatt scanned behind them. "So where is Rollins?" Better yet, where was Marcus Benton? He held the latter question. No sense riling his brother further, given the situation.

Sawyer led them down the ridge before the mining team. Most of the miners lined the trail, carrying tools, a few with weapons at their disposal.

Wyatt exchanged glances with Brett who wasn't a man who played any kind of cat and mouse for too long. He'd offer Sawyer a bit of time to play lawman, but he wouldn't hold back if things got tense.

Sawyer stopped his horse and dismounted. "You men have no right at this point to be on this property with your equipment. No land has changed hands, and you are trespassing. Not sure who gave you permission, but you can take this equipment right back where it came from, and I am giving you six hours to do so."

Frank Lloyd unfolded a piece of paper from his shirt pocket, stomping toward his brother. "Sheriff, I have in my hand the supporting documents that gives us permission to begin digging within the said mine on property twenty-three, forty-seven five, eighty-eight with minimal access and tracking on the property, signed by Federal Judge Hanson McGuire, yesterday, Washington. We are at liberty to begin mining the copper from this mine as of twelve midnight tonight. Documents for the other mines will arrive within the week."

Sawyer looked at the document as Brett approached, glancing over his shoulder to read it himself.

"Shit." Wyatt rushed to dismount, with Evan bringing up the rear. Keeping himself in line was one thing, but keeping his youngest brother out of trouble was another. He scurried to block his path. "Far enough."

"You broke jail early." Evan tried to push past him.

"Sorry, brother, holding you right here." He put a hand against the youngest McCade's chest, grinning. "Let Sawyer do this, or you'll be my new cell mate. My, how I would hate that. You snore."

Evan rolled his eyes and folded his arms. "Sawyer better handle this one, or the whole mine's going up. Brett wired it. If you aren't going to let me tell him, you'd best get to it."

He eyed his younger brother with suspicion and then trotted toward Sawyer. If the mine blew that would be trouble sure enough. Leave it to Brett to pull off something as drastic as blowing things to kingdom come.

He stopped beside Sawyer and tugged his brother's shirt sleeve. Lloyd eyed him with a stern glare, but the man never stopped talking. He used his arm to nudge his brother who was listening to more of Lloyd's explanations while studying the document.

Wyatt eyed Brett, who stood stoic though the veins in his neck visibly pounded.

"Looks like the document is legal." Sawyer glanced toward Brett, who turned to walk away without as much as a word.

"Sawyer?" Wyatt tried again, snatching his brother's sleeve this time.

"Give me a minute, will ya?" Sawyer spat, scanning the paper further.

Thundering blasts began inside and outside the mine, scattering the men to take cover. Some dove for the wagons as rock, dirt, and clumps of trees sprayed the area, thick black smoke rising in the air as the explosions continued. Wyatt dove farther away into the high grass, grabbing his ankle and glancing back up, surprised he'd kept his hat.

"Son of a bitch!" Sawyer settled in the grass beside him, looking back at the mine which continued to implode on itself, collapsing in a heap of smoke and fire.

"I, uh, was trying to warn you, brother." Wyatt rolled and held the hat to his head at the next explosion the complete rise of land sank. "Apparently, Brett's knowledge of working with black powder is paying off real well today."

"Shit." Sawyer was back up once the explosions stopped, though the smoke was thick in the air.

Wyatt followed, scanning the tree line for Dawson who would have been rather close to the festivities.

Lloyd dusted off his fine suit with curses, trotting over to Sawyer. "That man must be arrested, the bastard. That's a blatant misuse of government assigned property. I demand he be detained and brought before the judge for such a crime."

Wyatt smirked, stifling a chuckle. His one thought was Brett had now become his cell mate, not Evan. Sawyer would have to bring him in.

Sawyer narrowed his gaze. "You clear out this hell of a mess like I said, or I'll set fire to all of it myself."

"Is that a threat, Sheriff?" Lloyd bristled, bulking his shoulders and chest out.

"Yep." Sawyer never batted an eye as he turned back toward where Brett and his men remained.

Wyatt slammed his hands to his hips. *This ought to be good.* Sawyer having to arrest the man who'd taught him and his brothers about the ranching business as they had grown up. Brett was a good man, a really good man, but he had a fierce temper. For a moment he was glad he wasn't the sheriff. Maybe that was why he preferred bounty hunting. Less rules and regulations just lasso, or shoot the man and bring him in.

Brett stood with his arms folded, then took off his hat and ran a calloused hand through his graying hair. He met Sawyer's gaze.

Wyatt stepped closer. Shit. This couldn't end well. He folded his arms as Dawson rode up and dismounted. "Tell me Brett didn't do this?"

Wyatt gave his brother a nod.

Sawyer surveyed behind him at the men with Lloyd who were beginning to pack up their equipment and turned back to Brett. “This wasn’t what was needed to keep your land.”

“I figured.” Brett spat tobacco to the ground and never dropped his gaze.

Wyatt wasn’t sure just how old Brett was, somewhere younger than their father would have been and older than Dodge who was nearing sixty. But if there was anything he had learned from the man, it had been integrity.

“Rollins will have the federals out here in a matter of days, not to mention the circuit judge.” Sawyer surveyed the imploded mine once more.

“You gonna arrest me, best get to it.” Brett removed his gun belt and handed it off to Evan who cursed and walked away, well aware not to tangle with Sawyer when he was playing sheriff.

“You can ride in. I’ll wire to see if you can post bail after ten days.” Sawyer held his ground, serious and as sure as usual.

Brett turned to his men. “Evan’s got the ranch, follow his orders and clear out this mess.”

“Sawyer, you can’t do this.” Evan turned back with a roar, challenging his oldest brother after all.

Brett mounted up on his horse, turning it toward Evan. “He doesn’t have a choice in the matter.”

Evan shook his head and stomped off shouting orders to the men at the wagons.

Sawyer grabbed Colonel’s reins speaking to him and Dawson. “You two hang around and make sure things stay quiet.”

Wyatt figured he’d have been hauled right back in

like Brett. Either his sheriff brother was getting soft or he was getting tired of Miles Rollins' ploys to rile him. It was at best the latter. He nodded as did Dawson, both looking on as Sawyer and Brett rode side by side back up the ridge toward town.

"You could have given me a little warning." Dawson stuck a finger in his ear, opening his mouth.

He had to chuckle. "The warning came about thirty second before the blast."

Dawson held a hand to his wounded brow, still covered with a dressing. "There can't anything good come out of this one."

"Nope," he agreed. "You look kind of peaked, you holding up?"

"I'm good." Dawson folded his arms.

"Well, why don't you check on Zane at the ranch?" His suggestion was to get Dawson back to the ranch for a rest, and he'd expected protest, but his brother only nodded heading toward the horses.

Wyatt remained behind and by dusk, the group of miners had moved every wagon down the trail. That didn't mean they wouldn't be back for the other mines. Brett had never had an interest in making money off the mines he owned. He was adamant about keeping the land untouched. Well, this mine would be worthless. Vegetation would grow to fill things in, though the fallen rise would change the appearance of the landscape for years.

He glanced across the trees in the distance, the rocks near the river and the imploded mine. Marcus Benton was near, maybe not here at the mine, but aware of today's happenings no less. The hair on the back of his neck stood on end with the blowing of the wind and he heard his father' voice. *Wait for the fight, son, as it will come to you and then, you be ready.*

He held his ground a moment longer, mounted the palomino that hadn't shied at all with the explosions, and turned him a full circle. Eyes were on him, he was sure of it, but if the bastard was present he didn't let on.

****

"Sawyer is going to arrest you all over again." Tess dipped a bowl of stew for Wyatt and sat it beside a plate of corn muffins.

He chuckled and dug into his steaming bowl with the metal spoon. "He knows good and well where I am, but he's got his hands full tonight."

"Arresting Brett, what good will that do? Can he hang?" Law wasn't her specialty, but she didn't think that would be the case, though without a doubt Dodge would not be happy.

"Nahh, Sawyer will let him post bail, and he'll be fined, but not much more. We're thinking the deeds will prove the ownership of our lands, and then blowing the mine won't matter anyway." He sipped his coffee and set the mug back on the table.

"And you think Mr. Rollins will leave?" She was worried more than she let on, and if the man was connected to Marcus Benton, what then? Maybe Mr. Rollins would find some other way of earning his money, but Mr. Benton—he wouldn't let things go and there was no doubt that Wyatt wasn't done with the revenge he was bound to have.

"No. I think he'll appeal though I don't think it will get him far, but he isn't done and—" Wyatt's blue eyes were serious, though he stopped mid-sentence.

Tess whispered the rest of what he hadn't said.

"And neither is Mr. Benton."

Wyatt held her gaze for a moment and went back to his dinner.

She'd given up on talking him out of his ideas about the fate of the evil man who had nearly killed him. As hard as it was, and even though they were married, there was no point in thinking she could change his mind. He was better every day, and while she had missed him since he'd been jailed, at least his brother had kept him in check. She smiled, there was also the possibility she might keep him just as safe and the thought amused her as she took his hand tugging him from the chair.

He stood planting his mouth on hers and lifting her into his arms to carry her to the bedroom. Funny, he heard the unspoken words loud and clear.

She held on by wrapping her arms around his neck and toed her slippers off one at a time.

He chuckled as they dropped to the floor and laid her on the bed as he kicked from his own boots, making short work of his shirt, trousers and long underwear. Her breath quickened as he stood before her naked. Her eyes dropped lower where there was no doubt of his desire for her. She quivered in anticipation as he helped her with her dress, tossing it aside and pulling her to him.

She began with the buttons of her chemise and dropped her pantaloons as he watched her. They fell in the bed together with the impact of his tortuous kiss.

"Doc?" Wyatt laid himself across her, holding his torso off her, his furry legs adding to the sensations that were already building within her. "Tell me what you want."

"Wyatt?" How could he ask something like that? She wanted him; she wanted his touch all over, but to discuss it. Heat warmed her cheeks even though they were married.

He tugged a nipple into his mouth, his left hand tracing to her abdomen and then below, letting his hand rest between her legs rubbing wantonly. He left one nipple for the other. "I want to make you hold on so damn tight I think you'll crush me. Now what do you want, Doc?"

"Only you."

"Answer the question." His voice was a whispering growl and his rigid member rubbed against her thigh. Oh lord, but his hands touching her, his lips tasting her. He knew he was driving her crazy and she met his intense blue eyes and whispered.

"Just touch me; all of me…make me cry your name." Her words came in between her short panting breaths.

He smiled and his hand left her and pushed her thighs apart. She obliged, opening her legs for him, but he pressed further, pushing them so wide, her hips caught.

Her breath hitched as he entered her, her breasts flattened between them, her nipples puckered against the rasping hair of his chest, his breath on her neck. Her body relaxed as his hips pulled from her and pressed again. She moaned at the sensation, the fullness he brought that always tugged pleasure from deep inside. His hips rose and fell against her one solid stroke at a time until her body clenched around him of its own will.

He moaned but never changed his pace as he raised

his head to look at her. And she built, his body pressing with earnest against the nub of her each time he stroked deep inside. When her body shuddered again he raised his chest from hers and lifted himself up onto his hands, placing them on the bed on each side her, pressing against her with ferocity. How was it he sensed her reaction so well. She held his gaze as she met him stroke for stroke, tracing her hands to his hips urging him. She was almost— "Wyatt…"

And he held her, pumping as her body writhed through her climax beneath him, coursing pleasure taking her breath. She closed her legs around his hips as he lowered his chest to hers again, but never stopped the motion as he growled through his own release, his body trembling through and a final gasp leaving him. God, she loved him, and she held tighter to him wanting the crush of his large body against her own, the weight of him more comfort than she'd ever known.

She closed her eyes, his breath against her neck, his body wracked in aftershocks. And she held him, having missed him with his time in jail.

And then he whispered. "So many times, I've seen all the bad the world can hold, but every time I think of the good and beautiful things, it leads me to you, Doc."

"Hold me." She brushed the hair away from his brow and memorized his words, clinging to keep him deep inside her. This was love, this was all she'd ever dreamt of, and if she never took another breath in her life, Wyatt McCade was all she would ever need.

Chapter Twenty-Three

Miles Rollins slammed his fist on the table before the judge, agitated at his nervous personal lawyer who hadn't haggled enough to prove the deed they held. "This deed is legal according to the laws of the United States government, and I will not sit here and let anyone say otherwise."

Wyatt wanted to chuckle. With Circuit Judge Patrick Carter presiding, that wouldn't go over well. The judge jerked a glance at Rollins for a long moment, stopping the man in his verbal tracks. "The question of possible falsified deeds is in order and let me not remind you again, Mr. Rollins, while you are not sitting in an official courtroom, I make the rules here and further outbursts will find you tossed onto the streets of Cheyenne."

Rollins held his tongue, posturing in a huff back into his chair.

The judge dropped his gaze again studying the deeds Sawyer had set before him with brief explanation of the concern for deceit. Before the judge were the three land division deeds that were legal, the four-thousand McCade acres along with Brett and Marcus Benton's deeds for one-thousand acres each. The judge continued as he eyed all the documents, including the one that matched the one Rollins held. "I believe, given the McCade's and Mr. Morgan have owned this land since the time of these deeds, that I have to understand what is being presented, and you will remain quiet until I do so."

Rollins sent a scorching gaze his way, but Wyatt held his poker face, amused as the man didn't have the good sense to shut his mouth. "Judge, with respect, these men do not want to lose their land or homes, and why would they not produce these obsolete deeds, no longer current in the eyes of our fine government, in order to see our plans for progressing the railroad and the mining of copper thwarted?"

The judge ignored Rollins this time and moved the documents around. Judge Carter was a decent judge, respectable and true to his word, and at this point Sawyer seemed to be playing it right by remaining quiet.

Wyatt scanned those around the table. Sawyer sat before the judge to his left, everyone around a large table. Dodge and Brett were across from Rollins and his lawyer. Brett had remained stoic with Dodge also holding her tongue, which was amazing on both counts. Sawyer had warned them all to keep quiet and let him do the talking. He glanced to his right where Zane sat beside him fidgeting as much as ever, but interested in the court proceedings. Dawson was on the other side of Zane and had shocked them all by showing up in court in a shirt, vest, and trousers. He hardly looked like the same man without the leather tunic and buckskins. Evan had been instructed to remain with the herds with Brett still being detained except for court proceedings.

"Judge, you can compare all you like, but the fact is, this is a legal document issued on the said date and that fact cannot be denied, with all due respect, sir."

Rollins' counselor appeared as if he were sweating blood as he spoke, his eyes wide and his voice shaking.

The judge glanced up once more with his cold dark eyes. "You will refrain from telling me how to run my courtroom. Do I make myself clear?"

"Yes. I mean, yes sir, Judge. Yes, sir. Fine, Judge." The counselor stuttered, slinking back from the table.

Wyatt turned to Zane who tapped his arm and leaned closer to whisper. "Does he know about the left-handed slant?"

Wyatt gave his nephew a quick wink.

The judge glanced up, speaking to Sawyer. "Tell me again how you acquired these documents."

Sawyer took a deep breath and began. "My father purchased and sold land for a living, incredibly meticulous about legal documents and deeds, getting government issued numbers for plots of land and making two deeds for each plot. One for safekeeping and one saved in his office files. The three deeds we have presented are the six-thousand acres that my father divided in eighteen-forty-four. One thousand each to Mr. Morgan, and a man named Marcus Benton. The other four thousand he kept so each of his four sons would retain a thousand upon, well, should our mother one day pass."

Wyatt wanted to chuckle as Dodge rolled her eyes. Hell, she wasn't going anywhere soon, not that he'd want her to, but she'd likely live to be one-hundred and three.

Sawyer continued, "The copies of these deeds, the second and only copies were in crates filed at my father's railcar office years ago but were taken after my father's notary was killed. My brother, Wyatt, was able to uncover these deeds in Denver and at the same time, saw proof of recent tampering of the crates where they were held. He also found the deed you have there that is signed with a likeness, but not my father's signature, and this deed seems to match what Mr. Rollins has presented which we believe is falsified as the six thousand acres was originally sold from Jefferson Rollins to my father, John McCade, not the other way around."

Wyatt leaned back farther in his chair, folding his arms. Sawyer was playing it safe, speaking in a calm manner and telling a clear story of how things had happened.

"My father's notary, Da Ming, a Chinese, worked for my father for many years, and when he died, his things were taken by his brother and the deeds were in those crates," Sawyer explained, his gray eyes serious.

"You recovered these deeds?" The judge glanced at Wyatt.

"Tell me more of this search." The judge folded his arms behind his head, sitting back in his chair to listen.

Wyatt's pulse raced. What to tell and what not to tell. "My father's notary worked for him long before we were born. He was very meticulous in writing and copying deeds for my father's purchases and sales. You can see his fine penmanship there on all three of those deeds we own. He was the record keeper and had an incredible eye for detail. He never made mistakes or error, very precise. If he even had a blot of ink, he burned the deeds and started over."

Rollins postured, shaking his head. The top hat from New York knew most of this very story himself.

Wyatt straightened his leg, adjusting in his seat and

continued, "I happened to remember Da Ming's personal belongings were taken without my father's knowledge, retained in Denver by Da Ming's brother."

The judge angled his head with a curious gaze. "This man's brother is?"

"A Chinese named Chan, owns the meat market in Denver." He waited.

The judge gave a knowing smile. "It's a small world, the same Chan that smuggles opium among other things, I suppose?"

He nodded. "Chan was estranged from his brother at the time and hadn't a liking to work any longer for my father. Da Ming died in a railcar accident that was no accident. He was beaten, the documents were taken, and he was sent down the tracks in a burning railcar."

"So…Chan had something to do with his own brother's death?" The judge's concern was apparent with his narrowed frown.

"I saw it myself as a youngster," he added, uncertain he should have gone that far.

Judge Carter glanced at Sawyer and back. "What reason would he need those documents and what reason for such a forgery?"

"As questionable a character as Chan, I think he took the documents thinking there would be money somewhere in stocks or bonds," Sawyer answered.

Rollins piped in. "Please, Your Honor, this is preposterous and in no way plays into why we are here today."

The judge glared hard at the man.

Sawyer picked back up. "There is much more to this story than a burning railcar, and my family and I have been putting it all together for the last couple of years."

"Enlighten me." The judge leaned back in his chair once more.

Sawyer hesitated, with an apparent struggle where to begin. "A constant rival of my father, Marcus Benton had it in for Da Ming because he wouldn't falsify the deeds as he was very loyal to my father. The false deed is dated two years later, and the signature on it isn't my father's. It's the exact replica of the blank deed Wyatt located, but the signature isn't my father's hand. The inking on that deed is fresh if you look closer, and the slant of my father's signature isn't correct, and it's smudged. Da Ming's ink never blurred."

The judge grabbed both documents and held them to the light. "Where is this Marcus Benton now?"

"He was scheduled to hang for the death of my father from years before but was pardoned about the time all this trouble started." Sawyer nodded and continued, "Since his release, Wyatt was beaten and left for dead, and Dawson took a bullet a few weeks ago. This man has had a personal vendetta against our father and family for some time, and some of his scheming and planning goes back twenty years or more."

The judge pondered for a moment, then Rollins interrupted again. "Judge this is absurd. My father purchased this land from the United States Government and on his death became my own. This country wants the railroads built. Even though I have this deed, I have still assured the McCade's they may keep their home and lands. Even Mr. Morgan here was to keep his land until he blew up the copper mine *that I own*."

Brett spoke for the first time. "Mighty generous of you that the train will plow right up to their home, and a working mine will devastate the cattle business that I have spent my entire life building. I can guarantee I won't sit idle for you to take over either property."

Dodge placed a slim hand on Brett's, and he stopped talking. Shit, all they needed was Brett to escalate, and there would be bloodshed right on the premises. Wyatt exchanged glances with Sawyer, his brother then settling his gaze on Brett.

The judge studied the deeds comparing them again as he talked. "And you think this Marcus Benton is behind this deed and the actions to take over both pieces of land, using Mr. Rollins here to do so?"

Wyatt nodded along with his brothers. "They want to build a rail past the Black Hills and into Rapid City, where Benton owns a great deal of land along such a path. And that would stand to be right profitable."

"This is totally out of hand gentleman. I know of no such plans other than the ones I have placed before you." Rollins stood and raised his voice, though his counselor tugged him back to his seat.

"Mr. Rollins, might I ask the relationship you have with Marcus Benton?" The judge glared.

"I am aware of who he is. He was in the papers when he was sentenced more than a year ago. I'm afraid I don't know the full story, or nothing of his pardon." Rollins lowered his tone, and his beady eyes dropped.

"I didn't ask what you knew of his story. I asked if he is an acquaintance of yours," the judge snapped.

"Yes, I know him, but he has nothing to do with this rather outrageous concocted story." Rollins gripped his hands into tight fists.

The judge turned to Wyatt once more. "And what

of this wrong slant in your father's signature?"

Wyatt reached a hand toward the judge's inkwell and pen. "May I?"

The judge shoved the small bottle of ink and quill toward him. Wyatt pulled a small sheet of paper closer, dipped the quill and signed his full name, left-handed as he spoke. *Wyatt Zachariah McCade.* "My father was left-handed, and he taught me to write. I am left-handed and our slants were very much the same." He finished his name but didn't stop there. While the ink was still wet, he laid the paper face down on top of another. Then he drew them apart and laid them beside the false deed, and pulled the correct deed next to it. "I believe it had been inked and reversed just enough to change the signature, too much to be my father's signature."

The judge studied all the deeds for some time. He used a magnifying glass to scrutinize each, and then scanned around the room making eye contact with each person as he spoke. "Well, I believe the evidence at hand to be very clear. I am siding with the McCade's and Mr. Morgan, as the three deeds dividing the land were processed first with legal Government Issue. The one that Wyatt McCade pulled from Denver shows a clear case of forgery due to the blank deed that matches it with the falsified slant of John McCade's signature. Now, I am not saying that you, Mr. Rollins, know anything of this, but forgery can wind a man jailed for a very long time. I suggest you clean up your future endeavors."

The judge stood to the protest of Rollins who jumped up, red faced with anger. "This cannot be solved that easy. My father paid a great deal of money for all that land, and it is rightfully mine upon his death.

What about my compensation for that?"

"Take it up with the United State Government, sir." The judge turned back to Brett and Sawyer who stood. "But might I ask Mr. Morgan and Sheriff McCade, just why would this Marcus Benton benefit from this land going to Rollins?"

Sawyer stole a glance at Brett who deferred back to him with a nod. "My guess is that he would gain a percentage of the copper profit while selling land he owns in northern Wyoming clear though to Rapid City. But as you see, he isn't here, choosing to hide while others do his bidding for him."

The judge glanced at Rollins who fumbled to gather his files. "I believe you are right to assume there is a gamble to make money off miles of rail built and the sale of land. Your rebuttal to this idea?"

Rollin's stern face relaxed into a sardonic smile. "Judge with all due respect, once more this is a heinous disreputable scheme to cheat me out of doing what needs to be done to maximize the potential of the United States' railroad. As for Marcus Benton, he is not of my concern. My goal is to get the railroad spur built through to Rapid City, an up and coming town. My father purchased that land long ago, and this is robbing me of my deserved inheritance."

Finally, the judge spoke, folding his hands on the table as he leaned closer to Rollins. "Are you finished? Mr. Rollins, while I believe you have a deed that seems government issued, there are still too many questions and actual proof of forgery. In my opinion and according to the laws of Wyoming Territory, my decision is final. You may, of course, appeal at your leisure."

"Your honor, this is an absolute injustice. This is a legal deed, and of course, I will appeal as high as the supreme courts, if necessary." Rollins hissed.

The judge slammed his gavel on the block of wood and rose. "Gentleman, Mrs. McCade, I bid you a good afternoon. I will have the paperwork ready for pick up here at the bank by morning." And with that, the judge grabbed his case, loosened his tie, and stepped from the room.

Wyatt sat back in his chair and took a deep breath. The issue was hardly over, and things were about to get interesting.

As if on cue, Rollins turned looking once at his lawyer, who never made eye contact with him, and back at them all, focusing on Sawyer and Brett. "I assure you all this is by far not over." The man flung a glare at each of them. "I will appeal, and this time, to take it all, your land, your homes, your cattle, and the remaining mines." He took a breath and tromped to the door, turning back with a quick huff to them all before leaving. His lawyer scooped up the piles of paperwork before him, the tiny man hobbling to follow.

Wyatt stood, stretching his leg, and rubbing his thigh. "We may have won the battle…"

Sawyer finished for him. "But we haven't won the war."

Dodge got up from the table, adjusting her skirt. "Well, it's over for now. With this final decision, he could appeal, but that would take a heap of time and more of his precious money."

Brett spoke then, tilting his hat back and shoving his hands into the pockets of his trousers. "Needn't sit idle, boys. This roughs up Benton's plan, and when riled, he fires back first. He's not done. Not even a little."

Wyatt grabbed his hat, waved a hand through his short locks, and put the hat on his head. He didn't have to be told anything more to know Brett was right, and damn it to hell, he'd been waiting and not so patiently for long enough.

*****

The grayness of early morning streamed through the edges of the closed blinds, darkness still cast across the room. Tess woke with a start, her head pounding and nausea erupting from nowhere. She sat up, jerking from the blankets, trying not to disturb Wyatt. Trotting and pulling her hair back she was sure she wasn't going to make it to the washroom as bile rushed her throat. She bent and heaved, gagging over the porcelain basin. Nothing returned as she continued to gag, but her head whirled, sweat forming across her brow. She sucked in a breath and fought to remain standing.

"My word, where on earth did this come from…" She panted, whispering to herself as she closed her eyes and held the small counter.

She and Wyatt had eaten leftovers the night before and quite late at that. Perhaps the food had upset her stomach. She gagged again, trying to be quiet about it and thought for a moment she might pass out. This was bad, and today had promised to be a busy one. Dodge would be by early as she had planned to ride along with her to check on her patients.

"Doc?" Wyatt stood in the hallway in his long underwear. He squinted as she heaved once more, holding a hand up to stave him off.

She sucked in a breath and took the small cloth

from the counter to her mouth. She was ill, very ill. "I'm fine. I need to lay…back down. I think the food from last night…" She gagged again, still producing nothing but bile. Something was wrong. She'd been ill before but never had nausea that pulled heaves from deep inside her.

"Doc, you aren't all right, you're as pale as a ghost." He ran a hand through his messy dark hair, still squinting away his sleep.

She turned and staggered past him into the hallway, wondering if she could stop the world from spinning by lying down again. "Just need to…"

He caught her and lifted her into his arms.

"I need to lie down for a bit. I have to see my patients…this morning." She closed her eyes and hung on tight.

"You might want to think about that, Doc." He laid her on the bed and tugged the covers over her. "I'll get Dodge."

"She'll be here soon enough; she is…riding with me today." She opened her eyes. The nausea somehow gone, but the pounding inside her head brutal. Good lord, maybe she had a brain hemorrhage. No, it wasn't that, but she had something.

Wyatt laid a cool cloth across her brow, touching her forehead. "I don't think you have fever."

"Thank you." She used the cloth to wipe her face.

"I've gotta meet Sawyer this morning, but if you aren't well…" He sat on the side of the bed, resting a hand on her thigh.

"No, I'll be fine. The nausea's subsiding. I'll rest a bit, if you can get Anna hitched to the buggy for me." She smiled, though let it fade to the nausea. It had been a long time since a man fretted over her, and maybe some part of her liked it, even if it didn't seem worth the illness.

He got up and began dressing as he talked to her. "I shouldn't be long. Sawyer wants to ride, to check the pass near Brett's, to make sure Rollins' men moved everything along. You stay here if you don't get to feeling better. You can see your patients tomorrow."

"I'm sure I will be fine." She lied. She'd never had nausea hit her like that. She placed the fingers of her right hand to the wrist of her left. Her pulse was bounding, but steady and he was right, she had no fever, though her brow was damp. "You go. Dodge will be here in a short time, and I'll let her drive the buggy."

He finished dressing and stepped closer, tucking his shirt into his trousers, then leaned to kiss her forehead. "Maybe I should stay here."

"I'm a physician. These things hit and then pass. Probably the food from last night. Are you taking the new horse?" She was curious, even though another wave of nausea passed through her.

"Yep." He nodded, having picked the gelded palomino in spite of the animal's light coloring, which offered little camouflage, if it came down to it. She suspected he'd picked the horse because she had loved the color and the animal's gentle nature.

"So what did you name him?" Tess thought the animal beautiful enough to be worthy of a name.

He chuckled, his brows together. "Horse."

"He is a beautiful animal, and he deserves a real name." She giggled, then placed the cloth to her face as nausea hit once more.

He contemplated her suggestion for a moment.

"Let me see how he runs at the pass, and I'll think about it. You and Dodge don't go too far, take the pistol with you either way."

"I have it in my bag." She wanted to cringe. She'd been carrying the weapon for days now at his insistence but didn't like it one bit. Guns were dangerous, and even though he'd taught her to shoot the darn thing, she hoped she never had to use it. "I've gotta check on poor Mr. Golden as the fall from that ladder was a bad one, and I've got two expecting mothers."

He held her gaze. "Maybe I should ride along?"

"Where are you and Sawyer riding off to anyway?" Dodge moseyed in carrying her large sun bonnet and a lunch basket.

He glanced at his mother as he stepped into his boots. "Probably out to check the pass, make sure things are clear. But the doc is feeling rather poorly."

Dodge set the basket and hat aside. "Tess?"

"I'm fine, we ate a late supper, and it didn't agree with me I suppose." She closed her eyes as Dodge placed a hand to her forehead.

"Well, you have no fever." Dodge sat on the bed beside her.

Wyatt grabbed his hat, kissed her forehead, and plopped it on his head. "If you aren't back in a few hours, I'm coming for you."

"I'll be fine." She gave him a forced smile.

He lingered a moment more, and she waited until his boots had clomped down the front stairs to look at Dodge.

"If I can rest for a bit, I think the nausea is passing." She sat up and propped the pillow better behind her head. And come to think of it, her head had lessened its pounding, and while she thought it was the food from the night before, she was of all things, very hungry.

Dodge considered her for a long moment, tilting her head.

"Oh, you worry for nothing. I'll get dressed, and I think if I have a bit of broth, I'll feel much better." Why wasn't she saying anything? "What?"

Dodge folded her arms. "Did this illness catch you this morning?"

Tess nodded, and then frowned. Why was her mother-in-law and best friend glaring at her with that look of certainty and knowing?

"And you and Wyatt have been intimate for quite a while now?" Dodge questioned, calculating in her head and settling her gaze back on Tess.

"Dodge!" At first Tess was put off by her inquisition, but then a jolt of nerves flickered through her as she caught the real meaning. No, that wasn't even possible, was it? "Dodge, I hardly think that is the case." She'd been disappointed so many times in the past, and Dodge, of all people, knew how painful that had been for her.

"When was your last monthly?" Dodge wasn't letting the issue go.

She tried to remember, then it dawned on her. It had been at least six to seven weeks before. Oh, lord in heaven, could she be carrying a child? She sat farther up in bed, hardly able to take a breath—pregnant with Wyatt's child. "Six weeks, maybe seven. I've been…so busy. Dodge?" Her voice cracked at the hope.

"Well, I would say things are very clear, and you are indeed not sick. You, Doctor Elizabeth Sullivan

McCade, are pregnant." Her mother-in-law beamed with pride.

Tess shook her head and burst into tears. This couldn't be true, and she could hardly let herself think it might be. "How on earth can that be?"

Dodge chuckled and sat again on the bed hugging her close. "The McCade men are rather potent."

She giggled, covering her mouth. "I should know better than to ever be surprised by what comes out of your mouth."

Dodge stood. "I speak things as they are, and I happen to have had four sons, and what you need right now is a hearty breakfast to stave off the nausea. Every night, leave a small snack at the bedside to gobble before you move in the mornings, and you can fight it off."

She thought of Wyatt and talked through her happy tears. "Wyatt said children didn't matter, that we could perhaps adopt one day and he…will he be happy?"

"He will be as happy as you, Tess. As happy as I am this very minute." Dodge kissed her cheek. "Congratulations, Doctor."

Tess used the sheets to wipe her eyes, her pulse racing along with her thoughts. "How could I not know this?"

"You have been busy, but I knew right away with all of my boys except Dawson. I was so busy caring for Sawyer and Wyatt. I didn't have time to think of being pregnant, though I knew when Evan came along later." Dodge reminisced and turned for the door.

"Dodge?" Tess sat to the side of the bed. "I want to be the one to tell Wyatt."

Dodge smiled. "Of course you do, and your secret

is safe with me. Enjoy this time. Embrace the days even when it's hard and even when you are ill. There is nothing like a baby kicking and moving inside and knowing that it's a part of you both."

Tess waited until Dodge was busy in the kitchen. She touched her low belly. How had she not known? And what would Wyatt say? They both thought her unable to conceive. So perhaps her issues when married to Israel hadn't been due to her own body, but his. Sadness gripped her for a moment, but she rubbed her belly and smiled through the tears. Life was unpredictable, and once again her life had taken another turn. "Your Daddy will be so proud." And then she let go of the real tears, crying for the woman who had so wanted a child, for the husband she'd lost and for Wyatt, who had deserved this moment and her love long before now.

Chapter Twenty-Four

Wyatt dismounted outside the jail, tying the palomino to the hitching post. He patted the animal, happy with his sturdy mount, a comfortable ride for his size. He entered the jail office, swiping the hat from his head, ready for a real ride to see how well he'd done in his choice. He'd been on the horse and galloped along a bit, but he hadn't given his full efforts where the new horse or his leg was concerned.

Sawyer glanced up, signed the ledger before folding the book closed, and slid it aside. Across the room, Zane swept the floor, glancing up but returning to the task.

"How's the horse?" Sawyer stood and grabbed his hat from the hook by the door, his brother as anxious for the jaunt.

"He's a good animal, thinking about naming him, leastwise Tess says I should because she thinks he's *pretty*." Wyatt smirked. Maybe he would name the animal to please her if nothing else, but there weren't many bounty hunters famed by the riding of a pretty horse, especially one with the fair coloring.

His brother chuckled and followed him outside. "You coming, Zane?"

"Yes, sir, can't pass up a chance to race a horse with no name." Zane tossed the broom aside and joined them, grabbing the reins to his own horse and quickly mounting up.

Wyatt tugged himself to the saddle, the burden of his full weight on his left leg still not easy when climbing up. There was no doubt Zane's mustang mix would win given that was what it was bred for, but it would be nice to ride hard and feel the wind across his face. "I don't know. This horse is strong, might give Shadow a run for his money."

He hit the reins and the horse took to a trot, Sawyer close behind him on Colonel and Zane bringing up the rear with his comment. "Well, I know Shadow will get to the pass first, but the question remains who will take the win between Colonel and yours."

Well, there was nothing like a challenge even if his leg ached. Sawyer's horse, Colonel, was damn fast and for a reason. There were times a sheriff needed a fast horse for escape, but he was a temperamental animal. He responded to Sawyer most of the time, but on his own terms bringing his brother to curses.

Sawyer gave Zane a wink. "Colonel can take him; we'll say go outside of town."

"Wasted breath boys, this animal wants to run." Wyatt tugged the reins, the new horse anxious to move faster. "You heard anything more from Rollins?"

"Naahhh. He packed it all up and headed toward Denver, and an appeal should take him months. Just want to make sure he got all the equipment from the rail at the pass farther down from Brett's." Sawyer stood in the stirrups and settled to comfort in the saddle.

"Well, I doubt it's done." Wyatt scanned the countryside. He, like his brothers, had been on the ready. Though there had been nothing from Marcus Benton, uneasiness had ridden with him all morning.

He'd pushed it aside, thinking it the worry over Tess being ill, but he wasn't so sure. He glanced behind him. Just because things were quiet didn't mean they were still.

Sawyer narrowed his gaze on Zane, who rode ahead. "Yep, but men like Rollins don't give up, and we both know Benton isn't done."

The comment surprised him as Sawyer hadn't been sharing much of his thoughts where Benton was concerned. But that was how his brother did things, thinking, watching, and waiting. He had no patience for that when it came down to it. He'd given up sharpening the knife in his boot. Hell, the thing was now sharper than the razor he used to trim his beard each morning. He scanned the rolling prairie once more as they caught up with Zane. The early morning sun was bright and sweat ran down his back at the intense heat. No matter, it was good to be back on a horse and for more than a slow ride. The horse could feel it too, tugging against the reins for the run. Well, it was time, past damn time. His leg was healed and whether his brother knew it or not, this ride would tell him a thing or two about how much and what his nearly healed body was capable of taking.

Zane turned Shadow and the horse reared, kicking his front legs high in the air. "I'll give you boys a head start."

"That's a bit cocky given you don't know much about my horse." Wyatt raised an eyebrow and lined his horse up, grinning at his nephew.

"This is gonna be easy." Zane gave him a knowing smile.

Wyatt chuckled along with his brother. Zane's

enthusiasm did something of bringing him back to his own youth, when he and his brothers had raced their various horses.

Sawyer measured up with Colonel, lining him up with the other horses. “A head start huh? To the curve in the road?”

Zane gathered Shadow’s reins and glanced toward the bend Sawyer had nodded to. “All right.”

Wyatt met gazes with Sawyer, both counting off and on the mark, taking their horses to the wind. That Zane had given them a head start might help, but the new horse took to the kick and left Colonel by a length. Damn fast. Maybe he did deserve a name.

The wind hit his face, and he closed his eyes for a half second, wanting to feel the animal against the earth. He’d missed riding for speed. This was where he felt free, this and when he was wrapped within Tess’ arms.

He thought again about the night before, when he coaxed her body to yield to him. Watching her tremble and clench and hearing her soft cries, was enough to drive a man damn insane. She was so beautiful and while he’d loved her since the first day he’d ever laid eyes on her, it wasn’t until now that he knew what love was all about. Having her meant hope and forgiveness and each day being a new journey together. And now he was getting soft, he kicked the horse to urge him faster.

The muscles in his leg tightened and his foot tried to cramp against his boot. A little pain was good and a reminder Marcus Benton was near. He glanced behind him, his senses taking over where his mind wanted to remain rational. He couldn’t shake the feeling something was wrong somewhere and it didn't have to do with the current race. Sawyer and Colonel now rode a full two lengths behind him, and Zane's horse Shadow was bringing up the rear.

He rode harder, letting the reins slack. His horse stretched to full length, but Zane rode comfortable and loose, never looking at either him or his father as he passed them both, his lighter weight to his advantage. Wyatt leaned in closer to the horse, but Zane flew ahead with Colonel closing in close behind.

Wyatt clucked his tongue. His horse found a bit more energy, catching Shadow's tail wind with Sawyer's Colonel at his flank. Wind hit his face along with the sting of dust. He squinted, loosened his grip, and let the horse run on his own.

Zane pulled ahead by a length or more leaving them behind. So, it was he and Sawyer. Colonel against no name. Brother against brother. He urged the horse, neck and neck, racing as when youngsters. Glancing at Sawyer, he caught his brother's half smile as Colonel nosed ahead. He kicked again, and the horse beneath him picked up the pace and took a head past Sawyer just as they met their mark. He'd beaten his brother and ran the animal farther turning right and watching as Sawyer reined Colonel to the left both animals slowing.

Sawyer leaned across the saddle horn, catching his breath. "You got us."

Wyatt nodded, but was uncertain if he could get off his horse with the pain in his leg. He leaned down to rub his calf. "Barely, brother, but we both take the loss."

Zane was all smiles, but at least humble. "He likes to run as much as Shadow and Colonel."

Wyatt gave the horse a pat. “Looks to be so, but Shadow remains the champion.”

“He’s bred for it.” Zane pulled his hat off and wiped his sweaty brow with the sleeve of his shirt. His gray eyes were so much like Sawyer’s it was like seeing his brother again at a younger age.

Zane stood in the stirrups, glancing in the distance. “Hey!”

Sawyer and Wyatt followed his gaze. In the meadow they had raced through was a mare, still a single rope around her neck, hanging free and dragging behind her.

“Dawson’s mare.” Sawyer grabbed his looking glass as Wyatt turned his horse.

“I’ll get her.” Zane galloped off in her direction.

“Careful.” Sawyer warned.

Wyatt rubbed his thigh. “He’ll be fine. He’s got one just like her.” It was true. Shadow was a horse that was hard to handle for all, except Zane. The boy and horse had a bond like no other.

“Dawson said the mare was even tempered. He’ll be glad to have her back.” Sawyer glanced around them.

“Well, as least she didn’t end up with Benton and his men. And it looks like the railroad’s thwarted plans left the area clear.” Wyatt urged his horse to follow Sawyer, not having been out to the point since Brett had blown the mine.

“I figured, but he’ll still file his damn appeal.” Sawyer stopped Colonel, scanning the area.

“He won’t get far—”

Rifle fire scattered across the ground around them, startling the horses and sending them both from their mounts. Wyatt scrambled for his rifle from the saddle. Damn, his leg. Scouring pain clamped down on his ankle. He'd landed too hard, though he limped after Sawyer, letting his horse go. *What the hell?*

"Shit!" Sawyer rolled into the high grass, lifting his revolvers.

"Son of a..." Wyatt slid in place on the ground next to him, cursing the pain in his ankle. His horse trotted to follow Colonel, toward the tree line behind them.

"You hit?" Sawyer looked up toward the blown mine with its covering of charred boulders and fallen trees.

"I'm good." He laid the rifle beside him on the ground and pulled a revolver. He normally held both, but his right hand still didn't give him straight aim, the heavy revolver painful to cock.

"How many you count?" Sawyer peered off toward where Zane had gone for the mare, now out of sight.

"Three, one rifle and two pistols." Wyatt answered, having heard the three distinct weapons.

"Three." Sawyer held steady, revolver poised, eyes narrowed.

Wyatt glimpsed the side of the rise. With the mine blown, there were downed trees and lots of charred wood in fallen piles. Shambles of rock and bare dirt were piled at the mine's entrance, giving cover to their attacker and leaving them sitting ducks in the high grass.

They waited, brother to brother, for a breath of seconds and as the smoke cleared from the haze of rifle fire, a voice echoed across the ridge. "John McCade was prophet according to these parts."

Wyatt's blood turned to ice and his pulse stopped for an instant. Marcus Benton. "Well, at least the bastard finally showed."

"He can't have been here for long." Sawyer's voice was steady as he held his revolver, still searching for Zane. "Hudson tracked him to Aurora, outside Denver a day or so ago."

Wyatt lifted the site on his rifle, closing one eye and scanning the clutter at the opening of the mine. "Thanks for sharing the news. The son of a bitch knew we'd be back here, sooner or later, and Hudson had better watch his back."

Benton continued his words echoing around them. "Some people in these parts think he walked on water, but the sins of the father will be paid by his sons."

"Where is he?" Wyatt whispered, squinting against the sun. All he needed was a glimpse, and he'd fire whether his brother liked it or not.

Sawyer spoke back in the same whisper. "Quiet. It's echoing due to the mine. He's near the mouth."

Wyatt gazed across the fallen opening. *Just step out you bastard.*

"Wyatt McCade, didn't I leave you to your fate? I'll have to do a better job next time." Benton's guttural laughter roared across the distance.

Wyatt's gritted his teeth, the bitter need for revenge coursing through his entire being. "What are you waiting for?"

His words were met with a spray of bullets that plowed up the earth all around them. Sawyer ducked, covering his head, but Wyatt grabbed his rifle, taking aim where the fire sparked near the mine. He waited a second more and pulled the trigger. A yelp emerged from the fallen trees at the front of the mine. One down. He smiled at Sawyer with satisfaction, but his brother turned to look for Zane again.

"You know Wyatt; there are worse things than death." Benton's voice filled the void. "If you want to see the doctor again, Eleanor and Morgan will sign those deeds over in full to Miles Rollins."

Wyatt's heart all but stopped, physical pain searing right through the middle of his chest as if a shotgun blast had taken him. Not Tess. He wouldn't let her be a pawn in this game. He gulped for breath, the visceral pain so deep he wasn't sure the air entered. "I'll kill that fucking bastard with my bare hands."

Sawyer grabbed him, his voice strained at the effort of keeping him down. "You don't know he has her. Dodge was with her, she'd shoot him in a heartbeat. This doesn't make sense. He couldn't be here and have had time…"

Wyatt pushed harder still, fighting off his brother's fists, rolling across the shotgun. "Let go Sawyer, before I hurt you." If Marcus Benton had Tess, he'd cut the man's heart out with a spoon, but their movement gave them away, and more gunfire shook the ground around them.

"There's Zane to think about. Now sit still." Sawyer growled, still holding tight.

Wyatt lessened his fight and hit the ground with a fist, the hard earth crushing to sand beneath it. Benton had Tess and he knew it. The uneasy feeling from earlier hadn't led him wrong.

Sawyer eased his grip with the next spray of bullets, and Wyatt scrambled up. His brother cursed behind him as he stood erect and stepped ahead. "All right, you got her, and right here, and right now you got me. But regardless what happens, you will never own McCade or Morgan lands."

"Wyatt!" Sawyer yelled at him in a loud whisper.

He stood still, though his pulse pounded through his head. He and Sawyer had dealt with situations like this for years. When dealing with hostages they didn't give in. Giving in meant certain death for the one in jeopardy. By holding out, he was in charge of the game. That Marcus Benton was before him meant Tess had been taken by his men. He waited, expecting a bullet right through his chest.

"Very unwise, McCade." Benton surfaced from the mine, revolver in hand and the cronies with him stood with their rifles poised, one bleeding from the shoulder, but still maintaining his weapon.

Benton cleared the rubble. "Oh, I can assure you her safety—for now."

Wyatt held his tongue, it being insane he was standing out in the open and holding both revolvers at ready, not that he'd be accurate with his weakened right hand.

"I give you a week, of which time the deeds for McCade and Morgan lands will be signed over to Rollins, or it will be such a pity for the beautiful doctor to meet with disaster. Wouldn't that be a shame?" Benton laughed sadistically, his voice echoing.

"You hurt her in any way, and there will be no force this side of hell to stop me from taking you down," Wyatt yelled, his voice steady and sure. He was in prime position, and the fastest draw if it came down to it, but Benton had him because he had Tess.

"There *are* worse things than death, check mate,

Wyatt McCade." Benton's chuckle vibrated around him, but the man's fondness of chess wasn't amusing, and this was no game of chess where Tess was concerned.

A rifle shot blasted the dirt at Benton's feet, and the man lost his balance, tucking back near the mouth of the mine. Benton's men plowed up the area with gunfire in retaliation. Wyatt ducked once more, avoiding a hit as he came up with his revolvers still in hand.

"Holy hell!" Sawyer fired rapid rounds from his rifle, taking careful aim.

Out of the smoke, Benton made off on his horse, riding hard toward the north, away from the mine, but his men continued to fire.

"Where's Zane?" Wyatt asked, firing back at the men. It was apparent his nephew had in sorts saved the day with the blast, but Benton was getting away.

"Not sure, but I believe he bought you time," Sawyer spat. "We both know if he'd have tried to hit Benton, he'd be laying dead."

Wyatt ducked along with his brother as Benton's men hammered gun fire too close for comfort. His brother was right. Zane was an accurate shot from any distance and chances were he had fired for distraction and to give Wyatt a quick escape. But that was short lived as Benton's men gave them no breathing room.

Zane continued firing, but Wyatt couldn't tell from where. One of Benton's men fell with a scream, the other taking a hit and disappearing behind the mine and riding off the same path Benton had taken.

Sawyer stood, rifle remaining poised.

Wyatt jumped up, making his way to the mouth of

the mine. Benton's man was dead which would add to the issues they were already dealing with. But he didn't have time to worry with that. He had to get back to town to make sure about Tess. Nausea hit the pit of his stomach, and his belly rolled as he turned for the clearing. Where had the damn horses gone? He took a chance and whistled.

Zane galloped in on Shadow, holding his rifle across his lap and Dawson's mare tied along. He said little as he dismounted, Sawyer trotting toward them.

"I thought it might be the one way to stop them." Remorse filled his nephew's voice.

Sawyer spoke to his shaken son. "You didn't have much choice, son, and good or bad, it never feels like the right thing." Sawyer untied the mare from Shadow and continued, "Take Shadow for our horses, I'll get this one loaded up on the mare."

"Well, I'll be damned," Wyatt whispered. The palomino had stayed close by and had responded to the whistle, coming right to him. He took the reins and climbed into the saddle. Looking back once he was all but sure he would suffocate before he got back to town. His chest was crushing in on him and his mind was spinning. Tess. Anything, but her. He kicked hard and the horse took off against the wind.

"Wyatt, no!" Sawyer called to him, but he never stopped, even to the sound of his brother's heated curses. Maybe, Benton was bluffing, and Tess would be there in town waiting on him. Dodge had been with her, and if they had been far enough from town, Benton's men wouldn't have found them. He urged the horse ahead, leaning into the wind, terror streaking through him. He thought his heart might explode in trying to breathe. He'd lost Tess once, and he'd not let that happen again—ever. And while Marcus Benton didn't bluff, he was a walking dead man.

When Cheyenne came into view, he was aware that behind him, Sawyer was gaining, mounted on Colonel and racing hard. Well, his brother needn't stop him at this point. He'd take down Marcus Benton, as soon as he knew what had happened for sure. The man had always pushed the edge, but this time he had crossed the line.

Sawyer caught him, out of breath. from racing. "Wyatt, you don't know what's happened."

He said nothing and pushed his horse harder toward Cheyenne. Regardless if Benton had Tess, it was his men who had taken her; the bastard couldn't be in two places at once. There might be the chance he could track those men and get her back. His gut clenched again at thinking of her in Benton's possession. He couldn't fathom it. She had to be frightened and the thought crushed him.

He slowed his horse, heading past the depot and then the saloon, riding right up to the jail. He dismounted ignoring the throbbing pain in his ankle. He tied the horse, giving the winded animal a pat on the rump as it watered in the trough. Sawyer dismounted beside him, tying Colonel and leaning against the animal to catch his own breath.

Wyatt's body shook in a rage he wasn't sure he could control, and he didn't know what to do first. He couldn't breathe. He turned a full circle, jerking his hat off and running his fingers through his dark hair, confused as hell and coming apart one second at a time. He needed to pack his gear, things for the trail, a staple of food, and more ammunition. He needed a damn shot of whiskey. He needed—Tess.

“Dodge?” Sawyer turned abruptly, taking off on a run.

Wyatt followed close on his heels. Dodge was driving the buggy toward them. Tess’ horse Anna, struggling at the pace.

“What happened?” Sawyer stopped the horse, running to the carriage and assisting a disheveled Dodge from the wagon. She had scrapes across her face and her wrist was wrapped in her shawl and bleeding through, dripping to the dirt at their feet.

Wyatt’s heart sank in the truth being realized, his pulse all but stopping.

“Men came on us with horses…” Dodge stepped to the ground. “We tried to fight them, but there were too many. They took Tess. We both fought hard, Wyatt, but I couldn’t stop them. Marcus did this didn’t he, the rotten coward.” Dodge fell into Sawyer’s arms, unsteady and near tears.

“Which direction, Dodge?” Wyatt asked, figuring they had headed in the direction of Denver just where Benton would have turned when he was out of sight

“West.” Dodge eyed the other side of town, finding her stance. “Wyatt?” She focused on him leaning into Sawyer, holding her injured arm to her chest. “Tess was ill this morning because she…is with child.”

Wyatt took a step back, moving his head back and forth in disbelief, no words leaving his open mouth. What had she said? Confusing thoughts flooded his head. Tess pregnant? But she couldn’t be, could she?

“She wanted to be the one to tell you, but you have to find her son, hurry…” Dodge’s voice faded, and she collapsed, Sawyer lifting her in his arms and taking her toward the clinic. "Send Zane to bring Rose back here, and you wait, Wyatt, and I damn well mean it."

A jagged arrow had pierced Wyatt's heart and torn its way through. He'd hardly ever seen Dodge cry, and he'd never seen her pass out. His knees tried to buckle, and he slammed his fists hard into the side of the buggy, ignoring the pain in his weak right hand. Tess was with child, pregnant…but how? She'd not been able to conceive and…a baby, his child. Marcus Benton would die a slow and agonizing death if it was the last thing he ever did.

"Wyatt?" Zane's voice turned him. The boy had ridden in with the mare carrying the dead man's body, and he wouldn't know much of what to do.

Wyatt swallowed the bile that had risen in his throat. "Benton's got Tess and Dodge is hurt. Go straight to the ranch and have one of the hands bring Rose here. Send another to ride for Evan and Brett. You stay with Mei Ling and your brothers. Go now!"

Wyatt grabbed the reins to the mare. "Send another hand out to get Dawson at his cabin."

"Yes, sir." Zane turned Shadow, riding out of town once more, the boy disheveled and white as a ghost.

Wyatt glanced at the dead man on the back of Dawson's mare. Blood dripped from the man and ran down the horse dripping, falling to the ground. He'd take the body to Henry at the end of town. Wasn't like this man needed more than a hole in the ground being he worked for the likes of Marcus Benton. His pulsed raced as he headed toward the church. Time was wasting, and he had to get on the trail.

West. Dodge had said they headed that direction.

That meant one thing. Benton's men had taken Tess to Denver. Chan's would be the one place the man could hide. He took a deep breath, eyeing the mid-day sun. Two to three days hard riding, being the train wouldn't run for another few days. Hell, he'd be faster on a horse anyway, and once he checked that Dodge was all right, he'd be on his way to slit Marcus Benton's throat.

****

"I'm fine." Dodge fussed as Sawyer used a cool cloth to clean the knuckles of her right hand.

"Hold still," his brother scolded. "And start from the beginning."

Wyatt said nothing, though he was falling apart on the inside and filled with a rage he was sure he couldn't hold for long. Apparently, his mother had a nice right hook, but that wasn't a surprise, the woman had taken on the likes of many men and women in her past. She was tough as they came and he had a feeling the men who'd taken Tess were nursing their own wounds between the fight she and Dodge had put up.

"I told you, it wasn't Marcus, but three of his men. They came out of nowhere, and one grabbed the horse. The other two the buggy. They said very little in taking Tess. We both fought hard, but they got her from the buggy and the other held me, though I kicked him right in his trousers. When he doubled over, I ran to grab Tess, but that man had a knife. I still tried, but he grabbed her and put her on the horse with him and they all rode away." She tugged her fist from Sawyer. "It's fine, but Rose will need to stitch this." She held up the wrist for Sawyer to wrap for the time being.

Wyatt met his mother's gaze.

"I tried so hard, Wyatt. I begged them to take me

instead." Dodge fought tears, swallowing hard, as discouraged as he'd ever seen her.

"I'll get her back," he said, surprised at the audible stress in his voice. He couldn't breathe. He wouldn't lose her, not now or ever again, and he was losing time.

Rose trotted into the room in a hurried flurry of skirts. "Sawyer?"

He hugged back her tears and nudged her toward Dodge. "Her arm is cut pretty bad."

"Dodge, oh my lands." Rose gave her a hug and slowly unwrapped her wrist and looked at the wound.

"I'm all right." Dodge held her arm out, where she sat on the exam table. "Stitch it up and there's some sulfur salve in the cabinet there to keep it from becoming infected."

"And Tess. Zane said she was taken?" Rose turned to Sawyer, tears streaming down her face as she glanced at Wyatt.

Sawyer nodded, his gray eyes dark. "Benton ambushed us at the blown mine, lucky enough Zane had ridden off to get Dawson's mare he'd sighted earlier. But it's Benton's men who attacked Dodge and Tess, taking her. "

"And I assume there's no need to hold this a secret anymore. Tess is with child." Dodge spoke it again and Wyatt's heart stopped for a brief second.

"But Tess couldn't…" Rose glanced up from Dodge's injuries.

"It appears that situation has remedied itself." Dodge rested her gaze on Wyatt.

"Time's wastin'." Wyatt placed a hand on Dodge's cheek and turned to leave the room. He limped as he paced down the darkened hallway, Sawyer behind him.

He took one glance into the bedroom that had become his own with Tess. He could see her, smell her, feel her, and he would get her back come the wrath of hell itself.

He turned to his brother. “You know this won’t end well, and I can’t ask you to go. You have a family to think about.” Either he or Marcus Benton would die before it was all over, and Sawyer damn well knew it.

All Sawyer did was nod, checking his weapons and glancing behind him once at Rose. “And if it were my family, you’d do the same.”

Wyatt’s chest tightened the air thin as he fought his emotions and swallowed the thick lump in his throat. He and his brother had fought side by side since a young age, but this wasn’t an outlaw robbing a bank or train. This was the man who had menaced his family for all these years, had his father killed, and had now taken his wife.

Sawyer hugged Rose once more. “Zane will watch out for you, Mei Ling, and the boys.”

She wiped her tears, touched his cheek, and offered him a gentle supportive smile. “I love you, Sawyer, come home to us.”

Then of all things, Rose stepped from her husband and then to him, wrapping her arms around his middle. “Bring her home, Wyatt. I’ll be praying every day.”

Wyatt blinked hard, letting her go and led the way outside to the porch. Lifting his gaze, he froze. Before him were Dawson, Evan and beside them, Brett Morgan, standing next to their saddled horses, ready to ride with him.

“This time, you don’t go alone, brother.” Dawson handed him the reins to the palomino, fully saddled and packed.

Brett tilted his hat back. "Been a long time coming."

Evan held his gaze, his younger brother humbled for once, saying nothing.

Sawyer stepped off the porch and shoved his rifle into the saddle, mounted Colonel and faced him.

Wyatt eyed each man in turn. "When we get to Denver, Marcus Benton is mine." Mounting up, he pulled the palomino ahead to lead the way. They were all aware of the stakes in this game, and he had no doubts about what he stood to lose.

Chapter Twenty-Five

Tess sat in a fancy Asian decorated room on silk covered bedding. If nothing else, it had been comfortable to rest on a real bed after three days on a horse night and day, not that she'd slept. The men who had taken her had said very little, but other than the immediate skirmish of her capture, they had been very polite in making sure she drank and ate and the ties on her wrists were not too tight. She was well aware, even though they had blindfolded her during the night that she was deep inside Chan's meat market in Denver. The coppery smell of blood and animal wafted through the small room now and again, and the sweet fragrance of Chinese spices caused her stomach to groan in hunger.

She'd thought of refusing the food and water she'd been given on the trail, but she had to eat for the health of her baby. Tears filled her eyes. She hadn't had the chance to tell Wyatt he was going to be a father. She'd been in this same room for hours now, but had yet to see anyone save the very large Chinese man who had shoved her in the room and opened the door once in the last few hours to make sure she was still there. She had tried the doorknob and it had been locked, but she wouldn't make it to the end of the long hallway or out of the compound without being discovered.

Wyatt would come for her. He would, though she had to wonder how long it would take, and at what cost.

Even if she hadn't seen him, the men who had taken her worked for Marcus Benton, and that made things incredibly frightening. She'd been around him several times in the past, and once had even helped him when he'd fallen ill. He'd always been very well spoken and paid her in excess, but there was something of evil that always surrounded the man. No one had spoken his name, but she was well aware she'd been taken by him.

The Chinese man opened the door again speeding toward her and grabbing her arm. "Come."

She jerked her arm free, scowling at him but following. He smirked at her and led her down the long hallway to a set of four steps and into a room on the right. There, he bowed and left her alone. She had the slight urge to bow back to him, given it was something she had often done with greeting Mei Ling over the years.

She glanced around the room at the beautiful Asian rugs hanging on the walls and the finely set table with its porcelain dishes carrying designs from China. The red silk curtains that covered the windows were of finer silk than any of her dresses, the quick glimpse showing the darkness from outside. So, what now, dinner? She turned as an elderly Chinese man entered the room, the silver eye giving him away. Chan.

He stopped before her and bowed holding his posture until she did likewise.

She'd seen him the night before in the darkness when her blindfold had been removed, and she had been whisked away to the fancy bedroom.

He stood erect again and met her gaze with one good eye for longer than made her comfortable, and it was clear. He was trying to intimidate her, and as was his culture the women would drop their eyes. She would not give him that satisfaction. She stood taller and forced herself not to look away. It reminded her of the times in medical school that she had been placed in front of the lead physicians to explain the actions she had taken for a patient's care and because she was a woman, they were more than harsh at trying to trip her up. She held the old Chinaman's gaze with purpose.

"I suppose no formal introduction needed. I hear many good things about lady doctor." He smiled, but it wasn't genuine as his one eye scanned her up and down.

"No. Mr. Chan, they are not." She let him know she was well aware who he was and where they were.

He pointed to the table, speaking in his broken English. "Please, I had fine meal prepare in your honor this evening."

She looked on as two Chinese women emerged from behind the silk curtain to set the table with various dishes of stewing meats, steamed rice and vegetables. Her stomach groaned again as the fragrances wafted around them, strongly sweet. She was so hungry, too long since her last meal and nausea edged through her. She fought the urge to gag, not wanting him or any others to know she was pregnant. Mind over matter…at least for a little while. She sat with caution as he did.

He picked up a dish spooning pieces to his plate and handing it to her. "Spicy pork." Pork, with all she had smelled for the last few hours. Her stomach turned, but she had to eat something. Perhaps she would put the meat on her plate and eat the rice.

She took the dish and as he did, placed a few pieces on her fancy porcelain plate. The thing she had to do was play along and learn as much as possible. If she behaved, she would be treated better than if she acted out and she couldn't chance getting hurt for the baby's sake. She eyed the chair to her right at the head of the table where a third place setting waited.

"We will have guest soon." Chan passed a bamboo basket of white rice to her. She used the wooden spoon to add a small pile to her plate. He continued eating as she lifted the meat to her mouth with the use of chopsticks. Had it not been for Mei Ling, she wouldn't know how to use them. She chewed the spicy pork and coughed, reaching for the small porcelain cup of steaming tea before her.

"Spice very strong." He chuckled gruffly though he never looked up at her.

"It's fine." She lied and her next bite was of the white fluffy rice. Was this how she would be held, with a fancy room closed off to the outside world and fine dining? "I'd like to know why I have been abducted."

Chan continued with his chewing, his expression unchanging. He had thinning hair, though the length of his white hair was braided, hanging down his back. He wore a yellow silk shirt trimmed in black, with pull through buttons and high collar neck. He took another bite of his food, ignoring her question.

"I have patients to care for, and they are at risk without me checking on them." She did worry of those in her care, but right now she needed to know what was planned where she was concerned.

The curtain to her left flung open and she jumped. Before her stood Marcus Benton. She hadn't seen him since he'd been sent back East for sentencing, and while he appeared basically the same, he'd aged. His beard was full of gray and so was his hair. He was tanned from the sun, but his evil dark eyes remained just the same.

He removed his hat and adjusted his chair with a nod to her. “I hope, Doctor, that you have found the accommodations to your liking.”

She fought her racing pulse with a gulp of air. “The accommodations are well enough, though I don’t understand why you have brought me here.”

Benton piled a heap of rice, then pork to his plate and began eating along with Chan, at first ignoring her question.

“Unfortunately, Doctor Sullivan, oh, sorry, Dr. McCade is it now?” His dark eyes scoured across her. “I do apologize for the inconvenience, but it’s what I call one of the necessary evils to let’s say, make the move on a rather large game of chess.”

Tess held his gaze, determined to keep eye contact. “I have always been fair to you and your men when you had injuries. As I recall, I kept you alive when you fell ill several years ago.”

He nodded, drawing his lips in a frown. “Yes, Doctor, your diplomatic and efficient care has been appreciated. But now your services are needed to create a little havoc for your—*husband*.”

She was well aware of his reasons and while she was afraid, she would never let him know that. She hadn’t lived all these years in the rugged West to back down that easy, and she was a physician, capable of holding her ground against any man in conversation. “Tell me, Mr. Benton, is the land you seek worth all that you, the McCade’s, and Mr. Morgan have paid over the years.”

His eyes narrowed, cold and black. "You're being the pawn, the one most at risk in this game, is unfortunate doctor, but I need you to control your husband, and we both know it won't take much for Wyatt to rush to your rescue. When he does, I won't leave room for error again."

Tess held his gaze, her pulse racing. She had already figured she'd been taken because Mr. Benton knew Wyatt would fight for her. And whether or not he got the land he wanted, Wyatt would come, as nothing on God's green earth would stop him. "Wyatt will kill you."

The slap to her face snapped her head back. For a moment she was dumbfounded. She fought tears as she remembered to take a breath, glaring at him in disbelief and placing the back of her hand to her stinging lip, where blood threatened to drip.

His dark eyes pierced through her once more. "I will have the land, but better than that I will have the showdown with Wyatt McCade that has been coming for years. It would be wise for you to hold your tongue, madam. Do I make myself clear?"

"Yes." She answered trying not to let her voice crack and remained quiet as the two men went about chatting on the price of illegal whiskey from China. It was surprising how Chan had not even reacted to Mr. Benton hitting her. It was as if he were in a stupor, not seeing the things around him. She took a moment to focus on eating once more, if for nothing else for the baby and when she finished she took a chance to speak once more. "I would like to return to the room where I am being kept."

Benton glanced at her plate and held her gaze with

a nod.

Chan snapped his fingers. “Zihao.”

The large Chinese man returned, waiting with a bowed head, and she placed her napkin on the table and spoke to Chan. “I thank you for the gracious meal.”

Benton stood, and she examined him saying nothing. How could he think manners were important given he’d just slapped her? She turned from the table and followed Zihao, then waited as he’d locked her inside the small fancy room.

She moved to the tiny glass window that had been boarded up. There was a small corner where she could see the darkness of the sky. The stars were visible and Wyatt would be following them to find her. And her prayers were for him and for the tiny life inside her. “Oh, God, please protect them both.”

Marcus Benton was a ruthless man. She touched her swollen lip, it occurring to her that she had never been hit by anyone in her life until now. He had knocked her senseless and her top lip was swollen three times its size. It would take Wyatt several days’ ride to get to Denver, but what then?

She thought of Dodge who’d fought hard to keep her from being taken. Her friend had been beaten and cut and in spite of her injuries had still tried to keep the men at bay. “Oh, Dodge…”

Tears flooded her eyes, and she didn’t stop them from spilling down her cheeks. She had slept little in the last few days dozing on and off, her body in a heightened state of fear. And she had to wonder if the dream she’d had a while ago where Wyatt couldn’t find her had something to do with why this was happening now. She lay down on the heavy silk blanket, drawing it around her. Her hand found its way to her low belly in protection, and closing her eyes she whispered. "He will come for us, you'll see, your father is the best bounty hunter this country has ever seen. And we are the bounty he is hunting."

Chapter Twenty-Six

Wyatt stood along the river's edge, staring across the black rippling water that glistened with the light of the moon. It was long past dark, and he'd yet to give in to sleep. How did a man sleep when his wife had been taken by his worst enemy? How could he even think of rest when he didn't know if she was all right? He shook again with rage he'd been trying to control, his fists tight. If he lost his mind, he would lose Tess. Sawyer's words echoed though his head, and his brother was right. No matter what happened he had to keep himself together—as he broke Marcus Benton's damn neck with his bare hands.

The night was cool, and the rushing of the water filled the void of the quiet that seemed to keep him on edge. They shouldn't have stopped for the night once again. It was three days hard riding to Denver and he, his brothers, and Brett had ridden their tired horses far longer than they should have. There was no doubt Tess was being kept in Denver at Chan's compound. It was the only place that rotten bastard, Benton, could hide.

"Wyatt?" Sawyer handed him a tin of steaming black coffee.

He took the cup and sipped. The hot liquid fell to the pit of his hollow stomach.

"There's a bowl of stew near the fire. You need to eat and try to rest." His brother sipped his own cup of the hot brew. "Dawson's rabbit stew, it's the best."

He shook his head. His brother meant well, making small talk, but he was restless. Sleep wouldn't come even if he tried. "We should've kept going."

Sawyer's gray eyes narrowed. "You don't rest yourself and your horse and you won't make it to Denver. If you think you are getting her back the minute you ride into town…"

Wyatt turned back to the river. Not one bit of this was to his liking and while he hadn't the best idea of how to go about it, nothing sounded good at all since they'd quit moving forward.

Sawyer sighed. "We'll get her back, Wyatt, but we have to plan well."

Wyatt spun back around to face him again. "This is no bounty hunt, this is my wife, and I'm not sitting idle and weighing in on things for long, brother."

It was obvious that Sawyer was losing patience. "Wyatt, you move too soon, stir it up in town, and you may lose the right chance to get her back."

"And if we don't move soon enough, we lose her anyway." He shouted, the coffee spilling around the edge of the cup, burning his fingers. "Shit!"

Sawyer's voice rose to match his own. "We're all at risk, Wyatt, but we are all here. Now you need to get your hind-end over there and eat and try to rest so you don't get us all killed."

His body stiffened as his brother marched away. "You're not my father."

Sawyer spun back around on a dime, pointing at him as he spoke. "No, but was he here he would tell you the same damn thing."

Sawyer held his gaze a moment longer and

returned to camp. Why was his brother always right? He idly followed and grabbed the plate of rabbit stew and sat on the rocks, where Dawson was using a firelight twig to study a map.

He shoved the food in his mouth not intending to taste it at all. He chewed slower. Dawson had always been a good cook and the rabbit gravy was thick around the tender bits of meat and was flavored with wild onions. He took another bite. It was good or either he was damn hungry.

"Stew's good." He tried.

"You need the food." Dawson never lifted a glance from the map.

He wanted to curse but thought better of it. If Sawyer wasn't enough of a mother hen, he could always count on Dawson. Things in Denver would get heated and he'd need his brothers, if for nothing else to watch his back. Marcus Benton was luring him there for more than the signed deeds or getting Tess back. Neither Dodge nor Brett would sign over any part of their land to the bastard. It was a trap, no less, as Sawyer had mentioned earlier that morning.

He took another bite of stew and pictured Tess' face, wondering if she were as bruised and battered as Dodge had been. There was no doubt she would have fought just as hard and given her condition—he was about to come apart at the seams to have her back and Benton damn well knew that, too.

But Denver was a problem. They already realized the trouble they would have with Benton and Chan. Getting into that compound would take some doing. But then there was also Chance Barlow and the lowlifes that worked under him that would be watching every corner in town. Barlow might be Denver's sheriff, but the jackass had an understanding of some kind with Chan, allowing his illegal sales to go unnoticed.

Dawson sat the map aside and blew out the flame on the small twig, tossing it back in the fire. He surveyed behind them and whistled like a bird.

Wyatt rested his left hand on his revolver, but Dawson touched his sleeve stopping him.

Out of the darkness Leaning Bear approached. He'd missed the call the Indian had made before approaching. Hell, it was likely the Cheyenne medicine man had been watching them for the last hour before he'd decided to join them.

Dawson greeted his friend in the Cheyenne language. The medicine man tugged a painted horse behind him, the same horse Wyatt had faced on the long ride back to Cheyenne when he'd been hurt.

The Indian spoke his native tongue and exchanged glances with Wyatt.

"He says he must be seeing a ghost in seeing you alive and well," Dawson translated with a glance to Wyatt.

"Tell him I know he speaks English and to cut the crap." Wyatt scowled.

Leaning Bear laughed, walking closer with a nod to the others still speaking in Cheyenne.

Dawson chuckled. "He likes annoying you better."

The Indian helped himself to the stew and squatted near Dawson, the two conversing in Cheyenne for several minutes.

Wyatt glanced at Sawyer who'd taken a place on the ground near the fire. "Think it's best we all ride into town together?"

Sawyer put a halt to the idea. “Nope, you and I are going into town. We’ve done enough in Denver with the courts to act as if we are there on business, which will throw off Barlow and his men. Dawson will keep scout. Watch who comes and goes.”

Dawson acknowledged with a nod as the Indian ate noisily beside him.

Evan snorted in his sleep on the other side of the fire and rolled over with a moan.

Wyatt didn’t see the plan working, hell, he needed no plan. “Barlow will be on us like a leech.”

“But with any luck he won’t know what we are up to. Chan doesn’t keep him up on of things, though Zihao is a concern. And Benton will avoid the risk of letting Barlow in on anything. Even he knows the man can’t be trusted.” Sawyer pulled his boots off one at a time.

Dawson stretched out on his rolled buffalo hide. “They’re just waiting Sawyer. Benton, Chan, and Zihao. Even Barlow.”

Sawyer contemplated things with a sip of his coffee. “We’ll have a look around town, wait, and take the men one by one. Get Barlow and his men out of the way first. Hudson’s been working out some details to make that easier.”

Wyatt slammed the tin mug to the rock beside him and leaned back. Waiting wasn’t part of the bargain for him, and apparently, his brother had mapped out all the details.

Dawson adjusted his position. “My question is what does Benton think is going to happen? He knows we’re on the way, but what then? Denver’s a busy town, not much fight’s gonna happen there, and that compound of Chan's is locked down."

"I wired Judge Hargrove to let him know what's going on. There's a chance he can render a search warrant for Chan's property, though I don't expect that to be of much help," Sawyer added.

Brett sat forward, resting an arm across his knee, setting aside the rifle he'd been cleaning. "The judge can write and sign anything he wants, but that won't get us into that compound. You boys would be wise to remember the fact Chan's no longer running things, but those Chinese working for him remain loyal and so is that mountain of a son he has. They don't play at all by the white man's rules, any better than the Indians."

Dawson caught Leaning Bear by the arm as he jumped up pulling the knife from his belt.

Brett chuckled, tossing up his hand in defense. "Pipe down there, medicine man, no one's got a fight here."

The Indian spoke to Dawson and sat once more, putting his knife away and glaring at Brett with a huff.

Dawson interpreted with a quick glance back at the medicine man. "He says the Chinese can be seen near the old railway in Aurora, and he's seen a fancy dressed man walking along the tracks."

"Word has it that's where Miles Rollins is holding up; just waitin' it out until he can pull together what he needs to build that railroad through to Rapid City." Brett tilted his hat back and laid his rifle aside.

The Indian mumbled again and slurped his stew.

Dawson glanced at Brett and then Sawyer. "He says there are new engines on the track there and lots of activity with a new rail being put down."

Brett smirked. "Well he's banking on making

money for every mile of that track laid down, but with us halting his initial plans, he very well may be thinking of laying a separate track to go north."

The Indian continued speaking in Cheyenne then stood to walk back to his horse and galloped off into the night.

"Why can't he speak damn English?" Wyatt hissed, gripping his fists. The medicine man could speak English as well as any, and all the Cheyenne chatter was enough to grate across his nerves.

Dawson sighed. "You know you might try a little respect, Wyatt. Had he not found you…"

"Well, when he did find me, he told you I was a dead man." Wyatt hissed, folding his arms.

"The spirits told him it wasn't good, not that you'd die," Dawson corrected him.

Wyatt ignored them all and stared into the fire. How could he focus on anything more than rescuing Tess? It had taken him years to hold her in his arms and now, not knowing if she was all right caused him as much pain as when he'd left Cheyenne thinking he'd never see her again. And that she was carrying his child…hell, he could hardly breathe at times.

Sawyer settled back against a log and pulled his hat over his face.

Brett kicked Evan who snored in a gurgle beside him, the older man chuckling and stuffing his duster behind his back for support.

After a while, Dawson broke the silence. "I've been praying, Wyatt. We'll find her, but you have to listen to Sawyer, and we have to work together, all of us."

He took a deep breath and met his brother's intense

blue eyes. Hell, Dawson didn't even pray to God but to all the damned Cheyenne spirits and forefathers. But for reasons he didn't understand, he nodded his approval. If the Cheyenne gods saw fit to make things right, then who was he to knock his brother's beliefs where Tess was concerned.

He swallowed the lump that held tight in his throat. "Father always told me to listen to both of you. I think he knew my quick temper was much like his own." He'd always been in the middle, stuck between the perfect son, Sawyer, and Dawson, the lone wolf, or so their father had called him. He'd always felt he'd fallen short where his father was concerned, and that had been reason enough for his father's voice to haunt him over the years.

Dawson smiled. "He always saw the good in you that you never saw in yourself, Wyatt."

"All I ever gave him was trouble. Wish I had listened more. What the hell would he tell me to do now?" Wyatt's voice trailed off. His father's voice had spoken to him for years, but gave him no answers now.

"That's just it; he wouldn't tell you what to do. He'd make you figure it out on your own." Dawson offered a slight smile.

Wyatt nodded. When had his little brother gained such smarts? If nothing else was true, their father had pushed them all to think on their own. He glanced at Dawson, then Sawyer and even Evan, who continued to snore. While he didn't have any clues on getting Tess back, he had in each of his brother's a different part of his father's wisdom. Maybe that was his father's doing as well.

"I keep running things through my head why

Father would have given him the land when it came down to it. I mean, I know Dodge said it was to protect me, but that never slowed him all these years." Wyatt picked up a small twig on the ground breaking it into tiny pieces.

Brett's deep voice rose above the night. "He did it to keep Chan out of Cheyenne."

"Chan?" Wyatt held Brett's gaze from across the fire.

Dawson sat up again and Sawyer rolled to his side with interest.

Brett took some time to answer, spitting a plug of tobacco from his mouth into the woods behind him. "Chan was set on operating in Cheyenne due to the Union Pacific's plans to build a railroad hub there, but there was controversy as to Denver coming up with the money to have the first hub. John caught onto Chan's ideas and played that part up, pushing him to choose Denver. Making it easy by selling him the land he has now for a right cheap price."

"I didn't know Father had land in Denver." Sawyer sat up, tilting his hat back.

Brett explained further. "Your father pulled together every cent he had at the time to buy the land in Denver and then sold it to Chan at a loss. It worked, and Chan was happy until the Union Pacific backed out of Denver and brought the rail through Cheyenne. So, while he is playing both sides by letting Wyatt into those deed boxes, he stands to benefit from the rail going farther north where he can ship his goods into unknowing territory."

Wyatt added to the story that was scrambling through his mind. "So, Benton chose sides, going with

Chan, and Da Ming didn't figure into their scheming and that got him killed."

"He wants your mother and me to sign over the deeds. If I thought that would save that pretty doctor of yours; I'd sign my land over in full right now, Wyatt, every last acre. But I think we all know, Benton doesn't play fair. If you want your wife back, we'll have to take her back, and working together is part of it. The other part of it is no one getting anxious, and that means you."

Wyatt sucked in a deep breath, aiming to slow his racing pulse. Brett was right, but how was he to remain sane for even a minute of this?

Brett's lips pressed tightly for a moment and he twirled the end of his gray mustache. "Now I know you are hurtin' with the thoughts you can't lose her. If the Indian has seen Rollins in Aurora, then I'm taking Evan, and we'll check out things there and pull Rollins and his men from the game. Hold 'em up in a railcar in one of the mines there."

Wyatt couldn't grasp any of this happening. "We need every man we got in Denver."

The older man cut him off. "Benton's a coward. He'll run with Tess if you boys get in, and we'll block him from the rail there in Aurora, cut off his escape north or south. Send Dawson for us if things get out of hand, but you boys do what you do best. Pull in Barlow and the men with him. Hell, get Chan and his son if you think you can. Eventually, Benton is outnumbered, and he'll run. But with no help he won't get far."

"Sounds good if it all goes as planned." Sawyer shook his head.

Wyatt scoffed at the idea with a quick reminder.

"But what the hell are you going to do with a handful of men. We have no jail access and nowhere to put them without a damn big attraction in Denver."

"Hudson has secured the vagrants from an abandoned warehouse outside of Denver, opposite end of town from Chan's. He's set up things on the second floor there," Sawyer explained with a nod.

"You been wiring him, and you think Barlow doesn't already know about that?" Wyatt sat forward. There was no one to trust in Denver at the telegraph office or elsewhere. "And wiring the judge wasn't such a good idea either. Hell, might as well announce it to the city."

"You got a better plan?" Sawyer hissed, gripping his fists.

Wyatt only glared, gritting his teeth. No, he had no better plan, but there was too much chatter, too much unknown, and Tess wasn't in his grasp.

"Why is it Benton wants the deeds signed in full to Rollins and not himself?" Dawson glanced from his brothers to Brett.

"My guess is Rollins is holed up in Aurora to get started on the spur once the deeds are signed. But there's more." Brett nodded. "I figure Benton isn't banking on getting out of this alive. He's angry as hell his brother was killed, his plans for this spur were thwarted, and he isn't back to see that rail line be built…he's back to take us all one by one. So, you have to get the doc because I don't think he is going to give her up without a fight. But while I am telling you all to be careful, I'm not telling you to take it slow as time's wastin'."

Wyatt's nerves frayed. It would be Tess who paid

the price if things didn't go well. He jumped up, not willing to wait one more minute. He grabbed his revolver and rolled the barrel, picked up his saddle bags, and stomped toward the horses. He slung the saddle blanket over his horse's withers and lifted the saddle, but turned to find Brett standing in between him and the horse. He glared hard at the man who had practically raised him.

"That fight you got inside you." Brett hit his mid-chest with a balled fist. "You store that up, you hold the fire and the anger right there inside, and once you have her back, then, and only then, do you cut that rage loose."

Wyatt gripped his fists tight, fighting tears. "I won't lose her even if I have to pay the devil himself. I will kill him."

"Sure you will, and we're gonna let you have him, but not before we get the doc out of his hands." Brett hit his chest once more. "You ride into town alone in the dark; you are as good as dead. How is that gonna save her? You're gonna be a father, it's time you acted like one, choosing to do things even if they aren't easy."

Wyatt fought emotions he wasn't sure he'd ever control.

"I've known you since you were a boy, and I knew way back then you'd be as tough as they came. But the fight's not here." He pointed to Wyatt's mid-chest. "It's here." He placed a finger at his temple.

"You're taking Evan to Aurora for the same reasons." Wyatt questioned.

Brett narrowed his gaze. "He's a dead-eye shot from more than a hundred yards away, and a lot like you, but he's young yet, not able to rein that temper like I am asking of you. He about got himself killed at the river a while back, and I think this time we let him do some growing."

Wyatt allowed a smile to slip. Evan had always been looking for a fight, and he'd ridden right into the bullet he'd taken some time back while driving a large herd of cattle across Marcus Benton's side of the river. He was young, and it was best he went to Aurora for now, no matter. Brett had always watched out for them all, but he had a special fondness for Evan that went beyond that protection. Evan had been a ten-year-old boy when their father had been killed, and Brett had stepped in to teach him the cattle business from a tender age. "It's just as well, wouldn't want to see him hurt because things got out of hand."

Brett smiled. "At least we agree on that. Now you get yourself some rest, and tomorrow we'll see about starting on the wrath of the devil you want to bring down."

Wyatt looked up across the vast darkness of the sky as Brett moseyed back to camp. There were the stars that Tess so loved. She had told him how when he was gone from Cheyenne, that she had looked at them for hours, hoping he was seeing them too. Perhaps she was glancing at the same part of the sky he was seeing now, big damn sky. Somehow, she was all around him, and he wouldn't give up until he had her back in his arms where she belonged. He glanced into the heavens once more and whispered to the God she often prayed to. "She's mine; you can't have her just yet."

Chapter Twenty-Seven

The afternoon sun set hard in the sky, heat scorching across Wyatt's shoulders. He tugged on the reins of the horse beneath him and waited on Sawyer to catch up as he scanned the town of Denver that rested before him. Somewhere on the other end of town was Tess. The want to race in and take her was overriding the well laid plans Sawyer had sworn him to follow.

Brett and Evan had turned south miles back to set up their watch outside Aurora. If Miles Rollins was there, they'd hold him and any of the others who'd have potential enough to cause trouble. He wasn't sure Rollins was worth much to Marcus Benton, but if they managed to take one man at a time in the game Benton was playing, it would leave the man with few options. Dawson had left them to scout the surrounding areas around Denver.

"It's now you gotta hold back." Sawyer stopped Colonel beside him, glancing at the town they both knew well.

"I know." Hell, he did know, but why did he feel like he might suffocate with the fact Tess was just within his reach?

"Then best we go." Sawyer took Colonel ahead.

Wyatt gave the palomino a gentle spur to the side, the animal following. It would be best that they rode into town, pay for a room, and make everything seem as normal business for any onlookers. Sawyer would meet with the judge for the warrant, not that it would do any good. And while his brother played sheriff, he had a few things to take care of as well, starting with a quick spy of things at Chan's compound.

"Let's have a drink and see about a room." Sawyer took the lead as their horses trotted gingerly into town.

Wyatt said nothing but scanned the faces of men and women along the streets. He had to think with the bustle of the popular town, it wouldn't be easy to pull off much of anything. Outside the railroad office, two Chinese men eyed him and his brother. Probably Chan's lookouts and they had to know he was coming. Hell, they knew right where Tess was, the sons of bitches!

Sawyer dismounted outside Barlow's saloon, tilting his hat back and eyeing Barlow's deputies across the street.

Wyatt climbed down taking a look at the same men, ignoring the swelling in his ankle, his boot tight.

"Barlow's on us." Sawyer lifted his saddle bags and tossed it across his shoulder.

"Yep." He tied off his horse and followed his brother into the noisy saloon. The stench of alcohol and sweat greeted them, the piano music from the corner drowning out voices to muffles. Tables of men played cards while others were belly up to the bar, and another group cheered a young man who was having his first taste of Barlow's rotgut whiskey. The boy tossed back the small glass and coughed and sputtered until he dropped to his knees. Wyatt thought to chuckle, but he needed his own hot burn to ease him through the next few hours. His head pounded, and he gripped his fists tight.

He followed Sawyer to the long bar and leaned on it, glancing at the large mirror behind the counter and studying the faces in the room, eyeing Hudson who sat alone at one of the far tables.

The bushy browed bar tender stopped before them, wiping the counter with a cloth.

"Whiskey." Wyatt held up two fingers, and he wasn't ordering for his brother.

"Make that two sarsaparillas." Sawyer interjected, slapping coins onto the counter with a nod to the man who glanced from one to the other and shrugged.

Wyatt gave him a hard glare. "What the hell, Sawyer, we've been riding for days, and I want a drink."

Sawyer narrowed his gaze. "Need you thinking clear, now take the damn sarsaparilla and go sit with Hudson."

The bartender placed two shot glasses of the thick syrupy liquid before them. Wyatt grabbed one and left Sawyer, mumbling curses as he walked toward the deputy. He set the glass down hard and took the chair across from Hudson picking up the already dealt cards like he might concentrate on the game.

Hudson lifted his own cards, peering over them. "How you holdin' up?"

Wyatt sorted the cards in his hands. Hell, too bad he wasn't playing. A pair of deuces. How was he holding up? Not good, fraying at the seams and about to implode just like the damn mine Brett had blown. "Some days are diamonds."

"That good, huh?" Hudson discarded and drew another. "I've been watchin', but there's no sign of her.

Chan's got the place locked down tight."

Wyatt dug in his trouser pocket and laid down several coins as Sawyer settled in the chair beside them, turning it around to rest his arms over the chair back.

"Building's secure, the second floor's empty, escapes, a door in the front and back and a window on the third floor. Got a lot of rats, so we'll add a few more of the larger version?" Hudson tossed another card face down.

"I'm meeting the judge later for the warrant." Sawyer tilted his hat back, wiping his sweaty cheek on his sleeve.

"We're not getting into Chan's that easy." Wyatt gulped the sarsaparilla, waiting for the burn that never came.

"No, but if we have it, we'll have reason to keep Barlow busy, and take a look as far as we can get." Sawyer lifted his hat and ran his fingers through his dark hair, returning it.

Hudson laid down a key, and Sawyer slid it across the table pocketing it in his vest. "Room seventeen at the hotel. Wyatt, Mattie has a room for you, the one at the end of the hallway, keys across the door ridge. I've seen nothing of Benton, but the man at the livery has seen him twice in the last two days, word has it he arrived alone."

Wyatt drew another card. The hair stood on the back of his neck at the mention of Benton. If the man was here, then so was Tess, and it was a sure thing he was awaiting their arrival. "You sure the building's secure."

"Yep." Hudson leaned back in his chair glaring over Wyatt's shoulder, a smirk crossing his face.

"Here's trouble."

Wyatt didn't turn, aware Chance Barlow had entered the saloon. Well, that hadn't taken long.

Sawyer's knuckles turned white as he gripped the chair back. His brother hated the likes of any crooked law man and had been waiting without luck for the corrupt sheriff to be voted out of Denver.

Barlow stopped before them, folding his arms, the two deputies from outside behind him. He sniffed wrinkling his nose. "You boys smell anything?"

The men behind him chuckled.

"You got business here, sheriff?" He spoke to Sawyer.

Wyatt continued the game, lifting another card, focusing to keep his head about himself. His fight wasn't with Barlow who was more of a nuisance, though he'd just as soon take a quick fist to the man to shut him up.

Sawyer stood. "As a matter of fact, I do, not that it is any concern of yours."

Barlow took a step closer, his dark eyes narrowing in threat. "If it's in my town, *sheriff*, it's my business."

Wyatt waited on Hudson to draw, holding the pair of twos and three eights. Hell, a full house. He sucked in a deep breath to stave off the impending doom that pressed in on him. *Steady. Shit! It isn't Barlow you want.*

"Then you make it brief. There's always trouble when you boys are in town, and take this, sorry excuse for a deputy with you when you go. He's been hanging around long enough." Barlow examined Hudson, his eyes dark. "Your time is short, best you find your way somewhere else."

Hudson winked at the man with a big toothy smile. “Just enjoying spending my hard-earned dollars right here in support of Denver’s fine economy.”

Wyatt held his chuckle. Hudson could make anything sound like a joke, and what he was doing was riling Barlow as was usual.

Barlow leaned both hands on the table in the saloon he owned and whispered in a growl. “You know, it must be a hard thing to overcome your roots. I can still see your father right there on the streets, drinking and pissing himself to death—such a pitiful man.”

Hudson jumped from the table, and Sawyer was quick to grab him. Wyatt stood, blocking Hudson and narrowing his gaze on Barlow. It wasn’t the first time that he had used such a ploy to stir things up where his friend was concerned.

Barlow turned to go with a sardonic chortle that echoed from outside.

It was all Wyatt could do to wrestle Hudson toward the chair again. The saloon had gone quiet, and every eye seemed to be on them.

“Sit, we’ve got an audience and too much at stake.” Sawyer spoke through gritted teeth and took his own chair, lifting the scrambled cards and shuffling.

Wyatt sat, annoyed at not moving things faster. He had things to do, and time was wasting.

“He has no right.” Hudson focused on the swinging saloon doors and lifted his cards.

“He’s just riling, let it go,” Wyatt urged.

Hudson glared at him, discarding, and jerking up another card. “Some things never change, but one day…he’ll get what’s coming.”

“Both of you get your heads together,” Sawyer

warned and tossed down a random card.

They weren't playing; they were holding their cards and going through the motions. Too damn bad, a full house was a damn good hand.

Sawyer lifted another card and continued, "I'm going to the hotel. I'll make my way to the judge at dusk. You boys finish the game. Wait it out at the brothel. I'll be done with the judge by nine and meet you at the warehouse for a look around." Sawyer rested a glance on Hudson, squeezing Wyatt's shoulder as he stood. "Keep this one out of trouble."

"Gonna pay hell to do that." Hudson's pout let go to a smile, but the uneasiness in his eyes never dissipated.

Wyatt shrugged his shoulder from Sawyer's grip. He didn't need any coddling. He needed his wife back.

Sawyer made his exit from the saloon, and Hudson drew another card.

Wyatt shuffled his cards, eyeing the men around them, but he held onto the full house. Nothing but a few miners, men from the railroad, saloon girls, and the bartender. "Where's Barlow when he isn't here?"

Hudson spoke without looking up. "Out back at the brothel every couple of nights. He's a wife who pays little attention, I suppose. His men walk the city after dark, pretty predictable in their path, taking the main roads and walking the back alleys to return. They never hit Chan's area, leaving the Chinese to themselves."

Wyatt placed another coin on the table. That made things easy enough. All he had to do was make it to Chan's, but then he'd have the Chinese to deal with. "Roof tops?"

Hudson tilted his head, eyeing him with suspicion.

"No, they don't check the roof tops, and Sawyer will kick my ass if you are thinking what I know you are."

"What Sawyer doesn't know won't hurt him?" Wyatt narrowed his glare.

"You sneak off to Chan's, and either his men or Benton will kill you before you have a chance to get her back, Wyatt." Hudson whispered through his teeth.

He laid down his cards, spreading them wide. "Full house and the queen of hearts, is mine."

Hudson cursed, "Damn it, Wyatt, that's insane!"

"Gonna take a look around, map it out in my mind." He shuffled the cards once more.

Hudson cursed, "Shit! You mess up, and you could lose her. Are you listening?"

Wyatt raked the coins and paper money back, his direction and leaned back to pocket it. "That's why I'll have you backing me up. Lookout from a distance."

Hudson threw his cards down, shaking his head. The deputy had known him long enough to know how he worked, and he couldn't wait on Sawyer. If he could at least take a look, they'd make better time bringing the men in one at a time and move this production a bit faster.

He thought of Tess again. Some parts of missing her were so visceral the pain squeezed the air right out of his lungs, and other times her tender voice echoed inside his head. He'd give his left arm to hold her again even for one second. Well, it was a matter of time and he'd add Marcus Benton to the list of outlaws he'd taken to their grave.

****

Tess held her belly and heaved again, spitting into the chamber pot on the floor in the corner of the room.

She was hungry and white rice alone hadn't been enough to keep her sated. She'd refused to have her meals with Marcus Benton, and the price was heavy as she'd been given two small bowls a day of the plain tasteless mush. Nausea wracked her body, and she clamored back to the small bed, falling on top of the silk linens. This could not be good for the baby, and if she didn't die at the hands of the man who held her, she was sure it would from the nausea.

It was late, darkness beyond what light she could see through the boarded window, and there would be no more food until tomorrow morning. She wretched again, swallowing hard at the dry gag and closed her eyes. She'd been careful not to let on she was with child. If Benton was aware of it, he might hurt her, or worse yet, the baby. But if she didn't get more consistent food and water. *Oh, Lord in heaven, please…*

Opening her eyes once more, her gaze fell on the small black bag under the empty wooden set of drawers. Was that her medical bag? Slowly, she lifted herself from the bed. She had a gun in there if they hadn't bothered to take it. She shook her head, of course they would have searched it, but why on earth would they have left the bag with her? Making her way across the room, she lugged it free and went back to the bed opening it. How had she not seen it before now? She hadn't thought about it since the men who had kidnapped her had taken it from her.

She searched the contents. No gun, but all her supplies were intact. She jostled through the various medications, finding a small pouch of ginger—one of the herbs she had gotten when in Denver the last time. The bitter root was good for nausea, and she'd used it the last few weeks. While it didn't always work, she'd welcome even a little relief. She took a tiny pinch of the raw root and placed it under her tongue, ignoring the burn. She held her lips tight, her mouth watering and tucked the pouch into her chemise, in case the bag should be taken from her later.

Noticing the bottle of chloroform, she lifted it, reading the label. The noxious medication she had used more times than she could count…what if—

"Oh, my lands what am I thinking," she whispered and glanced at the door behind her. When the man called Zihao did return, perhaps she might be able to sedate him.

"Physicians are sworn to the Hippocratic Oath, Doctor." She spoke to herself in a whisper wondering if she should dare. Even if he was well over six feet, chloroform would bring him down in seconds. Yes, that was it, she could run then, and it seemed most of this part of the house stayed quiet. If she could make it out of the compound and into Denver, she'd find safety and Wyatt. He was here; he had to be. Lifting her skirt, she tore a shard of her petticoat away, folding it several times and looked at the glass bottle once more.

Dousing the liquid onto the cloth, she let it saturate and folded it again. It wouldn't be long before the Chinese man would return to bring in more water for the evening. He would parade in and set it on the dressing table and leave without a word, but there was that one second he would turn his back.

Careful not to inhale the putrid liquid herself, she curled it into her hand and set the capped bottle back into her bag. With that, she kicked the bag back under the wooden chest. She wouldn't need the bag, not wanting anything else to hinder her attempt to escape. She sat back down on the bed, holding the drenched cloth to wait, which turned out to be less than a minute. Her pulse raced as she heard the heavy footsteps becoming louder.

Zihao entered with a bow, though he never really made eye contact with her. How could the man use the Chinese custom of respect when he was holding her hostage? He turned to place the small porcelain pot of water and one saucer and cup on the dressing table across from her. He would set it up precisely and then turn to go. She had a quick second while he was turned and…

She jumped on his back, not believing what she was doing and fought to get the cloth to his face. He yelled at her in Chinese swears as she scrambled for a hold, wrapping her legs around his large middle as he swung about. He tried to grab her, but she clung to him and wedged the cloth of chloroform across his mouth and nose. He fought hard to free himself of her, and then both of his hands went to the cloth, though his fight lessened and his swears diminished. He hovered with her riding on his back and then swayed. She held tight with both hands across his nose and mouth. *Oh dear God, what if this kills him?*

Zihao fell toward the bed carrying her with him, and she broke the fall with her arm, rolling him to the floor. He fell with a thump and moved no more. He wouldn't die, but when he came too, he'd be useless for a while. Chloroform was indeed a strong drug, and while it was needed medicinally, the side effects could be with a person for days. Headaches with unclear thought processes and confused lack of judgment were very common. She stood above him, making sure he didn't move.

Turning to the door, time was of the essence for her escape. The long hallway was clear, but she hadn't any idea which way to go. She glanced to the left, the longer hallway leading farther into the house, and she wanted the shortest way out which was the way, she'd been taken to eat with Benton and Chan. She went to the right. Reaching the end of the hallway, she waited and eased a glance around the corner. Stairs. She bent to peer through the slats of the railing seeing no one below, in the small parlor. Off that was the room where she had eaten the one meal before she had angered Mr. Benton. With a deep breath, she took the stairs, cringing at the creak of one of the boards toward the bottom. She was still deep in the center of Chan's home as there were no windows, but the faint hint of smoke caused her to stifle a cough. She went ahead to the next room, entered and froze. Two Chinese men stood just outside the room she'd have to get through to be free of the house.

She crouched behind the curtain contemplating how to get past them. She'd have to find another way as it didn't appear they were planning to go anywhere soon. Taking a step back, she screamed as she was grabbed from behind, startled.

"Well, now, I would think you would learn to follow the rules, Doctor." Marcus Benton's voice hissed in her ear. He pulled her into the room behind her.

She tried to shrug from his grip and yelped at the pain he inflicted with his grip on her upper arms. She bent, seeking relief from his grasp. And then she made the mistake of looking at him and was rewarded with a back hand across the jaw. Her head snapped back, and she tasted blood but didn't drop her gaze.

"Seems you and I have a little problem, Doctor." Benton dragged her back the way she came. "Apparently, your refusal of dinner and lack of food hasn't been enough to assist you in learning your proper role here."

Tess dug her feet in, not wanting to be taken back. She had to break free of him and run, if nothing else.

He turned and swung a fist into the side of her head, pulling her by the hair when she tried to free herself. She held her head, thinking she might faint, her ears ringing. He never relinquished his hold and continued to drag her back up the stairs and toward the little room. She bobbled and tried to keep her footing. Fighting was futile, and she had to protect the baby.

Mr. Benton slung her inside the tiny room against the bed. He glanced at Zihao out cold on the floor. Then he knelt and lifted the cloth which held the Chloroform, eyeing her with suspicion.

Tess froze on the bed, afraid of further eye contact, but meeting his gaze anyway.

He scowled and slammed the dresser over, lifting her bag and tossing it out into the hallway, where the contents spilled and bottles of medication shattered.

He grabbed her once more by the wrist. "Chloroform? Ingenious, Doctor."

Tess yelped at the pain of his grip but didn't break eye contact.

"Pardon, sir." A very small Chinese woman appeared at the doorway.

Benton turned. "Can't you see I am busy here?"

The woman bowed, dropping her gaze. “A woman comes from Cheyenne and asks to speak with you.”

“Dodge.” The whisper escaped Tess before she could halt it.

Benton waited for the woman to leave. “Well, now, this changes the game of play.”

Tess stood, trying to free herself from his grasp. It had to be Dodge, but she would be in so much danger here. But she hadn’t another chance for any help at all and inhaled both lungs full of air and screamed. “Dodge, I’m here, Dodge.”

Before she could yell further, Benton grabbed her and shoved his hand over her mouth, wrestling for a hold, but she yelled for Dodge once more as his fist came across her brow. She clutched her head falling back to the bed, confused until the cloth of chloroform pressed against her mouth and nose. No, not the chloroform, which wasn’t good for the baby. She held her breath until Mr. Benton slammed a knee into her ribs, the crunch forcing air from her in a heaving cough. Oh, God, broken. Her body rhythmically sucked in another breath, and pain coursed through her entire chest. She tried to pry his hand away from her mouth, but her strength and thoughts blurred as she gasped again, her mind fading. Her eyes closed as if of their own will and her body floated into a sudden darkness.

Chapter Twenty-Eight

Dodge narrowed her gaze on the man she'd despised since she was a very young woman. The two-faced jackass had never been anything but a coward. Her remark that she had come to ask for Tess had been met with a shake of his head, and the deep guttural laugh had turned her stomach. She folded her arms, the pistol in her corset, uncomfortable at the gesture. "I want her back, she has nothing at all to do with any of this, Marcus, and you know it."

Marcus Benton allowed a sadistic smile to emerge. "No, but I need her to control Wyatt, while I gain back the lands that are mine. Tell me Eleanor, did you come with the signed deeds?"

She narrowed her gaze with caution. "All these years, Marcus, all the deception and it still boils down to you not getting what John had. What's in it for you now, Marcus, if you gain the land, make the sale to the railroad? You'll always be on the run and hiding in pigsties like this. Has it been worth it? No, I didn't come here with those deeds. You'll never realize the ownership of John's land."

He leaned against the far wall folding his arms, his dark eyes narrowing. He'd aged well she thought. His hair was still dark and thick, and his skin showed the hint of a few lines, but he hardly appeared his sixty years.

"You should know better, Eleanor, that I play to win, and even after all these years, I have still beaten John at his own games." His smile was smug.

"How by killing his sons, my sons, what does that get you in the fine scheme of things?" She wanted to send a fist into his belly, though her newly stitched wrist was still very tender. "Your brother nearly killed Sawyer, and you left Wyatt for dead, Marcus. You left my son to die, and don't tell me it wasn't you that shot Dawson a few weeks ago, because he saw you. It grazed his head, Marcus! His head! Where does that kind of hate come from? Release Tess and end this nonsense. You're a very smart man, move on to something more, leave here for Mexico, the Orient. With your connections, you could set up a fine swindle of others somewhere else."

"I'm sorry, Eleanor, but I need the physician as collateral." He gave her a sardonic smile, adjusting his collar.

"She has never wronged you, and if this is because of Wyatt, he was a boy who got scared half to death because he watched Da Ming die a horrible death at your hands. You cannot blame him for John's actions that were to protect him and the Cheyenne Territory from someone as corrupt as you and Chan. And for that matter, I don't know where you unearthed that blasted Rollins, but he isn't worth the two cents you probably paid him." She hissed her flurry of thoughts.

Benton chortled. "John's still very hard at work here, is he not?"

Dodge took a step closer. "John is dead, and you should have hung for that, Marcus."

"Harsh words from such a beautiful woman." He

smiled and glanced the length of her body. "And if John had lived, would he have approved of you finding your way to Brett's bed? Oh, but then, that's right, he was well aware of your promiscuousness even back then."

She raised her hand to slap him, but he caught her wrist mid-air and caressed it. "You and I, things could have been more than pleasant. We could've had it all, Eleanor, and I'm sorry my men were rather rough on you."

"You, bastard!" Dodge jerked her arm away from his grasp, careful to protect the other.

"John and I had no secrets, not even about Brett. He and I were better at business than being married, but we loved our sons, and I will not have them fall at your hands. Even if I signed the land over to you, full and clear, your plans wouldn't last very long. You are in so deep, Marcus, that you will be paying the devil soon enough."

"John had his own illegal dealings, swindling Chan out of Cheyenne and into Denver, though it has remained relatively profitable here." He picked at the dirt underneath one of his nails and lifted his gaze to her once more.

She took a step back. "Look around you, Marcus; this is a slaughterhouse. A pig sty."

"That land was meant to be mine," he shouted. "Mine!"

She shook her head. "It was never yours and never will be. And you only need Rollins as an endorsement for the signature of the land. You are in so deep you can't even have your name on it."

"Oh, the webs John weaved that you will never know about, Eleanor. You don't know, do you?" His tone lightened. “John planned to deed Brett’s land to me until Brett schemed with Da Ming, changing the deeds himself.”

“That’s not true. John promised Brett that land long before the night you killed Da Ming.” Dodge clenched her fists. Brett would never have done John wrong, he had too much integrity.

“Oh, but I assure you that it is very true, and Da Ming paid the price for it all.” He chuckled.

She didn’t let him finish. “You killed Da Ming because he wouldn’t forge the deeds the way you wanted. You got the land you had so John could protect Wyatt. And as for Brett, he would never have his land without John’s approval. He is a man of great integrity, very unlike you.”

He considered it for a moment. “Brett Morgan is a coward, but I wouldn’t say that about Wyatt. It took five men to take him down. You should be proud. He fought until he couldn’t stand up. Too prideful to let go and die respectably. As for Dawson, he was in the wrong place at the wrong time, shall we say. Why, I believe John would roll over in his grave if he knew one of his sons was roaming the countryside looking like some kind of half-breed Cheyenne Indian.”

“There is a special place in hell for you, Marcus.” Dodge wanted to strangle the man with her bare hands and she wanted Tess, who carried her grandchild, released.

He laughed.

Enough was enough. “I want Tess back and right damn now. It’s over, or it will be very soon, I assure you.”

His amusement seemed to stop as Chan entered the

room.

Dodge glanced at the elder Chinese man. He'd aged with his long silver hair and wrinkled features. She met his one-eyed gaze and watched as he bowed, a gesture she didn't return his blind silver eye unblinking.

"Ms. McCade, your presence is vast shining star." He glanced at her. That was odd as he seemed confused to what was going on, though he turned and smiled at Benton murmuring some exchange she wasn't sure she understood.

She shouldn't have come here, and it was late making things even worse. The darkness of Denver was one thing, but the pure evil before her made her draw her weapon from her corset, pulling back the hammer and taking aim.

"Why, Eleanor, why is this no surprise?" Benton glanced at the weapon and back to her.

"You have been warned, both of you. I know Tess is here; I heard her scream, and so help me, if you lay a hand on her, I will put you in the ground myself, Marcus." She stepped backward until she was out the doorway and across the path to the edge of the compound. Chan's men followed her outside to cut her off from her escape. It wasn't far to the gates, and the shadows of several men in the darkness made her turn to a run. Before she was off the grounds of the compound, someone grabbed her, covering the scream that never escaped.

****

Wyatt spun Dodge around to face him, having jerked her off Chan's grounds and behind the buildings at the edge of Denver. "Damn it, Dodge, what are you doing here?"

"The same thing as you." Her chest heaved, and she pulled from his grip in anger. "You scared the hell right out of me."

"I should've known to have you jailed before we came here." He gripped her elbow and tugged her along behind the back alleys of Denver.

"I thought I might have the upper hand in a chance with Marcus, but he isn't negotiating." She struggled to keep pace with him. He slowed once they had crossed two more streets.

"Where is everyone?" she whispered when he let go, leaving her to walk on her own.

How the hell did this always happen, Dodge meddling where she didn't need to be? He should have had Sawyer lock her up for good measure.

Dodge touched his arm. "She's there, Wyatt. Tess. I heard her call me."

Wyatt's knees wanted to buckle and throw him right on the ground. He stopped, unable to take the next step. He scanned across the city, turning to make sure they weren't being followed. His throat was tight, and his chest held so deep a pain he wasn't sure he could inhale the next breath. He turned away from Dodge and raked air into his lungs, his head spinning.

"She's alive, and we'll get her back," Dodge said, her voice tender.

He tugged free of her grasp, swallowing another gulp of air and continued to walk back into town. "Of all things, you took the train? You have no business in the middle of this."

She followed but slowed her pace again, her reply stern. "Wyatt, she is my friend, and my daughter-in law. I have every right to be here. She is also carrying my grandchild. I had to do something. The better question is why are you are out here alone at Chan's?"

Wyatt pondered the question he wasn't about to answer. "Sawyer is with the judge about the warrant for all the good that will do us. I'm meeting him, Dawson, and Hudson as soon as I get you to the hotel, where you will stay put."

"What about Brett and Evan?" She followed him across the street where he stopped before a hotel.

"They are in Aurora keeping an eye on Rollins, and you are going to room seventeen and stay there. I swear I will hogtie you to the chair in the room if I see you step one foot outside until one of us comes back for you."

Dodge narrowed her glare. "I am capable of following directions. When will you be back?"

"Not sure." Hell, he'd still be spying around Chan's if he hadn't caught sight of her running in the darkness. "But you'd best be right here when we do return."

"Mind, you all be careful." And with a huff and a flurry of skirts she disappeared inside.

Wyatt turned toward the back alley behind the hotel, using the lamppost light for checking his pocket watch—the picture of him and Tess' wedding day riding just inside. He angled the picture to pick up more light. She'd been the most beautiful thing he'd ever seen that day. He touched the picture with his thumb and closed the cover over the face of the clock. He was late for meeting Hudson as planned. His partner in eavesdropping on Chan's would have cleared out once he grabbed Dodge.

He cursed to himself. Adding Dodge to the mix

was adding a bit of trouble none of them was expecting. It was lucky enough Benton hadn't kept her. She could have gotten herself killed, but she well knew that Benton held her in high enough regard not to take her life. At least the bastard had respected her enough to know she carried a pistol and well knew how to use it. He turned toward the other end of town, making sure he wasn't followed. Staying clear of Barlow's men and looping through a variety of back alleys, he stopped outside the abandoned building Hudson had secured. Nothing, or no one moved, and after a time, he scampered inside and up the stairs.

Hudson leaned against the far wall, blocking the door where they planned to lock the men they captured, and he and Sawyer stopped their conversation at his entry. He had heard the last bit of their conversation. They'd been talking about Tess, and he had an idea or two about what they weren't saying now.

"So, let the games begin." He glared at his brother, not willing to think more on what both men held back.

Sawyer played it off by tossing a thumb over his shoulder. "We've already scored. Barlow's two deputies are inside."

Wyatt glanced at Hudson who couldn't hide the grin as he spoke. "They made it easy; they always follow the same path, but I think Barlow isn't gonna be the least bit happy."

Sawyer ran a hand through his dark hair, returning his hat. "There's more. I found the judge dead in his office. Strangled."

Wyatt couldn't slow the thoughts in his head, the blow to his belly intense. Tess being held, the judge dead, and then Dodge shows. Things were going downhill and fast.

Sawyer narrowed his gaze, folding his arms. "And you had no business going to Chan's on your own, Wyatt."

"I suppose it's a good thing I went. I just put Dodge in your hotel room." He defended, kicking at the cracked wooden boards of the warehouse flooring, eyeing Hudson who'd likely given him away.

"Dodge?" Sawyer's brows drew together, and his hands dropped to his sides.

"Apparently, our mother thinks herself immune to Benton's wrath, but she had to pull her pistol to escape. I nabbed her inside the gates and got her back to town." He shoved his hands in his trouser pockets.

"She's not hurt?" Sawyer asked, concerned.

"No, but Benton has Tess for sure." Wyatt sucked in a breath so painful he thought his chest might collapse. So damn close to her, and yet so far that he was dying one slow breath at a time.

"You know as well as I do she won't stay there." Sawyer shot him a challenging glance.

"She will. I believe it's the first time I have seen her white as a ghost in fear."

Wyatt turned, drawing his revolver at the shuffle of feet coming up the stairs.

A whistle came out of the darkness, and Dawson shoved Chance Barlow into the large darkened room.

Hudson trotted over to help secure the struggling sheriff. "My, my, my, what goes around comes around."

Barlow spat a hiss of curses through the gag, his words muffled but understood.

"Quiet, or I'll find a larger gag." Hudson chuckled,

though he didn't smile as he sent a fist into the sheriff's belly, doubling him over.

Dawson was quick to grab the man and lug him off as Wyatt shoved Hudson away. "Take a walk."

Hudson jerked from his grip and trotted away in a huff.

Dawson shoved Barlow ahead, unbolting the locked room that contained the man's two counterparts, tied and gagged, sitting on the floor. He shoved the resisting man inside, slammed the door, and bolted it once more, turning back to them. "Three down, a couple of more to go."

Sawyer sighed. "Not that this is going as planned."

"What?" Dawson glanced between them.

"Wyatt rescued Dodge from Chan's. Apparently, she thought she could talk Benton into releasing Tess who is inside. And you…" Sawyer turned to Wyatt, "had no business being at Chan's alone in the first place. Judge Hargrove is dead. Found him in his office." He turned back to Dawson.

"Dodge is here?" Dawson shook his head unbelieving.

Sawyer nodded. "At the hotel."

Dawson's brows lifted. "Best you lock her up somewhere safe."

"She'll stay put. It got tense enough at Chan's she had to pull her pistol to escape." Wyatt explained as Hudson returned.

Dawson leaned against the iron door. "Brett has Rollins and his men detained in an old railcar inside the mine, leastwise until they are discovered missing. The area was deserted. So, what do we do now?"

Sawyer lifted his gaze, saying nothing for a long

moment. Then with great show, he removed the star from his vest and shoved it into his trouser pocket. He steadied his gaze on Wyatt, and after a deep breath spoke. "This is Wyatt's bounty, and now we play with no rules."

Wyatt held his brother's gaze, giving him a simple nod. That his brother had removed his badge meant for the moment, he was no longer a man of the law and was giving him full rein to run things how he wanted. He glanced at Dawson, then Hudson and back to Sawyer. "I can't ask any one of you to go farther than here."

Sawyer stepped up. "We've taken down worse than the likes of Benton over the years, and we did it together. Nothing's changed."

Dawson nodded as did Hudson, who tilted his hat back with a grin.

Wyatt held all three in his sights for a time, brother to brother, Hudson somehow a part of that. Brett and Evan waiting as posted. Damn and even Dodge along for what she thought was good measure. He lifted both revolvers, twirled them once and holstered them. "Then the time has come."

Chapter Twenty-Nine

Wyatt waited in the shadows outside the back entrance of Chan's compound, leaning against the house, surprised he'd made it that far without being noticed. The lack of a full moon and a cloud covered night, an added protection. The Chinese men in town, put there to watch things, had been distracted by Sawyer who'd idly acted as if he were on some mission several streets behind Barlow's saloon. And now, alone in the darkness, with Tess so close—his chest pounded in anticipation.

A whistle, sounding much like a night owl came from the roof above him. Dawson was in place, and at any moment, Sawyer would arrive to his spot near the side door. The plan was to get inside, taking a man or two at a time. Each taken would limit Benton further, putting Tess in more jeopardy, but this was about timing, and the sand in the hour glass had all but run out.

If things went well, he'd have Tess in his arms, and Marcus Benton would be on the other side of hell. Or he himself would be the one, facing off with the devil. No matter, anything would be better than the purgatory he'd been living in since Tess had been taken. If Marcus Benton wanted a fight, he was about to get one.

He ducked back as a young Chinese man from inside Chan's stepped to the porch to light a smoke, a rifle over his shoulder. The short Chinaman took his time lighting a cigar and blew out a puff of smoke as Dawson snaked a noosed rope down from the roof. His brother managed to snag the hatless man around the neck and jerk him upward before he ever had a clue, the burning cigar and rifle the only evidence the man had once been there. Wyatt grabbed the rifle cocked it and set it behind the trees against the house, just in case he needed it later on. There was a slight scuffle on the roof, followed by a chirp that Dawson had the man secured.

Wyatt shook his head. If Dawson wasn't his brother, he might have an inkling to be frightened of the man's silent but deadly skills. He was swift and efficient, if nothing more. He hadn't killed the man but had put him out for a while.

Zihao came to the door and whispered in urgent Mandarin, cursing as he drew his weapon and scuttled back inside. Wyatt stifled a chuckle at the man's Chinese rendition of *son of a bitch*, one of Mei Ling's favorite curses over the years; though she would be hard pressed to ever admit it.

Movement across the other side of the compound caught his attention, and Dawson whistled. Sawyer was in place. He could make out the shadow of his brother and got the nod Sawyer sent his direction. His brother disappeared around the corner of the house, and Wyatt turned back to the door, drawing both revolvers as a succession of bullets blasted the direction Sawyer had taken.

"Shit." Wyatt held his position a moment longer and ducked under one of the windows making his way around the main house. The gunfire wouldn't attract any attention in the town of Denver, given Barlow and his men were out of the picture. Chancing a quick look, he caught a glimpse of Sawyer trapped behind a small shed with two Chinese men firing from two directions. His brother was trapped. *Holy hell!*

A rifle shot from the roof, and one of the men firing on Sawyer fell dead. Dawson had taken him from his vantage point. The other pulled back, not showing himself for some time. Wyatt held steady, waiting. So much for keeping the loss of lives to a minimum as now they were known. A streak of gunshots flared from the bushes, where the one man had hidden. He held his revolver steady and waited. When a second shot came, he fired, and a yelp sounded. Two down.

Things went quiet, though he ventured a few of the bullets had come from Hudson who was placed on the roof of the last buildings in town with the long rifle. A stalemate, but Benton had to know good and damn well they were here now. Hell, everyone inside knew, including Tess. Commotion sounded from inside the house, a group of five Chinamen took their place on the edge of the front porch of the meat market, firing toward Sawyer.

Wyatt scrambled back into the bushes at the side of the house as another Chinese man rounded the house in his direction. He held his breath and waited as the man closed in.

He bent and tucked himself under the edge of the raised porch, his ankle aching. Seconds passed. He waited as the man stepped closer. He grabbed his wrist, wrestling for the pistol and slamming the man's head against the side of the house. The small man went limp, and Wyatt shoved him beneath the porch.

Shit. Another Chinese crept onto the porch, slinking his way. Wyatt didn't move. One more step and—the man fell with a thud of Wyatt's pistol butt across the back of his head. He eased the limp man's body to the edge of the porch and then rolled him off to join the other underneath the porch. These men were as innocent as Tess, but they well knew who they worked for, and if they'd stay down, they'd live. He glanced from the porch, Sawyer running toward him to the corner of the house and Dawson firing to keep the men on the far side of the porch in check.

Sawyer slammed down into the bushes next to him, out of breath, revolver poised.

"You good?" Wyatt eased closer to his brother.

"Zihao's back…inside. Two are…on the porch. I don't know where the hell Dawson is, but he is picking them off one at a time." Sawyer jerked the barrel of his revolver free and tugged another barrel from his vest pocket to replace it with little effort.

"He's on the roof; I'm taking these last two and going inside alone." There was no point in waiting and the time had come.

"Nope." Sawyer hissed in a whisper.

"You have a family, Sawyer. Cover me." He growled, easing up against the side of the house. He'd be faster if his damn leg didn't hurt like hell, but at least his long healed broken hand was handling the revolver with ease.

Sawyer hopped up, doing the same. "And so do you."

Wyatt contemplated a swift left hook to knock his brother out, but the men on the porch began firing in their direction. Dawson blasted from across the compound. Evidently, he'd jumped to other rooftops to get a better angle, but the spray of bullets, kept them trapped against the wall of the main house.

A rifle blast left the house firing in Dawson's direction. Where in the hell had that come from? He glanced at the windows above him, where smoke hung in the air. Dawson was in direct line of fire, and Hudson wouldn't have a shot from where he was placed, the distance too great.

"Get those two and cover Dawson." Wyatt didn't wait on Sawyer's response but climbed the large bushes to grab the upper roof. Heaving himself up, he gripped the narrow ridge and pulled up to the lower roof. If he could take the man shooting from the window, he'd have a way inside to Tess. He eased closer and waited until the rifle emerged from the broken window again and fired. He jerked the hot barrel toward him with all his might, and the man screamed as he flew out the window and to the ground, ten feet below. It wasn't until he glanced at the unmoving man—*Shit!* It had been a woman, and while it had been a hell of a fall, she was up and running.

Rapid fire tore the frame of the window around him; someone from the inside was firing on him. He ducked, but the splintering wood followed him to the edge of the porch where he had no other option but to drop to the ground. The impact of the ground on his bad leg, took his breath and he hopped, stifling his curses as he rolled. He dropped his revolvers to grab the leg. "Ahhhhhh…son of a bitch!"

Surely he hadn't broken the leg again, but now he'd lost his chance of getting inside the house. He had to get up. He grabbed both revolvers, shoving one in his holster as he pushed with his good leg gaining his stance, unable to limp at first on his bad leg. Holy, holy hell! He tried again and managed several hops on the way to the back of the house, the gunfire following him until he was back where Dawson had pulled up the first of the men to the roof. He hid in the safety of the bushes once more and bent to grab his ankle, which was a mistake.

Zihao grabbed him, slinging him out into the open, his revolver firing as it was kicked from his hand. He'd let his guard down. The man had come out of nowhere. Wyatt reached for his second revolver, but Zihao swung his body and a left boot caught his right hand, sending the weapon flying and him grabbing his hand. He spun back, struggling to keep his footing on his weakened leg. Damn Chinese and their fancy kicks. Why didn't the giant of a man have a gun and fight like a real man? He eyed the revolver closest to him, but Zihao kicked it away. They eyed each other a moment longer, and the hulk of a Chinese man smiled, a sure sign he wasn't interested in a gunfight.

Wyatt stood erect, gripping his fists tight. The man might be bigger, but he'd always held a punch that knocked a man right to his knees. Zihao swayed his arms around in front of him, planning one of those fancy Asian chops.

Wyatt cursed. He didn't have time for a fight with his brothers still exchanging gunfire in the front of the compound.

The man struck then, whirling to kick, and landing to slice a hand across Wyatt's shoulder. He growled. Hell of a hit, but he waited. He'd take a bit of abuse and then lower the boom. The man kicked twice catching him in the ribs with the last. Zihao whirled again, but this time Wyatt caught him by his boot and shoved him backward until he fell in the dirt, the breath knocked from his large frame. Wyatt grabbed his boot with one hand on the top, and the other at his heel. twisting with every ounce of energy he had left. The snap of bone pulled a squall of Chinese curses from Zihao as he grabbed his ankle.

Wyatt let go and retrieved both his revolvers, the exchange of gunfire quiet now. Something wasn't right, and it dawned on him that this unnecessary fight had all been a distraction, and he was a fool. Brett had been right. There wasn't a doubt in his mind while he and his brothers were fighting, Marcus Benton had taken Tess and left the compound.

"Front's clear." Sawyer and Dawson ran to him, both stopping cold in their tracks.

"She's not here; all this was so Benton could take her without us knowing." His mind raced, and his leg begged for mercy. Behind him, Zihao began laughing as he held his knee.

Wyatt turned and stepped closer, cocking his revolver and placing it against the man's forehead. The laughing ceased.

"Wyatt!" Sawyer called him out.

His hands shook with anger. "Ahh, you're not even worth the cost of a bullet." With that he tossed the revolver in the air, caught it backward, and swung it across Zihao's brow. The large Chinese man fell back against the dirt, clutching his head.

Dawson led the way to the corral and bent to touch the dirt. "Tracks are headed right toward Aurora."

Wyatt slammed both revolvers back into the holster

low around his hips. The horses waited at the edge of town, and he might be able to catch Benton if they hurried, and if he could damn walk that far. He headed for the palomino, thinking the leg was surely broken again, his boot the only thing holding it together.

Sawyer spoke to Dawson. "Go with him. I'll have to see Dodge on the stage to home and help Hudson keep Barlow and his men from causing problems. I need to report what happened to the judge. Brett can help, but keep Evan out of the way. Wyatt?"

Wyatt turned, stopping for a moment.

"Wyatt, use your head when you find him. He'll be waiting on you." Sawyer urged him ahead with a nod.

He held his brother's gaze, no words other than the ones they were both thinking. More times than he could count, he and Sawyer had worked together to apprehend outlaws and renegades and had always come out on the right side of the law, but now—now his brother was purposely giving him the freedom to take down Marcus Benton all on his own. It was as it should be. He turned and made his way to the horses, not looking back.

Dawson scrambled ahead, tossing him the reins to his horse, and he climbed into the saddle, kicking the palomino into motion. Oddly, it crossed his mind that he should have named the damn horse as Tess had suggested. The animal was steady and solid, and with any luck they'd catch Benton before he took Tess off in one of the engines.

He glanced ahead. The few miles to Aurora were already taking longer than his patience would allow. He should have known as Brett had told him that Benton would run, taking Tess with him. He gazed into the darkened sky, the stars clear and bright, and he touched the heaviness of the pocket watch in his vest pocket. As long as the stars were leading the way he'd damn well find her and put an end to Marcus Benton once and for all.

Chapter Thirty

The rocking motion of the train tugged Tess from a medicated slumber. It took a moment for her to gather her bearings, remembering she was still in the darkened railcar. It had been hours ago that Benton had taken her from Chan's, forced her onto a horse, and threw her into the old train car a few miles from Denver. Still feeble from the chloroform and broken ribs, she had taken back to closing her eyes, in spite of her fear.

She shuddered at the memory of Mr. Benton carrying her when she gave out due to her injuries and inability to run fast enough. And when he'd thrown her inside the railcar, he'd sworn to beat her further if she so much as made a sound. She'd cried in pain for hours, praying Wyatt would find her and that the tiny life inside her was safe.

She was thirsty, and in so much pain she could hardly move. She traced her tied hands to her side, breathing an incredible effort. She was sure the ribs were broken, at least two of them. Tugging at her ties and using her teeth, she tried to loosen them, but with her wrists raw and her strength dwindling, she gave up.

The train chugged along, and the wood burning engine sent wafts of black smoke through the car, choking her further. She still had a raging headache from where Mr. Benton had hit her. The swollen lump was tender as she touched her forehead, her ear bloody.

Good Lord, no wonder she woke each time a bit startled and confused. She was concussed, and the chloroform hadn't helped the situation at all, but she could hear at least. *Physician heal thyself...*

How was she to do that with her hands tied on a rolling train? She needed to tighten her stays to keep her ribs more comfortable but couldn't manage it given the situation. The fact that the engine rolled tirelessly through the darkness, rocking her to and fro in the clutter of spilled furnishings confused her further.

She tried to sit, but the effort was difficult with her bound hands. She thought of Wyatt as she managed to lean against the wall in the darkness. She was here on the train because he had come for her. She'd heard the echo of gunfire before Mr. Benton had dragged her along to the horse. And she still worried of Dodge and what may have happened to her. While there had been no secret that Mr. Benton had always held a fondness for Dodge years before, there was no doubt in his current state of anger that would matter little.

She sucked in a shallow breath and let her hands slide to her low belly. Tears spilled down her cheeks. She wasn't even sure which direction they had taken but suspected as Wyatt had mentioned, Chan had all kinds of connections along the rail to San Francisco and even south into Mexico. But what then? No matter where he took her, Wyatt would come if he hadn't—no she wouldn't think he'd been shot with the noise that had taken place long behind them.

She had wanted to tell Wyatt he would be a father. She'd dreamt of seeing him hold their child and of him watching her care for the baby, but now…would she even hold this child herself?

"He'll come for us, your papa. He's a very strong man, and he knows how to track bad men. He will be so proud of you." She closed her eyes at the same time the train began to slow, slinging her hard against the wall and the pain taking her breath. They were stopping. She waited until the noisy engine ground to a halt, holding her side and fighting to stay upright at the hurried stop. Surely Mr. Benton would return and shove her around, and she wasn't sure she could take the pain. Whatever he did, she needed to cooperate so she wouldn't be hurt further. More would kill her, and she was certain of that.

Voices sounded from outside, the first hint of morning lighting the sky, though she could see little from inside the darkness of the railcar. She needed to stand to look out the boarded windows, and perhaps see what was going on. Mr. Benton was yelling along with another man but their voices were muffled.

She used both hands to grab one of the tattered tables to stand. She bit her bottom lip and pulled, pushing with her legs, stifling a cry of pain. It seemed to be that Mr. Benton was conversing with the conductor. His voice was enough for her to cringe as she held to the table, sucking in panting breaths. She moved a bit farther toward the end of the railcar, careful of making any noise.

Gunfire blasted from beside the train, causing her to jump and use both hands to grab her side. Tears filled her eyes. Perhaps Wyatt had come, but the returned fire startled her when it ricocheted inside the cab, causing her to slide back down to the railcar floor.

"Best you find your way to sign those deeds, Morgan. I'm going to enjoy taking what is mine." Mr.

Benton yelled, and Tess lifted her head from where she had crouched in pain.

"Brett?" she whispered. Lord, if Brett was here, then was Wyatt as well? The dreaded gunfire continued, and she wished she could have held her ears. In spite of the danger, she tugged herself to standing once more, shaking so hard in the effort she thought she would pass out. She had to call and let Brett know she was here, to let anyone with him also know.

Gathering all the effort she could muster, she took the two needed steps and grabbed the door, which was bolted. Focusing on a deep breath, she debated that calling for Brett would get her hurt or worse yet, killed, but then there was a yelp in the distance, and the gunfire ceased.

She froze, listening. It was now she had to scream. She leaned against the door, holding her side giving it all she could muster. "Brett!"

It came out as no more than a raspy whisper and she tried again. Pushing hard from her lungs. "Brett…" She coughed and grabbed her side, tears streaming at the awful soreness and she collapsed, sliding down the door to sit. It was no use, she hadn't the breath needed. She closed her eyes trying to breathe, but then the train began moving once more.

"No!" She tried to stand but fell back down calling for Brett, nothing but a hint of whispered air escaped her moving mouth. "Brett…Brett…"

And now, what would become of her? Brett, had he been shot and what about Wyatt and his brothers? She had no idea where Mr. Benton would take her, but they were riding east, given the hint of early morning sunlight that peeped through the tattered windows. East to where? And Wyatt…he would still come. She knew he would, but if Brett…

She thought of her aunt and uncle so many miles away. They would have been ecstatic to learn she was expecting. And what if she were lost to them forever? Wyatt would come for her, he would, and she knew it. No matter where Mr. Benton was taking her, Wyatt wouldn't stop until he found her. *Lord, in heaven, please…*

****

Arriving outside Aurora hadn't come soon enough. Wyatt's horse held as steady as Dawson's mustang, Viho. The animals sprinted the last leg as the scrap metal and rail cars that belonged to Miles Rollins came into view. The mine in the distance would be where Brett and Evan were keeping Rollins and his men under guard. That price would be right costly if Rollins pressed charges, but the situation couldn't be helped, and they had needed Rollins out of the way for a time.

He slowed the palomino just behind Dawson's mount

"The engine and car aren't here." Dawson turned to him.

"Let's check the mine." His pulse raced as the morning began rising over the hills to the east. Time was wasting, and he'd pay hell trying to catch the train on horseback. Approaching the mine, he froze. Things were too quiet as he dismounted.

Apparently, Dawson had the same thoughts. Dismounting and lifting the revolver from his belt as he led the way inside the opening of the mine. The darkness enveloped them, but in the distance a lamp flared golden. The sound of a revolver cocked, stopping them both in their tracks.

"You boys better be glad I recognized you in the dark." Evan spoke from behind them as he stepped closer un-cocking his revolver and sliding it back into the holster around his hips. "Brett's been hit."

"What the hell happened?" Fear ripped through Wyatt for Tess' safety once more.

"Benton rolled an engine and railcar out of here, and Brett went after him. He stopped the car and began firing." Evan led the way farther inside the mine where Brett was sitting and leaning against a rusted railcar.

"He got me, but he didn't get me good." Brett held his side, seeking a comfortable position with a growl.

"You gut shot?" Dawson asked, bending to take a look at his side.

"Don't think so," Evan answered, meeting Wyatt's gaze. "Benton has Tess, and he took her on that new track Rollins men were laying north. Wyatt, that rail isn't finished."

Wyatt's pulse raced, and his gut turned into knots so tight he thought he might vomit. He'd never catch the rolling train at this point. What the hell was he to do? Allow Benton to run that train right into the ground with Tess on it? He turned back to his brothers and Brett. "Both of you get him to a doctor in Denver, I'm going after her."

Evan turned to face him. "Where's Sawyer?"

Wyatt walked away, his heart pounding hard inside his chest. He had to think, cover as much ground as possible the shortest route.

Dawson tugged his medicine pouch free, mixing an herb with a bit of water and then using a cloth to place it against Brett's wound. "Dodge showed up in Denver, confronting Benton alone. Wyatt got her out of Chan's compound, and Sawyer stayed to put her on the stage this morning. Seems someone killed the judge last night. Sawyer will meet us here as soon as he and Hudson do something with Barlow and his men we'd apprehended."

Wyatt turned back to them all. "Time's wastin'."

Dawson jumped up and blocked his path. "You don't go alone, Wyatt."

He lifted his hat and ran a hand through his dark hair. Damn it to hell! He could hardly breathe. "I'm not waitin' another second, and you both need to get Brett to a doctor. Been waiting my whole life to end that bastard's life. Gonna do that in a very short time."

Dawson and Evan protested at the same time, but Brett spoke above them. "Let him go, the track isn't complete and that coward, Benton, likely doesn't know that he is about to plow that engine right into the ground." Brett closed his eyes at the effort, but opened them again. "You go, Wyatt, but there's only one way to cut off that train as fast as it's rollin'."

Dawson shook his head, folding his arms in protest. "That's a drop off, clean to the canyon floor. No horse can make that!"

Brett acknowledged with a nod but held up a blood-stained hand to stop him from speaking further.

Wyatt was aware of the canyon and how high the walls on the west side were. His brother was right, no horse could make that fall and survive it, much less a rider.

Brett sat up higher, groaning in pain. "Wyatt, the closest side is damn steep, but the farthest edge will work if your horse doesn't shy. Keep him light, let him have the reins, lean forward, and hang the hell on."

"That's plain suicide!" Evan challenged, kicking at the dirt of the mine floor. "No horse or man ever made a drop like that!"

"One man did." Brett narrowed is gaze on Wyatt once more. "Your father, and I watched him with my own two eyes."

The mine went still, and Wyatt had to steady himself on both feet to remain standing. Damn his paining ankle. He'd never doubt Brett's words, and if any man could have taken a horse on a drop like that, it would have been his father.

"Take the far side, go down at an angle, and hang on tight at the end, ground's soft there." Brett explained and set his sights on Dawson. "Evan can get me back to Denver. Dawson, you'll need to go with him, catch up taking the regular trail. If he loses the horse, he'll need yours."

Dawson gave a reluctant nod.

Wyatt held Brett's gaze for a long moment, then took off on a full run ignoring his searing ankle once more. If his father could take the size of that drop, then so could he, and he'd been waiting his whole life to prove he was the man his father had made him. He mounted the palomino and urged it ahead, aware of Dawson following on Viho. All he could see before him were the tracks and the steep grade he needed to climb in the distance. At the end of that climb would be the drop off, and with any luck he'd make it. And without luck, he'd fall to his death, and he would be justified in not naming the damn horse beneath him.

Dawson caught him. "Slow your horse or his legs won't have the strength to pull the climb, or the wall of that canyon."

He let off the reins. The grade of the miles ahead would tax the animal regardless the speed. They'd already ridden miles, but there were still miles to go, and his brother was right. His heart pounded in his chest, and his breathing was as rapid as the horse beneath him. He'd lost Tess once, and he'd promised he'd never let her go again. Picturing her in his mind, he could hear her voice and feel her touch.

Sweat rode down his back as the sun rose before he and his brother. As they galloped along, reaching the first rise in the land, he began unloading the animal of the items attached to the saddle. If he carried less, he lightened the load for the animal and the dangers for himself. Turning, he untied the bedroll and let it fall from the horse into the dust behind him. He stuffed one revolver in the back of his belt. Struggling to remove his holster, he pulled it free and slung it to wrap it around itself and the second revolver. He wouldn't need but a single revolver and the knife in his boot to do what needed done. He tossed it to Dawson who caught it, tucking it into his belted tunic.

Lifting his saddle bags, he held them out. No words were needed as his brother took them, laying them over the saddle before him. He withdrew the rifle from the side of the saddle where it rode secure most all the time. He handed the butt end to his brother, the exchange smooth, but the look of fear in his brother's blue eyes intense.

He glanced away and unhitched the coiled rope from around the saddle horn and let it fall away, urging the horse onward. The palomino was damp with sweat, but eager. He inhaled, turning toward the lesser drop off, which was still a mile or more. It hadn't taken as long as he thought to get to this point, and now he had to hope the train wasn't farther than expected.

Why was it now that Tess seemed so far away, though she was nearly close enough to be in his grasp? The sharpened knife in his boot weighed heavy, a constant reminder of the task at hand. He'd hunted men, some worse than the evil that drove them and claimed the bounty on most. At times it had been hard and a few times the call was so close he'd almost lost his life, but never once had he held any fear—until now. Until—Tess.

He'd fought with his father the last time they had exchanged words but as the wind whipped around him, his father's' voice spoke again, freeing him of the fear and driving him. *Relax in the saddle, son. Let the horse do the leading, follow his stride. A good horse is better than any weapon. Ride as one with the animal.*

He'd somehow come full circle to this moment, where his father's voice found him once more and led the way to Marcus Benton.

"Watch yourself. I'm not slowing this horse one damn bit, you bastard!" He spoke a whisper into the wind glancing back to his brother, whose horse was losing ground. The mustang, bred for quick flight didn't have the stamina of his own horse, with no true breeding at all. A random animal with a bit of spirit and heart enough to do the job before them.

His attention diverted to the trees ahead. Black puffs of smoke filled the distant sky. The train. *Fight for what is right. Make me proud, Wyatt. Always fight with your head, not your hands.*

His father's voice was a comfort, assurance of

some kind, though puzzling. When he had thought he would die on the prairie, his father had been before him in the shadows of the dark night in protection. And now, he'd have his father with him as he drove the horse down the side of the godforsaken cliff ahead.

He glanced back for Dawson who had now fallen out of view. He supposed his brother would turn back to make a lesser grade, catching up to him, but not before he caught the train. He urged the horse further, and the animal slowed as the ridge inclined higher. The wind and the heavy breathing of horse filled his ears, though the steady pace of his heart wouldn't lead him wrong.

Chapter Thirty-One

Time stood still as Wyatt reached the edge of the drop off to the canyon floor. Ahead was the place he was sure Brett had mentioned. He swallowed the wind in a gulp of air he needed to fill his lungs once more. Thinking too much would slow him and the horse, and in an instant he jerked the palomino's reins heading him off the bank. Gripping his thighs tight against the animal and leaning full back to counter his weight, he held fast. Falling, for what seemed longer than his next several breaths, he then held tight, leaning forward. The horse's hooves caught and he slammed forward, gripping the back of the saddle with one hand, pain coursing through his leg at the effort to hang on.

The horse met solid ground again, jolting them both, and they fell farther, several lengths of the animal. The pounding to his back was fierce, the breath knocked from him enough that he coughed from the stir of dust that blinded him. He tugged the reins tighter, guiding the airborne animal down the jagged earth with his father's voice as clear as ever. *Slow and steady son, when you break a horse, do not break their spirit, become one with the animal, one thought, one being, one motion.*

They fell again, but he relaxed his hold, not fighting the fall, allowing the horse to take control. Hooves caught again, and he leaned back farther to counter the angle, struggling to settle his weight center. Then the horse fought for footing at the last drop. He held stronger, sure they would go off sideways, but the palomino righted himself and scrambled toward the canyon floor in a flurry of dust. He hung on again, waiting and falling, gripping tight with all the strength he had left, countering his weight with the animal.

The impact of the ground pounded through him, taking his breath. He didn't fall and neither did the horse that trotted from the silted earth in a huff of snorts, rocking his large head. They weren't broken, they were alive as near as he could tell. He coughed away the dust and sucked in a breath of relief, not believing it for a second. He rubbed his leg, bending across the saddle horn, and lifted his gaze to the train in the distance.

He coaxed the horse ahead, walking him at first, and to his amazement the winded animal didn't appear to be injured. He stroked the palomino's side and urged a faster pace, little by little. It was a wonder the horse would do another thing besides try to buck him off, but he picked up speed, the train still in the distance before them.

He kicked and the horse gained ground. He shook his head and pulled his bandana over his face, leaning across the animal. The horse raced along and snorted, perspiring as the back of the train moved closer. His gut clenched at the memory of Da Ming and the fire engulfed railcar. No, he wouldn't lose Tess to the train plowing through the end of the tracks and into the dirt. Hoping the horse didn't shy, he urged the pace, and the animal gave it his all, catching the tail of the two-car train. He stretched a hand close to the back railing of the train and the horse went wide. *Shit!*

He angled the animal in once more and reached, jumping and clinging to the railing, the horse falling behind. Wyatt's body swung in the air, and it was all he could do to pull himself onto the side of the railcar, clinging tightly to stay there. Kicking a leg over the railing, he pulled himself to stand on the back and bent to his knees to catch his breath, holding his lower leg. If the damn thing wasn't broken again after all this he'd be surprised. He closed his eyes trying to gain enough breath to stand again. The palomino continued running, following the train, but losing ground. He gave the animal a brisk nod in awed respect.

Forcing himself up, he listened at the bolted door, struggling to break the lock free. "Doc? Tess?"

He'd given himself away if Benton was with her, but he needed to warn her there would be an abrupt halt of the train. He listened, shaking his head and trying once more. "Doc?"

From inside, the slightest sound of her voice reached him. "Wyatt…" She knocked several times.

He jumped up to pry at the door, but it wouldn't budge. He cursed, but had to warn her to steady herself. "Tess, I can't get in, but the train is going to stop fast. Brace yourself on the front end. Stay low, Doc. Can you hear me, Doc?"

Another knock followed, making him smile. That meant Benton was on the engine. He glanced above him and grabbed the railing of the top of the train, pulling himself up with great effort. Kicking with his boots to gain leverage to the top of the railcar. It took some doing, but he made it, fighting to keep himself atop the slick roof, the wind pounding against him just as hard as his pacing heart.

He scooted, crouching, to the front of the car and lay down, peering over the piles of wood that were there to feed the engine. The conductor was standing with Benton holding him at gunpoint. He lifted himself to his knees, having no idea how he would go about things but needing to stop the damn train. It couldn't be far before the track ran out, and even if he'd just survived the biggest jump of his life, he had no intentions of being on this train when it ran out of track.

He jumped to the woodpile across from the attached railcar, cursing his tender leg once more, and several bullets flew his direction. He'd been seen and ducked behind the wood pile pulling the revolver from his belt. Six rounds, a knife in his boot, and the raw earth ahead of the tracks, so much for even odds.

Rapid fire plowed near him, and all he could think was the ricochet could enter the car behind him hitting Tess. When Benton halted fire, he made a dive to run across the piled wood, firing twice as the man ducked behind the engine doorway.

He met his mark firing again, to keep the man where he was. Three rounds gone, but Benton had one left and would have to reload. He lifted his head and Benton fired again, and the wood before him splintered in his face, burning his eyes. Son of a bitch…he rolled, trying to blink but not rub the dirt away. Never mind his vision, Benton was busy reloading.

He forced himself up, squinting, and made for the engine in a single leap. The air knocked from his lungs, as he scrambled to lift his revolver, a moment too late. The cock of Benton's hammer sounded in his ears, and the barrel touched his temple.

"Sit where you are, McCade." Benton jerked his revolver from him and tossed it from the moving train.

Wyatt sat, favoring his leg, the frightened engineer meeting his gaze.

"Turn back around, you coward, and speed up this train!" Benton snarled at the engineer whose hands were shaking.

Wyatt's right eye burned as he blinked several times. Now his fate was sealed just as it was for Tess.

"You know, I should have finished you off instead of wishing you to suffer after your well-deserved beating," Benton yelled over the engine.

Wyatt only glared, contemplating a move. That was all he had. Perhaps one kick to take the revolver, or the crotch to bring the man to his knees. Pace this slow, he thought. Wait for the right moment, but don't wait too long.

"Faster!" Benton ordered the engineer.

Wyatt edged down, keeping his hands up. He could reach the knife in his boot, but Benton had the upper hand with his loaded revolver.

"Do you think I thought Eleanor or Brett would give up those deeds? That land is mine, and I will have it still. Killing you McCades will be easy now that Morgan has paid his own price. That deed will go back to your mother with him dead, and when she owns the lands, Rollins will claim title to them all with the courts. The line to Rapid City will be built, and I'll live like a damn king in Mexico where I will sell your wife off to the highest bidder. Such a shame for the pretty physician."

"Sir?" The engineer yelled.

Benton ignored him.

The engineer tried once more. "Sir? The tracks run out very soon."

Benton back handed him, and the man slumped across the controls, the train slowing with the impact of his body slamming against the controls.

"Sir, please! The tracks end a few miles ahead, you must let me stop the train!" The engineer tugged himself upright.

Benton's eyes went cold. He pulled the man toward him and sent him whirling from the moving train.

Wyatt jerked the knife from his boot, stood, and scrambled toward Benton, who fired. The bullet ricocheted, pounding around the large metal engine car. Wyatt grabbed the man around his middle wrestling hard, the gun firing twice more, but falling away from Benton's grasp. They both scrambled for it, the train beginning to bounce along uneven track. Wyatt fought for stance, his vision blurred, gripping the knife tighter.

Benton grabbed the revolver as they bounced within the unsteady car, and Wyatt dropped the knife to keep the gun from blasting in his face. He grabbed Benton's wrist and pushed with all he had to keep the gun pointed away from his face, with the bastard riding over him. The train slowed further with the unsettled track, and both men were tossed across the railcar.

Wyatt head butted Benton in the face, sending the man back and just about knocking himself out. He blinked his blurry eyes as the man lifted the gun toward him. Damn, but that was six rounds fired, wasn't it? He smiled, hoping he was right.

Benton pulled the trigger, fired and all that sounded was a metal click. Empty. The train bounced and bucked, slinging them to one side, both eyeing the knife, lying nearby. Benton got to it first as Wyatt wrestled against him, the blade whipping across his chest with a burn. He slammed a forearm across the man's face, and Benton's head popped back. The train began slamming hard against broken track, the grinding a roar of twisting iron. Wyatt pushed with all his might, thinking of Tess, and bracing for impact.

The engine hit hard, riding into a ridge of piled dirt, slinging both men apart and across the dusty engine car. Wyatt's head slammed hard against the wall of the car, and he lost his bearings as wood piled up around him. The jostling hurt, and he lost sight of Benton and grabbed hold of something, trying to brace once more. It seemed to take an eternity, but the engine sputtered and hissed. then stilled, smoke filling the air.

He coughed with the dust. Pain scorched his back and leg, and he groaned trying once again to see where he had landed, confused for the moment, and his eyes blurred. "Tess?"

He sucked in a breath and tossed wood from his body. Using what strength he had left to stand, he swayed at the effort, holding his bleeding chest. Damn, another shirt ruined, but he had to get to Tess.

He turned, scanning for Benton, who lay splayed over a pile of wood at the front of the railcar. The man held the knife handle, unmoving. The blade had impaled into the side of his neck, the handle sticking out and blood seeping onto his shirt. Benton met his gaze, the bastard's fate sealed once and for all.

Wyatt struggled to walk across the debris, haggard from fatigue. He held his hand to his bleeding chest. Benton gurgled a curse, holding the handle of the knife steady.

Wyatt took a ragged breath and spoke between breaths. "Take your medicine. It never had to be like this. You were never even close to being the man my father was, and that made you damn near crazy to have what he had. But he saw right through you and always outsmarted you no matter what you thought you would pull." He picked up the revolver which rested next to the man. *Well, that was damn convenient.*

He leaned closer to Benton who was now gurgling blood with each breath but watched him with wide dark eyes. He tugged a revolver barrel from the man's vest pocket, Benton grabbing his arm to try and stop him. Dropping the barrel out of the revolver he held, it clanked away on the metal floor of the engine. He popped the new chamber of bullets in place. He ripped his father's pocket watch from the man's vest and stuffed it into his own pocket.

Benton stared at him and tried to speak, managing a slight growled whisper. "Do it." He sputtered blood and his hands dropped, his chest heaving for breath.

"My father was a great man, and he never had to prove that to anyone." Wyatt opened the newly placed barrel of the weapon and let five of the bullets fall to the floor of the engine, leaving just one. He rolled the barrel and closed it and cocked the hammer. "This is for my father, my family, and *my* wife."

With that he placed the loaded revolver in Benton's right hand and placed the man's finger on the trigger, the heavy gun weighing down his limp hand. "Do it yourself, you bastard. Check mate."

Wyatt wiped a sleeve across his eyes, trying to clear his blurry vision, but the right eye continued to drip tears. He grabbed his bandana and padded it against his chest and ran his heart in his throat as he made his way to the passenger car which hadn't overturned like the engine. As he got closer a gunshot blasted behind him. He froze for a second. It was done. Marcus Benton was dead.

"Doc?" He scrambled to the door of the car, jarred open from the impact. The wooden frame splintered in half even though the bolt had held. He pulled up and crawled through the opening and found his stance among the tangled spill of tables and chairs.

"Tess?" He moved farther into the car. She had to be all right, but the train had hit hard. He ignored his own pain tossing tables away behind him and digging through.

"Wy…att…"

The most beautiful voice he'd ever heard drifted to him from behind the tables at the front of the car. He tossed the wreckage away and found her lying against the front of the railcar as he'd told her. He lifted debris from her and knelt. "Doc?" He smoothed her hair from her face not believing she was before him.

Her voice was but a whisper as she tried to lift herself up and grimaced.

"Don't move, Doc. Lie still, I'll carry you."

"I'm all…right." She whispered, holding her side.

"He hurt you?" He touched her swollen lip as he sat and pulled her to him, afraid of hurting her further.

"I'll…heal. My ribs…are broken." Tears dropped from her eyes in her struggle, but she touched his cheek, fighting for short breaths. "I knew…you'd come. Just hold…me."

He leaned against the front wall of the railcar and tugged her gently into his lap and worked to untie her bound wrists. She winced as he removed the ropes and touched the tender burns, and some part of him was afraid to ask, but he did anyway. "Are you hurt anywhere…else?"

She took his hand in hers and placed it on her low belly. "We're fine, Papa." With that she leaned into him and wept, her body shaking hard enough to cause her pain.

"It's all right, Doc. I'm taking you both home." He held her then, until her tears stopped, unsure of how much time had passed, his own tears spilling into her hair. He rocked her with tenderness, never wanting to let her go again.

"You must…help me…tighten my…stays." She lifted her head. "You're hurt?" She touched the blood-drenched cloth at his chest.

"I'm all right, Doc." The cut on his chest burned, his eyes stung, and his leg throbbed, but he'd take all that and then some to be where he was at this very moment. He gently touched her side. "Broken ribs, Doc, they hurt a might." How could any woman stand that kind of pain and ask to be bound tighter?

He stood, gently easing her with him, setting her to her feet. She turned, holding the wall, and he grabbed the ties, pulling the laces tight with great care. As brave as she was trying to be, he'd sooner take another ride down the side of that cliff than tighten the stays. "Doc, there's a physician in Greely, can't be far from here."

She yelped as he tugged again, and he froze, afraid to touch her.

She stole a glance at him over her shoulder as she held to the side of the railcar. "Mr. Benton?"

He shook his head.

She nodded. "Tighten it a bit more…it will help." She waited as he tugged again, biting her lower lip.

He turned her and touched her face still not believing he had her in his arms again. Her gentle gaze met his own and he lifted her gingerly into his arms and made his way outside the wreckage, Tess clinging to him.

They had no food or water, no horse, and they were miles from nowhere. The pain that ripped through his own body was enough to make him want to give up, but as bruised and sore as he was, he was somehow whole again. And he would manage, carrying Tess as far as the ends of the earth if needed. He continued walking for a time, the train long behind them.

"Wyatt, you can't carry…me so far." She laid her head against his shoulder holding tighter to him as her body shook in pain and fatigue.

"Damn well gonna try." He glanced west, the heat of the sun scalding, but it would set in a few hours and perhaps by then he'd find a bit of water or his brothers would arrive.

"Dodge?" Tess asked, still hanging on to him. "And Brett…there was gunfire and…"

"Dodge is on the stage to Cheyenne by now. Brett took a bullet to his side, and Evan took him to Denver. He'll be all right I think. Dawson and Sawyer will find us soon enough, and Hudson's in Denver, cleaning up the mess we left there." He ignored the pain in his leg and kissed the top of her head as he continued his slow pace.

She laid her head back down against him and sniffled in relief.

"Don't cry, Doc, it's all over," he whispered and

squinted, his vision still blurred in his right eye, and he blinked is disbelief. "I'll be damned."

He stopped and set her to her feet, still holding her against him. In the distance was the palomino trotting toward them, still wearing the saddle. Who would've ever believed it? The animal who had saved her and him had followed them, even after the fall and the race to the train.

Tess lifted her head. "Your horse."

He shook his head as the horse stopped before them and gave a rumbling neigh. "You saved the day, Boy, more than you know."

He steadied Tess and patted the animal's damp fur. "Damn amazing. Gonna have to give you a name after all."

Tess touched the horse. "He's soaking wet and winded. How on earth did he get here?"

Wyatt glanced at the horse once more. "You have no idea, Doc but he brought me to you, racing to catch the train for more miles than I can count and for a fall I thought we both wouldn't survive."

"Oh, my lord." Tess' mouth dropped open.

"I had a bounty to hunt down, and she was carrying a very special package of her own so, I believe he is deserving of a name. You take the honors, Doc." He held her steady as she kissed her hand and placed it to the palomino's large nose.

She thought on it for a long moment. "Bounty, we should call him Bounty, so…we never forget what he did for us."

"It's a good name. If I put you on him, can you ride?" He tugged at the saddle to make sure it was still secure enough to carry her.

“I think so.” She held her side as he settled her with care. He grabbed his canteen, thankful he hadn’t tossed it from the saddle and was surprised it had remained on the horse after the fall. He handed it to her, and she drank a few sips and coughed holding her painful ribs.

“Easy, Doc.” He took the canteen and sipped, wanting much more, but capped it again. Settling a hand on her thigh, he took the reins to the horse and clucked his tongue to urge Bounty ahead.

“Will you be happy, Wyatt…a baby and all?” She gazed at him, her body broken but her smile his reward.

He was surprised at her question. Of course, he was happy. “Only if she is as beautiful as her mother.”

She smiled and rubbed her belly, a happiness she deserved. “And if it’s a boy?”

“Nah wouldn’t be right for a boy to look like you.” He chuckled and squeezed her thigh. “Are you all right, Doc?”

She smiled though her eyes closed, clasping her hand on his. “I will be.”

Ahead, two men on horseback raced toward them. He chuckled. Either he was hallucinating with his blurry vision, or his brothers had found them. He stopped Bounty, and Tess opened her eyes.

He looked on as they got closer. “We’ll have you to a doctor in no time. Drink.” He handed her the canteen once more.

She drank, the pounding of hooves echoing around them, even though his brothers were a half mile away.

“I love you, Wyatt.” Tess handed him the canteen.

“You have no idea, Doc, not even a little, how much I love you.” He smiled. “But hold onto this horse, it looks like they have another mount with them. Can you make it, Doc?" He could hardly stand up himself he was so tired, his leg fatigued.

"As long as you are…with me." She held her side, though a tear slipped down her cheek.

"Doc, I'll never let you out of my sight again, not even for a minute." He rubbed her hand and wished he could kiss her, the deep passionate kiss he'd been longing for since he'd lost her, but that could wait. Staring into her tired green eyes, everything was clear. Some kind of hint at the beauty the world held for them now. Things were bright and new, even if he could hardly stand up.

Never again would he take his sight from her, and come winter, he'd wait as she brought their baby into the world, and he'd relish in watching her happiness at holding the child she had waited a lifetime for. And next spring, he'd surprise her by starting on a real house on the ranch. Yep, and then he'd spend his time, seeing to her happiness in any way he could, even if that meant giving up bounties. Well, maybe just a few. She had closed her eyes again, and he increased his hold on her in case she fell. But then, if she did, he'd always be there to catch her as he'd promised.

Epilogue

The early spring sun played across the McCade ranch, offering no relief from the heat in Cheyenne. Wyatt stood along the river's edge, scanning the horizon on the other side to the home he'd completed with his own two hands with a good bit of help from his brothers.

And now he'd spent most of the afternoon in wait of Dodge's Sunday evening meal, walking by the river admiring his handy work and contemplating the move back to the ranch. It had always been home, but he'd not lived on the ranch much the last few years. Bounty hunting and covering town as deputy, it was easier to bed down at the jail and then, of course, at the clinic. If he were being truthful to himself, he'd not called the ranch home since his father had died, never having taken the same liking to the cattle business as his brothers.

He bent to pick up a stone and threw it across the water watching as it skipped several times. His father had taught him to skip rocks, but his father's voice had remained quiet for the first time in years, and his own vivid dreams of disaster had faded.

"It's almost time for supper, what are you doing out here." Tess approached, carrying their infant daughter, Ella.

He turned back to the water for a moment. "Ahh,

just thinking."

Tess shaded the baby's eyes from the sun, by tilting her across her forearm. Ella kicked and flailed her tiny arms and legs, the infant excited to be outside. "Brett came by for dinner, and Dawson is back from Gillette just in time."

He chuckled, reaching for his daughter, and tucking her into the crook of his arm. She was, besides her mother, the most beautiful thing he'd ever laid his eyes on with his dark hair and Tess' green eyes. He hadn't expected his deep paternal instincts to take over from the first moment he'd held her after Tess had given birth, but this daughter of his had him wrapped several times around her tiniest finger.

"You see all that, baby girl?" He turned a full slow circle. "One day, you'll be the matriarch to every bit of it as Dodge's name sake, though that might be your downfall." He laughed.

"It's a very appropriate name and Eleanor is very elegant. Besides, Dodge is the best friend I have ever had." Tess defended, folding her arms with a pout.

"That was your first big mistake a long time ago." He put an arm around her, and together they moseyed back toward the main house.

"Oh, you love her as much as me and besides, I want Ella to be head strong and confident. She can be a doctor or lawyer, or maybe a rancher in her own right." Tess raised her voice an octave, touching the baby's dark hair.

He thought on it. "A woman rancher? I suppose if any daughter of mine has a hankering she'd do a fine job of it."

"So, Sawyer got a telegram that Miles Rollins had

dropped the appeal?" She raised her brow, waiting on his response.

He took a deep breath and nodded. "He'll scamper off to swindle a deal somewhere else. Barlow and his men are being held for the federal marshal, going down for all the crooked dealings in Denver. The new judge has offered Hudson the position as Denver's sheriff. He'll sure as hell gloat, but he had the satisfaction of closing down Barlow's and Chan's operations."

She smiled. "Well, let him gloat, he'll make a fine sheriff, after all, you and Sawyer taught him all he knows. And Chan and his son?"

He shrugged. "Likely high tailed it to San Francisco or off to China."

"Sawyer says he will just start up again somewhere else," she added.

"Yep." He tucked the baby onto his shoulder.

"And you are destined to ride a wagon for years to come, Wyatt McCade." She laughed, and for a moment he looked at her. She was all that was good, all that held him together. And now it was when he'd make good on his promise. "I'm getting used to wagons; in fact, you and I are going to have a good bit of time running wagons full of items to the new house."

Tess stopped in her tracks, narrowing her brows. "Wyatt?"

He smiled. "You didn't think I did all those months of hard labor to build Sawyer and Rose such a fine house, did you?"

Her mouth dropped open as she turned to view the beautiful cabin across the river. "All this time, you had me thinking Sawyer was building that house, and Rose played along?"

"You should know good and well Sawyer isn't leaving the big house. He's the one who added on to it several years back." He touched her cheek. "I want to make you happy, Doc, and I want this one to be raised here." He kissed Ella's cheek, tugging her hand from his beard with a grimace.

"But my clinic and…" She shook her head.

"Well now, there's a bit more to the story. You'll keep your clinic, and you and the baby can ride in a buggy into town every morning with me. Of course, I will be riding Bounty."

She considered him, not understanding.

"I made you a promise. With Hudson taking off for Denver, Sawyer's gonna need a full-time deputy. It makes perfect sense to me." He acted as if it were nothing, shrugging.

"I know you promised, but will you be happy not bounty hunting?" Her serious green eyes were so bright he wanted nothing more than to kiss her.

"My father wanted Sawyer and I to work together, and while we have a lot of the time, this will make it more like he wanted, I suppose." And he would be happy that he could be home a lot of the time and besides there would be a good bit of work to keeping up a homestead.

She kissed his cheek. "You said your father's voice was finally quiet, and if I didn't know better, a part of you has calmed."

Hell, she had always read him like a book, knew his thoughts and understood things about him that he might never comprehend. He nodded. "It's as it should be. Me being here to take care of you and Ella."

His father's lands were once again preserved for

them all. And the birth of the little girl in his arms and the love of the women beside him were every bit enough. Looking around he thought of his father. He'd forgiven himself for thinking he'd always fallen short where his father was concerned. And since his short ride down the side of that cliff, he'd come to terms with the loss of the man he'd always loved.

He glanced at Tess. "I love you, Doc."

"And I you." Her green eyes sparkled in the warm sun as she beamed at him.

"No, I really…love you, and to prove it, we won't be moving into the house just yet." He'd waited on purpose.

"Well, why not?" She asked.

He tugged the baby's tiny hand from his beard once more with another groan. "Well, we'll be in Boston for a few months, leaving next week."

Her mouth dropped open and her eyes filled with tears. "Oh, Wyatt…"

"Reckon this one will make it an easy trip?" The last few months had been a challenge with a new baby keeping them up nights.

"Oh, Wyatt…well…" She used her sleeve to wipe her tears. "I so wanted to share the baby with them. My aunt will adore Ella, and we'll make sure to take all Ella's things, and I'll have to call in another doctor for a few weeks. And then, there, well, there will be so much to do in just a week."

He chuckled and grabbed her hand, leading her to the house. "You can make a list later; come on, Doc, its dinner time."

"Yes, well, I'll start that later tonight when Ella is asleep."

"Sorry, Doc, you'll be quite busy later tonight." He winked at her and kissed her on top of the head, wrapping an arm around her once more.

"Busy?" She eyed him with suspicion.

"Yep, busy. Dodge made up my old room and plans to keep Ella while you take a nice long hot bath and go to bed early for some much needed rest." He'd planned the idea with Dodge a few days before, and his mother had been elated for the time with her granddaughter.

"But the baby…"

He interrupted. "The baby will be fine, and you and I are going to get some rest."

"How come I think maybe this rest is to your advantage." She nudged him with her elbow.

"I do promise not to keep you up long, and we can sleep in. You can open the clinic in the afternoon." He stopped her again, intending to kiss her but taking the time to study her in all her beauty, flustered but ready for the challenge of getting the family to Boston.

"How many bedrooms did you put in that house?" She smiled, her brows rising in wait.

Wyatt eyed her with suspicion. "Doc, you holding out on me?"

She couldn't hide her grin. "It's true."

Well, that wasn't what he'd expected, not that he was a bit disappointed. He'd been awestruck in watching her care for Ella, her sweet voice talking to the baby. She was so happy, maybe happier than he'd ever seen her since becoming a mother, given that had been long overdue. He lifted Ella high in the air, the baby grinning at him. "Well, now, it seems you are going to have some company in keeping us awake at night."

The baby cooed her first laugh and chewed her tiny fingers.

"Wyatt, she's laughing…oh." Tess hugged him and spoke to the baby. "Are you laughing at your papa?"

The baby grinned again while sucking her fingers.

"I'll let you sleep tonight, Doc. Apparently we're going to need it." He pulled her against him, savoring her lips. She tasted of spring and hope and all things good. Holding her and his daughter closer, he led them toward the main house. His father's voice was still, and for the first time in more years than he could count, he was sure of where he belonged.

A word about the author…

Kim Turner writes western historical romance and discovered her passion of writing at the age of eight by writing poems, short stories, and journals. Kim graduated from Clayton State University with a Bachelor's of Science in Nursing and holds a Master's Degree in Adult Education from Central Michigan University.

Working as a registered nurse for over twenty-seven years, she enjoys studying the medical treatments of the Old West as well as keeping up with the latest western movies and television series. While she loves reading anything from highlanders to pirates, she claims to have an unquenchable thirst for the American cowboy when choosing her reads.

Kim lives south of Atlanta with her husband and calls her greatest accomplishment the birth of one daughter and the adoption of another from China—neither of which came easy.

Kim is a member of Romance Writers of America and Georgia Romance Writers.

Kim's Motto: It's All About A Cowboy and the Woman He Loves.

kimturnerwrites.com

www.ingramcontent.com/pod-product-compliance
Lightning Source LLC
LaVergne TN
LVHW020523100826
845148LV00010B/1325

* 9 7 8 1 5 0 9 2 1 3 7 6 4 *